best
intentions

best intentions

simran dhir

HarperCollins *Publishers* India

First published in India by
HarperCollins *Publishers* 2021
A-75, Sector 57, Noida, Uttar Pradesh 201301, India
www.harpercollins.co.in

2 4 6 8 10 9 7 5 3 1

Copyright © Simran Dhir 2021

P-ISBN: 978-93-5489-151-9
E-ISBN: 978-93-5489-159-5

Typeset in 11.5/16 Adobe Caslon
Manipal Technologies Limited, Manipal

Printed and bound at
Thomson Press (India) Ltd

For my parents, Nimmi and Suresh Dhir,
and my husband, Ankur

1

'GAYATRI WILL ALSO get married, Nina,' said Ashok Mehra to his wife consolingly as he contorted his cheek against the shaving razor in his hand. 'Let's just be thankful that Nandini's wedding went off so well.'

Nina's face appeared beside her husband's in the large bathroom mirror. She shook her head. 'You don't know how many people asked me about Gayatri during the wedding. I'm sure everyone was saying *how* can the younger sister be married before the older one?'

Ashok splashed water on his face, then peered at his chin in the mirror to judge the results of his labour.

Nina walked back into their bedroom and sat on the edge of the dark teakwood bed, unconsciously straightening the edge of an old Kashmiri rug with her toe. Ashok followed her a few seconds later, wiping his face with a towel. He sat next to her and circled her shoulders with one long arm. With his still-slim, athletic frame and her plump but exceedingly pretty face, they made for an unusually good-looking pair, even now in their fifties.

'I just don't know what to do with Gayatri,' said Nina. 'She didn't even dress up properly through the wedding. Hardly any make-up, and she refused to wear my gold set on the wedding day.'

'Nina, she's thirty-two. You can't treat her like a baby.'

'Even if she's eighty, I'll still be her mother, no?' replied Nina, sharply.

'Let's talk about this later. There's so much work still to be done to wrap up the wedding.'

Nina didn't seem to be listening. 'Do you know what Anjana told me?' she asked softly. 'I feel so odd even repeating it. She heard a rumour that Gayatri is ...' She paused before continuing, 'That she likes girls.' She looked at Ashok and half-whispered, 'Do you think—'

Ashok cut her off as he stood up. 'Why do you have to listen to that stupid woman? And even if she does, you know ... Anyway, I'm going for a bath.' He walked back towards the bathroom. Pausing at the doorway, he turned to look at his wife's troubled face. 'And listen, don't worry. I'll also speak with her regarding the boy Prakash Uncle told us about.'

Nina looked far from satisfied as he closed the bathroom door behind him.

The grand Mehra family bungalow at No. 7, Jagjivan Road, Old Delhi, was purchased by Ashok's long-deceased father when he migrated to India from Pakistan in 1947. The senior Mr Mehra, a savvy property dealer in Lahore, had set up a bureau to facilitate the exchange of houses of elite Hindus, Muslims and Sikhs on either side of the border before Partition. Later, he transitioned smoothly into being one of

Delhi's leading property agents, ensuring that his family's fortunes flourished again within just a few years of their chaotic and tragic shift from Lahore.

The large-sized bungalows in the area and broad, quiet roads lent to this part of Delhi an air of calm exclusivity and old money that could be incongruous with the crumbling mansions and unkempt lawns often hidden behind tall walls. Ashok Mehra's lucrative career as a senior executive in a machine tool manufacturing company and Nina's taste for elegant living had, however, spared their house such a fate.

Nina entered the dining room. Gayatri was sitting at the breakfast table, across from Ashok, eyes focused on the newspaper before her. Her hair was gathered in a loose bun, and small silver earrings dangled from her ears. Sunlight streamed in from the large French doors behind the table, which led into the garden where newly flowering pink and purple petunias signalled the beginning of winter.

'Hi, Mom,' said Gayatri cheerfully, looking up as her mother walked in. 'Slept well?'

Nina murmured a response as she sat in her usual spot at the head of the table. 'Where is Dadi?' she asked.

'Still very tired,' replied Gayatri. 'She said she'll have breakfast in her room.'

'I can't begin to imagine how tired Mama must be at eighty-eight,' said Ashok, pouring himself a glass of the carrot and beetroot juice he drank religiously each morning before leaving for office. 'It's been a few days since the wedding and my legs still haven't stopped aching.'

'Malti Didi!' Gayatri called from the table. 'Omelette jaldi, please.'

'Gayatri, don't shout like that,' said Nina irritably.

Gayatri, used to her mother's admonitions, did not react. Turning over the page of the newspaper, she started to read as she nibbled on a piece of toast.

Nina looked at her elder daughter, her mind still preoccupied with her seemingly bleak marital prospects. But maybe thirty-two is not that old, she thought. Just four years older than Nandini. And everyone says she's so pleasant looking. She didn't get my features like Nandini, but her eyes are nice and large like mine. That nose and jawline she's inherited from her Dadi must be what's scaring all the boys away. If only she would make up her eyes, leave her hair loose. At least she is not dark. Is that a wrinkle near her mouth? Nina squinted at Gayatri's face.

She was jolted out of her thoughts by her daughter's voice. 'Ma, can you please stop doing your staring thing?'

Nina blinked and looked away. 'One can't even look at one's own daughter now,' she sniffed as Gayatri directed her attention back to the newspaper with a frown.

Nina caught Ashok's eye and gestured with her chin towards Gayatri. Ashok pursed his lips and shook his head. Nina raised her eyebrows insistently, but her husband just frowned at his plate and started to butter his toast.

'Okay,' said Nina in a challenging tone, 'then I'll tell her.'

Gayatri looked up from the newspaper. 'Tell me what?'

'Nothing, beta,' said Ashok, glancing at his wife. He could see that she was not going to relent. He cleared his throat and said, 'There is a boy whom … I mean … you know …' He broke off.

Gayatri lowered her eyes and glared at the newspaper as if it was the one suggesting she meet yet another prospect for an arranged marriage.

'Gayatri, your father is saying something,' said Nina sternly.

'Do we really have to start this now, Papa? Chhoti just got married a couple of days ago. Don't I get a few days' rest?'

'Rest!' said Nina. 'We are not telling you to climb Mount Everest. Just to meet a boy. He's from a good family, and earning well also.'

Ashok added gently, 'Beta, you just meet him, and if you don't like him then we'll leave it.'

'The answer is no,' said Gayatri firmly, folding the newspaper and setting it down. 'I'm tired of meeting boys with their mummies and daddies in tow, asking me stupid questions. I cannot choose a partner this way. I hate them before I've even met them. I'm too old for this now.'

'This is not a good attitude, Gayatri,' said Nina.

'Ma, you had a love marriage,' snapped Gayatri, her face reddening. 'So stop pretending that you can even begin to understand what it's like to be rejected by men whom, frankly, you don't even feel like talking to in the first place.'

'Beta,' Ashok said patiently, 'we didn't want to trouble you during Chhoti's wedding because you were so busy. At least hear us out now.'

Gayatri propped her elbows on the dining table and covered her face with her hands as her father continued.

'His name is Ujjwal. He is an engineer and has done an MBA from IIM Calcutta. Works for Google. His parents live in Agra.'

Gayatri remained silent, her face still buried in her hands.

'We are only telling you to meet him. If this were a few decades ago, you'd have been married off without even being asked.'

'Please, beta?' Ashok said, giving his wife a warning look at the same time.

Gayatri took a deep breath.

'Your father is practically begging you, Gayatri,' said Nina. 'Is this really that difficult for you?'

Gayatri clicked her tongue in irritation. 'This is so unfair. Fine, but on one condition: this is the last one I will meet. I refuse to be emotionally blackmailed by the two of you ever again. I'm giving you notice of that now.'

Her father smiled. 'Spoken like a true lawyer.'

'I'm late for work,' said Gayatri, standing up. 'And thank you, but I'm not a lawyer any longer.'

'Oh, that reminds me,' Ashok said. 'Sunil Uncle called me about your quote ... The one that was published in the *Indian Times*, on the Aryan invasion issue. He sounded very impressed, though honestly, I don't think he understood the point you were making.'

Gayatri shrugged, still angry with herself for giving in to her parents. She picked up her purse. 'I'll see you in the evening.'

'But breakfast?' asked her mother.

'I'm not hungry.' She marched out of the room.

Nina shook her head. 'This is what it's come to, Ashok, begging and pleading with our own daughter. So headstrong she is. I pity the poor fool who marries her.'

Gayatri's office was a twenty-minute drive from her house, a short commute by Delhi standards. Entering a residential colony, she parked her car near a black wrought-iron gate through which a two-storey red-brick house was visible. The low boundary wall of the house was covered with a bougainvillea creeper dotted with a few pale flowers that were fading as winter approached. Come March, it would burst into pink flames, taking its place on the frontlines of the hot Delhi summer, second only to the soft golden abundance of the laburnum trees that lined the lane outside. On the grey letter box hanging on the gate were the words 'Indian History Review (Regd. Off.)', and below that, in smaller letters, 'Kailash History Foundation and Library'. The paint was a dirty yellow colour and the edges of the letters were peeling off.

Still sitting in the car, Gayatri finished the omelette sandwich that had been forced into her hand by Malti Didi as she left the house, then made her way into the office.

Leela, the peon, was dusting a shelf of books by the entrance. She smiled as Gayatri walked in. 'Gayatri Didi, namaste,' she said. 'Shaadi sab ache se ho gayi, Didi?'

'Namaste, Leela,' responded Gayatri, now cheerful. 'Haan, sab theek se ho gaya.' She handed Leela a bag and told her to distribute the boxes of sweets in it among the staff.

Walking into a room to the left of the main door, Gayatri settled down at her desk. Switching on her computer, she untied and then gathered her shoulder-length hair into a bun. A minute later, Leela placed a mug of hot coffee on her desk. Gayatri acknowledged her absently, her attention on her computer screen as she fiddled with her earrings and typed at short intervals.

Her forehead was still furrowed in concentration forty minutes later when a voice called from the door. 'Gayatri, you're back? I thought you weren't supposed to return until Monday?'

Gayatri turned in her chair with a grin. 'Farah, hi! Yeah, I decided to come in today itself. So many emails clogging my inbox. And I felt so guilty about leaving you to handle all the editing for this month's issue.'

Farah Alvi walked in with quick steps. Her delicate features were framed by straight, long hair. Like Gayatri, she hardly wore any make-up but for the kajal lining her eyes. 'I won't lie,' Farah said as she lowered her bags onto her desk, 'I'm really happy to see you. It's been a crazy week. Recovered from the wedding?'

'I'm just glad it's over,' Gayatri said. 'If one more bovine aunty asks me about my wedding plans, I swear ... I've had visions of strangling each one of them with the thick gold chains around their necks.'

Farah laughed. 'It was that bad, haan?'

Gayatri raised her hand, holding her forefinger and thumb just a centimetre apart. 'I was this close, Farah. I wanted to run away.'

'Let's sit outside and chat, na,' said Farah. 'I'll bring my coffee there.'

'Okay, give me a minute, I'll just send off this email.'

A few minutes later, they walked through glass sliding doors to a veranda that lined the garden, and sat on the cane chairs laid out there.

'I really didn't think it would be this bad, you know, Farah,' said Gayatri, cupping her coffee mug in both hands. 'I've been going through it for so long now. But this wedding just awakened some matchmaking monster in family, friends, everyone.'

'Well, at least it's over,' said Farah, picking up her cup.

'It will never be over. Chhoti will go on her honeymoon, have children, the children will grow up and get married. And through all of that, everyone will be looking at me to see if I'm feeling bad. And worse, suspecting that I'm not really happy for her.'

'Come on, Gayatri. It won't be so bad.'

Gayatri sipped her coffee and continued in a complaining tone, 'And, to top it all, now my parents are making me meet another one of these moronic boys.' She shook her head.

Farah looked at her sympathetically. She knew it would be impossible to cheer Gayatri up while on the subject of marriage. 'How is Nandini?'

'She's fine,' said Gayatri with a faint smile. 'She's left for her honeymoon with Amar. To Italy.'

'For how long?'

'They're returning on Monday, because they both need to get back to work. They have such busy lives, it's crazy.'

'But these corporate lawyers earn so well also,' said Farah.

'Still, I don't know why they do it,' said Gayatri, shrugging. 'They spend an equal amount of time cribbing about their work as they do actually working. And Amar's father and elder brother have such a huge litigation practice. He could easily join them instead.'

'I saw the brother at the wedding, but didn't spot his wife anywhere.'

'Who, Akshay? He's not married.'

'Isn't he much older than Amar?' asked Farah.

'Yeah. I almost had a fight with him at the wedding. Can you imagine,' Gayatri said, widening her eyes, 'he bribed the waiters to serve alcohol before the wedding ceremony was over, despite us telling them that the bar should open only after.' She shook her head. 'And he wasn't even apologetic when I told him to stop. You know, that typical aggressive south-Delhi type. I didn't like him one bit.'

Farah grunted in disapproval as she sipped her coffee.

'And even when we had spoken at the engagement earlier, he was so full of himself. When I told him I had quit law to study and work here, he was really dismissive, like he couldn't understand why someone would do that.'

'He does sound like a bit of an ass,' said Farah.

'It's that self-important air that some people derive from thinking that only their work is important. I probably shouldn't say this, but even Chhoti is a bit like that. Full of my-firm-this and my-transaction-that. It's just a job. She doesn't get it.'

Farah smiled patiently, accustomed to Gayatri's bouts of irritability whenever she was forced to meet an arranged marriage prospect.

'Anyway,' Gayatri said with a sigh, 'I'm just happy to be back at work now. How have things been?'

'Okay,' said Farah. 'I finished fact-checking and editing the article on the sculpture section at the National Museum, and sent off the article from P.R. Goswami for review, and ...' She looked at Gayatri hesitantly.

'What?'

'Actually, I received an odd call last week,' said Farah. 'We were sent an article for publication. It was biased, all propaganda, terrible language, no research. Not even one source cited. Basically, just a rant.'

'And?'

'Some guy called to threaten us, saying we have to publish the piece.'

Gayatri frowned. 'What?'

Farah nodded. 'I didn't want to bother you during the wedding—'

'Threatened means… What did he say exactly?'

'Vague stuff. Like, we will not be responsible for consequences if you choose not to publish this … your journal is completely one-sided. You know, stuff like that … and in chaste Hindi. Someone called Visheshwar Dutt.'

'You told Kanthan?'

Farah nodded. 'He said he would discuss it with the trustees, but he was worried. He's still in Lucknow at that conference.'

'Probably some old nut, desperate to have his article published,' said Gayatri.

'Maybe,' said Farah. 'But he had quite a few rude insults handy when he realized I am Muslim.'

'Really? This is serious then, Farah. Shouldn't we go to the police?'

'I told Kanthan not to, for the time being. Maybe we should wait and see if it goes any further.'

'You know,' said Gayatri, 'this sounds similar to what happened at the *Indian Age* last month. Remember? They got random threatening calls and then those two journalists were thrashed for publishing some pieces on Gandhi.'

Farah looked worried as she said, 'I don't know. I googled the guy, this Visheshwar Dutt. He's written bits and pieces on some blogs, all Hindu right and might.' She stood up. 'Come, let's go inside, I'll show you the article.'

A few minutes later, Gayatri was hunched over her desk, reading Visheshwar Dutt's article. Her nose was wrinkled as if assaulted by a foul smell. 'The grammar is bad, but the substance is even worse,' she said. Skimming through a few paragraphs, she started to read aloud, 'Akbar history is work of jihadis and terrorists. All histories that he was great and kind-hearted ruler are fraud and should be rejected. All tombs and monuments built by him were conversions of Hindu temple and structure. The Muslim foreigners, all of Turks, Afghans, Mughals, Uzbeks, have come and looted all temples and all cultures of Hindus. Then they have created false histories by paying their servants to write of their great works. Akbar has taken Hindu wife by force to please—' She broke off and looked at Farah. 'This is a joke, not for an academic publication.'

Gayatri continued to read, 'The Hindu Muslim unity is a lie, nothing like that has been there. The Muslims never allowed Hindus to do their cultural, religious and moral duties, even Akbar's Din-e-Illahi was a fraud. There was no mixing of cultures, only loot and violence. That is the reason for stagnation of Indian thought since 1000 ad. Why there have been no thinkers of any repute since Adi Shankaracharya? If Israelis are invaders, then also are the Muslims, and they should also return to where they come from.' She shook her head. 'What rubbish! This is a fine rant for some right-wing type publication. Why send it to us?'

'I guess they think that if they manage to get it published in the *Review*, even this kind of nonsense gets legitimized.'

'Well, the least these people can do is read the submission guidelines on our website. What is all this baseless stuff? Maybe we should add one more—threats will not be considered helpful in our decision to publish.'

Farah frowned. 'I just hope this doesn't snowball into anything bigger.'

When Gayatri returned home that evening, she offloaded her bags on the first sofa near the door and went straight to her grandmother's room, as usual. Her parents were there too.

'Ram Ram ji, Dadi,' she said, bending to give Dadi a kiss on her fair, still reasonably taut, eighty-eight-year-old cheek. 'How are you feeling now?'

'Tired,' Mrs Nirmala Mehra replied, kissing her back. 'At my age, it goes without saying.'

She sat regally in a high-backed chair with sturdy arms. Her short white hair was perfectly combed, her pale pink salwar–kameez was immaculate, and her fingers and ears sparkled with diamonds. Gayatri looked pale and tired in comparison.

'How was your day, beta?' asked Ashok as she sat on the couch beside her mother.

'Fine,' replied Gayatri, her tone turning sulky as she remembered their conversation that morning. She smiled at her grandmother. 'What's the news, Dadi? Have your great sisters given their verdict on the wedding? What all have they criticized?'

Mrs Nirmala Mehra was the eldest of seven sisters, of whom only four were still living. 'Criticize?' said Dadi sharply. 'What will they criticize? They were too busy trying to close their gaping mouths. In fact, they can't stop talking about the guests who attended.'

'That's true,' said Ashok, nodding as he sipped his daily quota of whisky and soda. 'All those politicians. I know Amar's father is joining the BSD, but I didn't expect the chief minister to turn up.'

'I know,' said Nina, 'Even that fellow … Rajan Cheema was there. He's supposed to be the biggest fixer in the government, no?'

Ashok shook his head. 'Not just fixer. He is the PM's right-hand man. Anything you want done, you have to go through him.' He spoke with the confident insider air typical of all Delhiites discussing politicians, and Bombayites speaking of actors. 'But it's a dirty world, and I'm not thrilled that Nandini will be exposed to their sort.'

'Woh Sadhuji bhi toh tha,' said Dadi. 'I was wondering how he wasn't feeling cold in that dhoti and the flimsy cloth around his shoulders.'

'Yes, that Chhatarpur Baba,' said Gayatri. 'He looked just like a Bollywood villain na, with his long red tikka and flowing white hair.'

'Mama,' said Nina, ignoring Gayatri's comment and looking at her mother-in-law, 'isn't he the same baba that your sisters have been going to?'

Dadi nodded. 'Haan, he's the one. They say if you have the tea at his ashram, all your ailments get cured. Knee pain, gas, skin problems, everything.'

'That's why your sisters have been looking so young and pretty lately,' teased Ashok.

Dadi snorted. 'They are greedy, all of them. They just go for the free tea and the laddus. I know them very well.'

'In their Mercedes and BMWs?' asked Gayatri sceptically. 'You really think they go all the way to his ashram in Chhatarpur for free tea?'

'You don't know them,' replied Dadi, shaking her head. 'I was the one who raised them after our mother passed away. They stayed with us for months after Partition in Delhi. Only I know what my poor father went through with these naughty girls. The losses he suffered during Partition were one thing, but these girls took full advantage of my mother's absence.'

Gayatri smiled. 'And your father?' she said, looking at Dadi. 'How did he manage?' She loved hearing stories of her grandmother's childhood, even if she had already heard them many times.

Dadi said, 'What could he do, poor man? He had lost his wife and was saddled with so many girls in a new land, having left everything behind in Lahore. He used to tell me to keep my sisters straight so he could get them married well. And I did, I found boys for all of them myself.'

Nina could not resist. 'And now, Mama, we need to find one for our Gayatri too.'

Gayatri frowned at her mother and opened her mouth to reply, but before she could say anything, Dadi said, 'Of course, that will also happen. My Gayatri will marry a very lucky boy.'

Gayatri took a deep breath and looked at the floor.

Nina pursed her lips and shook her head slightly.

Ashok Mehra poured himself another drink and changed the topic.

2

Two days later, Gayatri made her way to Green Park market and parked her car. Usually, she enjoyed the cheerful chatter of people walking about the chaat shops and pavement stalls, which stocked everything from make-up to mobile phones. Today though, the sounds grated on her ears as she trudged towards C for Coffee, where she was due to meet Ujjwal Mehta.

She scrolled through her phone to bring up the photograph that her mother had sent her, then pushed open the door of the coffee shop and looked around. Not finding anyone resembling the person in the photo, she sat down at an empty table for two and started reading an article on her phone. A few minutes later, a group of three people—two men and a woman—walked up to her table. 'Excuse me?' said one of the men.

She looked up at them distractedly, and indicated that the other chair was taken.

The older of the two men asked, 'Beta, are you Gayatri?'

Gayatri felt a stab of annoyance. This one had brought his parents along without warning. She forced herself to smile politely, and gestured for them to sit down. The prospective groom pulled up two more chairs, and the mother settled noisily into the seat that was too small for her generous bottom and too close to the table for her large stomach.

Gayatri sized Ujjwal up. He fidgeted nervously with his sleeve, not making eye contact. I know this type, she thought with an inward sigh: quiet, ordinary and dull. She had long given up efforts to be non-judgemental at first sight; after all the practice she had had, she found that her first impressions very often matched her last.

'Beta, mummy–papa nahin aaye?' asked the father.

'Uh, no,' said Gayatri. She enquired how long the Mehtas had been in Delhi, and learned that Ujjwal's parents had come from Agra especially for this meeting. There was some obligatory small talk about the weather and pollution levels in Delhi, a brief comparative analysis of the traffic in Delhi and Agra, and then everyone fell silent.

Accustomed to the lulls that regularly punctuated such meetings, Gayatri no longer felt awkward when no one had anything to say.

After a few seconds, she looked at Ujjwal and asked, 'So you work in Bangalore?'

'Yes, at Google,' he answered, but did not ask her anything in turn, deviating from the routine she was familiar with.

The father spoke, 'Beta, you're a lawyer?'

'Yes, Uncle,' she said, not bothering to correct him.

This was followed by a number of questions put to her by Mr and Mrs Mehta, while Ujjwal sat silent on the sidelines. After ten minutes of practised questioning and experienced answering, when Ujjwal's father asked if she was willing to move to America after marriage, Gayatri's eyes brightened. This would be easy, thank god.

'No, Uncle, I'm sorry, but I'm not open to living abroad,' she said, a little too happily. She quickly adjusted her expression to look slightly apologetic.

Ignoring her answer, Mr Mehta announced that his son had received an offer to work in California, which he had accepted.

'That's great, congratulations to … uh … you all,' said Gayatri, 'but I really don't want to live abroad, I'm sorry.'

Ujjwal's father, however, didn't seem like he was ready to give up. 'It's a great opportunity, beta, you'll see,' he said. 'His salary is amazing, top in his class right now.' He looked at Ujjwal proudly.

Gayatri nodded. 'I'm sure it is, it's not easy to get jobs in the US nowadays.' In her relief, she was feeling kindlier towards the Mehtas, even genuinely wishing Ujjwal well for his new life in California. Who knew, maybe he'd get lucky, find a gori and disappoint his parents. Bringing her attention back to the conversation, she continued, 'It's just that, personally, I've never wanted to live outside India.'

The father persisted. 'But everyone wants to go to the US. Good parks, big-big department stores, no pollution aur, sabse important, good money.' He paused. 'And best thing, you'll have to change only one letter in your name— "r" to "t", Mehra to Mehta, hai na?' he said with a self-satisfied smile.

He definitely came up with that one before coming here, thought Gayatri. A little weary now, she tried again: 'I'm very sorry …' Seeing the father open his mouth to say something, she added quickly and firmly, 'In any case, I don't think I want to marry Ujjwal.' She glanced at Ujjwal apologetically. She wouldn't have had the gumption to reject anyone to their face a few months ago.

The Mehtas were visibly offended. The mother looked at the son who was looking at the father as he stared at Gayatri. Mrs Mehta attempted to rise from her seat, but given her ample proportions, only ended up jolting the person sitting behind her and falling back into her chair. Ujjwal dutifully rushed to help her.

Gayatri winced as Ujjwal and his mother walked off without saying goodbye, leaving Mr Mehta sitting across her. He made no attempt to leave. Gayatri started to put her phone and wallet away in her bag when he said, 'Beta, let me tell you something.'

She knew she had offended the whole family, so she smiled apologetically, and said, 'Uncle, I'm sorry if I—'

'If you had to go to Agra today,' he interrupted, 'and you went to the bus station in the morning, you would find many buses, right?'

Gayatri looked at him blankly.

He continued, 'And if you went in the afternoon, you would also find quite a few buses. Yes or no?'

She nodded in confusion.

'And if you go at six or seven or eight in the evening, again, there may be a fair number of buses.'

Gayatri was wondering whether he wanted her to go to Agra to meet the boy again. Surely not by bus? And why was he giving her travel advice?

He lowered his voice. 'Now, if you go at ten, you will find only a couple, maybe three, buses. But at eleven at night, you'd be lucky to get even one bus. So you'll have to board that one bus, correct?' He paused. 'See?' he finally demanded in a triumphant tone. 'You see or no?'

'Uh, I'm sorry, I don't understand,' said Gayatri.

'You are thirty-two years old,' he said, sternly. 'It is 11 p.m. for you now. If you are getting a bus, climb on. There is no line of boys waiting for you, so better to stop thinking you're above everyone else.' Mr Mehta stood up as he spoke and left.

Gayatri's eyes followed him blankly as he worked his way around the tables to his wife and son, who were waiting for him outside. She was lost in thought as she walked to her car and started to drive home. Though she hadn't invested anything in this meeting and was glad it was over, she couldn't shake off the feeling of indignation at a complete stranger telling her that she needed to compromise on whom she chose to spend her life with because 'it was 11 p.m.'

When her parents had started introducing potential grooms to her, she had agreed to go through the motions to avoid the drama and fights at home. Very soon, she concluded that these meetings were futile. Her parents' social circle regularly threw up men completely mismatched with her: either moneyed and intellectually vacant, or studiously intelligent but dull in every other way. And so, she had switched off from the process early on.

Now though, in this moment of weakness, as her anger over Mr Mehta's words subsided, and those ever-lurking djinns of insecurity and doubt reared their ugly heads, Gayatri had to summon the strength to resist falling prey to them. Her brow furrowed again as she remembered his words, her mind overflowing with the smart replies she had not made to him.

'Gayatri, is that you?' her mother called from the living room.

'Yes, Ma.' Gayatri walked into the living room and dropped into an armchair.

'They called me.'

Gayatri looked at her mother wearily and shrugged.

'What happened?'

'Ma, please,' replied Gayatri, 'I can't do this.'

'What do you mean, Gayatri? Here we are, going crazy trying to find boys who are good, educated, earning well. Do you have any idea how tough it is? And you go around rejecting everyone. At least give me a reason—'

'Then don't do it any more. You don't need to do this. Please. This guy … I just can't, Ma. You should have met him yourself, then you'd understand.'

'What do you mean? He's well-educated, from a good family, earning well. What more do you want?' Nina asked, in an agitated tone.

'Ma, I need you to stop badgering me about this marriage thing.'

'Really? And what do you propose to do instead? Go on living like this? Don't you want a family of your own?'

'I thought I have a family,' said Gayatri, unable to stop the tears welling up in her eyes. 'But if this is such a big deal for you, I'll move out.'

Nina was surprised to see her usually tough daughter in tears. 'Don't say such hurtful things, beta,' she said softly.

Gayatri had intended that to hurt. 'Mom, I am thirty-two now. I will not be bullied into meeting more useless guys. This is becoming humiliating.'

'But, beta,' began Nina.

'No, don't start that now,' said Gayatri, swallowing as she tried to control the tears that were streaming down her face.

Nina walked over to her and sat down. She tried to turn her daughter's face towards her, but Gayatri resisted. 'Please, beta, don't cry, I'm sorry,' she said. 'We just want the best for you. My strong girl.'

Gayatri pushed her mother's hands away, stood up and went to her room.

The next morning at ten, Gayatri and Farah entered Ramesh Kanthan's office for their weekly Monday meeting.

'Good morning,' Kanthan said, looking up from his computer screen. He was dressed in a crisply ironed green kurta and white pyjamas. His greying hair fell in scanty waves over his head. Widely acknowledged as one of India's foremost historians, Kanthan had started the *Indian History Review* twenty-three years ago. His writing had the unique distinction of being critiqued by both the right and the left, and being labelled 'Marxist', 'pseudo-secular' and 'conservative', depending on the labeller's proclivity. Though he had been influenced chiefly by Marxist theories as a young scholar, he had later developed a fanatical focus on research from original sources, even learning several languages to be able to study these first-hand. This resulted in a study of history that was more human and broad-based than Marxist blinders permitted, but also more factual than the 'nationalist' narrative required. When pressed to slot him, as this age of 140 characters and limited attention spans frequently demanded, people often referred to him, rather lazily, as a 'popular' historian.

Once they sat down, Kanthan got straight to the point. 'So, Farah told you about that call?'

Gayatri nodded.

'There's another development there,' he said. 'I got a call from Anil Bhargav last night.'

'Who?' asked Farah.

'Anil Bhargav. He's the secretary of the Shri Seva Parishad, SSP. You must have heard of them?'

'What does he want now?' asked Gayatri.

'He told me they don't like the sort of research we are publishing,' Kanthan said. 'He mentioned your piece on Godse, Farah's article on Kabir and Chandrappa's on the Indus script being non-linguistic. He also insisted that we publish that Dutt fellow's article to demonstrate that we are balanced.'

'This is just getting crazier,' said Farah, shaking her head.

'I've met Anil Bhargav a few times,' said Kanthan. 'I remember having a pretty interesting debate with him some years back at a college event or something. He was quite intelligent, he made a couple of points on archaeological evidence at Harappan sites that I went back and researched.' Kanthan paused. 'Look, I'll be honest with you two. My priority is that you are not dragged into some kind of mess. We have to think through this carefully.'

'But—' Gayatri started.

'Do you remember what happened to those journalists at the *Indian Age*?' continued Kanthan. 'And the Urdu Festival event organizers? They're still recovering from that attack. All I'm saying is, we need to be sensible. Things are changing, you know that. A few years ago, I might have reacted differently to something like this, but now …' Kanthan broke off, then added firmly, 'I am not going to invite trouble, particularly for you two.'

'But surely we're not thinking of publishing that rubbish?' said Gayatri, looking from Kanthan to Farah incredulously.

'Gayatri, that's not what he is saying.' Farah turned to Kanthan. 'Anyway, why is this Sri Seva Parishad so interested in us?'

'So you know that SSP is a religious cult headed by that Sadhu chap.'

Farah nodded. 'He is also like the patron saint of the Bharat Sanskriti Dal. He channels funds to the party through his multi-millionaire devotees, and also puts his armies of goondas at its disposal.'

Gayatri clicked her tongue impatiently. 'I don't know that much about this SSP, but we work very hard on our journal, Kanthan. We can't just publish any bullshit someone sends in. How can we give in to these nutcases? Let's go to the cops.'

'You know it's not that simple, Gayatri,' said Kanthan. 'The BSD is now part of the central government. The cops will not act against these people unless we reach out through someone with influence. And those sorts of favours always come with strings attached.'

Gayatri bit her lower lip thoughtfully. 'I can try speaking with my sister's dad-in-law. He's joining the BSD, or maybe he's already joined.' After a pause, she added, 'In fact, that Sadhuji fellow came for Nandini's wedding.'

'Do you think he can help?' asked Farah. 'I mean, does he know this Sadhuji well?'

'I'll check with Nandini,' said Gayatri. 'And this will be a personal request, not exactly a favour.'

'Fine,' said Kanthan. 'let's all have a think and meet tomorrow evening to discuss this. I'm not saying we will publish that piece, of course, but let's figure out how to deal with this situation sensibly, without anyone getting hurt. I'll also talk to a few friends. Okay?'

'Yes,' said Farah. 'I think that's a good idea.'

Kanthan and Farah looked at Gayatri.

She shrugged. 'Fine, but I can tell you now, I will not vote for giving in to this kind of pressure, no matter how much I think about it.'

A few hours later, Farah and Gayatri took their afternoon coffee break. They sat on the broad step that led from the veranda to the lawn, their bare feet on the green grass. There was a slight nip in the air. It was getting to that point in November when Delhiites seem to instinctively turn their faces to the sun, like sunflowers.

'When is Zaheer coming back from New York?' asked Gayatri. 'Have you guys decided on a date for the wedding?'

'Not yet, but his parents are really pushing him now. Let's see.' Farah sighed. 'Anyway, is Nandini back from her honeymoon yet?'

Gayatri nodded. 'She got back last night. I haven't seen her yet.' She paused. 'It's funny actually, I was never excited when she came home after spending months away in college, and now she's been away just a week and I can't wait to see her.' She stared thoughtfully at the grass around her feet for a few seconds, then said, 'Can you imagine, I told her she should not marry Amar?'

Farah looked at Gayatri, but didn't say anything.

'I really regret that, you know. I apologized to her before the wedding. I should not have said that to her.'

'You're her older sister, Gayatri. You were just looking out for her.'

'I really didn't think that Amar was good enough for her. He's not as smart as her. They used to fight non-stop, and they had dated for less than a year. But now that they're married, I feel really bad about the things I said.'

'I'm sure she knows that,' said Farah. 'Did she bring up your argument again?'

'No. But you know, one thing she said to me that night stuck in my head.' Gayatri paused. 'She said, "I don't want to end up like you."'

'Ohho,' said Farah, 'don't be silly, Gayatri. I'm sure she didn't mean it.'

'No, it's not that,' said Gayatri quickly. 'I don't mind what she said, but it did make me wonder whether seeing me single pushed her to say yes to someone whom she didn't love all that much.'

Farah thought for a couple of seconds, then said, 'Look, Nandini is a smart, intelligent girl. She's financially independent. She would have thought carefully about such an important life choice.'

Gayatri looked at Farah. 'I hope you're right.'

Later that evening, Gayatri entered the house to see Nandini lounging on an armchair, typing on her phone. 'Chhoti!' she squealed, hurrying over to give her sister a hug. 'You're back!'

'Hi, Didi!' said Nandini. 'How are you?'

'I'm okay. You tell me. You look so good,' said Gayatri, stepping back to look at her. Nandini's long hair hung loose over her slender shoulders. Her face, almost exactly like their mother's, looked tanned and beautiful. 'Why are you sitting all alone here?'

'Mom and Dad are not home yet, and Dadi's sleeping.'

Gayatri perched on the arm of Nandini's chair, and gazed at her with a broad, affectionate smile.

'What?' asked Nandini, looking over her shoulder.

'Nothing, I'm just happy to see you.'

'Didi, you're such a drama queen.'

'Anyway, tell me, how was the trip?'

'It was amazing, you have to go.' Nandini proceeded to describe to her sister in detail the moment she first saw the statue of David in Florence like a near-religious experience.

Gayatri asked, 'And how is it being in your new house?'

'It's a bit strange. Even going directly there from the airport felt very weird.'

'You'll get used to it soon, I'm sure. Why didn't Amar come with you today?'

'He's playing squash with Akshay Bhaiya at the club. They'll pick me up on their way home. I just wanted to get away from that house actually.'

Gayatri clucked in disapproval. 'That's not nice, Chhoti. You should make an effort with his family.'

'You try making an effort with that sister of his—Priya. What an irritating specimen,' she said, rolling her eyes.

'At least she lives in the US, so you won't have to deal with her that much.'

'No, Didi. She is staying here for a few more days. I hate her already. She's always going on about her Bobby and his diets and their gym and their fabulous life in the US. I can't stand her.'

'Don't be silly, you barely know her. Anyway, enough about her. Are you comfortable in the house otherwise?'

'I just miss my loo so much,' said Nandini with a groan.

'Thanks, Chhoti,' said Gayatri with a laugh. 'We miss you too.'

'Achha, tell me, did you meet that boy? Ujjwal? Ma told me about him before the wedding, but said I shouldn't tell you or you'd bite my head off.'

When Gayatri finished telling her about Mr Mehta's bus analogy, Nandini burst out laughing.

'Oh my god, Didi,' she said, trying to catch her breath, 'I can't get over it. How did you sit through that?'

'What could I do?' said Gayatri, smiling. 'This is the price you pay for being an old maid.'

Just then the doorbell rang, and Nina and Ashok entered the house. Nandini was swept up in a wave of parental love and anxious questions, before being whisked off to Dadi's room.

An hour later, Gayatri was sitting on the bed in Nandini's room as she picked out clothes to take to her new home.

'Chhoti,' she said. 'I wanted to ask you something.'

'Haan?' Nandini folded a kurta and placed it on the bed.

'Last week, we received some random calls at the *Review* pressuring us to publish some right-wing nut-job article, not to publish some of our own research, that sort of thing.'

'Really?' said Nandini, turning to face her.

Gayatri nodded. 'From someone called Anil Bhargav.'

'Who?'

'You know SSP, Shri Seva Parishad—that Sadhuji's organization? This Bhargav is supposed to be an important guy there.'

'Oh.'

'So, I was wondering if I could speak to your father-in-law about this. He is joining the BSD, na? And he knows Sadhuji?'

Nandini paused before answering. 'Yes, he is joining. I think the announcement is going to be made tomorrow.' She shrugged. 'Sure, speak with Amar's dad. No harm. They definitely know this Sadhuji quite well.'

'That's what I thought.'

'But, Didi,' said Nandini, 'please take care. You guys shouldn't do anything stupid. I mean, no point taking risks with all this.'

'Of course, we won't,' said Gayatri.

'You should have stayed a lawyer,' Nandini continued, shaking her head. 'Look at all this jhamela you have got into. And they hardly pay you. I don't understand why you had to go running off to do this history and all. You could be working in a perfectly safe job right now, and earning so much more.'

'Oh, so now that you're married, you're also going to start lecturing me about my life choices?' Gayatri frowned.

'Why are you getting so touchy?' asked Nandini, taken aback.

Gayatri's face immediately softened. She took a breath and said, 'Sorry, I didn't mean that.'

Nandini gave her a small smile and went back to folding her clothes.

'Then I'll come over tomorrow maybe?' said Gayatri.

Nandini nodded.

'Thanks, Chhoti.'

The doorbell rang. 'That must be Amar,' said Nandini, standing up and stuffing her clothes into a duffel bag.

Ashok would not hear of his son-in-law leaving without first having a drink, so when Amar explained that his brother was waiting in the car, Ashok went himself to invite Akshay to join them. By the time they entered the house, Amar was sitting in the drawing room, a drink in his hand, surrounded by the Mehra women.

The brothers looked similar—the same broad foreheads and sharp jawlines, but while Amar had glossy, black hair, Akshay had a head of rough-looking, unruly hair with hints of grey at the temples. Also, at six-feet-two, Akshay was four inches taller than Amar. Akshay seemed embarrassed to be standing in the Mehras' drawing room in a faded sweatshirt and shorts. His hair was matted with sweat, and his face was still slightly flushed.

'Beta, would you like to wash up?' Nina asked kindly.

He accepted the offer gratefully. Gayatri led him to the family study down the corridor and switched on the light. 'You can use that bathroom,' she said, pointing to a door at the far end of the room.

'Thanks.' Akshay glanced at the tall, dark-brown wooden bookshelves that covered two walls of the room. 'Whose books are these?' he asked.

'Mostly mine,' she replied. 'And my father's.'

'You like reading,' he said.

Gayatri wasn't sure whether that was a statement or a question. 'Yes,' she said. 'You?' she added, after a few seconds of awkward silence.

Akshay nodded, then abruptly walked towards the bathroom and shut the door. Gayatri shook her head and went back to the drawing room. She sat down next to Nandini, who was smiling happily at Amar's account of scuba diving in the Maldives a few years ago. The entire Mehra family looked thrilled, and even Dadi was pretending to understand what scuba diving was, laughing loudly.

'Amar is so sweet,' said Gayatri in a low voice to Nandini as he continued to entertain everyone with his anecdotes.

Nandini smiled. 'That he is. He's very social, na. He can make conversation with anyone.'

'He and Akshay look very similar, no?'

'Yeah, everyone says that.'

'But they don't seem alike in their manner. Amar is so easy-going, and Akshay is … a little … uptight.'

'Yeah, Akshay Bhaiya isn't very talkative.' She turned to Gayatri. 'He wasn't rude to you again, was he?' She had heard about the argument over serving alcohol at the wedding.

'No, no, don't be silly,' said Gayatri, smiling. She turned her attention back to Amar.

Akshay entered the room a few minutes later and sat beside Amar, sipping his drink silently. The two brothers rose to leave after they had finished their drinks, but their protests were no match for Ashok's powers of persuasion, which were fuelled by a desire for some company during his second round.

Akshay offered to make the drinks this time, and walked over to the wooden bar in a corner of the drawing room.

'Thanks,' he said to Gayatri a few minutes later as she placed a bottle of soda on the bar. He handed her two glasses. 'These are for your father and Amar.' She carried the glasses over to them, while he brought her mother and grandmother a glass of wine each. 'Your grandmother drinks,' he remarked as they returned to the bar for their own drinks. 'I've never seen someone so old have alcohol.'

'How does age matter?' asked Gayatri quickly

Akshay stood behind the bar and sipped his drink. 'I didn't mean, … I meant, I haven't seen women that age drink.'

Gayatri fiddled with her glass awkwardly. She looked back at the rest of the family, engrossed in conversation, and wondered whether it would be rude of her to just walk back to the sofa.

'So, where's your office?' asked Akshay, interrupting her thoughts.

'Not too far, Underhill Road,' she replied.

'That's a nice area,' he said. 'You've done law, right? And now you work with that journal … uh …'

'*Indian History Review*.'

'Haan, yes. I remember it from my college days. So did you actually study history?'

'I did a few short-term courses, but no formal degree. Before that I was litigating for a couple of years.' She sighed. 'We've already had this conversation.'

'Sorry, I remember now. Where did you say you used to litigate?'

'Girotra and Partners.'

'So why did you leave? Long hours?' he asked.

'No,' said Gayatri. 'I found something more interesting.'

'Studying history?' Akshay raised his eyebrows as he took a sip of his drink.

Gayatri detected a hint of condescension in his tone. 'Yes,' she said flatly.

'It must be very academic, and um … steady. I mean, compared to litigation.'

'To some extent. But we have our moments of excitement.'

'Really?' he said, his scepticism now apparent. 'Like what?'

Gayatri did not feel like continuing the conversation, but she knew she couldn't be rude to him for Nandini's sake. 'Like when we come across something fascinating in our research and discussions, or meet people interested in similar subjects. When you kind of put two and two together, that sort of thing.'

'Interesting, I can understand. But surely it's not exciting?'

'It is for me.'

'What are the readership numbers of your journal like?'

'About ten thousand per issue in terms of physical subscriptions,' she said. 'And we have a growing online presence now. It's freely accessible online because we are trying to draw lay readers, so it's not easy to track readership.'

'That's a pretty good number. Still, the *Review* is something you mostly see in college libraries. The ordinary person is not really interested in an academic type journal, na?'

Gayatri, already irritated, bristled at his dismissive manner. She said impulsively, 'Actually, there are a fair number of people who seem more than a little interested in history nowadays. The papers are full of it. Politicians can't get enough of it. In fact, some people are desperate enough to threaten us so we publish their pieces.'

'Threaten you?'

Gayatri paused. Might as well tell him, she thought. 'You know the SSP—Shri Seva Parishad? The one run by that Sadhuji … I think he was at the wedding,' she said.

'Yes, of course.'

'Well, we got a call from somebody called Anil Bhargav at the SSP. Apparently, they're not happy with the kind of stuff we publish and want us to publish some right-wing conspiracy theories instead. In fact, I was planning to come and speak with your father tomorrow, just in case he knows someone who can help.'

Akshay shrugged. 'So just don't publish controversial stuff that riles these people up. Why do you want to get caught in this sort of mess?' He continued after a pause, 'I'm just saying that talking to these people may not help much, because they genuinely believe that their versions of history are overlooked. They are not likely to be convinced by anything you say. And frankly, they probably have a point. Most academic discourse in this country is seriously skewed to the left— that's what is provoking such reactions. For that matter, I'm sure you wouldn't publish many "right-wing" historians at the *Review*.'

Gayatri shook her head imperceptibly, her opinion of Akshay now converted from mild disapproval to definite dislike. 'It's obviously not that simple,' she said testily. 'We have a journal to run, and need to maintain some academic honesty and rigour. If we start bowing down to this kind of pressure, we may as well shut down. And, by the way, we have published lots of articles contradicting what is perceived as "left-liberal" history, and even agreeing with some parts of what is now mistakenly called the Hindu discourse. In any case, threatening us is surely not the way to correct a skew, if there is one. They are free to write and publish their own stuff too. Anything that's well-researched and has sound sources will pass our peer-review process, that's the whole point.'

Akshay looked at her intently for a few seconds, then looked away. 'Shall we sit down?' he said, picking up his glass.

'Sure,' said Gayatri coldly. She picked up her glass and went to sit next to Nandini, irked by the conversation.

Akshay pretended to listen to Mr Mehra's story about how he was mistakenly arrested in Ghana many years ago, but was actually thinking about Gayatri. What an idiot, he said to himself as he sipped his drink. This is how people get themselves into trouble, and cry later.

He glanced at her. I know her type. Aggressive activist. Probably indoctrinated into left-wing fantasies by her education and has zero contact with the real world. Even a man selling paan on the road has more insights into life than people like her.

Akshay brought his attention back to Ashok's account of spending the night in the air-conditioned office of the commissioner of police in Accra. Poor guy, he thought. Stuck in a house full of headstrong women with no male company. No wonder he's so fond of Amar.

Later that night, Gayatri sat up in bed with her laptop propped on her knees. The wedding photographer had emailed them some pictures. She browsed through a few, and came across one of Nandini and her. She smiled. Their happy faces were cheek-to-cheek and they had their arms around each other's necks, careful not to smudge their wet mehndi.

I hope she is always, always, happy, thought Gayatri, squeezing her eyes shut for a long moment.

As she scrolled through more photographs, her eyes locked on one of her holding a dupatta above Nandini's head as they walked to the havan kund, where the groom and the pandit waited for the bride in the glow from the fire. Everyone in the picture was focused on Nandini's smiling face. Gayatri too, holding up her corner of the dupatta, was gazing at her sister. Nandini looked perfect. Next to her, Gayatri seemed quite plain. She frowned and closed her laptop. Ujjwal Mehta's father's words flashed in her mind.

A few seconds later, she shook her head. What's wrong with me? I'm happy and so lucky. I love my job, I'm healthy, and I don't need to marry anyone just for the sake of it. She closed her eyes and took a deep breath as she recalled her decision a few years ago not to marry Chirag, whom she had been dating for a while. He had surprised her with a proposal just as she had begun to realize that she didn't want to be with him for the rest of her life. She knew she had deserved to bear the guilt of causing him pain, but the way her own family, especially her mother, had treated her had devastated her at the time.

When she opened her eyes after a few seconds, they fell on her bookshelves. She spotted her favourite hardbound copy of *Pride and Prejudice*. Three books away, her bulky, much-thumbed edition of *Middlemarch* stood sturdily on its own bulk, right next to *Emma*.

Just as a common word begins to seem unfamiliar when stared at long enough, as she looked at them now, she saw her beloved books in a new light: still beautiful and comforting, but no longer because they stirred hope that a Darcy or a Knightley would one day whisk her away in a rush of romance. Instead, she felt grateful for the romantic adventures she had been on vicariously through them because, she sighed inwardly, such experiences seemed more and more unlikely in real life.

3

THE GREWAL FAMILY, of which Nandini was the newest member,
lived in a bungalow named Devaki Sadan in Nizamuddin East, one
of Delhi's more affluent neighbourhoods. Older residents of the city
remembered these coveted residential areas of today as nothing more
than scrubland a few decades ago, converted to large colonies after
Partition, in the 1950s.

Gayatri turned her car into the lane where the bungalow stood.
The guard at the entrance to Devaki Sadan enquired briefly about her
business, then pressed a button to open the mechanized gates, which
revealed a long driveway flanking a manicured garden. The driveway
led to a large, white, three-storey house decorated in the signature
style of 1990s Delhi: faux-Corinthian columns and ornate cement
corners moulded in a garish Punjabi interpretation of Renaissance
architecture. A man answered the doorbell and led her into a sitting
room. A few minutes later, Amar's mother, Rupi Grewal, entered. She
was dressed in a bright-orange silk salwar–kameez, a string of pearls

casually strung around her neck. Time had eroded only a little of her beauty since she had become Gyan Singh Grewal's wife at twenty-one. Many guests at Nandini's wedding had commented that Mrs Grewal looked more like the groom's sister than his mother; Nina Mehra's expression had become frostier each time she heard a variation of this comment.

'Hi, Aunty,' said Gayatri, standing up.

'Hello, Gayatri beta,' said Mrs Grewal graciously. 'How are you?'

Gayatri smiled. 'Fine.'

'Sit, sit.'

'Thanks, Aunty. I hope you've recovered from the wedding madness.'

'Oh, yes,' said Mrs Grewal with a wave of her hand. 'Most of it was handled by the office people. And then Akshay was here. Sons are so useful in times like these, you know.'

Gayatri nodded, suppressing the urge to roll her eyes. No wonder Akshay is such an arrogant ass, she thought.

Just then, Nandini entered the room. 'Hi, Didi,' she said, walking over to her and giving her a kiss on the cheek. 'Amar's father is free.' She looked at her mother-in-law and explained, 'Didi had some matter to discuss with him, so I thought I'd call her here.'

'Of course, beta, go ahead and meet him now. He may get busy with this party business later. All these press people have been buzzing around the house ever since the announcement,' said Mrs Grewal. 'You must have seen it in the papers?'

Before Gayatri could reply, Mrs Grewal held out a newspaper towards her. She took it with a nod, saying, 'Yes, I did see it.' She looked at the newspaper anyway and politely skimmed through the article on Mr Grewal.

GYAN SINGH GREWAL JOINS BHARAT SANSKRITI DAL

PTI, New Delhi: Reputed senior advocate Gyan Singh Grewal has joined the Bharat Sanskriti Dal, following the path of senior journalist T.K. Ramakrishnan and army veteran Maj. Gen. P. Pillai, who joined the party recently.

In a statement, the party spokesperson said, 'Gyan Singh Grewalji is a highly respected lawyer and preserver of the rule of law, and we are sure he will contribute immensely to the BSD's service to the nation. He will be one of the party's spokespersons with immediate effect.'

According to sources, Mr Grewal is likely to get a ticket to contest the by-elections in Chandni Chowk due in April next year and has already negotiated a junior berth in the Law Ministry with the Centre, provided he wins this election.

Criticizing the move, the spokesperson for the National Party said, 'It is sad that the BSD has to recruit persons who have defended the most notorious criminals and scamsters in recent history. True to the party's slogan, "Bharat Udega", the last pretence to any moral standards seems to flown out of the window for the BSD.'

Looking up with a smile, Gayatri said, 'Congratulations, Aunty'.

'Come, Didi, let's go,' said Nandini, impatiently. 'I have to get to office by ten o'clock. You'll have to drop me. My car's gone for servicing.'

Gayatri followed her out of the room, politely nodding to Mrs Grewal. Nandini led her across the lobby and down a flight of stairs to the basement. A wooden door opened into a large, brightly lit room with several open-plan workstations separated by low partitions. Natural light filtered in through the ventilator windows lining the top of one wall.

Nandini walked over to a door and knocked.

'Come in,' boomed Gyan Singh Grewal's voice from the other side.

Nandini and Gayatri entered. Mr Grewal was sitting behind a large desk. Stacks of dull brown and pink-coloured files, each bound with dirty white string, stood on the large desk.

'Haan. Come, come, beta,' said Mr Grewal, 'sit.'

Gayatri and Nandini settled into the large comfortable armchairs facing Mr Grewal. His round, bald head shone under the harsh lights. Shrewd eyes peered at them from behind rimless spectacles.

'So, tell me, what's this mess you've got yourself into?' he asked, not unkindly.

Gayatri began to narrate the sequence of events. When she finished, Mr Grewal picked up the phone on the corner of his desk and dialled a single digit. 'Akshay, come in here for a minute,' he said in Punjabi.

A few seconds later, Akshay walked in. He was dressed in a crisp white shirt and black trousers, his unruly hair neatly combed. He nodded at Gayatri and Nandini.

'Akshay,' said Mr Grewal. 'Gayatri here has received some threats at the journal where she works. She says Anil from SSP also called them. I was thinking why don't you get in touch with someone at Sadhuji's ashram and see if this can be dealt with. Might be best to call Anil directly.'

Gayatri looked at Akshay. He seemed mildly irritated, but said respectfully, 'Ji, I'll see what I can do.'

'Don't worry, beta,' said Mr Grewal to Gayatri. 'We will do all we can to help. We have a very good relationship with Sadhuji, going back many years to when I was a young lawyer. But it's better for Akshay to make these calls—things are a little delicate for me now with this party business starting.'

'Thank you, Uncle,' said Gayatri gratefully.

Akshay said, 'I'll need a few more details.'

'Sure, shall we speak now?' Gayatri rose from her chair.

Akshay glanced at his phone with a frown. 'No, I need to leave for court now. Later in the evening, maybe?'

'Yes, of course,' said Gayatri.

'Thank you, Unc— uh, Papa,' said Nandini to her father-in-law.

Mr Grewal waved them off with a smile as Akshay held the door open.

'What time would you like to meet, then?' Gayatri asked Akshay.

Now that he was out of his father's room, Akshay's irritation was evident on his face. 'Can I text you a little later in the day and let you know? Somewhere near the High Court, maybe.'

'That works,' said Gayatri. 'Then—'

Akshay turned around abruptly and walked away without waiting for her to finish.

Gayatri waited for Nandini in the lobby of the house while her sister went to get her bag. Akshay seemed to be making such a big deal about making one phone call. She would never have accepted a favour from someone like him if she could have helped it. She looked around her and was struck by how much she disliked the décor: velvet upholstery and matching dark velvet curtains held open with a golden-coloured cord. Statues and artefacts cluttered the floor and tables. She wondered whether these surroundings would cause a change in Nandini's tastes after a while.

'Didi, I'm ready, come,' Nandini called from the doorway.

'Akshay seemed a bit irritated, no?' asked Gayatri as she got into the car.

'Nah, don't worry about it,' said Nandini. 'He's a bit crabby these days. But his dad's word is like gospel for him. He'll try his best, I'm sure of that.'

Gayatri entered her office an hour later, exhausted. 'Such a bad jam on Lodhi Road,' she grumbled as she walked towards her desk. 'My calf muscles are hurting from the constant clutch-brake-clutch-brake I've done for the las—'

'Gayatri, I was just going to call you,' interrupted Farah. 'Come here. Look at this.'

Gayatri walked over to Farah's desk and read through the email open on her computer screen. It was from Visheshwar Dutt. She scowled. 'How very innocent—offering to come here with some friends and discuss the matter.'

Just then Kanthan entered, holding a piece of paper, looking upset. Farah looked at Gayatri and said softly, 'I forwarded the email to him.'

'I have such a bad feeling about this,' he said as he approached their desks.

Gayatri said, 'I just met my sister's father-in-law. His elder son, Akshay, has promised to speak with someone at SSP. Let's see if anything comes of that. They know this Sadhuji very well.'

Kanthan sighed. 'I've also spoken to a few people. Everyone is connecting the attacks on the *Indian Age* journalists with these people. This kind of thing is happening at many places now.'

'We should get the papers to cover this,' said Gayatri, frowning. 'Get some news reporters to write about it. And I still think we should go to the cops.'

'That will not help anyone,' said Kanthan. 'I don't think these people are bothered by what someone says in a newspaper. And what will we tell the cops? So far, we just have a couple of emails from this guy asking for his piece to be published. We don't even have proof of the phone calls.'

Gayatri's frown intensified. 'I hope you both know that you can record calls on your mobile phones?'

'Both calls came on landlines,' said Farah.

'Look,' said Kanthan, 'I think the sensible thing is to let matters cool down. I've said this before: I will not compromise on your physical safety.'

Gayatri knew well that Kanthan disliked any form of attention, good or bad. She admired him for refusing all requests to appear on TV debates, preferring instead to communicate through his writing

and his lectures at Delhi University. Now though, she felt he was
taking his reticence too far.

'I don't agree,' said Gayatri, 'but let's first see what Akshay can do
for us, and then take a decision.'

'I don't know how he will help, frankly. Are we going to have a
debate and convince these goondas to respect our freedom of speech?'
asked Kanthan irritably.

'At least let him try,' said Farah.

'Okay, go ahead and try,' said Kanthan. 'But I'm telling you now:
there is no way that this will end with them backing off. Bullies don't
see reason.'

They were all silent for a few moments. Then Kanthan said, 'If this
is the state of this country, so be it. It deserves to be run by goons,'
before walking away.

Gayatri shook her head. 'So cowardly. I didn't expect this of
Kanthan.'

'He doesn't mean it,' said Farah. 'And really, it's not cowardly to want
to save yourself and your loved ones from danger, Gayatri.' She paused.
'Even for you and me—it's not the same thing for us. You know, when
that Dutt guy started telling me to go to Pakistan with my histories
of Mughals and talking of ... I don't remember if it was kebabs, or
something equally ridiculous ... I was stunned. I shouldn't have been,
but it was the first time I was directly confronted ... taunted, really ...
with my religious identity at my place of work, and it just shook me up.'

Gayatri was silent for a few seconds. 'I don't know what the right
way to deal with this is, Faru,' she admitted in a calmer tone, 'but I
don't think bowing down is the answer. I know these situations are
different for you and me, but still ...'

'Well, I have no illusions about the lines that these people can cross.'

Gayatri sighed. 'Will you at least come with me to meet Akshay in
the evening? That way, we can both gauge the extent of the problem.'

Farah nodded. 'Yes, we'll go together.'

Later that evening, Akshay, Gayatri and Farah were in a café in Sunder Nagar.

Usually when she came to Sunder Nagar, Gayatri kept her eyes peeled for the exotic breeds of dogs being walked along the wide paths, their leashes invariably held by neatly dressed domestic help. Sometimes, she would ask to pet a particularly friendly looking St. Bernard or ruffle a husky behind the ears. She couldn't help but sympathize with these poor creatures, subjected as they were to Delhi's intense heat that their systems couldn't possibly survive, except in their air-conditioned homes. Today though, Gayatri had not noticed the dogs while driving to the café with Farah.

'Do you have the article this Dutt guy sent in?' Akshay asked. Gayatri handed him a few sheets of paper. He skimmed through them quickly. 'And did you bring along some older issues of your journal?'

'Yes,' said Gayatri, handing over four issues of the *Review*, with a few brightly coloured Post-its poking out of each. 'I've flagged some articles which might have irritated these fellows.'

'Okay,' he said, looking at Farah. 'So what do you want to do now?'

It appeared to Gayatri that he was deliberately addressing Farah rather than her. She spoke: 'I thought Gyan Uncle said you could make some calls to someone at that Sadhuji's organization, maybe to Anil Bhargav? He's the one who called Kanthan about this article.'

'I can, yes,' said Akshay. 'But before that, I think you should ask yourselves if it's really worth getting entangled in such controversial issues. I'm sure there's more than enough research to be done and published without courting trouble.' He shook his head. 'There's very little to gain by antagonizing these people, believe me.'

Gayatri took a deep breath to quell the surge of anger that had welled up in her. What a condescending ass. 'See,' she said, outwardly calm, 'we're a private society, not obliged to take anyone else's views into account. We don't work with an agenda. We, and our contributors, spend hours doing research, looking through archives that have not yet been mined. We will publish what we honestly believe deserves to be published when looked at through an academic lens, not random people's political preferences. And we definitely don't want to be forced to publish nonsense.'

Gayatri looked directly at Akshay as she spoke. He seemed a little ruffled by her straightforward manner.

'It's not that I don't get the seriousness of this,' continued Gayatri. 'It's just that there is a point, you know, beyond which prudence and holding back is just cowardice.'

'And what about you?' Akshay asked Farah. 'And Mr Kanthan? Do you also think that you should be pursuing a battle with these people?'

Farah's eyes darted towards Gayatri before she said, 'I don't know. If there is a way to sort this out without getting into a fight, that would be better. But I'm not sure what options we have, really.'

Akshay nodded. 'Look, I can try speaking to someone at the SSP, in particular about this Dutt fellow's article, but after that I think it would be better to lay low for a while and see what compromises are possible.' He glanced at Gayatri. While her face did not betray any emotion, her eyes were flashing. 'I will call someone at Sadhuji's office tomorrow,' he continued, 'and let you know how things go. I'm not promising anything.'

'Of course,' said Farah. 'Thanks so much.'

Akshay stood up and gathered the papers they had given him. 'Do you guys need to be dropped anywhere?'

'No,' said Gayatri, her tone bordering on cold. 'We have a car.'

'Okay.' Akshay held out his hand to shake Farah's, then turned to Gayatri. 'Bye, Gayatri.'

She nodded and said formally, 'Thank you for doing this.' After he had left the café, she turned to Farah. 'I don't like him one bit.'

'He's only trying to help.'

'I know, but his superior attitude, the way he looks at me like I'm some sort of idiot for wanting to resist this, is getting to me.'

'Kanthan and I don't want to pick a fight either, Gayatri.'

'I know, Farah. And I get where you are coming from, really, I do. But people like Akshay don't know how it feels to do something meaningful. What does he do on a daily basis? He's just a paid spokesperson for criminals. Advises his crooked clients on how best to avoid getting caught by the cops.'

'You can't blame him for doing his job.'

'His solution is "stop doing whatever is pissing these people off". People like him can't even begin to understand what makes someone want to take a stand on anything.'

'What stand, Gayatri? Aren't we also asking him to do some back-channel talking to help us?'

Gayatri fell silent and frowned.

'Anyway, let's not argue,' said Farah. 'This whole thing is depressing as it is.'

'That it is,' muttered Gayatri.

That night, as Akshay sat at his desk in his office studying some papers intently, the door to his office creaked open.

'Still working, beta?' asked Mr Grewal.

'Yes, Papa,' said Akshay, looking up. 'I was working on tomorrow's land dispute hearing. I've also been reading some back issues of Gayatri's journal, just to get a sense of what these people have been writing about before I speak with Bhargavji.'

Mr Grewal crossed his arms. 'And what did you think?'

Akshay shrugged. 'It's pretty high-quality academic research and writing. The contributors are all well-respected historians, and, to be fair, they have people from across ideologies writing for the journal.' He paused and added, 'A piece Gayatri wrote even inspired me to order a book on the subject.'

'What have Sadhuji's people taken offence to then?'

Akshay clicked his tongue. 'They did a special issue on Akbar, with a detailed study of his religious policy, accounts of inter-faith dialogues that he promoted, some pieces on his military conquests, promotion of the arts ... You know, that sort of thing. There was also one critical piece, but anyway ...'

Mr Grewal nodded.

'And Gayatri wrote an article on Godse in a recent issue. Ripping apart his defence and all that. Maybe that's what has riled up these people.'

'Very likely.'

'Although the journal seems to keep things balanced. For example, they did a special issue on Rajput warrior culture, Shivaji, Hindu epics, stuff like that. Honestly speaking, I don't see such a great bias.'

'How many people work at this journal?'

'They have a pretty prominent editorial board. The major editing is done by Gayatri and another woman called Farah, and they have a staff of another seven or eight people. And, of course, it's headed by Ramesh Kanthan.'

Mr Grewal grunted. 'These girls should be careful. Sadhuji and the party are on the rise now, they are in that mode where they think they can get away with anything.'

'I know, I tried to tell them, but I don't think this girl understands.'

'Achha? Matlab, stupid type?' asked Mr Grewal.

'No, no, not stupid at all.' Akshay paused before continuing, 'She seems intelligent, judging from her writing. And I guess in some sense, even brave. But then bravery and foolishness, they're almost the same thing.'

'Means?'

'I don't remember the last time I came across someone so—' He struggled to find the right words. 'So pointlessly stubborn. This standing up for her right to publish and speak freely, without any other agenda—it seems like such a naive view of the world.'

'Chalo, see what you can do. If nothing else, we must try for Nandini's sake.'

'Yes,' said Akshay with a sigh. 'Anyway, I'm going upstairs for dinner soon. Ma hasn't eaten yet. Are you coming?'

'No, no, you go ahead. I have some work to finish, I'll eat downstairs with my team,' Mr Grewal mumbled.

He didn't notice Akshay's face harden as he shut the door behind him.

Akshay was still in his office twenty minutes later, when there was a knock on the door. He frowned. 'Come in.'

He saw Neelam Bedi's elegant figure framed in the doorway. She was dressed in a simple black saree with a dull gold border. Her long hair was tied in a neat bun, and a small black bindi marked the centre of her brow.

She smiled. 'Hungry?'

'No, thank you,' Akshay replied tersely, and went back to reading the papers on his desk.

'Busy?' she asked, with an air of exaggerated innocence.

'Er … yes, actually.'

'Oh. I was just briefing Grewalji on the Kapoor land acquisition matter. Maybe you could also give us your thoughts for the final hearing tomorrow. We were just going to order dinner, we can all eat together.'

'No, thanks,' he said.

She stood silently for a few seconds, then entered the room and closed the door behind her. Akshay grit his teeth. His eyes focused on a single word on the paper before him.

'Akshay.' Her soft voice sounded loud in this small space.

He looked up at her stonily. 'You need to stop this.'

'You're always in a foul mood,' Neelam teased.

'I have work to do. I think you'd better get back to my father.' He returned his gaze to the file on his table.

'He's gone upstairs.' She walked up to his desk and rested a single finger on the glass that covered the surface of his wooden desk. Akshay noticed her manicured nail—perfectly oval, painted a dull, almost unnoticeable pink.

'I haven't seen too many girls come by lately. After … What was her name? Pooja?'

Akshay remained silent.

'I'm just asking generally, you know,' she said. 'There's no need to be rude.'

'Neelu!' Mr Grewal called out from his room.

She smiled, and walked out of Akshay's office.

He took a deep breath and closed his eyes. After a few seconds, he packed up his papers and left.

On the other side of town, Gayatri knocked on her grandmother's door. Malti Didi let her in. Dadi was sitting up in bed, facing the television set.

'Ram Ram ji, Dadi,' said Gayatri.

'You just came?' her grandmother asked as Gayatri settled on the chair beside the bed.

'Yes, I was with some of my school friends for dinner.'

'Beta, you should be careful when you are out so late. Why don't you take a driver?'

Gayatri smiled. 'Next time.'

'You always say that. This city is not safe, Gayatri. You should be more sensible about these things.'

Gayatri nodded. 'You're right, Dadi, but I keep safe. I lock my car in one motion as I shut the car door, I try to drive only on main roads, and always keep my phone at hand next to me. This driver business is too complicated.'

Her grandmother appeared unsatisfied with her answer.

'Anyway,' said Gayatri, gesturing to the television, 'what happened in *Bahurani ki Kahaani* today? Did Rohan come back to life?'

'I don't know what happens in these wretched serials half the time,' said Dadi, shaking her head. 'Sometimes people are dead, sometimes alive. Then they jump one generation, and then they show flashbacks. If Malti wasn't there to explain things to me, I would not understand anything.'

Malti tore her gaze from the television set to Gayatri, her eyes bright. 'Rohan apna mummy ka beta phir se born hua. Koi pregnancy nahin, aise hi.'

Gayatri stifled a laugh. 'At least makkhi nahin bana.'

'Did these friends you met include any boys?' Dadi asked, casually.

'Ohho, Dadi. I went to a girls' convent school. How will there be any boys?' She continued with a smile, 'Some of the girls did bring their husbands though, do you want me to try and snare one of them?'

Her grandmother ignored Gayatri's remark and turned her eyes back to the television.

'Anyway,' Gayatri said, 'I've decided to not go to these school dinners any more. All anyone talks about is their maids and drivers. Unless they have kids—then there is absolutely nothing else you can talk to them about. Today, I told my friend that I want to go to Greece next year. She starts off, "Oh, Greeece! Do you know, my Aryan knows the capital of Greece! I mean, he is just seven."' Gayatri raised her eyebrows. 'What is so amazing about that? Meera Didi, from next door, her son is five and he knows many more capitals. Of course, I didn't tell her that.'

Gayatri could tell Dadi wasn't really listening to her rant. When she found something disinteresting, Dadi just channelled a look of dignified disengagement. I should also develop this skill, thought Gayatri. It'll help me deal with these over-enthusiastic mommy types.

Her phone beeped. It was a message from Farah.

Dadi's eyes darted towards her, alert. 'Who is it?'

'Just work.'

'So late?' asked Dadi disbelievingly. 'I'm telling you, if there is someone—'

'Uff,' said Gayatri. 'Ever since Chhoti's wedding, you've all become more hyper about me. Why don't you just give up now?'

'Why should we give up?' demanded Dadi. 'Aaj kal so many new things are happening. Today on TV they were talking about some programme on mobiles to find boys called … uh …' Dadi closed her eyes, mumbling, 'Koi sabzi ka naam tha.' She looked at the TV intently, and then said, 'Haan, Tinda!'

Gayatri almost choked on the water she was drinking as she let out a laugh. Through her laughter, she felt a sudden stab of sadness. She missed Nandini. Without Chhoti around, having Dadi advise her to get on 'Tinda' just wasn't as funny as it should have been.

She kissed her grandmother goodnight and trudged up the stairs. She remembered how she and her sister had howled at the vidai ceremony after the wedding, Nandini refusing to let go of her. She paused as she crossed Nandini's now-empty room. This, she thought, looking at the closed door, is the quiet, sad reality of all that loud emotion.

As she shut the door to her room that night, Gayatri felt achingly alone.

4

N<small>ANDINI'S EYES OPENED</small> slowly as her phone began to buzz and beep.
The sound of the alarm was familiar; her surroundings were not. The
interjection of Amar's loud snores in the alarm's symphony reminded
her of where she was. She thought wistfully of Malti Didi, appearing
each morning with a cup of hot tea at the exact moment that her
alarm rang.

She stretched her limbs with a loud yawn and checked her phone
for messages before walking to the kitchen and turning on the electric
kettle. As the kettle gurgled, her still-sleepy eyes rested on the gulmohar
tree outside the kitchen window, its tiny leaves-within-leaves brushing
against the window grills.

The kettle turned off with a click as the water came to a boil. She
was reaching for a teabag when, suddenly, she recalled snatches of a
conversation she had overheard the previous day in office. Two senior
partners at her law firm had been discussing Amar. 'I'm glad Ritesh

didn't involve Amar in this deal. Asks the dumbest questions,' one had said. 'I mean, there has to be some limit on how far you can go on your dad's back, yaar,' replied the other. They had not known that she was in the adjoining conference room, waiting for a client. The client had arrived, and her busy day had taken over. She hadn't realized until now that her mind had tucked away the conversation to revisit later.

Sipping from the mug, she leaned against the kitchen counter. The hot tea, swirling across her tongue and down her throat, woke her up completely. She looked out of the window at the gulmohar again. When had she decided to marry Amar? She couldn't remember. She was twenty-eight and they had been dating for close to a year; marriage was never discussed, just assumed. So different from Didi, who had been forced to meet a series of random guys, and yet, was still single.

Nandini remembered the row she had had with her sister over Amar. What had Didi said? She squinted in an effort to remember: do you really love him or some filmy dialogue like that.

And now, here I am. She gulped down the last of the tea, flushing away her thoughts for the moment.

At a few minutes past five, Gayatri arrived at Café Nico in Greater Kailash. Akshay had called in the morning, asking to meet to talk about his discussion with the SSP. Farah had to go home early, so she hadn't accompanied her this time, but she had made Gayatri promise that she wouldn't be rude to Akshay.

Gayatri spotted him in a corner of the café and sat down opposite him, saying, 'Hi, so sorry, I know I'm late.' She was slightly out of breath.

Akshay had arrived ten minutes early for the meeting. 'It's fine, I just got here myself,' he said.

Gayatri set her bag down on the chair next to her and faced him expectantly.

He frowned slightly as he looked at her. She was dressed in a beige salwar–kameez, her hair was loose, and her cheeks were flushed from what he presumed had been a brisk walk from her car.

To Gayatri, his gaze seemed disapproving. 'So,' she said, tentatively, 'you said you managed to speak with someone at SSP?'

Akshay blinked a couple of times to bring himself back to attention. 'Yes, I spoke with Anil Bhargav.' He took an audible breath before continuing. 'He told me, informally of course, that this is part of a campaign they are running against many publications and news channels, big and small. They think the whole liberal, left-wing school of history has dominated for far too long, and they want to correct this by pushing their own version. And they have the support of the BSD and the government.'

'He said all that?'

'Not in so many words, obviously,' said Akshay. 'I'm simplifying it for you.'

Gayatri brushed away a twinge of irritation at his manner.

'So Bhargav is very set in his views, and this is one of those issues that can get them news headlines and publicity. But,' he paused before going on, 'I also managed to speak to Sadhuji. I made two points to him: one, that your journal is not popular in the first place and hardly anyone reads it.'

Gayatri's eyes flashed. What? The *Review* was one of the most well-respected journals in India.

Akshay added quickly, 'Relatively, I mean, and that it's mainly got academic value and is unlikely to sway public opinion.' He took a sip of water and continued, 'Second, I told him that you do try to publish all kinds of writing to balance things out, not just stuff his people disagree with. I mentioned that you have written many pieces on Hindu culture, like the one on Rajput warriors, the one on the Chola dynasty, and one on ... Ashoka, wasn't it? And the issue you had on alternative histories that included some of their hero historians like Vivekananda, Majumdar and all.'

Gayatri nodded, calming down as she realized that Akshay had taken the trouble to read the copies she'd given him. 'What did he say?'

'Look, to be honest, Sadhuji doesn't have a ... a personal view on history and all. He just thinks of himself as a holy man. It's Anil Bhargav who believes that they can use this "distortion of history" issue for a larger purpose. And Bhargav genuinely feels that the right must wrest control away from Marxist historians. When I spoke with him, he had plenty of examples of fact-twisting by leftist historians, and their arrogance. And they were bona-fide examples, no one could disagree.'

Gayatri frowned as she said, 'Even if that is true, surely they can't paint everyone who doesn't agree with them with the same brush? Anyone who has read Kanthan knows that his writings are almost ideology-neutral.'

'With all due respect to Mr Kanthan, I don't think that's possible. Ultimately, history is written by people, not machines. And all human beings, intelligent ones at least, have opinions.'

'As do stupid people,' said Gayatri, a little too quickly. She took a deep breath and adjusted her tone. 'Whatever you might say, at least Kanthan doesn't have an agenda, unlike this Mr Bhargav, whose agenda seems quite clear.'

'That's relative. Bhargav sees Kanthan's narrative, or lack of support for the right-wing view of history, as pushing a particular agenda. Anyway, to cut a long story short, Sadhuji seemed reasonably satisfied with the arguments I made, so I think your journal should be fine for now.'

'But do you think Sadhuji will be able to get Anil Bhargav to back off? You said this Bhargav person was quite aggressive.'

'Well, Sadhuji is the head of the organization. I expect he has some say in the matter.'

'Okay, yes, I guess they can't do anything he doesn't want them to.' Gayatri nodded, though it was evident she was not convinced. 'Okay,' she said again. 'Thanks so much for this.'

'No problem. These conversations can be tricky, but the right points needed to be highlighted. Plus, it helps that we have a personal equation with Sadhuji, that's why he was willing to listen in the first place.'

Gayatri smiled politely. This is probably the oily salesman part of his lawyer personality, she thought. 'And what about the others they are targeting?'

'Who?'

'We've heard from many people that other publications are also being threatened.'

'So?' asked Akshay.

'So they will continue to bully others? Can't this Sadhuji make his people see sense?'

Akshay looked at her incredulously. 'Surely you don't expect me to plead on behalf of every publication in India? I've sorted out your mess, that's all I was meant to do.'

Gayatri swallowed. There was no point in engaging with him on anything to do with the greater good, she thought. 'No, I didn't mean it like that,' she said.

Akshay shook his head slightly. She doesn't understand the real world, he thought. She is living in some fairyland where Bhargav will suddenly have a change of heart and roll back his agenda, convinced by an academic argument on the freedom of speech.

'And there is one more thing,' he said. 'Sadhuji would like to meet you.'

'Me?' she asked, puzzled.

'Yes, you,' said Akshay flatly.

'But why?'

'I don't know. He is a holy man, or a powerful one at the very least. They do things their own way.'

Gayatri sighed in exasperation. 'I don't—' she began, but Akshay interrupted her.

'Listen, Nandini and Amar have to go and get his blessings soon. You can go along with them, if that makes things easier. You've got what you want, now just complete this formality. It's not such a big deal.'

Gayatri nodded reluctantly. After a moment, she said, 'Akshay, thank you for this. We really appreciate it.'

'It's no problem. Just try to stay out of trouble,' he said with a small smile. He looked at his phone. 'I'd better get going.'

As she started to reach for her bag, she turned to him suddenly and asked, 'Why did we need to meet in person for this conversation?'

Akshay looked slightly uncomfortable. 'It's just that ... you know ... with my father joining the BSD, there is talk of phones being bugged. Maybe I'm being overly cautious. Sorry.'

'No, no, that's fine. Thank you again,' said Gayatri, suspecting an inflated sense of self-importance at work again. Who does this guy think he is? Saying a polite goodbye, she left the café quickly.

Once she was in her car, she remembered that her parents were expecting guests. Not in the mood for company, she turned on the radio and drove around aimlessly for a few minutes. How nice it would be to have a place of my own, she thought.

She took a U-turn at an intersection, and turned into N-Block in Greater Kailash, which housed one of her favourite Delhi markets, with its shops arranged around a small rectangular park. As a child, she had loved tagging along with her mother to such markets on hot summer afternoons. The days had seemed longer then, people seemed to have less to do, and there wasn't so much traffic between every person and their destination.

The market wasn't too busy. She walked in and out of shops, lightly running her fingers over the rows of cool cotton clothes perennially on display, no matter the weather, browsing through the magazines in a stall set up in the corridor, and finally, descended the steep staircase to the basement bookshop.

'Hi, ma'am!' called the person at the counter as she navigated the last step.

'Hi, Vinod, kaise hain aap?' she replied, immediately cheered by the sight of the cashier's familiar face surrounded by piles of books.

She pulled up a stool beside a shelf and started to pick out books, thumbing through them. After a few minutes, her eyes fell on a book titled *Listening to Silence with Sadhuji*. She pulled it out and found herself looking at Sadhuji posing serenely on the cover. He sat cross-legged on a tiger skin with a large image of the god Shiva visible behind him. Shiva too sat on a tiger skin, but unlike Sadhuji, he had a trishul in his hand and a serpent around his neck. His lustrous hair was tied in a macho bun from which the River Ganga flowed. Mount Kailash, topped with snow, glistened behind his head.

Gayatri tried to picture the scene when this photograph of Sadhuji was taken. The image of Shiva would have been carefully placed, and Sadhuji's face positioned strategically to allow for good composition. The photographer must have taken twenty or thirty shots, maybe more. Was there an umbrella dispersing light when the photoshoot was on? Did Sadhuji alter his expressions as the photographer clicked the shots? Thoda chin down kariye, sir, yes like that. She imagined Sadhuji tilting his head, softening his gaze, until the perfect shot was achieved.

Why does this person think he has a say over what our journal publishes, she thought resentfully.

She pulled out another book. *Godmen: Their Stories*. It had a chapter on Sadhuji. She started to read:

Kartar Singh Doljat, now known as Sadhuji, was born into a farmer's family in 1965 in Doljat, a village near Faridkot in Punjab. When he was eight, his teacher claimed he had miraculously turned ink into water in the classroom. This was followed by claims of other miracles: revealing the hiding places of lost objects, predictions of unseasonal rains, curing of fevers with herbs.

Kartar had amassed a small band of young followers by the time he was fifteen, but most village elders considered him a mere prankster. He dropped out of school and began to spend time wandering in the fields around Doljat. His excursions became longer, until one day at the age of eighteen, he disappeared. His parents gave him up for dead after a few weeks.

When he returned to Doljat eleven years later, Kartar found that his father and two younger brothers had died, and his mother and remaining siblings were labouring in the fields for a pittance. The state had experienced one of its worst floods in memory the year before and conditions in the village were even worse than when he had left; a shadow of poverty hanging over all.

Within two months of his arrival, one of the two major landowners in the village perished with his entire family in a road accident. Their heirs lived abroad, who hastily sold their inheritance to the villagers at the price negotiated by local brokers. That year, the rains were perfect and Doljat reaped a bumper crop. Word spread that credit for heaven's largesse was due to young Kartar. His followers grew in the inexplicable manner characteristic of such cases.

By 1999, he had built a small ashram in Doljat. People began to throng the place to seek his blessings. The villagers set up shops and rest houses to cater to the growing crowd. Prosperity dawned on Doljat.

Gayatri skimmed through the rest of the chapter, which listed the growing number of his ashrams operating under the Shri Seva Parishad banner, and his mentorship of the BSD: 'No office of the BSD is complete without a photo of Sadhuji looking over their operations.'

Kartar, she said to herself. I wonder if he even remembers his real name.

'We're closing now, ma'am,' said Vinod.

Replacing the book, she climbed the stairs, her mind still occupied with thoughts of Sadhuji. The knowledge that her safe, ordered world had intersected with an unfamiliar, unpredictable one made her nervous.

When Akshay returned home after meeting Gayatri, he found his younger sister, Priya, sitting with Amar and Nandini.

'Hi Bhaiya,' said Priya, going over to him and putting an arm around his waist.

'Hi,' he said, kissing the top of her head. 'I met your sister today,' he said to Nandini as he sat down.

'Oh, any progress on that front?' asked Nandini.

'I think so, let's see. She will have to go and meet Sadhuji, though. I told her she could go with you and Amar.'

'About that, Bhaiya,' said Amar, 'can you also come along? Sadhuji knows you better, and I've never really been to his ashram on my own. It will be much easier for us.'

After checking their calendars on their phones, Amar and Akshay decided to go the next day.

Priya interrupted them in a high voice. 'What is this about?' She turned to Nandini. 'Why does your sister have to see Sadhuji?'

Nandini opened her mouth and then closed it, unsure of what to say.

'Nothing, Priya,' said Akshay. 'She edits a journal, it's something to do with that.'

'Oh,' said Priya, looking at Nandini inquisitively. 'But why does she need to meet Sadhuji for it?'

Nandini tried not to let her irritation show. Thank god she lives on another continent, she thought.

'Just something she needs to discuss with him,' Akshay answered. 'Are you going out somewhere after this?' he asked, in a bid to change the subject.

'No, why?' asked Priya. She was dressed in an expensive-looking knee-length dress with gold stones stitched on its neck and sleeves. Her earlobes were all but covered by huge diamonds, their brilliance and cut matching those of the ones on her fingers. A handbag marked with monogrammed letters lay by her side on the sofa. Her sandals, with their single red strip running up the high heel, betrayed, to those in the know, their astronomical price.

'No, nothing, you're very dressed up, that's all,' Akshay said, instantly regretting his choice of subject. 'You look nice,' he added.

Priya looked down at her clothes. 'I can't dress the way I used to earlier now, can I?' she said. 'Bobby is so social, you know. Someone or the other is coming over all the time, or we are going out. And my mother-in-law doesn't like it if I don't have jewellery on. And why not—if we have the money, I shouldn't go around embarrassing them by dressing down, na?'

Nandini fiddled with her earlobe uncomfortably. She was still wearing the salwar–kameez and flats she had worn to office, and had on a chain and small earrings. Her purse, lying on top of her files next to her, had no discernible label.

'Anyway, I'm spending the night here. Tomorrow is my last day, na, before we leave for New York. I wish could stay longer, but Bobby is insisting I go back with him,' Priya grumbled.

Nandini closed her eyes for a moment, thanking the heavens for Bobby's insistence.

Mrs Grewal entered the room just then, and Akshay rose to kiss his mother on her cheek.

'Nandini, beta,' said Mrs Grewal after a few minutes of conversation, 'I was wondering … Would you like to go and spend a few days with your parents? In our family, brides usually do that after the wedding. Of course, we are only too happy to have you here, but I just thought you may enjoy that.'

Before Nandini could reply, Priya said, 'When I got married, Mummy, remember, I didn't come home to stay.'

Nandini sighed inwardly. 'Maybe I'll do that, thank you,' she said, finishing with an awkward 'Mummy'.

Akshay stood up, and stretched his shoulders. 'Okay, I'm going down to the office,' he said. 'Amar, let me know what time you want to leave for Sadhuji's ashram tomorrow.'

'Okay, Bhaiya.'

As Akshay walked towards the stairs, Priya stood up. 'Bhaiya, wait,' she said. 'I wanted to talk to you about something.'

Akshay stopped and turned to look at her. 'Yeah?'

Priya glanced at her mother as if checking whether to speak, and then looked at Akshay again. 'There's this cousin of Bobby's—'

'Please, Priya,' Akshay interrupted. 'We've spoken about this earlier. I'm not interested.'

'At least look at her photo. She is really pretty, and from a very good family. They are very close to Bobby's parents. She's an interior designer.'

Akshay took a deep breath, willing himself to not be rude in Nandini's presence. 'Just drop it, please. Anyway, I have work. I'm off.' He turned around and hurried down the stairs to the basement.

Mrs Grewal looked at her daughter sternly. 'Why do you trouble him like this, Priya?' she said. 'Even after I've told you so many times not to.'

'What, Mummy?' asked Priya petulantly. 'I've not committed a crime. I'm just trying to help. Is there something wrong with the rest of us that we got married? Or is there something wrong with him?' She looked at Amar for support.

'Priya!' admonished her mother.

Nandini shifted uncomfortably in her seat. She had returned after an especially stressful day at work, and was in no mood to witness a family row. Her stomach sank a little as she imagined more evenings like these. A sudden wave of homesickness overwhelmed her. She glanced at Amar, but he was fiddling with his phone, seemingly unconcerned.

Priya muttered, 'I was just asking because Bobby's mother told me to.'

Mrs Grewal seemed to have collected herself as she said calmly, 'What your older brother does or does not do is none of your business. He is intelligent and knows his own mind. Let him be.'

'And no one can question him, of course,' Priya said caustically.

A heavy silence descended on the group for a minute, before Amar said, 'Achha, Mom, Nandini was telling me that her cousin Tarun—the one who lives in the US and couldn't attend the wedding—is coming to India next week. Her parents are planning a little get-together and have invited all of us.'

'I'll check with Grewalji and confirm, but I think we should be free,' said Mrs Grewal.

'Bobby and I will be gone by then,' said Priya sulkily, but no one took any notice.

That night, as Nandini and Amar were watching a TV show in bed, Amar's phone rang.

'Ji, Papa,' he answered. There was a pause and then, 'Okay, give me two seconds.' He got out of bed and shuffled around for his slippers.

'What happened? Where are you going?' Nandini asked. 'Let's finish this episode, na? It's almost over.'

'I can't, Papa is calling me.'

'Now?' She couldn't hide her irritation.

'Yes. Why?' asked Amar.

'It's late, that's all. We've just come up after five hours of being downstairs, with your sister going on and on—'

'What about my sister?' Amar demanded aggressively.

'Nothing,' she said quietly.

'Are you upset because you didn't have a drink? Because I did ask you if you wanted one. You were the one who stupidly said no.'

Nandini glared at him. 'It's not the same as you having a drink in my house. Your mother was clearly not happy when you asked me. She made it obvious.'

'I've told you, it's fine here. Stop imagining things. If you want to make yourself uncomfortable, I can't help you. You're welcome to be miserable.'

'Why are you being so rude? You've been talking like this ever since we returned from Italy. Just because we are married now, do you think you can talk to me any way you please?'

'Look, Nandini, you will have to adjust to this house, the people here are not going to change for you. You need to understand that. It's the way the world is.'

'You think I'm not trying? After that crazy day at work, I smiled and talked to everyone for hours. The least you can—'

'Papa is calling me again,' Amar said abruptly, glancing at his phone, and walked out of the room.

Frowning, Nandini grabbed her phone from the bedside table to call her sister, but replaced it a few moments later. Didi will just be all preachy, she won't understand.

Nandini rested her head on the pillow, still frowning. Amar's family was so different from hers. She hadn't anticipated having to spend so much time with them every single day. The separate floor where she and Amar lived wasn't so separate after all. She closed her eyes. Maybe things will get better once this Priya goes back to the US, she thought.

When Amar returned half an hour later, he found Nandini asleep. He turned off the light and got into bed, relieved to have avoided the full-blown fight he had been sure awaited him.

A few seconds later, Nandini opened her eyes. She could make out the outline of Amar's body, turned away from her. She didn't know why she had pretended to be asleep when he entered the room. She considered sliding closer to him, but then decided against it. She turned her back towards him, and stared into the darkness.

5

'Listen, don't you have to go now?' Farah reminded Gayatri the next evening as they sat at their desks, working.

Gayatri glanced at the digital clock at the corner of her computer screen and nodded grumpily. 'I really don't want to go, Farah. I can't tell you how angry I am that I have to do this.'

'It's just a formality. You could hardly refuse after everything Akshay did. And Nandini will be with you. In any other situation, I would have come with you too, but here—'

'Yes, I know, it doesn't make any sense for you to go. The last thing we want is some confrontation. God knows if they'd even allow non-Hindus into the complex.' She paused. 'Seriously, who the hell is this con man to threaten us, and force me to meet him? And now I'll have to pretend to be all grateful.'

Gayatri's phone buzzed. 'That's them,' she said, getting up.

A large SUV stood in front of the gate. She was surprised to see Akshay in the driver's seat. Is he going because of me, she wondered. She really didn't want to take another favour from this rude and condescending fellow. She climbed into the backseat beside Nandini and gave her a hug.

Amar grinned at her from the front passenger seat. 'Hi, Didi.'

'Hello,' said Akshay formally, looking at her in the rear-view mirror as he started the car. She nodded to him. Seeing how calm he was made her even more irritable.

Nandini tugged at the sleeve of Gayatri's plain white kurta. 'Here, Didi, see our Italy photos, na. I didn't show them to you the other day when we met,' she said, swiping her phone's screen.

It was a long journey to Sadhuji's ashram. Amar, Nandini and Gayatri kept up cheerful conversation. Akshay hardly spoke. In time, the city receded, and was replaced by rows of shabby houses and shops, which gradually gave way to high-walled farmhouses. Finally, Akshay manoeuvred the car through a large white gateway into a parking lot, and found a spot between a Mercedes and a Bentley.

'Wow,' whispered Nandini to Gayatri as they walked across the parking lot, 'this Sadhu has some seriously loaded devotees. There must be at least a hundred cars here. On a weekday.'

Two women in white T-shirts and caps printed with the word 'Sadhuji' stood at a booth where all visitors were required to exchange their shoes for a round red plastic token.

Gayatri and the others paused before a large board outside with a map depicting the various shrines in the complex. 'This is huge,' she said to Nandini, curious despite herself. 'And so organized.'

The chill of the cold marble seeped through Gayatri's socks as they followed Akshay down a path into a massive room marked 'Sadbhavana Hall'. Inside, Gayatri blinked at the bright lights reflecting off huge chandeliers. A figure was seated on an elevated stage at the far end. She looked up at the television screens mounted in different parts of the hall, displaying Sadhuji's face as he chanted, his eyes closed. His long white hair flowed down freely, grazing the border of the cream shawl draped around his shoulders. His front teeth protruded slightly from under his lips.

Kartar Singh, thought Gayatri, has come quite a long way.

Throngs of devotees sat on the carpet, swaying and chanting along with Sadhuji, their eyes following the words lighting up on the screens.

Amar tapped Gayatri's shoulder. 'Shall we sit until Sadhuji calls for us?' he asked.

As she and Nandini sat down, Gayatri glanced at Amar and Akshay across the aisle separating the women from the men. Akshay looked up just then and caught her eye. They both looked away instantly. She started to fidget with her phone.

A few minutes later, Nandini nudged her. 'They're calling us.'

The four of them were guided into a private audience room, where incredulity overtook Gayatri's impatience. On one side of the plushly carpeted room stood a golden throne on an elevated platform, its arms carved in the shape of fierce-looking lions. Gayatri was reminded of the movie *Tahalka*, in which Amrish Puri played General Dong, the evil leader of an imaginary country called Dongrila.

They sat down on a long sofa, Gayatri between Nandini and Akshay. The air was heavy with silence. Gayatri began to feel a little suffocated in the seemingly surreal surroundings.

At last, Sadhuji entered, followed by three attendants, and strode towards the throne. He looked much smaller in person than he had on the screens in the hall. Akshay, Amar and Nandini stood up, folded their hands and bent their heads. Gayatri reluctantly followed suit.

After a few seconds, Sadhuji's voice rang out: 'Om Shivaay.' Amar and Akshay echoed his words as they raised their heads. He was seated on the throne. Akshay approached him and spoke in a low tone. Sadhuji nodded slowly as he looked at Gayatri, his face expressionless.

Gayatri shrank back slightly, a mixture of anger and revulsion gripping her. Sadhuji was gazing at her calmly. She felt a sense of déjà vu: an incident from her schooldays flashed in her mind, when she had been forced to apologize, for no fault of hers, to a classmate in front of the whole assembly. For the shy child that Gayatri had been, the experience had been akin to torture.

Akshay gestured to Gayatri to come forward, but even though she was standing, she could not move. She took a deep breath to calm her inner turmoil. He's just a con man, she told herself. She willed her feet to step forward, but they felt nailed to the ground.

Akshay came back to her and whispered, 'This will just take two minutes, I promise.'

When she stayed rooted stiffly to the spot, he placed his hand gently on her lower back and said again, gently, 'Come, Gayatri, it's just a formality. Let's just finish this off, please.'

Gayatri let herself be led towards Sadhuji. As she stood before him, Sadhuji placed his hand on her head, his fingers grazing the back of her neck. Tiny volcanoes of disgust erupted on the skin of her neck and arms, which seemed to rebel against his touch. She felt the pressure of his hand keeping her head bowed as he chanted calmly in Sanskrit, the sound of his voice grating through her body with every syllable. Her face muscles felt tight and her teeth were clenched as she stared at Akshay's feet next to her.

Sadhuji loosened his grip as he came to the final chant and she raised her head to meet his gaze. Her cheeks were flushed. He held out some flowers but she made no move to take them. Akshay stepped forward and took the flowers, instead, then held her hand and placed them in it.

Sadhuji stared at Gayatri intently for a few seconds. She did not look away. Then, he turned towards his attendants and said, 'Now prepare for the pooja for Amar and Nandini.'

An attendant guided Akshay and Gayatri out of the chamber. Akshay was still holding Gayatri's hand with the flowers, lest she drop them. They passed through a small corridor into the large grounds. He led her to a bench a few steps away.

'Are you okay?' he asked, looking puzzled, as they sat down.

Gayatri took a deep breath and nodded. 'I'm sorry, I don't know what came over me.' She bit her lip to fight the angry tears she could feel forming behind her eyes. Not in front of him, she told herself. She couldn't remember why her hand was in his.

'Don't worry,' he said. He placed her hand in her lap. It was trembling. 'Your hand, it's still shaking,' he said.

She looked down blankly.

'Are you sure you're okay?' he asked gently.

'I'm really sorry,' she repeated. 'I don't know what happened.'

'Just sit for a bit,' he said. 'You'll feel better.'

A few minutes later, Gayatri and Akshay left the ashram. He had insisted they leave right away, a little unsettled himself by her seemingly visceral reaction to Sadhuji, and feeling oddly responsible for her ordeal. He had called for another car for Amar and Nandini, even though Gayatri had hesitated to leave her sister behind. 'She'll be fine, she's with Amar,' Akshay had reassured her, saying that they couldn't interrupt the pooja, which would take at least another forty-five minutes. He had sent Amar a text explaining the situation.

Gayatri lowered the car window and took a deep breath. The polluted air felt fresher than the purified air in Sadhuji's chamber. They sat in silence as the car slowly wound its way through the narrow bylanes of Chhatarpur.

As the car idled at a crowded traffic light, Akshay turned to Gayatri. Her head rested against the seat and though her eyes were closed, worry lines creased her forehead. He looked at her intently for a few seconds, his face betraying no emotion. He noticed that one of her long silver earrings was tangled in her hair.

The noise of the horns that started blaring as soon as the light turned green interrupted his thoughts, and he resumed inching through the traffic. After driving in silence for a few minutes, he glanced at Gayatri again. Her eyes were open now.

'Feeling better?' he asked as he changed gears. She nodded as she sat up straighter and moistened her lips with her tongue. She doesn't look better, he thought. 'Do you want to stop somewhere for a coffee or something?' he asked.

Gayatri looked out of the window and shook her head. 'No. I'm fine, thank you. I'm sorry if I … uh … made a scene.'

He looked down at her hands. The tremble seemed to have disappeared. 'You didn't make a scene,' he said.

'Do you think Sadhuji will still keep his word about our journal and tell his people to back off?' asked Gayatri, after a pause.

Akshay shrugged. 'He expects most visitors to give an arm and a leg for the kind of audience you seemed terrified by.'

Gayatri frowned. 'I was not terrified, Akshay. I don't know what happened to me in that room.' She turned towards him. 'So you think he won't help us then?'

'I didn't say that. I don't think what happened today will affect anything.' He didn't want to tell her that Sadhuji had probably already forgotten about their meeting.

Gayatri looked out of the window again. She sighed. 'I really don't know what happened inside. I felt as if I was underwater, as if I couldn't breathe.'

Akshay remained silent. A few seconds later, he turned on the radio. Gayatri wondered why she had bothered to explain herself to him. When they reached her house, she got out of the car and thanked him curtly, before closing the car door and walking in.

Akshay's stiff smile dissolved into a troubled frown as soon as she turned away.

Caught up in her meeting with Sadhuji all of Friday, Gayatri had barely had time to plan for the lunch she had promised to help Nandini host at her new home on Sunday. After spending Saturday afternoon making and remaking lists and running errands for the lunch, Gayatri reached the Grewals' house at noon on Sunday, dressed in a plain light-pink kurta and cream trousers, despite, or maybe because of, her mother nagging her not to wear her faded old kurtas. She was not looking forward to the afternoon at all.

She picked up two dishes from the backseat of her car and kicked the door shut behind her.

'Here, let me help you,' a voice called out as she struggled to balance her purse and the food.

Akshay walked over and took the dishes from her hands carefully.

'Thanks so much.' She gathered some bags from the front seat and followed him up the stairs, which led to his and Amar's apartments.

He smiled, looking back at her. 'I can see Nandini's taken full advantage of you.'

She was glad he didn't mention the ashram. 'It's the only thing younger sisters are good for, in my experience.'

Akshay pushed open the door to Amar's flat with his back and placed the dishes on the table. Amar emerged from one of the rooms and came over to give Gayatri a hug.

'Where's Nandini?' asked Gayatri, carrying the bags into the kitchen.

'She's getting ready, I'll call her,' he replied.

Akshay took a seat in the living room, his eyes straying towards the kitchen every now and then. Gayatri's reaction to Sadhuji had been on his mind since their visit to the ashram. Her face as she had sat in his car—drawn and strained—had bothered him. Her genuine and violent revulsion for Sadhuji had stayed with him. He had started to type messages to her on his phone a few times on Saturday to ask how she was, then deleted them. He was sure she viewed him as part of the world that Sadhuji inhabited, and maybe even hated him as much as she did Sadhuji.

Just now, when he had watched her park her car and then struggle to get her things out, he had hesitated before jogging down the stairs to her, half-expecting her to brush off his offer of help.

Akshay hung around for the next hour, moving the furniture around and setting up the bar, surprising Amar, who couldn't remember the last time his busy brother had helped so much with tasks that could easily have been delegated.

Gayatri noticed Akshay talking and moving easily through the groups of people milling about on the terrace, beer in hand, quite unlike his brooding, unfriendly self. He was dressed in a white shirt and jeans, his spectacles replaced by a pair of sunglasses on this unusually sunny winter day.

She was helping in the kitchen when Akshay entered. 'Why don't you come out and get a drink?'

'Er, I'm just making sure the lunch is—'

'Already done. Come,' he insisted. He shepherded her out to the table doubling as a bar on the terrace. 'A sangria? I heard he's making them well.'

She nodded. He handed her a glass and leaned back against the railing next to her. A group of people came and stood next to them, forcing them to stand closer than they would have otherwise. Turning her face towards the sun, she took a few large sips of her sangria and felt a slow wave of cheerfulness course through her.

'Gayatri,' Akshay began hesitantly. 'I was wondering how you were doing. After the ashram visit.'

'Fine.' Her memories of the day were blurry. She recalled Akshay steering her towards Sadhuji with his hand on her back, her hands in his on a bench, and then him driving her home. She looked at him now, meeting his gaze, feeling exposed somehow. 'I don't know if I thanked you that day. I just … I don't know—'

'You don't need to thank me. That's not why I brought it up. I was just worried.'

Before she could say anything, a girl wearing a short red dress and huge sunglasses that covered half her face sidled up to Akshay and hugged him. 'Akshay Grewal!' she squealed.

Startled, he turned and smiled. 'Nitya, hi,' he said, not matching her level of enthusiasm. He looked at Gayatri, embarrassed. 'Er … this is Gayatri, Nandini's sister. Gayatri, this is Nitya, Amar's school friend.'

Gayatri noticed her ridiculously childish flower headband, and smiled politely.

'Hi, Gayatri. Why only Amar's friend?' Nitya asked with a pout. 'Not yours?'

Akshay smiled awkwardly as he extricated himself from a lingering arm.

'So, Akshay, how are you? You never respond to messages only. Now don't give me any shit about work, okay? I have many lawyer friends, no one is as busy as you.'

Akshay looked at Gayatri apologetically as Nitya continued chatting. 'Gayatri, no, wait,' he said when she turned to go inside. He looked visibly irritated.

'I'll just go check if Nandini needs help,' she said with a smile, nodding to Nitya as she left.

Half an hour later, she slipped away, duties done and further questions averted.

As the Grewal family sat around the dinner table that night, Amar could sense Nandini bristling at his mother's questions about the lunch, but he was determined not to intervene. She had fought with him just before dinner, and now he was enjoying watching his wife squirm a little.

Rupi Grewal had sent two maids to help with the lunch, and they had dutifully reported each mishap in detail, including Nandini having broken a dish that was borrowed from Rupi's kitchen.

'It just slipped from my hands. I'm sorry. I'll replace it,' said Nandini. Already annoyed because of the fight with Amar, she was finding it hard to be calm in the face of this inquisition.

'It's not available in India,' replied Rupi. 'It was bought twenty-five years ago in the US.'

Nandini apologized again. She looked at Amar for support, but he seemed immersed in his dal.

'I also heard that one girl vomited all over the guest bathroom. Is she a friend of yours?'

Nandini sighed inwardly, vowing never to let those wily spies of her mother-in-law enter her apartment again. 'She's a college friend. I think she drank too much on an empty stomach.'

Rupi murmured a few words in a disapproving tone.

'It was nothing, Ma,' said Akshay. 'It happens sometimes.'

'Not,' replied Rupi, in a slightly acidic tone, 'in our house.' She looked at Nandini, her voice slightly gentler, 'Take care next time. This is now a politician's house, you know. We can't have stories of girls getting drunk and vomiting all over the place getting out.'

Nandini said nothing, biting back the range of rude responses lined up in her head. She felt like kicking Amar, who was eating as if he had nothing to do with any of this. She had half a mind to tell his mother it was he who had forced her friend to have the vodka shots in the first place. She started to say something, then decided against it.

Pleading tiredness, she excused herself from the table and left the room before anyone could stop her.

Twenty minutes later, Amar entered their bedroom and found her watching TV. 'What the hell was that?' he demanded angrily.

'What?'

'Getting up like that from the table. Who do you think you are?'

'I was tired and came upstairs. What is so difficult to understand?' she said with a frown, her fury quickly matching his.

'Don't you dare,' said Amar, raising his voice. 'Don't you dare' he repeated, 'be rude to my mother ever again.'

Nandini's frown intensified. 'Did you by any chance tell her not to interrogate me as if I'm a criminal? When you're the one who got my friend drunk. I won't take this kind of interference in my own home.'

'This is their house, not yours. And you'd better behave yourself here.'

'What the hell do you mean by "behave yourself"? I'm not your slave,' spat Nandini angrily. 'And you and your family can keep your shitty house and fuck off. All of you.'

Amar rushed over to Nandini, his hand raised, face hard with sudden, violent rage.

Nandini instinctively stood up on the bed, grabbing a pillow to defend herself. Amar stepped back, shaking at the thought of what he had almost done.

His hand didn't come down on Nandini that night, but they both felt the impact of that near blow.

The next evening, Gayatri was sitting down to dinner with her parents and grandmother, when she received a text message from Akshay: 'Spoke to someone at ashram, all seems okay. Not to worry.' Gayatri let out a sigh of relief.

'What happened?' asked her mother.

'Nothing, Ma, just some work thing,' said Gayatri, keeping her phone face down.

They continued to eat their food, between bits of chatter.

A few minutes later, Ashok's phone rang. 'Oh,' he said, looking at it. 'I'd better speak to this fellow.' He wiped his mouth with a napkin and stood up. As he left the table, he looked at Gayatri and said, 'Come to me after you're done, I need to speak with you.'

'What's this about?' Gayatri asked with a frown once her father was out of earshot.

'I don't know,' shrugged Nina, looking at her plate.

Gayatri suspected her mother knew exactly what it was about. She took a deep breath and said loudly, 'You people are so frustrating. He wants me to meet some boy again, na? How many times do I have to tell you? No. No. No! Why do you keep torturing me with this nonsense again and again?'

'Gayatri, please don't talk to me like that, beta. I'm your mother.'

Gayatri's short temper was never more likely to flare up than when the target of her ire responded calmly. 'What kind of mother? Can't you see? I'm tired. I. DON'T. WANT. TO. MARRY. How hard is that to bloody understand? I have important things going on. Just because all you have in your life are those stupid judgemental cows you call friends, you want to get me married so they stop badgering you. This is about you, not me.'

Nina's eyes filled with tears. Gayatri swallowed, immediately feeling guilty. She knew she was shouting at her mother because she didn't have the courage to shout at her father. She stood up, went over to her mother and squatted by her chair. 'I'm sorry, Mama, I didn't mean to upset you.'

As Nina wiped away her tears, Dadi shook her head at Gayatri disapprovingly. 'What's happened to you? Is this any way to talk to your mother?'

'Oh god, Ma, please, don't cry. I'm so sorry … please, please. I don't know why I just …'

Nina continued to cry softly.

'Mama,' said Gayatri, elongating the last syllable pleadingly now, tears pooling in her own eyes. 'Ma, please, okay, just stop. I'm sorry. I shouldn't have said those things, I didn't mean th—'

'What is going on?' Ashok demanded, walking into the room and looking at his wife in surprise.

'Dad, I … uh … it's my fault. I was … uh … rude to Mama,' said Gayatri quietly. 'I thought you were going to pester me to meet a boy again. I'm sorry.'

Ashok placed his hand on his wife's shoulder. 'And so what if we were?' he asked. 'Have you grown so old that we should be scared of you? That you can make your mother cry like this?'

Gayatri looked miserably at her mother through her tears.

Ashok continued, in a raised voice, 'And yes, there is a boy we would like you to meet. Will you do us one favour and just meet the goddamned fellow? What will it take for you to do that? Shall I beg you? Fold my hands? Touch your feet?'

'Ashok, bas, enough!' reprimanded Dadi. 'Gayatri, why are you being so stubborn? Can't you see how much pain you are causing your parents? They are only thinking about what's best for you. You will meet this boy. No, Gayatri?'

Gayatri looked at her father. She nodded, tears still streaming down her face.

'Come here, beta,' Ashok said to Gayatri.

She ignored him and hugged her mother. Nina gave her a kiss on her head. Ashok, patting Gayatri, thought with guilty satisfaction that this coup, unplanned as it was, had been quick and effective. Though not without bloodshed, he reflected regretfully as he glanced at his wife, whose face still shone with tears.

6

At ten minutes to five on Sunday, Gayatri made her way into the Oberoi Hotel, dragging her feet in exactly the manner her mother so disliked.

The dull November evening faded away as a tall and heavily moustachioed doorman welcomed her into the elegant, brightly lit lobby of the hotel. Smartly dressed people milled around, guided by courteous staff. The cheerful smiles of the employees grated on Gayatri's downcast mind. Maybe when they drive home, she thought, these same happy smiles become sad and worn. Maybe the doorman hates his moustache and dreams of shaving it off every night.

She walked into the coffee shop and took a seat at a table near the large bay windows that overlooked the garden. Still five minutes to go, she thought, looking at her watch. Untying her hair, she ran her fingers through it, only to tie it up again. She was wearing dark blue jeans and a black sweater-top, which had a row of pearls sewn onto each cuff.

Her mother had chosen the top, and had insisted Gayatri put on some kajal at least. To be fair to Nina, Gayatri was looking pretty.

She glanced towards the entrance just as a tall man in a dark-blue suit entered, his gelled hair and pointy shoes conspicuous. She was sure this was the guy, but the clickety-clack of his heels went past her as he joined a group of men in a corner of the coffee shop.

Her phone rang. She sighed as she swiped the screen. 'Hi, Ma.'

'Beta, you've reached, no?'

'Yes. I'm sitting in the coffee shop. He's not here yet.'

'Okay, good. Achha listen, talk nicely okay. Don't be in a hurry. And don't get irritated please.'

Gayatri rolled her eyes. 'Yes, Ma. Okay, listen I'm getting another call,' she lied. 'I'll see you when I get home. Bye.'

A man was coming towards her. He was attractive and slim, and dressed in jeans and a rust-coloured sweater. This can't be him, she thought, too normal. He walked to the next table where a girl, Indian but with her hair dyed blonde, was sitting, fiddling with her phone. Ah, there you go, thought Gayatri. I'm becoming so good at this.

She peered out of the window beside her. It had become dark quite suddenly, and the window now reflected the bright lights and people inside the coffee shop. A head appeared above hers in the window, startling her. It was the man in the rust-coloured sweater.

She turned around quickly.

'Sorry, did I scare you?' he asked.

'No, no.'

'Are you Gayatri?'

'Uh, yes. Vikram?'

'Hi,' he said with a smile. 'Vikram Gera.'

Gayatri smiled back. Vikram took the hand she held out and shook it gently. Not a very corporate handshake, she thought.

'Have you already ordered?' asked Vikram, sitting down opposite her.

'No, not yet.'

'Okay. What are you thinking of getting?'

'A filter coffee.'

A server came to the table and Vikram ordered two filter coffees. As the server walked away, Vikram and Gayatri smiled formally at each other.

'So, how long have you been in India?' asked Gayatri.

'Just over a week now.'

Gayatri nodded.

There was silence for a few moments before Vikram asked, 'What do you do? My mother said you're some kind of a researcher, but she wasn't sure.'

'I work with Ramesh Kanthan, I'm not sure if you've heard of him. He's a historian.'

'I'm afraid I haven't,' he said with an easy smile. 'So you're a historian too?'

'Well, I studied to be a lawyer actually, but I then developed an interest in history and switched careers. I've been working with Kanthan for two years now. I help with his research foundation and manage a journal.'

'Interesting,' said Vikram, leaning back in his chair.

The server arrived with their coffees. As they fiddled with the little sachets of sugar, Gayatri stole a glance at Vikram. He was very good-looking, especially for the thirty-plus arranged-marriage market. How come he didn't have a girlfriend?

Sipping her coffee, she said, 'And you're a banker?'

'Yeah,' he replied. 'I used to work with Goldman, but now I work with a boutique firm in London that focuses on NRI clients.'

'Okay.' Gayatri took another sip as she tried to think of a follow-up question to do with his work.

'Have you ever been to London?' asked Vikram.

'Yes, I went a couple of years ago to visit my sister when she was working there. Where do you live in London?'

'Near Canary Wharf.'

'Oh, my sister also worked at a law firm in Canary Wharf, though she stayed near Hampstead. Canary Wharf is quite convenient, isn't it?'

'It's not the smartest area, but it's newly built and the rents are reasonable. And my flat overlooks the Thames, so I like it. Plus, it's close to work.'

Gayatri smiled and nodded. Even if he's kind of cute, we have nothing in common, she thought, her smile fading as she looked down at her coffee cup.

'So, how come you're not married yet?' asked Vikram. 'Bad break-up, or some deep dark secret?'

Surprised by his directness, Gayatri looked at him with a frown.

'Mine is no secret,' he continued casually. 'I broke up with my girlfriend last year.'

'Oh.' Gayatri was not sure how to respond.

'She got a job in the US, and before we could figure how to manage our trans-Atlantic relationship, she fell in love with an American,' he added matter-of-factly.

'Oh,' repeated Gayatri. How do people recount this sort of intimate personal history to strangers, she wondered.

'Now your turn,' said Vikram.

'Uh … no real reason, I'm afraid. It just never happened,' she said with a polite, formal smile. She wasn't about to tell someone she'd just met about her previous relationships.

'You're the first girl I'm meeting, you know,' said Vikram, 'like this.'

'Really?' That explains it, this one is new to the game.

'How does this work?' he asked. 'I mean, how many times do you meet one guy? Do you start dating someone you like or is this really all about the family?'

'It depends, really. I've never met someone more than twice or thrice.'

'And are you expected to decide in just a couple of meetings?'

'Usually. I mean, if the guy and girl want to meet a few more times, I guess that's okay, but there is always some pressure from the families. So people get cornered into deciding one way or another pretty soon. And there are some ultra-conservative families who won't let you meet more than once or twice.'

Vikram sipped his coffee thoughtfully, then asked, 'And how many guys have you met?'

Gayatri was quiet.

'I'm sorry, was that an impolite question?'

'Yes, actually. But I'll tell you anyway. Around ten.' The real number was closer to twenty.

'Wow,' said Vikram, eyes wide.

'Yeah, wow,' said Gayatri drily, feeling a sudden swell of irritation. She didn't want to waste any more time with him. Her parents had forced this meeting on her, and she had done what was required. The blonde girl would be more his type in any case.

'Look,' she said. 'It was nice meeting you, and I'm sure you'll—'

He interrupted her, 'Don't tell me you're leaving just because I asked you some questions about the process?'

'It's not that. If I'm being honest, I don't think we'll get along. We are obviously quite different. Let's just leave it at that and not drag this out. If you have any more questions about the process, I'm happy to answer them. Just call or text me.'

At his perplexed look, she sighed and tried again. 'Look, I know this won't work, and neither of us should be wasting our time. Trust me, I'm the experienced one here.' After a pause, she added, 'I'm not usually so direct, you know. It's just … I've been through too many of these meetings, so I know.'

'Why did you say we are quite different?' he asked.

'Well, for starters, I'm an academic researcher, and you're a banker. You live in London, and I don't want to move abroad. Isn't that enough?'

'I'm moving back to Delhi, as I'm sure you know. And I think it's nice that we do different things.'

Gayatri sighed inwardly. This one just doesn't want to make a mess of his first meeting, she thought. Would it be too rude if I just got up and walked away?

'At least finish your coffee,' he said.

She nodded. 'Okay.'

After a pause, he asked, 'So how did you develop an interest in history after doing law?'

'I studied history in school and college, but wasn't particularly drawn to it. Then I started reading history, and found that I didn't want to do anything else. What about you, I mean, how did you end up in London?'

'I went to the Kendriya Vidyalaya in Kishanganj, near Ghaziabad. Then did a B.Com. from Delhi University, an MBA from London Business School, and here I am.'

Gayatri was surprised. Not many kids from government schools ended up in investment banks in London. 'Do you have any siblings?' she asked.

'A younger brother. He's doing his undergraduate degree at Brown in the US.'

Gayatri was impressed. This family probably had an interesting story.

'What about you?' he asked. 'Siblings?'

'Just a younger sister.' She looked at her watch and smiled apologetically. 'Vikram, I'm sorry, but I really do have to leave now. I'm meeting a friend at seven.'

Vikram nodded. 'Actually, I'm sorry about the way this started off, you know, with the interrogation and all. I didn't mean to be rude. I was just curious about the process.'

'No, that's fine, don't worry. Call me, you know, if you need to speak or … whatever,' she found herself saying non-committally.

Vikram insisted on paying the bill. Once he was done, they walked out of the hotel together. He waited with Gayatri until the valet brought her car to the porch. She got into her car and, seeing that he was standing by the window of the passenger seat, rolled down the window. He lowered his head to smile at her and said, 'Bye.'

She nodded and smiled back.

Gayatri walked into the dimly lit living room and tossed her bag onto the sofa near the door.

'So, how did it go?' asked Nina, startling Gayatri.

'Ma! How long have you just been sitting here in the dark?' She switched on a light.

'Never mind that. Tell me, how was he? Are you meeting him again?' Nina asked with a hopeful smile.

Exhausted, Gayatri sank into a sofa. 'Probably not.'

'What does "probably not" mean? Did you agree to meet again or no?'

'Ma, I don't know. I don't know anything.'

'Gayatri, I'm asking you something. At least tell me what you thought of him.'

'Ma,' said Gayatri in a calm voice. 'Please don't pester me like this. I will not end up marrying him. I may speak to him again as a friend. He just wants to know more about this arranged marriage business.'

'Know more about this arranged marriage business?' Nina repeated, loudly. 'What does he think you are, the secretary of Gupta Marriage Bureau? What is wrong with boys these days?'

'Calm down, Ma. It's fine. I didn't like him like that either.'

'Achha, at least tell me what he was like. Why didn't you like him?'

'Ma, I don't know how you arrange these matches. He is a hard-nosed-banker type. You know I don't connect with those sorts. We don't have a common world view at all.'

'You and your world-view-shirld-view. Shama said this boy is very intelligent and good-looking. His parents just bought the house next to hers, so they must be very well off.'

'So she doesn't really know the family or anything?'

'She hasn't known them for long. Nice, simple people, she says, but they have made a lot of money. His father was in the government. Not at a very high post, I think. He is very ill now apparently. But the boy is doing very well … and so intelligent.'

Gayatri was quiet for a few moments. She lifted her legs and rested them on the arm of the sofa. Earlier in the evening, something about Vikram had struck her as out of place, but she hadn't been able to put her finger on it. It came to her now: his manner of speaking. He pronounced each consonant very precisely, with an evidently practised effort.

A few seconds had passed before she realized her mother was still talking.

'… and you won't be able to sit like this with your leg over the arm of the sofa if you live with your in-laws, you know.'

Gayatri looked at Nina, weary. She always marvelled at her mother's undying certainty that she would one day be married into a TV-soap-like Punjabi household.

'Don't stare at me like that, Ms Mehra. There is a lot to life that you don't know. I may not have your fancy degrees and your knowledge, but I know what it takes to lead a happy life.'

Gayatri stretched out her arm and squeezed her mother's hand, putting an end to the conversation.

Vikram fiddled with his phone while the television blared in the background. His mother sat next to him, her eyes fixed on the screen. The shelves below the television housed a set-top box, speakers and some devotional DVDs. The sofas were upholstered in black–brown leather, and a variety of glass bowls and objects stood atop the wooden table, on a white lace runner that ran along the length of it.

When a commercial break came on, his mother took off her spectacles and turned to him. 'You didn't tell me much about the girl when you came back,' she said in Hindi.

Vikram shrugged. 'Nothing to tell.'

'Shama Aunty said they are quite high-flying, you know. I only asked you to meet her because Shama insisted so much, and she has been so good to us since we shifted here. I couldn't say no. But this type of girl will have a thousand nakhras.'

Vikram nodded. He had gone along with the meeting partly to avoid an argument with his mother, who seemed very keen to maintain her friendship with her fancy new friend, and partly because he wouldn't have minded a casual hook-up on this trip.

'She will make a fuss to talk in Hindi, I'm sure,' said his mother.

'Mummy, relax. Let's see what happens. She was okay, but hardly my type. I met her only because you insisted.'

'Are you going to meet her again?'

Vikram looked at the TV absently. He didn't know what had made him press Gayatri to stay and finish her coffee. She was kind of attractive, but could do with losing a few kilos. Maybe he was just not used to a girl wanting to leave within a few minutes of meeting him.

'Vikki,' said his mother loudly. 'I asked if you were going to meet her again.'

He shrugged. 'I don't know.'

'There is another girl who is studying in Delhi. She's just come from Kitty Masi's town in Punjab. If you want, I can arrange something.'

Vikram's phone rang before he could say anything. 'Sorry, one minute,' he said as he got up and went into his bedroom, leaving his mother clicking her tongue in disapproval. He closed the door behind him and answered the call. 'Hello, sir.'

'Vikram, how are you?' replied a voice in a British accent.

'Fine, sir.'

'What's the status of the Cheema meeting? Was Rajaram able to help?'

'Sir, Rajaram is trying to set up a meeting for next week. I will let you know as soon as it's done. This Cheema is not easy to get hold of.'

'Rajaram is not worth his name as a fixer. He is supposed to know everyone in Delhi. What are we paying him for?'

'I know sir, I've been chasing him round the clock. I'll text you as soon as something is finalized.'

'You need to be quicker. I want to hear some positive news by Tuesday.'

'Don't worry, sir, I'll get it done.'

'If you don't, these clients will go elsewhere. And if we lose this mandate, I will personally screw you, Vikram.'

The call ended. His boss, Akhil Tandon, never said goodbye before disconnecting a call.

It's all so easy for Akhil, thought Vikram irritably jerking his chin to one side. All he has to do is sit in his large London office and bark orders. Why doesn't he fucking come here and try to fix meetings in South Block in that acquired accent of his?

Vikram sent a text message to Rajaram: 'Sir, any update?'

He waited for a few minutes, but when there was no reply, he figured it meant no progress. Dealing with these Delhi fixers was proving to be much harder than he had anticipated. This hustling job had seemed so much easier when Akhil had briefed him about the opportunity in London; it had seemed right up his alley. At the sound of voices from the living room, he opened the door to see who it was. Shama Aunty— no doubt here to find out how his meeting with Gayatri had gone.

Before he could close the door again, she spotted him and called out his name. He went over and touched her feet. She beamed at Vikram's mother.

'I just lo-oove the way you've brought up your son,' she said in a sing-song voice. 'Aaj kal no one touches feet and all in Delhi.'

Vikram's mother smiled politely.

Shama said to Vikram, in a teasing tone that assumed far too much familiarity for his liking, 'So, your meeting went well?'

Vikram wagged his head from side to side in an ambiguous nod that could mean anything and nothing at the same time.

'She is a very nice girl, you know. Her mother is verryyy good friends with me,' she drawled. 'I don't know why her rishta hasn't happened so far. She is nice-looking, na, beta?' she asked, looking at Vikram.

Vikram nodded politely. What am I supposed to say, he wondered. But maybe this was how Delhi's high-society women talked.

Shama turned to Vikram's mother. 'Her family is very well-respected in the city, you know,' she said in broken and accented Hindi. 'And her younger sister just got married into such a well-connected family, you won't believe! The who's-who of Delhi were at the wedding, all the top politicians.'

'Achha?' Vikram's mother said with a bland smile.

'That Sadhuji, you know, Chhatarpur-wale? He was also there. Everyone seems to be going to him these days. They say if you have the chai and laddu from his ashram, all your illnesses vanish. Sugar, heart problem, high BP, sab kuch! My husband is very regular there, he even wears a locket with Sadhuji's photo. You should take bhaisahib there. And the politicians who were at the wedding, toh don't ask. You name them and they were there. The CM of Delhi, all his top party people— Dixit, U.M. Agarwal and even that Rajan Cheema ... He's the PM's right-hand man, you know. I believe the groom's father has just joined some political party ... BSD, I think.'

Vikram's eyes flickered imperceptibly. What were the chances? So Gayatri was one-degree away from the power cats. He smiled absently as his mother and Shama Aunty went on talking. This is the way people got stuff done in Delhi, he thought. Someone knows someone who knows someone. And I have always been lucky, or was it a sixth sense that made me persuade Gayatri to stay and finish her coffee?

The sight of an old photograph of himself derailed his thoughts. It had been taken on his graduation day at Hindu College, more than a decade ago. He could almost smell the musty, unfashionable maroon sweater he had worn for the occasion. His parents had been so proud of him. They had travelled in a bus all the way from Kishanganj to attend.

He curled his lips in distaste. I must remember to tell Mummy to put that photo away, he thought.

Gayatri woke up to the sound of a text message. She reached for her phone and focused her eyes on the screen.

'Hi <smiley face>. So are you free for a tutorial on arranged marriages today?'

It had been two days since she had met Vikram, and she had wondered whether she would hear from him again.

After a couple of minutes, her phone buzzed again.

'Please, I really want to make up for our first meeting. I'm going out of town on Thursday, and I'd really like to see you before that. Can I pick you up from your place eight-thirty-ish?'

She sat up and replied quickly, 'No. I'll meet you somewhere.'

'Great <three smiley faces>. Let me know where you want to meet. See you then!'

She lay back in bed, trying to remember the last time she was asked out by someone halfway decent. But this is probably still a waste of time, she thought. And I don't know any guy who uses so many emojis when texting.

'Another drink?' asked Vikram.

'No, no,' Gayatri smiled. 'Two is my limit.'

They were sitting at a table on the balcony of a newly opened Spanish restaurant in Khan Market.

'Two? Really?'

'I usually don't even have two on a first meeting,' she said.

'Second meeting,' he corrected her. He noticed that the red wine seemed to have added a touch of colour to her lips.

'Anyway, what were we talking about?' she asked.

'I don't know,' he said, brushing his fingers against hers as he passed her the menu. She moved her hand away nervously.

'We should order some food now. I have to go to work tomorrow.'

'Of course,' he said, summoning a waiter. All day, he had wondered what he would achieve from this meeting, if he wasn't pushing his luck, expecting her to make his job in Delhi easier. But then, just as he was thinking of cancelling, a voice in his head rationalized that he didn't have anything to lose. He could even charge the dinner to the bank as an expense.

Their food arrived in a few minutes. 'This is good,' said Gayatri, taking a bite of her paella.

'You know, food was the toughest adjustment I had to make when I moved to London,' he said, taking a bite of a lamb chop. 'Everything tasted awful, just bland and so basic. I'd been a vegetarian almost my whole life, and the smell of meat was all around me. It was sickening.'

'But there are so many restaurants there, all kinds of food from all parts of the world,' said Gayatri.

'When I first went as a student, I couldn't afford restaurants, obviously. I used to take a bus to East Ham every alternate Sunday— it used to take an hour—then literally empty the buffet at this place called Madras Dosa. That was heaven. And even that cheap little hole was expensive for me.'

'And during the week?'

'I learned to cook. Dal, sabzi … I couldn't have survived otherwise.'

'Sounds quite painful,' said Gayatri, impressed. Most guys she knew wouldn't be able to fry an egg without calling for their Ramus and Chhotus in a panic.

'It was my own fault. I just wasn't adaptable enough, too rigid. That changed a little once I began working.' He smiled. 'Of course, the money helped.'

Gayatri nodded.

'But I have to admit, it didn't change all that much. There was this food truck that set up outside my office each day at noon. Aloo parathas, chicken curry, kebabs. It was a godsend. I ate there every single day the first year at my job. Now I earn enough to have someone come and cook Indian food at home three days of the week, and I eat leftovers on the other days. It's the best use of my money.'

'You sound really boring,' said Gayatri, with a laugh.

'That's probably right,' he said, glugging down the last of his drink. He signalled to the waiter to refill their glasses. Gayatri protested, but gave in after a half-hearted attempt to shield her glass with her palm.

'So, you mentioned you have a younger sister. Is she married?'

Gayatri nodded. 'Just recently. Last month actually.'

'Oh,' said Vikram feigning surprise. 'Was that arranged, or—'

'No. She'd been dating Amar … my, uh … brother-in-law. They work together.'

'Oh? What do they do?'

'They are corporate lawyers.'

He nodded, thinking of a way to ask about Amar's family.

'What's your India plan then?' she asked. 'Are you looking for a job? And why do you want to move back?'

'My parents need me. I want to be around for them.'

'That's nice,' said Gayatri. She sighed. 'I just want to get away from mine these days,' she continued, vaguely conscious that the alcohol was making her more talkative than usual. 'This marriage thing is so much pressure. You don't know it yet, you're just getting started. You're very lucky to be far away in a foreign land right now.'

'Why don't you apply for another degree and study abroad?' he suggested. 'I'm sure you'd have no trouble getting in.'

'I don't want to live abroad,' said Gayatri. 'I want to stay right here, in Delhi. Not in some place with depressing weather for half the year, eating shit food, and doing all the cleaning and washing and ironing.'

'Ohhh. The posh reason for staying in India,' Vikram said with a grin. 'No ghar ka kaam.'

'No, that's not it,' protested Gayatri with a little laugh. 'Anyway, at the risk of sounding super posh, do you know how the word posh originated?'

'No,' he said, interested despite himself.

'So, "posh" is an abbreviation for "Portside Onward Starboard Homeward". When the Brits used to travel to India by ship, this formula told them which side of the ship to book their cabins, so they could avoid the sun. They'd choose portside cabins for their onward journey to India, and starboard on the way back home. Get it? P-O-S-H. Portside Onward Starboard Homeward.'

He raised his eyebrows. 'Now that is fascinating. A genuinely posh fact.'

Gayatri smiled. 'Very funny.'

'No, really,' said Vikram. 'I think that may be the most interesting thing I've heard in a while.' And definitely the most interesting thing I've heard on a date, he thought.

They were both silent for a few seconds, then he said suddenly, 'Listen, could we see each other again?'

Gayatri tried to focus her thoughts. There's no point, she told herself, too much alcohol had been ingested. 'Okay,' she said, nodding.

'I'm away until the weekend, so Monday?'

She shrugged, smiling. What did she have to lose?

Akshay was eating dinner in his office when Neelam entered the room without knocking.

He frowned. 'I don't have time. If it's about the Sandeep Sharma hearing, we can speak tomorrow morning in court,' he said gruffly.

'Actually, I wanted to speak to you about something else.'

He wiped the corners of his mouth with a napkin, and looked at her coldly. She closed the door behind her.

'Leave the door open,' he said firmly.

'Akshay, can't we talk like we used to?' She paused, looking at him with a pleading expression. 'There's no one in the office.'

He closed his eyes and took a deep breath.

'Look,' she said, fingering the chain around her neck, and holding out the small pendant dangling from it.

Akshay looked at the pendant and then at her face in disbelief. 'Are you out of your fucking mind?'

'Why? You gave this to me. I need you to know how much you meant … mean to me.' She spoke softly.

'And I need you to get out. We just have to handle this damned matter until my father comes back from Bombay. Nothing else.'

'Akshay, I don't know what to do. Please. I've been feeling really awful, so guilty.'

Akshay stood up and started to pick up his papers. 'I can work upstairs too.'

'Please, Akshay, I really don't want things to be like this between us.' As he walked past her towards the door, she grabbed his arm, saying, 'At least listen, please.' Her eyes glistened with tears. 'Just once.'

He turned and looked at her for a moment. Then he clenched his jaw and jerked his arm away with such force that she was thrown backwards.

'Don't you dare,' he said to her slowly, his voice quivering with anger. 'Don't you fucking dare.'

'Don't you care even a little bit?' she asked. 'I've seen how your girlfriends don't last. Do you think I don't know how you feel?'

Akshay just shook his head and reached for the doorknob.

'Okay, then I'll tell your father,' she said challengingly.

He stopped, but didn't turn around.

'I will,' she said. 'I'll tell him everything. How things were ... before him.'

He turned back to her, his face consumed with hatred. 'You're pathetic.'

'I want you to listen to me. I need to talk to you.'

'Why? We have nothing to talk about. This is fucking blackmail.'

'Akshay, I ... I just want to say I'm sorry. I know it's been many years, but I still feel the same guilt I felt in the first few days when your father started ... I'm sure you know how he did it, he used to ...'

'For god's sake, stop this shit,' whispered Akshay angrily. He walked out of the room quickly, pulling the door shut behind him with a bang.

Later that night, as Gayatri climbed the stairs to her room, she heard a door creak on the ground floor. Her mother emerged, sleepy.

'How was it?' she asked.

'How was what?' asked Gayatri.

'I know you met Vikram. Shama told me,' she said.

Gayatri sighed in annoyance. This aunty-to-aunty communication network was infuriatingly efficient.

'Okay. It was okay.'

'What does okay mean? Are you meeting him again?'

Gayatri took a deep breath. 'Maybe. Yes. I don't know.'

Nina walked to the bottom of the stairs. 'I'm so happy, beta,' she said. Her voice sounded teary.

'God, Ma, are you crying? Please don't be silly.'

'When you become a mother, na, you will know.'

'I can't deal with this,' she muttered, then said, 'Fine Ma, we'll see then. Goodnight. I'm tired.'

'Goodnight, beta,' said Nina, padding back to her room.

Gayatri checked her phone as she crawled into bed. There was a text from Vikram: 'Have you reached?'

She smiled. 'Yes, a few minutes ago,' she typed.

'I wasn't sure it was such a great idea for you to drive, but I was afraid of pressing the wrong button if I said anything,' came the response.

'Goodnight,' she typed.

'See you Monday, Gayatri <smiley face>,' he replied.

She plugged her phone into the charger and switched off her light. Alone in the dark room, she allowed herself a tiny smile. She hadn't expected things to go in this direction at all.

Vikram put his phone down on the desk, the white glow from his laptop screen illuminating his face. He was thinking about the evening with Gayatri, how easy it had been to flirt with her, brush his hand against hers, to talk to her. He was surprised.

He searched in his inbox for 'Gayatri' and found an email sent by Shama Aunty, with some photos. He clicked on one, and Gayatri's smiling face appeared on his screen. It seemed to be at someone's wedding. She was wearing long gold earrings, but no make-up. Her hair looked nicer than it did on the two occasions they'd met. She is pretty if you look carefully, he thought.

Just then, a chat window popped up at the bottom of the screen. 'Call me.' It was Akhil. Vikram picked up his phone with a loud sigh and dialled the number.

Akhil answered on the first ring. 'Vikram?' he said in his clipped British tones.

'Yes, sir. How are you?'

'I'm being chased incessantly. We need to make contact with Cheema—and fast, or things will become slightly unpleasant. They'll channel their funds through someone else.'

'Rajaram is useless, sir. He seems to have low-level contacts, under-secretary types. But I have made a new contact today. I think I might be able to get a meeting with Cheema.'

'If not, I'll have to come to India myself, maybe next week. We need this to work, Vikram. Maybe I can ask—'

'No, no, sir,' said Vikram. 'Not to worry, I'll handle this.'

'Okay. This is a huge opportunity,' said Akhil. 'Once we push this through, the sky is the limit for us in India.'

'I understand, sir,' said Vikram. 'I'll get it done.' There was no response. Vikram looked at the screen of his phone and saw that Akhil had disconnected as usual.

Gayatri's face was still smiling at him from his computer screen. He bit his lip thoughtfully. He had never liked good girls like her, with all their rules and perceptions. It's easy to be goody-goody when you don't have to fight for anything in life.

No, she wasn't his type. But then, she didn't have to be.

7

ON MONDAY MORNING, just as she was about to leave for office, Gayatri had an extended argument with her mother. Nina insisted that Gayatri tell Vikram to pick her up for dinner from their house that evening. Despite her daughter's resistance, Nina triumphed, largely due to the fact that Gayatri was late for work.

Gayatri returned home that evening, dreading the meeting between Vikram and her mother. As she freshened up, she imagined her mother saying all sorts of inappropriate things, and giving all the wrong impressions. When she descended the stairs a few minutes later, she heard her mother's enthusiastic chatter interspersed with Vikram's polite laughs. Of course she likes him, thought Gayatri, she'd like a baboon if it was courting me right now.

'Shall we go?' Gayatri said to Vikram as she entered the living room, avoiding her mother's gaze completely.

He looked at Gayatri and then at Mrs Mehra. 'Sure, yes.'

'Yes, you kids make a move.' Nina got up and, with a broad smile, added, 'And, Vikram, don't forget dinner on Friday, haan?'

'Sure, Aunty,' said Vikram. 'I'll be here.'

Gayatri stiffened, then made her way out the door with Vikram.

Over at Devaki Sadan, Nandini ended a conversation on her phone. She had been watching television when her mother had called to tell her about Vikram.

Amar was sitting beside her, playing a game on his phone. 'What happened?' he asked, glancing at her sideways even as he continued to play. He pulled his headphones down to his neck.

Nandini shrugged. 'Just Mama being Mama. She's over the moon because Didi seems to have finally liked some guy she's been introduced to. Vikram something.'

Amar shook his head. 'I don't understand how your sister puts up with this stuff at her age.'

'It's mostly to avoid fights with my parents. Anyway, Mom has invited this Vikram guy over for dinner on Friday when my cousin Tarun and his wife arrive. So we'll meet him too.'

Amar didn't respond. Nandini saw he had pulled his headphones back over his ears. His eyes were on his phone, his body jerking every time he managed to shoot someone in the game as if he was truly in a gunfight.

Nandini looked at him for a few seconds, and then said loudly, 'Why do you play these mind-numbing games every free moment you have?'

'What's your problem?' he asked irritably. 'This is my way of winding down.' As he continued to play, he muttered, 'Never realized you were such a control freak.'

Nandini glared at him. 'And I didn't realize you were such a brain-dead moron.'

They had been squabbling almost every day. Feeling yet another burst of anger, she reached over and tugged off his headphones.

He put down his phone on the sofa and looked at her. 'What the hell is wrong with you? Don't ever fucking do that again. If you wanted someone who would read big fat books to you every evening, you should have tried harder with that asshole Nihar Jain.'

Nandini's eyes widened as she shook her head. 'I can't believe you're bringing up Nihar. That is so childish of you. But maybe I shouldn't expect better from someone who thinks playing video games at thirty-two is acceptable!'

Amar stood up. 'Fuck this shit. I'm done fighting. Every night it's the same fucking bullshit. I'm going downstairs where there's some peace. You can keep spewing your venom here.'

He left the room, slamming the door shut behind him. Nandini's eyes filled with angry tears. She turned up the volume of the TV, determined not to reveal any weakness.

At a quarter to eight on Thursday evening, Nina was pacing near the entrance to her house. 'It's so late. Tarun should have been here by now. I can't understand why his phone isn't connecting.'

Ashok didn't look up from his iPad as he said, 'Maybe he's been kidnapped, and any moment, we'll get a call for ransom.'

Nina sighed in exasperation.

'Relax, Ma, they'll be here any minute,' said Gayatri.

Ignoring them, Nina resumed her anxious vigil. Tarun was the only child of her beloved older sister, Saloni, who had died many years ago with her husband in a bus accident on their annual visit to Vaishno Devi. Nina, then newly married, had immediately taken it upon herself to care for her twelve-year-old nephew. Her in-laws had generously welcomed young Tarun as a new member of their family. Gossipy relatives put Nina's fierce protectiveness of Tarun down to her not having a son of her own, but the simple truth was that nothing had felt as natural for Nina as slipping into the role of Tarun's mother. She would later explain to her daughters that the word 'masi' literally means 'like a mother', and that they too would protect each other's children as fiercely as their own.

'It's been so long since Tarun Bhaiya and Prom made a trip to India,' said Gayatri.

'Two whole years,' said Nina. 'Poor Tarun. I was so upset with him for not coming for Chhoti's wedding. But the doctors could hardly let him travel after his back gave way … such bad timing.'

'At least they've come as soon as he could travel,' said Gayatri.

'Vaise, one thing is true,' said Ashok, with exaggerated innocence. 'Since he married Promila, we don't see Tarun as often as we used to.'

Gayatri sighed. She could not understand the deep and unwaning pleasure her father derived from needling her mother.

Nina reacted predictably. 'Hmph,' she said, 'you should have seen the girls I saw for him—all of them fair, beautiful, tall … all five-eight, five-nine. But he had to go and find this short, older Bengali girl to marry, even though—' She broke off suddenly as she heard the gate open in the driveway. 'They're here!'

There was a great deal of commotion as the couple was welcomed in. Everyone, except perhaps Nina, agreed that Tarun and Promila made a striking pair. At six-two, Tarun was tall and handsome, and Promila personified nearly all clichés of Bengali beauty with her lithe frame, wide eyes that slanted very slightly upward at the corners, and beautiful skin.

Once everyone had settled down, Dadi was wheeled into the room. She, like the rest of the family, was very fond of the couple. Prom and Tarun touched Dadi's feet, and began to answer all of her questions.

Their jobs, pay scales and absence of offspring were inquired about without a trace of embarrassment; no question was too personal and no time was to be wasted.

Gayatri slipped away to the kitchen to help with the elaborate meal that had been prepared. As she made her way back to the drawing room, her cousin's American-accented voice wafted out. They were speaking about Vikram. She paused outside.

'Masi, this is such great news,' Tarun was saying. 'Now we just need to push her a bit, so it goes through.'

Promila said softly, 'Tarun, I don't think a mature girl like Gayatri can be pushed in a matter like this. I was older than you when we married, right, but it was well worth the wait.'

Nina interjected, sharply. 'Mature means what? She's not old.'

Gayatri shook her head—her mother was too much. She entered the room with a quick step and sat down. An awkward silence followed, until Gayatri smiled at her cousin and said, 'We missed you both so much at the wedding, Bhaiya. Everyone was asking after you.'

'I know,' said Tarun. 'You don't know how disappointed I was. Ask Prom. I tried to persuade the doctor, but he just wouldn't let me travel.'

Promila nodded. 'We felt so bad, Gayatri. We took the first flight out as soon as Tarun got better. The silver lining is, we can stay for longer now.'

'Which brings us to the vital point,' said Tarun. 'When do we get to meet Nandini and her husband?'

'Tomorrow,' replied Nina. 'I've invited her whole family over for dinner.'

'Oh, good,' said Promila. 'I'm really looking forward to meeting Amar.' She added with a regretful expression, 'I was hoping to see a proper Punjabi wedding.'

'Well, your wedding couldn't be fully Punjabi, na,' said Nina, shaking her head as if to commiserate. 'We couldn't really do anything in Calcutta.'

'I think it was the best wedding I've ever attended,' said Gayatri.

'Don't worry, Prom,' said Tarun, nodding towards Gayatri with a wink. 'I'm sure you'll have other chances soon.'

Gayatri rolled her eyes and shook her head.

'Anyway, you're here now,' said Ashok impatiently. He had been waiting for a respectable few minutes to pass before sliding over to the bar. 'What can I get you, Tarun? A single malt? Promila, a glass of wine, or something stronger? Nina, I think you definitely need a glass of wine.'

After dinner, Promila and Gayatri settled down for a chat over coffee. Gayatri had been fascinated by Promila since their very first meeting many years ago. When she was fifteen, she had visited Calcutta with Tarun and Promila, travelling without her parents for the first time. She had fallen in love with the city: the view from the Mukherjees' spacious bungalow in Ballygunge, a trip to Victoria Memorial where she glimpsed a seemingly forgotten statue of squat Queen Victoria in an old corridor, leisurely meals with Prom's large family, the adventurous outings to eat egg-coated kabiraji cutlets and duck-egg Mughlai porothas in Calcutta cabins, evening swims at the Tollygunge Club, lavish dinners in Park Street. And, above all, the feeling of being thrown back in time.

Prom's father, Haren Mukherjee, was a well-known chartered accountant who had inherited many Marwari clients from his chartered accountant father, and her mother, Bharini, was a drama teacher at a school, and occasionally acted in plays herself. They had brought up their only daughter in the best of urban Bengali liberal traditions: Prom had attended La Martiniere for Girls and then studied English literature at Jadavpur University. Gayatri was enthralled by Prom's family and her cousins: something of import was always being discussed, whether it was politics, history, or cinema. Never was there a dull moment.

She also had one of her first grown-up revelations on that trip: it was not just her mother who was unhappy with Tarun and Prom's match. Tarun's relatively loud and brash Punjabi family was not the Mukherjees' first choice for their only daughter either.

A few years later, Gayatri and Nandini had visited the US, and stayed with Tarun and Prom. During long, lively dinners, the girls had heard stories of the couple's NYU days when they began dating. As Prom told them of how he had proposed marriage to her—reciting 'Banalata Sen', in Bengali, on one knee—Gayatri had felt like she was seeing a completely new side to her cousin. Prom's eyes had shone faintly with tears when Tarun offered a repeat performance for his cousins' benefit. Later, Gayatri had spent hours poring over different translations of this romantic poem by Jibanananda Das. Since that trip, the two had kept in touch. Prom would write to Gayatri about her and Tarun's lives, of personal matters such as their decision to not have children (which fed into Nina's unreasonable dislike of Prom, of course), and Gayatri found it easier to confide about her romantic relations (few as they were) in Prom than in her mother or sister.

'So, tell me about this Vikram,' said Prom. Sitting cross-legged on Gayatri's bed, she cupped her coffee mug with both hands. 'Are you really serious about him?' She always got to the point quickly.

Gayatri shrugged. 'I just met him. I don't really know.'

'Baba, tell properly, no. What is he like?'

'He's nice. Well … nicer than any of these other arranged-marriage guys at least.' She smiled.

'What does he do?'

'He's a banker, based in London. But he's looking to move back to India soon.'

'Delhi boy?'

'Not exactly, he grew up somewhere in UP. His parents then moved to Ghaziabad, but they all live in Delhi now.'

'And you get along with him? He's easy to talk to and all?'

'Yeah,' said Gayatri, shrugging. 'I guess it's not going to be red-hot love now, but there is comfort and liking. Of some sort.'

Promila sipped her coffee. 'Your mom seems to be quite keen on moving things along.'

'You know what she's like. But I can't blame her. I've really tried her patience. She had such grand dreams of marrying me into a nice, rich household, with samdhis that she could be proud of. Now, it's all she can do to restrain herself from pushing me into just about anybody's arms.'

Promila said quietly, 'I'm sure you'll think things through and make the right choice.'

After a moment's hesitation, Gayatri said, 'You know, Prom, for some reason, I feel maybe I should give this one a shot. I mean, I don't really have a reason to dislike Vikram.'

'Great, then maybe I will get to wear the clothes I had made for Nandini's wedding after all,' said Promila, smiling.

'Ha ha,' said Gayatri drily.

Promila laughed. 'Anyway, how is Nandini? Has Amar grown on you now?'

'Oh, yes,' Gayatri said, remembering the long phone call to Promila when she had shared her initial misgivings about Nandini and Amar. 'I can't tell you how sweet he is. I was completely wrong.'

'Amar's sister is settled in the US, right? So it's just his mom and dad at home?'

'Yeah, his sister lives in Boston. But there is Akshay also, na, Amar's older brother.'

'Oh, right, I'd forgotten. How are they all generally?'

'Amar's mom and dad are okay, the usual Punju-type. Akshay is…' Gayatri hesitated. She was going to say arrogant, but instead said, 'I don't like him too much, but he's okay. Doesn't seem like the interfering type. Keeps to himself.'

'How old is he?'

'He must be in his late thirties.'

'Not married?'

'No.'

Promila's voice dropped a notch. 'And what about Chirag? Has he tried to get in touch again?'

'No,' said Gayatri, looking down at her hands. 'We've bumped into each other a couple of times randomly, but he just looks right through me.' She shrugged. 'It's better this way, honestly.'

'You feel anything for him still?'

She shook her head. 'Just guilt.'

'Those were bad days, na?' said Promila sympathetically. 'I remember visiting just after you broke things off with him.'

Gayatri nodded. 'Mama was so upset with me. I think she'd been planning our wedding in her head for months. I still don't know why I put off breaking up with him for so long … And then he just proposed out of the blue.' She paused. 'It all seems so clear now, but back then, I was genuinely confused.'

'It happens to the best of us,' said Promila, patting Gayatri's hand. 'I think it was courageous of you to not marry him when you realized you didn't feel enough. Many a girl would have just gone with the flow.'

Gayatri sighed. 'There have been times, you know, after meeting some random guy suggested by some aunty or the other, when I've regretted my decision and wondered whether it wouldn't have been easier to just marry Chirag … Who knows, I might even have been happy. Sometimes I don't know what I was holding out for.'

'Vikram, maybe?' Promila smiled.

'Maybe.' Gayatri was quiet for a bit. 'Anyway, I tried to tell Mama to back off and give me time to think about him, but she just forced this dinner invitation on him in a very well-planned manoeuvre.'

'I think it's good, Gayatri—'

'Is it? I mean, for him to meet everyone, before we've even—'

'Did he object or sound reluctant?'

'No, actually. He sounded quite happy, even to meet Nandini's in-laws.'

'I would say, don't make such a big deal about him coming over tomorrow,' said Promila after a pause. 'But do start thinking about whether you like him seriously enough. I imagine these things don't take very long to accelerate once the parents get involved.'

Gayatri nodded, finishing the last of her coffee. They talked a while longer of books and of work. Gayatri told her of the threats to the journal and the visit to Sadhuji's ashram. Somehow, speaking with Promila, she felt more relaxed about the whole episode, like it was behind her. And, as she talked, she realized that somewhere she was more than a little grateful to Akshay.

Even before Gayatri could set her bag down on her desk the next morning, Farah asked, 'Have you seen the news?'

'No, there are so many people at home, didn't get a chance. What happened?'

'Look,' said Farah, turning her computer screen towards Gayatri. The headline on the news website read: 'JOURNALIST KIDNAPPED AND MURDERED'.

'Who is it? Someone we know?' asked Gayatri.

'Just read on,' said Farah, gesturing towards the screen.

Gayatri started to read the article. 'Megha Barua, a journalist with *The Nationalist* newspaper, was found dead in the Vasant Kunj forest area early this morning.' Her eyes widened. 'Oh, is she that Megha? The one who came to talk to us about our Godse piece?'

Farah confirmed with a look.

Gayatri continued to read. 'She was shot thrice, once in the head and twice in her chest. There were no signs of sexual assault. Her car was found on the road, about one kilometre from her body. Her purse and personal belongings were inside, suggesting that robbery was not the motive behind the crime. According to her colleagues, Megha left the office at about ten-thirty last night. She usually drove from the newspaper's office in Saket to her home in Gurgaon. She had most recently published a series of articles titled "Hounded by the Hindutva Trolls", in which she had taken on the internet trolls who regularly abused her on Twitter, Facebook and in the comments sections of her articles.'

'My god,' said Gayatri slowly, shaking her head in disbelief.

Farah scrolled down wordlessly, and showed her the comments.

'Go to Pakistan to Muslim dogs who wants to make noise.'

'Congratz, brave sons gave what she had to got.'

'These are not people to be messed with, Gayatri,' Farah said grimly. 'It's not just about a protest or standing up to some crazy professor in college. This is real. Life and death.'

Gayatri slumped into her chair. Picking at the skin under the corner of her thumbnail, she said, 'This must've been done by that fraud Sadhu. Farah, you should have seen him—dressed like an actor in a cheap play, sitting on a throne with lions as armrests. For god's sake, how the hell can he decide who lives and who dies for what they write?'

'We don't know for sure that his people did this.'

'They may well have. Akshay did say they are targeting others, that they're dangerous.' She continued after a pause, 'And just look at that spineless Akshay. He didn't even care to speak up for others who may be targeted by these people. I had asked him, you kn—'

'I don't think that's fair, Gayatri. It probably wouldn't have made a difference.'

'All the same, he didn't even want to try. I don't expect it, but I hope he feels some shame when he sees this.'

Akshay scrolled through a news report about the murdered journalist on his phone as he waited for his matter to be called in court number 10 at Delhi High Court. His brow furrowed as he thought of Gayatri. *I hope she understands what I was saying now.* He hadn't seen her since the lunch at Amar's place almost two weeks ago.

He caught a glimpse of Neelam coming towards him through the crowd of black gowns. Before she could reach him, he stood up and joined Mann and Singhvi, the two junior lawyers who worked with him.

'Sir, we are one matter away,' said Mann. 'We should go in.'

Akshay entered the courtroom, followed by the two of them. They stood at the back, among the crowd of bantering lawyers and nervous litigants, most sweating even in the November cold. Matter numbers flashed in red on the screen at the front of the court.

'Forty-five, Ratan Gupta,' shouted the court clerk.

Akshay pushed his way to the seats in front reserved for defence lawyers. The prosecutor for the case stood across the aisle.

'Your Ladyship,' Akshay began immediately, 'I am appealing against the order of the Hon'ble District Court denying anticipatory bail. There is a conspiracy to malign my client and engineer an arrest. All the facts are in the petition.'

'What charges do you anticipate?' asked Justice Rita Parekh, looking over her spectacles. Recently promoted from the lower court, she was known to be a tough nut to crack.

'If you will have page nine of the petition, we have shown evidence of a conspiracy to coerce one of his women subordinates to make rape allegations against him. This is nothing but an attempt to damage his reputation when in fact the relationship was fully consensual.'

The judge glanced through the application.

The prosecutor started, 'Your Ladyship, the defence's application has been rejected by the Hon'ble District Court as without merit. The order is in the file for your perusal. If you will please have para—'

Akshay interrupted him. 'Your Ladyship, the order does not address any of the facts that have been brought out in my application, including the text messages between the accused and the victim, and also between her and some of her friends. If you will permit, I will take the court through it. My client will cooperate with the investigation fully, and I will provide a bail bond for any amount as it may please the court.'

Sounds of protest arose from behind the prosecutor's bench. A shaky voice cut through the din. 'He is a rapist, no bail for him. Please, ma'am!'

Akshay glanced over his shoulder to see the father of the victim, neatly dressed and visibly angry.

The prosecutor addressed the judge again, 'Your Ladyship, a young girl has been raped by a man her father's age, and my learned friend is saying it was consensual? What are these messages they are trying to lean on? How have they obtained them? What about the injuries recorded at the physical examination?'

Akshay glanced at the girl's family again. Her parents were on their feet, their faces tense with pain and rage, silently willing the judge to hand down a death sentence to the accused today. For some reason, Akshay thought of Gayatri.

The judge's face betrayed no sign of sympathy. No one could tell if she was wondering what it was that made these people place faith in a system that had already failed them, or if she was thinking about what her government-appointed servant had packed for her lunch.

Akshay spoke in a calm voice. 'Your Ladyship, my client has his own house and family in New Delhi. His two children are currently studying for their tenth- and twelfth-standard board exams. He has no incentive to flee, given his deep bonds with family, and also his position as a public figure in this country. And there are health complications arising from the insertion of a stent in his heart last month.'

'And what complications are those?' asked the judge. There was a hint of sarcasm in her tone.

'He has been advised rest by cardiac doctors. In fact—'

'He may need to be admitted to hospital,' the judge finished. There were a few sniggers in the courtroom.

'Yes, your Ladyship,' said Akshay. He added firmly, 'The decision to admit him will be based on the written advice of his doctors. These are among the most reputed doctors in Delhi.'

The judge grunted. 'I will hear the matter in detail.' She looked at the clerk, 'Give a date, please. Not Tuesday or Thursday.'

Looking at the calendar on his computer, the clerk announced, '15 February.' The courtroom erupted in the din that typically followed as one matter concluded and the lawyers for the next pushed their way up to the podium.

Akshay spoke, trying to be heard over the noise. 'Your Ladyship, in the interim, please direct that no arrest be made. He will cooperate with the police, and make himself available to them as and when needed. He will also stop going to office for the time being, so as not to create a situation where evidence tampering can be alleged.'

The judge nodded, ignoring the protests of the prosecutor. She dictated to the stenographer, 'No arrest till the next date of hearing. Petitioner is directed to deposit his passport and to attend all investigations as required.'

'Grateful, your Ladyship,' said Akshay, bowing slightly. As he shoved his way out of court, he deliberately avoided looking at the victim's parents, feeling an unfamiliar stab of shame.

That evening, there was a flurry of cheerful activity at the Mehra residence as Tarun and Promila were introduced to the Grewals.

Rupi's exchange of pleasantries with Promila was hijacked by Nandini, who entered a couple of minutes after her mother-in-law and rushed past her to envelope Promila in a big hug. Slightly disconcerted, Rupi sat down next to Dadi. Ashok was relieved to see Mr Grewal take an instant liking to the very-American Tarun, and was secretly glad to be spared the brunt of Mr Grewal's one-way conversations that evening.

After Amar had chatted with Tarun and Prom for a few minutes, he joined his brother near the bar. As they stood there sipping their drinks, squeals of laughter erupted from the sofa where Promila sat between Gayatri and Nandini.

Amar subtly gestured with his chin towards the sofa. 'This Promila seems quite out of place in such a Punjabi set-up, no?'

Akshay shrugged as he looked their way, and his eyes settled on Gayatri. She was dressed in jeans and a grey and pink sweater instead of her usual salwar–kameezes. She looked happy, chatting and laughing. She seems different, he thought, when she's not in work mode.

He realized Amar was still talking and brought his attention back to his brother.

'… get married, adjust to the person, then their family, it's hard.' Amar leaned closer and spoke softly, 'Frankly, in this family, I like Gayatri Didi the best. Despite the fact that she wasn't thrilled that Nandini was getting married before her, she's always been nice to me.'

'How do you know that?'

'Nandini told me she was a bit jealous.'

Akshay sipped his drink. 'To be honest, she doesn't seem like the jealous type.'

Amar shrugged. 'Haan, I mean, maybe it's a combination of things that created a bit of resentment at the time. Like, she's not as attractive as Nandini, plus Nandini is younger and has this super high-profile, high-paying job—'

'I don't know about that,' Akshay interrupted. 'She seems to have consciously chosen to not make money because of this obsession with history.' He paused. 'And she's quite … I mean she's not unattractive or anything.' He looked around to make sure no one could overhear them.

'Nandini says Gayatri Didi thinks everyone who is making money is beneath her.'

Akshay finished the last of his drink and looked at Amar. 'Why are we wasting our time gossiping like teenagers? Come, let's get another drink.'

At a quarter past nine, Vikram rang the doorbell outside the Mehra residence. Though he had visited the house before, he couldn't help but notice again the casual, taken-for-granted elegance of old money that the place exuded.

Several people were already present in the drawing room when he entered. He halted at the threshold and looked around awkwardly.

Gayatri walked towards him. 'Hi,' she said, smiling.

'Sorry, I got slightly held up, I was on a call,' he lied, handing her a bottle of wine.

'Come, I'll introduce you to everyone,' she said, leading him towards her parents and Nandini.

Nina's smile couldn't have been broader if Vikram were Shah Rukh Khan himself. Tarun and Prom were summoned from their conversation with Mr and Mrs Grewal. They shook hands with Vikram, after which Tarun started to chat with Vikram about London and his work.

After the initial introductions, Nandini signalled discreetly to Amar, who was still huddled with Akshay near the bar.

'Vikram, this is my husband, Amar,' Nandini said as Amar walked over to where she was standing with Gayatri and Vikram. Turning to Amar, she said, 'You remember I had told you about Vikram?'

'Of course.' Amar grinned at Gayatri as he held his hand out to Vikram. 'Nice to meet you.'

Gayatri, rolling her eyes slightly, berated herself silently for not having pushed back enough when her mother had invited Vikram. This was a big step, introducing him to the whole family, and she was not happy that it had happened this way. She slipped off to the kitchen, where her mother was supervising dinner.

'You should take Vikram to Dadi's room, Gayatri,' Nina said, looking at her daughter happily as she walked in. 'Introduce him to her.' Dadi had gone to bed a few minutes before Vikram arrived.

'Ma, please. He shouldn't even be here. This is all because of you.'

Nina shrugged. 'Well, he's here now, so don't come to me tomorrow when Dadi gets angry that you didn't even tell her.'

Exasperated, Gayatri shoved a packet of chicken tikka in the microwave, and stomped off to Dadi's room. She peeked inside and sighed in relief when she saw that her grandmother had fallen asleep. As she turned to go back to the drawing room, she saw someone coming out of her study, down the dark corridor. It was Akshay.

He walked towards her with a sheepish smile. 'Sorry, someone was in the other loo, so I thought I'd use this one.'

'Of course, don't worry,' she said as she started to walk away, still preoccupied with her thoughts.

'Uh, Gayatri,' he called after her.

She stopped and turned around. He took a few steps towards her into the light, and she noticed the shadow of a beard on his face. He stared at her for a few seconds before starting, 'Uh, I was actually thinking … er, I mean … if you … if we could … uh …'

Gayatri wondered if he was drunk. Such incoherence from the usually calm and collected Akshay Grewal was out of character.

He took another small step towards her, which brought him close enough for her to get a whiff of something familiar. For some reason, she was struck by how tall he was. She had to crane her neck slightly to meet his gaze. His eyes betrayed some sort of nervousness.

'Are you okay?' she asked.

He swallowed. 'Uh, yeah, I was just wondering …' he hesitated, 'er, if you have Coke in the house.'

'Huh?'

'Sorry, there is only Pepsi in the bar and I prefer Coke. But only if you have some, otherwise, you don't have to—'

'It's no problem. I think we do have Coke. Why don't you go inside? I'll just bring it to the bar,' she said, entering the kitchen. A few minutes later, she walked to the bar with two bottles of Coke. 'Here,' she said, handing him one and placing the other in the small fridge behind the bar.

'Thanks,' said Akshay, appearing more collected. 'Can I make you a drink?'

'I have one, thanks.' She reached for a glass of wine kept on the bar. As she sipped from the glass, she saw Vikram talking easily to her father and Mr Grewal. He's making an effort to talk to everyone, she thought. Should I go and stand with him?

'… reading anything these days?'

Akshay's question startled her out of her thoughts. She looked at him blankly and then blinked as she replayed his words in her head. 'Uh, yes, I am. Re-reading actually. Some old R.K. Narayan novels,' she said.

'That must be nice,' said Akshay. 'He's somewhat like P.G. Wodehouse, no?'

She looked at Akshay questioningly.

'I mean in the way they both transport you to simple, happy places.'

Gayatri thought for a few seconds and said, 'That's true.'

'Why do you sound surprised?'

'I'm not surprised. I'd just never thought of the connection, and I love them both,' she said, giving him a small smile.

He nodded. 'I saw the row of Wodehouses in your study,' he said with a smile and sipped his drink.

Looking away, she noticed Nandini glaring at her from the corner of the room. 'Excuse me, I think Nandini needs me,' she said to Akshay.

Nandini gestured towards the corridor and Gayatri followed her. 'Didi, what are you doing?' she hissed as soon as they were out of earshot.

'What am I doing?' Gayatri asked, puzzled.

'You're flirting with Akshay Bhaiya.'

'Are you mad, Chhoti?' said Gayatri, looking at Nandini as if she was crazy. 'We were just talking.'

'You like him? Tell the truth.'

'Chhoti, don't be silly. Of course I don't.'

'Be careful, Didi,' said Nandini, widening her eyes. 'He's one of those complicated types. And he has some seriously messed-up history with women. I don't want you to get hurt.'

'Nandini, please. There's no need to behave like Ma. I don't like him. And anyway, how can you even think this when you met Vikram today?'

Nandini looked at Gayatri disbelievingly.

'We were just talking. About books,' Gayatri said. 'He's the one who started the conversation. He saw my books when he was here last time, that's why.'

'Okay. But I'm telling you, be careful. He had this weird smile on his face. Or maybe it was just weird to see him smile when talking to anyone.'

Gayatri waved her hand casually. 'It's probably because I'm closer to his age.'

'Maybe,' said Nandini. 'Anyway, why aren't you talking to Vikram? He's been stuck with Amar's dad for so long.'

Gayatri looked around. Vikram and Gyan Singh Grewal had moved their conversation to the sofa. Both were wearing serious expressions.

'They've been talking for like thirty minutes,' said Nandini. 'While you've been flirting in the corner,' she added.

Gayatri gave her sister a warning look. 'Shut up, Chhoti. It's not funny. I'll go and see how he's doing.'

'Yes, please rescue him. He must be so bored.'

Gayatri went over to Vikram and tapped him on his shoulder. 'Are you okay?' she whispered.

He glanced at her over his shoulder. 'Of course, don't worry,' he said and turned back to Gyan Singh immediately.

'Do you want to come and get a drink?' she asked.

'Thanks, I think both of us need refills. Sir, will you have another?'

Gyan Singh waved his hand. Vikram handed her their glasses, and went back to his conversation.

Gayatri walked away, irritated. He definitely didn't need any rescuing.

Gyan Singh took a long swig from his glass and let out the kind of satisfied sigh that only a great single malt could elicit from him. The fellow was still talking, but Gyan Singh had already heard what he needed to hear. He stopped Vikram mid-sentence. 'I'm travelling for a couple of days now, but come over to my office on Tuesday. We can discuss the funding opportunities in detail. If need be, I'll get someone in my office to connect you to Cheema.'

'Thank you, sir! That would be great,' said Vikram, pleased with his evening's work. 'I'll—'

'You know M.C. Jain?' interrupted Gyan Singh.

'No, sir,' said Vikram.

'He's not the sort of industrialist you investment banker types would focus on, but he is one of the ten richest people in India. If you include all colours in the rainbow and add a few dark ones ... You understand?'

'Of course, sir,' said Vikram, not really comprehending.

'He's into many businesses, including real estate. Once we have an idea of what you can offer, I'll introduce you to him. I think he is exactly the sort of person you are looking for.'

Vikram nodded. 'Sounds great. What time would suit you on Tuesday, sir?'

'Around four, once I'm back from court. After that I'm usually busy in briefings and those wretched television appearances.'

'I'll be there at four, sir,' said Vikram. Gyan Singh looked away and Vikram understood that the conversation was over.

'Thank you, sir,' he said as he stood up and walked over to the bar, where Amar was standing with someone he hadn't met yet.

'Vikram, meet my older brother, Akshay,' Amar said.

'Hi,' said Akshay, extending his hand. Vikram shook it, smiling warmly.

'Bhaiya, this is Vikram. He's Gayatri Didi's ... er ... friend,' he said awkwardly.

Akshay's face reflected a brief moment of confusion.

'Are you also a lawyer, Akshay?' asked Vikram.

'Yes,' replied Akshay, his eyes darting to where Gayatri was sitting.

'There are too many lawyers here.' Vikram laughed. 'Are you the arguing-in-court type or the firm type?'

'Court. I work with my father.'

'Great,' said Vikram. 'I have an appointment to see him in his office on Tuesday. I may bump into you then.'

'Oh?' said Akshay, mildly surprised. 'What about?'

'Nothing much,' Vikram said with a wave of his hand. 'I work with a London-based investment fund. There's a financial product we want to offer in India. Just wanted your father's advice, and a few introductions.'

Akshay nodded and took a large gulp of his drink.

'So, how long are you in India for?' asked Amar.

'I'm here to try and set up a client base,' replied Vikram, 'which will take a while to get going.'

'And what kind of clients are you looking at?'

'Oh, you know, NRIs, HNIs. They keep their money as cash or property or in boring fixed deposits. We want to give them an outlet to grow their money fast.'

'Where does your fund invest?'

'We have several products. We do small-scale venture cap, listed instruments, foreign currencies ... What we specialize in is tailoring investment baskets for different clients.'

Amar nodded mechanically, he had tuned out already.

Vikram smiled politely. He caught Gayatri's eye. 'Excuse me,' he said as he walked over to her.

'He's with Gayatri?' Akshay asked Amar in a low voice, his eyes on Vikram.

Amar nodded.

'They're seeing each other?'

'Not exactly. They've been introduced by family.'

'Oh,' said Akshay thoughtfully.

'What were you talking about for so long with Gyan Uncle?' Gayatri asked Vikram.

'Oh, just business.'

'What kind of business? He's a lawyer.'

'And a politician. He knows people. Anyway, let's not talk about all this. Should we go out into the veranda? The garden looks beautiful.'

Gayatri looked around uncomfortably. It would be very awkward if they were to disappear into the dark garden even for a few minutes.

'Come on?'

'It's a little cold. Maybe another time?'

'Sure,' said Vikram. His eyes scanned the room, then settled back on her face. 'You look nice,' he said.

She smiled. 'Thanks. I hope you haven't been too bored this evening.'

'No, no, not at all,' he said happily. 'It's been really great, in fact.'

She nodded nervously, surprised by his enthusiasm. She wondered whether inviting him to meet her family would be the point of no return.

'Hey, do you think it would be all right if I left a little early?' Vikram asked.

'Have dinner at least?'

'It's already quarter to eleven,' he said, looking at his phone. 'I have a call at eleven with my boss in London. I'll have to take it from the cab.'

'Okay, wait. I'll warm up some dinner for you, eat quickly before you leave.'

'Perfect, thanks.'

Gayatri went to the kitchen. As she stood before the beeping microwave, she closed her eyes for a few seconds. Is this really me, she wondered, heating up food for some guy I met a week ago? Am I going to end up marrying him? Her stomach suddenly turned. She placed the hot plate on a tray and sent it out for Vikram, and stayed back in the kitchen for a few minutes. When she went to the drawing room, Vikram had finished his dinner and her parents were fussing over him.

She ducked back into the kitchen, taking a deep breath.

Gayatri and Vikram were waiting outside the gate when his cab arrived. He looked at her. 'Given the safety levels in this city, maybe I'll have to see you back inside now.'

'I'll go in. Goodnight.'

'Listen,' he said.

'Yeah?' The cold November air made her shiver slightly.

He took her hand in his and looked at her. She looks prettier every time we meet, he thought. 'I enjoyed the evening,' he said.

She smiled. 'Me too. Thanks for coming.'

He glanced at the cab parked a few metres ahead of them before gently pulling her a step closer. She looked at his face, now close to hers, and felt herself blush.

'I feel I'm a little too old for this,' she said softly.

He leaned in and kissed her lightly, stroking her cheek. 'Go in now,' he said. 'I'll wait.'

She took a moment to collect herself, then smiled and nodded. 'Goodnight.'

8

Aᴛ sɪx o'ᴄʟᴏᴄᴋ on Tuesday evening, Vikram emerged from Gyan Singh's office with a cocky smirk. The meeting had gone better than he had expected.

Mr Grewal had interrogated him closely on every aspect of his proposal, from the identity and business interests of the NRI donors he represented, to the potential favours they could expect in return for the funds. Vikram had been well-prepared. Mr Grewal, seemingly satisfied, had made a call setting up a meeting with Rajan Cheema and also offered to introduce Vikram to M.C. Jain.

Akhil will be pleased with the M.C. Jain introduction, thought Vikram. Jain's network of shell companies was exactly the sort of vehicle they needed to set up to route their funds anonymously to India. If these introductions panned out, they would get the whole network ready-made, with hardly any legal risks.

Mr Grewal had suggested that Vikram wait to meet Sadhuji, who was expected to stop by the office within the hour.

Vikram strolled down a narrow corridor with wooden doors on either side. Expensive-looking artwork decorated the walls. One day, he thought to himself, I'm going to have a larger office with even more expensive art on the wall. He spotted Akshay sitting in a room, the door ajar. He knocked.

Akshay looked up with a distracted frown.

Vikram said, 'Sorry, I didn't mean to disturb you.'

Akshay's face cleared as he stood up and said, 'Not at all. Hi. Uh, come in.'

'I needed a place to sit and wait actually. Grewalji told me to hang around for an hour until Sadhuji gets here.'

'Oh?' Akshay raised his eyebrows. 'Er, you can sit anywhere really. Why don't you sit in the next room? I'll just finish what I'm doing and join you.'

'Sure, thanks,' said Vikram cheerfully, stepping back into the corridor and closing the door. He entered the adjoining room which was lined with shelves full of thick leather-bound legal books. A large conference table with a dozen or so chairs around it took up most of the space. He pulled out his phone and dialled a number.

After three rings, a voice on the other end said, 'Yes, Vikram?'

'Sir, he's in. Cheema is travelling for the next couple of weeks, but Grewal has set up a meeting once he returns.'

'That's great news,' said Akhil, pleasantly surprised. 'Well done, Vikram. This Grewal has turned out to be a very useful contact.'

'Exactly, sir. He's a brilliant lawyer and extremely well-connected, so that's cut down a lot of the work we would have had to put in to figure this stuff out. And,' he paused for effect, 'he knows many people who want to stash their cash outside India and wanted to know if we could help. It's through some godman contact of his.'

'Why not?' said Akhil. 'Say yes, no harm in talking.'

'Yes, sir, that's what I did.'

'Good. If it's going to take two weeks for these meetings to materialize, why don't you come back to London in the meantime? We can chart out our strategy.'

Vikram hesitated for a few seconds, then said, 'Absolutely, sir, that makes sense. I'll arrange to come back next week.'

'Great.'

This time, it was Vikram who disconnected the call.

While Vikram was speaking to Akhil, Akshay knocked on the door to his father's office and entered without waiting for a response. Neelam was standing there.

'Papa, do you have a minute?' he asked.

His father looked preoccupied. 'Now?'

'Yes, I need to speak to you.'

Neelam stood rooted to her spot.

'Alone,' Akshay said pointedly.

Mr Grewal waved a hand at Neelam, dismissing her. She pursed her lips and left.

'What is it?' he asked his son irritably.

'Papa, what is this business with this Vikram guy?'

'Nothing much. He needed a few introductions in India. He represents some business interests in Europe and the UK. They want some favours in return for donations to the party.'

'We've never done anything like this before.'

'It's very clean. There's no risk. All within RBI regulations. He will use the real estate company loopholes along with electoral bonds. That M.C. Jain does this all the time.'

'Let Jain take all the risks he likes. Why are you exposing yourself to all this now? Is it worth it?'

'What can I lose by making some introductions? Don't be so scared. What's wrong with you?'

'We don't even know Vikram, Papa,' Akshay persisted.

'Ufff! Don't worry so much. You're becoming worse than your mother. Politics is a different ball game. One has to take a few risks. And anyway, it's all counterbalanced by our contacts and political profile, na? No one can touch us.'

'At least tell me why you are doing this? Give me one good reason.'

'I have two. First, I like Vikram instinctively, and you know I always trust my gut. He's smart and ambitious—reminds me of my younger self in some ways. And second, if I can channel some funds to the alliance this way, my ticket will be sealed. That bloody fatso, Aastha Malhotra, is nipping at my heels, trying to impress the party with her high-flying funders and backers,' Mr Grewal said with a grimace. After a pause, he added, 'And anyway, Vikram is not an unknown commodity. I know of Akhil Tandon, his boss. In fact, that fixer CA, Vishal Sarkar, mentioned him to me a few weeks back, saying Tandon was trying to make some political contributions on behalf of some UK businessmen. So it's not completely out of the blue.'

Akshay shook his head, far from satisfied with his father's explanation.

'Beta, I will not be able to involve you in my matters if you start hassling me like this. You're no lily in the pond, you're such a street-smart lawyer. What did you expect when I told you I was entering politics? That I would lead hunger strikes and go on salt marches?'

'No, but I don't like you exposing yourself in this way. These days you never know who's carrying a recording device, and your reputation, all your life's work, can be gone in a second.'

'Beta, I have been practising law for the past forty years. Give me some credit for having an instinct about people.'

Akshay was silent.

'Look,' his father continued coldly, 'if you want, I'll keep this side of things away from you, but I don't want you stressing me out. And please understand: things will be greyer from now on. We can't be so scared to take risks.'

Akshay looked at his father doubtfully.

'Akshay, yaar, even in our practice there is risk. Sometimes to turn a judge's head, sometimes the public prosecutor's and sometimes the opposing lawyer's. Haven't we done it all? This is no different, but now we have graduated to the big league. Bahut ho gaya this running around these behenchod judges. Lordship, ladyship … bakwaas. I'm made for bigger things.'

'Fine,' Akshay said after a long pause. 'I just hope you're right.'

'Don't worry, puttar. This is politics, everyone does it. If I don't do this, I might as well not play the game.'

Neelam was waiting for Mr Grewal in his office when he returned from the conference room after his meeting with Sadhuji and Vikram. She locked the door and stood behind his chair massaging his shoulders gently. He took her hand absently.

'It went okay?' she asked.

'Haan, haan. Of course. I trust my instincts. I have a feeling this Vikram will be useful to me,' he said.

Sadhuji had connected with Vikram at the meeting, asking him his date of birth, then pausing dramatically and saying in his most soothing voice, 'Door se aaye ho, par abhi aur door jana hai.' Vikram had uttered a simple 'ji', looking slightly disoriented. Gyan Singh remembered feeling that way when he had first met Sadhuji. He had this gift of making people believe that he could really see inside them, see their greatness, their uniqueness.

Neelam interrupted Mr Grewal's thoughts. 'Akshay seemed grumpy.'

'I don't know what's come over that boy. He has never behaved like this before.'

'Maybe he's a little jealous,' said Neelam carefully.

'Jealous? Huh! What does he have to be jealous of?'

'Who knows?' murmured Neelam as she continued to knead his shoulders gently. She looked straight ahead at the door, avoiding the sight of his bald head.

'That's it, Neelu,' said Gyan Singh, patting her hand and pulling her in front of him.

Neelam perched on his table, her hands resting limply in her lap. He fingered the delicate chain around her neck, moving slowly downwards. Though his gaze was fixed on her breasts, she knew he was not thinking of her. Her eyes stony, she looked down at his chubby fingers, the knots of white hair below the knuckles, as they continued along their familiar path.

Gayatri sat across Vikram and his mother at their dining table. It was made of white marble, and had matching chairs upholstered in ivory and gold. Gayatri hated it.

She had been furious with her mother when she learnt that she had rung Vikram that morning, saying she wanted to send a cake for Mrs Gera with Gayatri. When Vikram had arrived to pick her up, Gayatri had been too embarrassed to look him in the eyes.

The conversation so far had been peppered with awkward silences. It was painfully obvious that Vikram's mother, like Gayatri, was not overjoyed by her visit.

'So, Aunty,' said Gayatri, making an effort. 'When did you shift here?'

'It's been two years now,' Mrs Gera replied in Hindi.

'The house is done up very well,' said Gayatri politely, also in Hindi.
I can't believe I have to try so hard, she thought. 'And the parks in this
area are so nice.'

'Whatever we have is because of Vikram.' She looked fondly at her
son. Another awkward pause followed as the three of them dipped
their spoons into bowls of rasmalai. 'I expect you don't do much work
around the house ...' Mrs Gera said to Gayatri.

Vikram said quickly, 'Why would she?'

'No, Aunty,' Gayatri said with a little laugh, 'I'm afraid not. But I
can make tea.' After a pause she added, 'And biryani.'

'Biryani?' repeated Mrs Gera.

'Yes, chicken biryani, mutton biryani, whatever,' said Gayatri good-
naturedly.

'Oh.' Vikram's mother looked at her coldly. 'We are vegetarian.'

Gayatri's smile shrank. She had forgotten.

This shit is getting real, thought Vikram. And I'm not even into her.
He had been far from thrilled when Nina Mehra had called, telling
him she wanted to send over a cake for his mother with Gayatri. His
mother didn't even eat cake. I just need to build my equation with
Grewal a little more before breaking things off with her, he had thought,
agreeing to pick Gayatri up that evening. It had been such hard work
convincing his mother that he was not serious about Gayatri, that it
was more of a work connection that he had to keep going.

Pushing back his chair, he said, 'Gayatri, come, why don't you say a
quick hello to my father? Then we can leave.'

Gayatri rose from the table gratefully and followed Vikram down
a corridor. He paused outside a closed door. 'Listen Gayatri,' he said,
his tone gentle, 'I had told you, na, that my dad is unwell? He has
Alzheimer's. He doesn't remember much, and is slightly unpredictable.'

Gayatri looked at him and said, 'Oh, I'm sorry.'

'Thanks, it's fine. It's been a few years now.' He opened the door, and they entered a large room where an old man sat in bed, propped up with pillows. The television was on and his eyes were vacantly glued to it. He did not acknowledge either of them. Vikram motioned to Gayatri to sit by him on chairs arranged near the bed.

'Papa,' said Vikram. When there was no response, he took his father's hand and said again, 'Papa.'

'Huh?' Mr Gera said blankly, turning to Vikram.

'Papa, main Vikram. Vikram. Ye Gayatri hai,' he said slowly, enunciating each syllable. 'Gayatri,' he repeated loudly. His father smiled blandly. He knew this meeting would be completely lost on his father. Vikram couldn't remember the last time his father had greeted a visitor. He just hoped that he wouldn't be rude to Gayatri the way he was to everyone else.

Mr Gera turned towards Gayatri. His smile faded all of a sudden, and he hesitated. Vikram nodded encouragingly.

Mr Gera looked at Gayatri again, and this time, the old man broke into a broad smile. He lifted his wrinkled hand with difficulty and placed it on her head. Gayatri folded her hands and smiled, nervous and unsure if she should say anything.

This rare reaction from his father brought a sudden sting of tears to Vikram's eyes. He looked at Gayatri as she smiled kindly at his father, and just for one unexpected and uncharacteristically foolish moment, imagined being with her, and allowing some real goodness to spill into his life.

'I like your father,' said Gayatri to Vikram as they were driving back. 'He has very kind eyes.'

'You mean you didn't like my mother?' asked Vikram.

Gayatri laughed. 'No, of course I did. She's sweet.'

'Don't worry, I know she was not on her best behaviour today. I'm sorry. I've never introduced a girl to her.' He saw Gayatri nod out of the corner of his eye. 'These things will work out in time. I'll handle her, don't worry,' he continued without thinking. He stiffened suddenly as he went over the words he had just uttered, wondering what had made him say them.

Gayatri looked outside the window. This was the first time Vikram had referred directly to a long-term future for them.

'Shall we stop for a quick bite?' Vikram suggested in a bid to deflect the awkward silence.

'Sure,' said Gayatri. 'Where?'

'Let's go to Alkauser. It's not fancy, but—'

'I love it. Let's go.'

Gayatri leaned her head back. The shiny emblem on the bonnet of the car caught her eye. I'll have to tell him to get a lower-end car, she thought. I can't imagine myself in one of these, it just feels so wrong.

She thought about the photographs she had seen in the house— they were all recent, except one. It was an old, grainy photo of the entire family: Vikram looked about fifteen and his brother, Virat, much younger. They stood with their parents outside a shabby building, a helmet in Mr Gera's hand. None of the people in the photo looked happy. She glanced at Vikram. He seemed to have changed so much since then.

Vikram rolled down the windows as he deftly parallel parked between two other cars in the narrow Chanakyapuri lane. Cold Delhi winter air filled the car immediately. Alkauser sold kebabs to what seemed like a permanent line of cars, its sprightly employees pacing up and down the narrow lane adjoining the little shop to ensure its patrons were served swiftly. A boy came towards them and memorized their order with no trouble.

Vikram reclined his seat and stared out of the window. He remembered his father's smiling face from earlier that evening. It had been years since he had seen that smile. He glanced at Gayatri, the catalyst for that unexpected reaction, and felt oddly connected to her.

'There weren't too many photos at your home from when you were young,' she said. 'What was your childhood like?'

Vikram was silent for a few seconds. 'It wasn't pretty,' he said at last. 'We grew up in a lower-middle-class household outside Ghaziabad. Till I was fifteen or sixteen, I didn't even know south Delhi existed.' He paused. 'My father fell ill when I was in class twelve, and my mother had to work as a salesperson in a clothing shop so we could get by. It was quite tough.'

Gayatri looked at him, unsure of what to say.

'Sounds like a tragedy the way that I'm narrating it, but it's not like we didn't have fun. Virat and I were actually okay—we had lots of friends, and we played all day long. We didn't dwell on our parents' issues when we were out. Life in the house was depressing, though. Especially for my mom, who had to bear the entire parental and financial burden. I can't tell you what she's been through.'

Gayatri nodded. 'But then how did you—' She broke off before completing her question.

'Get where I am? I studied like mad for my twelfth board exams. Like you would not believe. I had taken commerce, and I just worked like a dog. I got tuition notes from people, and just studied and studied. I had this epiphany, you know, that that would be my ticket out of there. Somehow, I got into the college I wanted.'

'And Virat?' asked Gayatri.

'Madam,' interrupted a slightly nasal voice, and a hand thrust plates of galouti kebabs, kakori kebabs and the slightly sweet varqi paratha into the car.

As the boy scampered away, Vikram and Gayatri arranged the food on the dashboard.

'Virat was even more driven than me,' said Vikram, helping himself to the food. 'I think seeing me go to a good college made him realize that there was no other way out for him, he had to follow me.'

Gayatri bit into her food. It was delicious, but given the context of their conversation, she knew it would seem callous to say so.

'My next break came when I got a scholarship to go and study at LBS. Everything paid for—we could not believe it. My mom made me go with her to Badrinath for some pooja before letting me out of her sight.'

'That's quite a journey,' Gayatri said.

Vikram put a piece of kebab in his mouth along with a few slivers of onion doused in green dhania chutney. He sighed and said, 'This is awesome. The one thing I miss in London.'

As Vikram continued to eat, Gayatri thought of her life, devoid of any moments of financial or intellectual insecurity. And, here she was, still living with her parents.

'You know, your story makes me feel useless,' she said. 'I've mostly just drifted here and there, and got by.' She took another bite. 'I mean, this marriage business is the most terrifying thing I've been through. Being rejected over and over, rejecting others and continuing to meet people whom you don't like … It's really shitty and saps all your self-confidence sometimes. But I can't call it a struggle.'

Vikram looked at her as she scooped a bit of the soft mutton kebab with a piece of the paratha and popped it into her mouth. He had never thought of the arranged marriage process in this light: it must be seriously depressing. A drop of green chutney slid down her lip and nestled in a little depression above her chin. He opened his mouth to say something, then stopped and handed her a napkin instead.

She wiped her mouth with an embarrassed smile. 'Let's go,' she said, finishing the last bite on her plate. 'I told my mother I'd be back for dinner.'

Though they didn't speak of their childhood on the way back, each was thinking of the other's journey, each a little envious of the other.

Nandini called Gayatri after dinner.

'Didi?' said Nandini. 'How did it go?'

'What?' Gayatri asked, walking to her own room.

'Vikram's parents, what else?'

'How did you know?'

'Obviously Mom told me. Anyway, tell na,' said Nandini.

'It was okay, his mother didn't seem too thrilled, but his father was very sweet,' said Gayatri, settling back against the cushions on her bed.

'That's good. These mothers are always possessive about their sons, Didi. You can't do anything. You should see Amar's mom, my god. One day if he says he doesn't want to eat something she has cooked, she behaves as if someone's stabbed her.'

Gayatri laughed. Nandini had been complaining about her in-laws a lot recently.

'And she's even worse where Akshay Bhaiya is concerned. I pity the girl who marries him.'

God help that girl in more ways than one, Gayatri said to herself.

'How was his house?' asked Nandini.

'Huh?'

'Vikram's house, Didi, how was it?'

'Uh, okay from outside, but inside I didn't like it. Everything was too shiny.'

'Uff, you shouldn't be so rigid, Didi. There's nothing wrong with a little shine and shimmer,' she said slightly defensively. 'Anyway, you can always change your part of it. They have more than one floor, na?'

'Yes, the first floor is empty, I think.'

'Oh, so that's where you'll stay,' said Nandini.

Gayatri felt the weight in her stomach grow heavier as Nandini went on about the first floor of Vikram's house. She interrupted, 'Anyway, Chhoti, you tell me, how have you been?'

'Fine, Didi, busy with office, you know how it is. I've hardly seen Amar this week. And now he's travelling for work for a couple of days.'

'Where?'

'Bombay. In fact, I was thinking I'd come over when he is away.'

'That'll be nice, Chhoti. Do that.'

'I'll call tomorrow and confirm. Okay bye, Didi. And well done, finally!'

'Bye,' said Gayatri, rolling her eyes even though her sister couldn't see her.

Vikram's face flashed before her eyes. She smiled. She definitely liked him. And what if she never found another decent guy? She thought of all the boys she had met over the last three years. Vikram was definitely different.

Remembering his remark that evening about handling his mother, she turned over to her side. Would she really spend the rest of her life with him? What kind of friends would they have? Would she be able to live with his mother? What if his mother expected them to have dinner together every day? She thought of Nandini's life and bristled. She didn't want a life like that.

She took a deep breath. It's all happening too fast, she thought. Everyone is assuming that I'll marry him, just like with Chirag. Maybe I should take a quick trip somewhere, to sort things out in my head before this gets out of hand.

Vikram was pacing restlessly on the terrace of his house, smoking a cigarette again after six whole months. He knew he had given Gayatri all the wrong signals that evening. Not only had he brought her home, he had also made that comment about how he would handle his mother for her. He had wanted to kick himself as soon as the words left his mouth.

He stopped pacing and sat on the parapet lining the terrace. He should have made some excuse to Mrs Mehra, and not introduced Gayatri to his parents. He had felt strangely protective of her when his mother was interrogating her about cooking and housework. She just didn't get that Gayatri was from a different world. As he blew out a well-formed ring of white smoke into the cold night, he thought of that brief moment with his father—even though Gayatri hadn't really done anything—and he felt so grateful for it.

He shook his head as he stubbed out his cigarette. There was no point in this unnecessary complication. It was a good thing he had to go back to London. Gayatri and he had planned to meet for lunch in a couple of days, and he would tell her then. Some time away from each other would solve the problem. And he had seen enough of Gyan Singh Grewal to know that even if things with Gayatri died out, Grewal would not let that impact business.

Vikram looked up at the cold and unusually clear Delhi night sky. Something niggled at him on the inside. He wondered if it was a twinge of guilt at stringing Gayatri along.

9

'So, when will you be back?' asked Gayatri when Vikram told her he was going to London.

They were sitting in a rooftop café in Delhi's Meharchand Market. It was a sunny winter's day. Bougainvillea creepers climbed the parapet bordering the roof, and pots of bright dahlias lined the corners of the café.

'Maybe in a couple of weeks or so,' replied Vikram.

Gayatri nodded as she continued to stir her coffee, careful to hide the feeling of relief that swept over her. Two weeks by herself was exactly what she needed to figure out how she felt about him. She couldn't have planned this better herself.

Vikram, for his part, had practised the conversation in his head on the way to the café. He had to let her down gently. He cleared his throat and started speaking in a low tone. 'I've had a really good time these past few days, Gayatri.'

She smiled. 'Me too. Shall we order?' she asked, signalling to the waiter.

They made small talk about the weather as they waited for the food. She expressed sympathy for him, having to leave this glorious Delhi sunshine for London's gloomy winter. He could not detect any disappointment in her voice or expression; in fact, she seemed to want to avoid the subject of their relationship altogether, instead talking about mundane things like some food festival she was planning to visit.

Once their lunch arrived, she was content to stop talking completely and concentrate on eating.

He decided to probe a little. 'So, now what?' he asked.

'Meaning?'

'I mean, uh, what will you do the next few days?'

'The next issue of our journal is coming out soon, so it's going to be crazy hectic,' she said, her mouth half-full of the fried fish she was evidently enjoying. Some of the tartar sauce seemed to have found its way to the tip of her hair, which was falling over her shoulder.

She is very clumsy with food, Vikram thought, almost affectionately.

'Good, good,' he said. 'I, myself ... I'll be very busy too. Some days I work till as late as one or two at night. And with this time difference, it might be, you know, tough—'

She cut him off. 'This fish is really good, haan. You should try some.'

'No,' he said. 'I'm fine. I'm not too hungry today.' He had this urge to reach across and wipe the tartar sauce from her hair.

'Would you like some dessert?' he asked when the waiter cleared their plates sometime later.

'Yes, let's get that triple chocolate thing we saw downstairs.' Her eyes seemed to brighten at the thought of dessert.

'Okay,' he said, perplexed. Had he misread her all along? Wasn't she concerned about what would happen to them? Or maybe, she was so certain about them that she wasn't concerned. But no, he thought, there's definitely a barrier today, as if she really doesn't care.

Dessert arrived, and she made some more pointless conversation about his flight and the movies he could watch onboard.

'I'll probably work the entire time,' he said. 'I just hope they don't ask me to stay on in London for longer, there's so much work piled up.' He looked into her eyes. There was no flicker of worry. They are actually quite nice, her eyes, he thought. Lighter than the usual shade of brown.

Soon, it was time to leave. He followed her down the narrow staircase and waited impatiently while she stopped to have a quick word with the manager to praise their meal.

As they walked to the car, Gayatri, relieved that she had got through lunch without any talk about their future, wondered how she would feel if things just died out once he went to London. A pang of something resembling fear pierced through her, but it was quelled quickly enough as she reminded herself how much she needed some time to digest all of this. The best thing to do would be to say a quick goodbye, she decided.

At the car, she turned to him and smiled. 'Take care, Vikram.'

He felt an unexpected rush of anger at her bland words. He wanted her to react, to feel bad because he was going, at least say that they would speak while he was away. 'I'll call you,' he said.

'Okay,' she replied, looking in her purse for her car keys, deliberately avoiding eye contact so as not to test herself. She reached for the car door.

Before he could think, he grabbed her hand away from the door, and pulled her towards him. Her face was now just below his. She looked up at him, surprised. He moved closer. Though they were standing by a large tree, she felt conscious of the assortment of drivers and street vendors who were doubtless staring at them. Then, just as suddenly as he had grabbed her, he pulled away. She looked at him in confusion. There was a strange mix of fear and worry on his face—or was that anger?

Vikram stepped back quickly and opened the car door for Gayatri. She got in without looking at him and started the car. It took a couple of tries before she got it out of its narrow spot. Finally, glancing at him with a small smile, she drove away.

'Going to London? Aise hi?' asked Nina Mehra loudly, her eyes wide with panic. 'Arre, only two days back toh you went to his house, he didn't say anything then?'

Gayatri nodded, flipping channels with the remote control. 'Something came up at work, so he has to go. That's what he told me at lunch.'

'Oh god, I must talk to Shama. He should have told us properly. This is not the way.' She looked around for her mobile phone.

Gayatri sat up straight and looked at her mother. 'No, Ma. Please don't do that.'

'Why? We just want to know, na. He has met you so many times now, met us, you've been to his house and met his parents. Now what has happened suddenly?'

'I'm actually glad he's going away for a few days. I also need some time to make up my mind. You know this has all happened too fast.'

'Fast? What fast? Thirty-two is fast?'

'I'm telling you, Ma,' said Gayatri. 'I mean this. If you call Shama Aunty or anyone else about Vikram, I will text him immediately to say it's off. Don't test me.'

Gayatri stood up and walked up to her own room, quite certain that her mother knew better than to follow her. Sitting on the armchair in her room, she looked out at the garden, thinking of the moment when Vikram had pulled her towards him. The expression on his face had been so intense—

There was a knock on the door. Gayatri didn't respond.

'It's me. Prom.'

'Come, come,' she said, sitting up.

Prom and Tarun had returned from their trip to Shillong that morning. She came in and sat on the bed, facing Gayatri. 'Your mother seems upset. Vikram's going away? She said you've threatened her, telling her she can't call the boy's side.'

Gayatri smiled despite herself. 'You're making me sound like a terrorist.'

'I'm glad at least you're still in good humour.'

'You know my mother, Prom, she'll go overboard and fix wedding dates if she has her way. I'm so glad he's going away for a couple of weeks. I told you, na, this is moving a bit too fast. I need some time.'

Prom looked at her for a few moments. 'You sure it's just that?'

Gayatri looked out of the window. After a few seconds, she turned to Prom and said, 'I like Vikram, Prom. But it's too soon, and I'm not sure if I want to ... if I will be able to spend the rest of my life with him, his family.' She sighed. 'Maybe it's the difference between being twenty-two and thirty-two. I know what I don't want, at least.'

'You'll have to make up your mind yourself. The only counsel I would give you is once you feel certain, don't overthink it.'

Gayatri nodded.

'Achha anyway, Nandini will be here soon. She's spending the night, right?'

'Oh, yes, I forgot. That's a relief, Mama will be distracted from her disgracefully unmarried daughter by her very-much-married one.'

Prom smiled. 'Think of somewhere to go. I want to eat some super spicy food.'

After they got back from dinner, Nina walked up to Gayatri's room to check if the girls needed anything. She found Promila settling down on some cushions on the floor, Gayatri curled up in the armchair, and Nandini sitting cross-legged on the bed.

'Come, Ma,' said Gayatri. 'Sit with us.'

'No, no, I just came up to see if you had everything you need. Tarun is okay?' she asked Prom.

'More than okay after all those whiskies.' Promila smiled.

Nandini said, 'Yeah, Mummy, I think Tarun Bhaiya and Dad really overdid it today. Sit for a while, na.' She patted the space next to her on the bed.

Nina pursed her lips and sat on the edge of the bed. 'I have to go soon. Ashok—'

'Ashok will need me to put him to sleep,' mimicked Gayatri with a laugh. 'Mama, he's not a baby. Sit with us for a change.'

Nina frowned. She didn't like to be teased in front of Promila. 'How are Grewalji and Rupiji?' she asked Nandini.

'Fine.'

'And Priya?'

'Thankfully far away. She was in Dubai a few days ago to shop for a wedding. I was so afraid she would come here and plonk herself, but she went right back, thank god.' Nandini shook her head. 'All the time, just into her clothes and hair and shoes. She is literally useless.'

'There's nothing wrong with being concerned about the way you look, you know,' said Nina irritably. 'And once you're married, you have to think about these things a little more. Just because your didi here'— she glanced at Gayatri reproachfully—'doesn't take care of herself, it doesn't mean you should learn all the wrong things from her.'

Gayatri rolled her eyes and smiled at Prom.

'Okay, I'm going now,' said Nina, standing up. 'If you two can talk some sense into my older daughter here, I'll be grateful.' She looked at Nandini. 'You know, na, Vikram is going back to London. Without any yes or no.'

Nandini gave her sister a furtive look, then said quickly, 'Okay then, goodnight, Ma.' She got up and shepherded her mother out of the room.

'You needn't be scared, Chhoti,' said Gayatri as Nandini walked back to the bed. 'I'm done with getting angry.'

Nandini crossed her legs on the bed. 'But, Didi, really, what about Vikram? Did he say anything at all?'

The agitated expression on Vikram's face as he had pulled her towards him flashed in Gayatri's mind. 'No,' she said shaking her head, 'nothing.'

Nandini opened her mouth to continue, but Gayatri spoke first. 'Chhoti, I need some time to sort through this. Imagine if you had known Amar for only a few weeks before you married him.' She thought of Vikram's house, his mother, his ailing father. 'I sometimes feel like I can't do this adjusting thing any more. How do you change yourself or your habits after thirty?'

'It's not that tough,' said Nandini, defensively.

'It's different for you,' said Gayatri, stretching her legs out. 'You married Amar after dating him for a bit.'

'And it doesn't end at marriage,' said Prom. 'Once you get married, then you need to have kids—'

'And they need to be brilliant at everything, and before you know it, you need to get them married,' added Nandini.

Gayatri shook her head. 'What a waste. And through it all, try to concentrate on your career and make something of your own life.'

There were a few moments of silence where each of them pondered their own situations.

Nandini was the first to speak. 'Actually, whether you marry for love or it's arranged, you have to be ready to adjust to a new life and, sometimes, a new family.' She stopped herself from saying more. She had amassed a great many complaints in the two months she had been living with Amar's family.

'I still think it's easier to do things you don't like if you love your partner already,' said Prom.

Nandini felt a strange hollowness hearing Prom's words, and looked away.

'But,' said Gayatri, 'on the other hand, in an arranged marriage, you know right from the start that you need to gel with the family.' She paused. 'I mean, I felt completely out of place in Vikram's house that day. But living there and getting along with his family is a precondition to being with him—it's a big part of the decision.'

Nandini said, 'I think work makes the biggest difference—working and earning. I mean, I earn more than Amar does. At least I don't depend on him financially.' There was a pause, and then she said, 'That will be a problem for you, Didi.'

Gayatri shrugged. 'I guess I could earn more than I do now if I really had to.'

'But you still wouldn't be able to afford an area like this,' said Nandini in the plain-speaking manner of younger siblings. 'I just feel such a huge sense of freedom because of my salary. Tomorrow, if I really need to, I could just walk out and lead the same life.'

'It's a different kind of freedom that I have, Chhoti,' Gayatri said quietly.

'Maybe, but I don't really get it, Didi. This interest in history that you have, couldn't you have pursued it part-time? Even Akshay Bhaiya was telling Amar that he knows so many lawyers who have other passions while doing law.'

'Why was this Akshay discussing my career choices?' asked Gayatri irritably. 'Ek toh he thinks he's so superior to everyone—'

'I don't know about superior,' interjected Prom, but he seemed a little aloof that day at dinner. Huddled in a corner with his brother.'

'You didn't see him flirting with Didi, then?' Nandini asked innocently.

'Flirting?' said Prom, surprised.

Gayatri glared at her sister. 'You're crazy, Nandini.' She looked at Prom. 'She's mad, Prom. He is a stuck-up, arrogant, complicated person.'

'I've never known you to be so harsh with your judgements, Gayatri,' said Prom.

'You'd be too, if you spoke to this guy for just five minutes. He's always full of himself. And so condescending. I told you, na, I needed a favour from him for work, and he … Well, he did help, I'm not denying that, but … I don't know. He's not a nice guy. He doesn't have any principles, at least none that I can respect.' She paused. 'He had an opportunity to speak up for some people, journalists, who were being targeted by some right-wing nuts. He had the influence, the access, but he just didn't do it. It didn't even cross his mind. He doesn't have a conscience.'

'Didi, that's not fair,' Nandini protested. 'I know what you're talking about, but you can't expect Akshay Bhaiya to have convinced those goons to stop troubling other journalists. He did what he could for you, na? He really went out of his way, I thought you'd be grateful.'

Gayatri exhaled loudly. 'I am grateful. But really, he did what he did because his dad told him to. That doesn't mean I have to like him or respect him. Anyway, can we please stop talking about him?'

After a few seconds of silence, Prom said, 'I think he's quite good-looking, though.'

Nandini and Gayatri looked at each other for a second, then burst into laughter as if on cue.

'I love how Prom gets to the point,' said Gayatri, still laughing. 'Not a nice guy, okay … Unprincipled, fine. But have you noticed how good-looking he is? Tall, all that greying hair at the temples, cute smile when it makes its rare appearances. Intelligent also. What more could a girl want?'

'For all her Bengali airs, Prom ultimately zeroes in on the Punju guy only,' said Nandini teasingly.

Prom looked at Gayatri carefully as she laughed along with them. She hadn't said anything about any greying hair at Akshay's temples or his smile. With all this time in a Punjabi family, thought Prom, smiling inwardly, I think I've developed the Punjabi aunty antennae too.

The next evening, Nandini sat at her office desk, scowling at her phone. She had just spoken with her mother-in-law, who was insisting she come home early to meet some important friends of Mr Grewal who were coming specially to meet her and Amar. Picking up the pack of cigarettes on her desk, she walked to her friend Suchita's room and waved at her through the glass door. Together, they walked to the smoking balcony on their floor.

'Why so pissed? Khambani's chasing you?' asked Suchita, lighting her Classic Mild.

'No, yaar,' Nandini grumbled, taking the lighter from Suchita and lighting up her cigarette, 'it's Amar's mom.' She took a long drag and blew out smoke. 'She is such a pain. She wants me to go home early today, and I have to turn around an SPA this evening. Jugal is working on it, he'll give it to me only by six.'

'Why does she want you home early?'

'Some friend of Amar's dad is coming over. They should tell their bloody son to return sooner.' She took another drag and let the smoke filter out from between her teeth. 'Why the fuck am I stuck with this shit, Suchi? And they do it so politely—beta this and beta that.'

'You should tell Amar.'

'I've tried, but he doesn't get it. It's only been a couple of months since we got married, but I swear I'm fed up.'

'Nan, you have to make them understand that your work is demanding. You can't be expected to get home when they want. Did they tell you about this dinner before today?'

'No, that's the worst part. She says she did, but I swear I don't remember her saying anything.'

Suchita shook her head. 'It's funny though, they should understand your work and lifestyle, it's the same as Amar's.'

'The thing is, because Amar's dad is such a big-shot lawyer, and with all this politics business that has started, they've developed a really inflated sense of self. Like they can't imagine that someone else might have something more important going on. My mom-in-law is like, "Grewalji has said so, so please come home by seven, beta."'

'She calls him Grewalji?'

Nandini nodded. 'It's all so pissing off. I never had random stress like this at my house.'

Suchita laughed. 'Maybe you'll also be calling Amar "Grewalji" in a few years.'

Nandini rolled her eyes. 'Shut up, Suchi.' She stubbed out her cigarette. 'I don't think I can take more of this saas–bahu bullshit. Come, let's go in. I'll take the draft from Jugal now and work on it at home. Fuck my life.'

10

A FEW DAYS LATER, Akshay was in his office with Mann and Singhvi when his phone rang.

'Yes,' he said into the phone. After a moment, he nodded. 'Coming.' 'I'll be back in a few minutes,' he told Mann and Singhvi and went to the conference room.

Inside, Sadhuji was sitting at the head of the large table. Mr Grewal was sitting next to him, looking sombre. Akshay touched Sadhuji's feet and took the seat opposite his father.

'We need your help, beta,' said Sadhuji, smiling, the three horizontal red lines on his forehead creasing slightly.

'Ji, Sadhuji,' said Akshay. 'Bataiye.'

'Akshay,' his father began gruffly, 'you know that Megha Barua investigation—that journalist who was murdered? Two of Sadhuji's people have been arrested in Karnal for the murder.'

Akshay glanced at Sadhuji. His head was slightly cocked, his eyes gave nothing away.

'We need to get them out,' continued Mr Grewal. 'The FIR is for murder under 302, along with the usual conspiracy sections. Of course, you can't go yourself, so send Mann and Singhvi. Those men should not say anything to the cops incriminating Sadhuji.'

The rush of contempt for Sadhuji that suddenly coursed through Akshay surprised him. 'Uh,' he hesitated, 'they ... they were involved in the murder?'

His father frowned. 'What kind of question is that? I'll give you their names and numbers. For now, just have them released. You know the Haryana Police is like the Rajhans government's private goonda army. They'll be waiting to make an issue of this.'

There was silence for a few seconds.

'Are you going then?' asked Mr Grewal, his voice wrapped in displeasure.

'Uh ... yes.' Akshay touched Sadhuji's feet again and walked out of the room.

Mann and Singhvi were still in his office. Akshay instructed them to make their way to Karnal. Neither batted an eyelid as he briefed them and handed over some wads of cash.

Leaning back in his chair after they left, Akshay stared into empty space, thinking of Gayatri. He would have to warn her to lie low. Suddenly, his father stormed in and slammed the door shut behind him.

'What the bloody hell was that?' Mr Grewal's booming voice felt even louder in the confines of the office.

'What, Papa?' asked Akshay looking up at his father. It had been many years since his father had used this tone with him.

'Who the hell do you think you are? I won't have you sitting in judgement over me or Sadhuji, that too in front of him. First that

Vikram business, and now flashing your eyes at us over this small favour for Sadhuji.'

'I've sent Mann and Singhvi,' replied Akshay calmly. 'The work will be done.'

'You listen to me,' his father said in a low tone, clenching his teeth. He rested both his palms on Akshay's desk and leaned forward. 'If you don't want to work for me, get the hell out of here. I don't need you. Don't think you're bloody indispensable. I've been in this profession since before you were born. So don't try to teach me.'

'I'm not trying to teach you anything, Papa,' said Akshay, averting his eyes.

'I want you to understand two things clearly,' said Mr Grewal, heavy breathing punctuating his speech. 'One, whatever you are, it's because of me. I'm the one who trained you, who gave you clients, this practice. It's my name you're earning off, my bloody plate you're eating from. Don't you ever forget that. And two,' he continued, 'I don't need a morality meter in my life. I follow my own judgement, and I don't give a damn for anyone else's.'

Akshay raised his eyes to his father's.

He wasn't sure if it was his father or himself who seemed more unrecognizable to him in that ugly moment.

When Gayatri awoke the next morning, she reached for her phone and saw a message from Akshay. It read, 'Can we meet for a few minutes today please?'

She frowned. What does he want now? She replied, 'Sure, I'll be done with work by six.'

He replied immediately. 'I have a client briefing then. Can we meet earlier? Around four? I can come to your office if that's more convenient.'

At a quarter past four that afternoon, Leela announced that a 'Mr Akshay' had arrived to see Gayatri. Farah was not at her desk.

Gayatri finished typing a sentence on her computer, then stood up. As she walked to the doors leading to the veranda, she ran her hands through her hair, wondering if it was looking messy, as it often did when she was working.

Akshay was sitting in one of the cane chairs outside. He looked at her as she stepped out. The fading afternoon sun shone a dull golden light on her face, and lent a glint to her silver earrings, tangled in her hair.

'Hi,' he said, standing up.

'I hope everything's okay?' she asked, sitting down. He seemed to have an odd, sheepish look about him.

'Everything's fine,' he said. 'I just needed to speak to you. I'll get to the point, Gayatri. Those threats you got … You need to take them seriously. I mean, don't take any chances.' He looked at her intently.

She stared at him for a few seconds, trying to figure out what he really meant.

'It's not worth it, Gayatri. These people can be ruthless, and may not care about personal connections. So just be careful, please.'

She was surprised at the note of desperation in his voice. 'Did you find out something else? Are they planning—'

He shook his head. 'No, no, nothing specific.' He added, gently, 'There's no need to worry.'

'I'm not worried,' she said contemptuously. She was sure he was hiding something, but before she could ask any questions, Leela arrived with two glasses of water.

Akshay took one and thanked Leela with a small smile. 'See, I spoke to Sadhuji's men when you asked me to, and they seem to have backed off for now. But please try to stay off their radar. These people, whoever they are, they're not done. And please tell Farah and Kanthan to take this seriously as well.'

He's probably been sent here to convey a fresh 'friendly' threat from Sadhuji, she thought, trying to remain calm. 'Akshay, I'm grateful to you for thinking of me—of us all—and coming here to warn us.' She took a sip from her glass before continuing, 'We will be careful, but this journal is very important to us, and we can't just sit around and be bullied like this.' She added testily, 'It is cowardly not to stand up for yourself against bullies, and for others as well, if you can.'

Akshay gazed at the floor in silence. She really can be quite stubborn, he thought. She's obviously still upset that I didn't speak up for the others targeted by Sadhuji. Whatever ideas she has about me, why can't she see sense for her own safety? And who is she to take this moral high ground anyway? She's seeing Vikram—doesn't she know what he's up to?

He looked at her and said, 'Can I ask you for one favour, please?'

'What?'

'Will you tell me in advance if you plan to say or write something controversial?'

'Why?'

So that if your body is found in a ditch, I'll know why, he wanted to say. Instead, he said, 'If I can help in some way, I'd like to.'

She pursed her lips. 'I don't see the point.' Why was he pretending to worry about them? It would be better if he came clear about the threats he had been sent to make, rather than sugar-coat them with fake concern.

'Gayatri, please. I'm just saying, let me know if you plan to reply to them, or write or publish something they don't want.'

'Fine,' she said grudgingly.

They sat in uncomfortable silence for a few moments.

'You found the place easily?' Gayatri said finally, breaking the quiet.

'Yes, your directions were perfect.' He looked around. 'This is a nice place you people have here. Is it someone's house?'

Gayatri nodded. 'Kanthan's. He lives upstairs, and we use the ground floor and basement as our office and library.'

'Library?'

'It's a small not-for-profit library.'

'What kind of books?'

'Mostly history, some politics and religion as well.'

'Do many people use it?.'

Gayatri shook her head. 'There aren't too many takers for the books, just the silence and space, and that too mostly to cram for competitive exams. It's sad, but we try.'

Akshay nodded. 'Can I see the library?'

Gayatri was surprised he was interested, but she led him inside. He followed her past a few shelves to the centre of the room, where sweater-clad students were sitting at the tables, studying from books labelled with combinations of acronyms for competitive exams: IIT-JEE, PMT, IAS, AIEEE.

He pulled out a few books from a nearby shelf, then sat down, thumbing through one titled *Prejudice and Pride*. It was a study of school history textbooks in India and Pakistan. Gayatri had contributed it to the library herself.

Why is he pretending so much, she thought. She walked up to him and tapped him on his shoulder. He looked up at her, smiling.

'Are you done?'

'Haan? Oh, yeah, sure,' he said, his smile disappearing at her stern tone. She could be such a dragon. He replaced the book on the shelf, and followed her up the stairs and outside. They walked to where his car was parked.

'Akshay, thanks for coming over and … uh …'

He unlocked the car. 'You don't need to thank me. Please just be careful.'

She nodded curtly and turned away before he had driven off.

Nandini was exhausted by the time she reached home. She had been dealing with a rude and demanding client all day, and was looking forward to curling up in her room with her laptop and watching her new favourite drama from across the border, *Dil ka Dariya*.

She started to climb the stairs to their floor, when her mother-in-law called from the downstairs living room. 'Nandini beta, just come here a minute.'

Nandini sighed. She was in no mood to make small talk, but she walked over and forced a smile.

'Sit, beta,' said Rupi.

'Actually, Mummy, I was going to go upstairs to rest. I've had a long day, I'm feeling completely drained,' Nandini said, tilting her head to one side tiredly.

'I just want you to talk to Bittu Bua. Her husband is very unwell.'

Nandini could not place Bittu Bua. She fought the urge to refuse and say that she was going up anyway, and that this Bittu Bua could go to hell. She nodded instead. Rupi dialled the number and proceeded to speak for a few minutes.

Nandini sat on the sofa across from her mother-in-law and fidgeted with her phone. With each passing minute, she grew angrier. Her neck and back hurt, her shoulders were tense with stress. She desperately wanted to lie down. How unfair was it that she, an equity partner at one of India's largest law firms, was being forced to sit and wait like a child by a woman who had done nothing of note except produce three children.

Rupi finally handed her the phone. Nandini mustered a smile. 'Namaste, Bittu Bua,' she said stiffly into the phone.

'Haan, beta, how are you? We are waiting for you and Amar to come over sometime. Once Uncle gets better, you must come.'

'How is he feeling now?' asked Nandini mechanically. It felt absurd to be asking someone whose face she could not remember how her equally alien husband was feeling.

'Ahista ahista recover kar rahein hain, beta. You know, after the operation it has been so tough.'

Nandini hmm-ed sympathetically, though she still had no idea what operation they were talking about. 'Okay, Aunty,' she said quickly, 'please give him our regards. We are really hoping he gets better soon.' Without waiting to hear the reply, Nandini handed the phone back to her mother-in-law and slipped out of the room.

Upstairs, the door to their apartment was ajar. Loud sounds could be heard from the bedroom. She entered to find Amar lying on the bed in his pyjamas, watching what looked like a Jackie Chan movie. He didn't notice her.

She turned around angrily and stalked to the kitchen, poured herself a glass of water and glugged it down. As she drank the last sip, the feeling that had been niggling at her for the past few days surfaced clearly in her mind: maybe she shouldn't have got herself into this marriage mess after all.

Meanwhile, at No. 7, Jagjivan Road, Gayatri was in her room, browsing through news reports on her laptop. There were still a few minutes before Vikram was supposed to Skype her. It had been a week since he had left for London, but she had spoken to him only twice.

She clicked on a report on the Megha Barua investigation. Two suspects arrested for the murder had been released on bail. A Karnal police inspector had reportedly said that they had received another tip-off which pointed towards professional robbers who were wanted for several other similar crimes. She frowned as she recalled Akshay's visit to her office.

She googled 'Akshay Grewal' and went through the first few links that came up. They were news stories related to cases where he had appeared in court for the accused. He had been quoted a few times, saying things like, 'Confessions in police custody have been questioned time and again by the highest courts,' and 'We are happy the court has agreed with us on this matter.' One report said he was defending a prominent academic who was accused of rape. Gayatri's nose wrinkled as she read about the case. Another link said he was an alumnus of SRCC in Delhi.

The peculiar ringtone of a Skype call interrupted her. Vikram's face came up on her screen.

'Hi,' she said, remembering that she had meant to brush her hair and wash her face before the call.

'Hi, Gayatri. How are you?'

'Fine.'

'Busy day?' he asked.

She started to say something about her conversation with Akshay, but stopped with just a nod. She realized just then that she hadn't told Vikram about the threats to the journal in the first place. 'You?'

'Oh, you know, the usual. Shitty weather, freezing to death and my boss is killing me. All par for the course.'

She smiled. 'Where are you right now?'

'Still in office. Want to see it?'

She nodded.

He moved his phone around his room. All grey and glass and devoid of any colour. No wonder people got depressed there. 'Very nice,' she lied.

'But I just want to come back now, you know. I'm so done with this London thing. I want some sunshine.'

'I can imagine,' she said. 'The weather here is better, but only for a few more weeks. Once the garmi sets in, you'll be dying for some London gloom.'

'I don't think so. Once I'm back, I know I won't ever want to leave,' he said softly.

She looked away and said quickly, 'Do you know when you'll be back, then?'

'No, not yet, but hopefully within a couple of weeks. I have some meetings fixed in Delhi with Grewalji, so once those materialize I'll take the first flight back.'

Gayatri frowned. 'I've asked you this before, I know, but do you really need to go through him for your work?'

He nodded. 'Once he comes into the picture, the whole deal changes. And it's not a one-way thing, we are helping him, too.' He clicked his tongue and added, 'This is what business is all about, yaar. Don't worry.'

She was not convinced. 'Is Akshay involved in all this at all?'

'No, no, what can he do?' said Vikram, condescension apparent in his tone. 'Uske bas ki nahin hai, yeh big game. He's not a patch on his dad. Grewalji has vision, you know, he wants to grow even at this age.'

'You mean in politics and all?'

'Of course, that's the only way up in India. That's where the real power is. Not in this lawyer-giri.' He added with a gossipy grin, 'And, he's a player.'

'Who?'

'Grewalji, you must have heard I'm sure?'

'Heard what?'

'Uh, about that woman?' he said tentatively.

Gayatri shook her head.

'Actually never mind, it's nothing,' said Vikram.

'No, tell me,' she insisted. 'Which woman?'

'Arre, it's nothing, don't bother with it.'

Gayatri sighed in exasperation. 'Please just tell me, Vikram. We are too old to play games like this.'

He paused. 'Okay, but you definitely won't tell your sister or anyone else?'

'Of course.'

'Grewalji is having an affair with some woman in his office called Neelam.'

'What?'

'Yes. It's been going on for many years. Even his wife is cool with it.'

Gayatri's eyes widened.

'Now please, don't go around telling anyone. Please! In fact, I should not have told you.'

'I'm not going to tell anyone, Vikram. I'm not a teenager.'

'It's not you, it's just that girls generally talk—I mean, anyway, just don't tell anyone.'

Girls generally talk … did he really just say that?

'Uh, look, I need to go now,' he said abruptly, 'I have a call in five minutes.'

'Okay,' she said. She wondered whether Nandini knew about the affair.

'Hey,' he said.

'Hmmm?' she murmured, still distracted.

'You look cute.'

She snapped back to attention, 'Goodnight,' she said, mustering up a self-conscious smile that vanished the moment she disconnected the call.

Far away in London, Vikram continued to smile for a few seconds after she had hung up.

For a large part of his flight from India, he had tried to lecture himself about why he needed to put an end to this Gayatri episode. He had even written down a list of reasons, and had emerged from the flight determined to forget about her. But when he wheeled his suitcase into his two-bedroom flat overlooking the Thames, he wondered what it would have been like if she had come with him. He had scrolled through his phone until he found a picture of her, and zoomed in on her face. And in that moment, he had known he was not ready to let go just yet.

Half an hour later, Gayatri went down to the living room where her parents, Tarun, Prom and Dadi were sitting.

She poured a glass of wine for herself and joined them.

'So,' boomed Tarun, 'how is the romance going?'

'There is no romance, Bhaiya, but if you're asking about Vikram, he's fine,' replied Gayatri good-naturedly.

'No romance? What kind of a Punjabi kudi are you? No romance?' He laughed at his own joke while Prom looked on in disapproval.

Not for the first time, Gayatri wondered how an intelligent woman like Prom put up with her loud cousin, even after accounting for all the opposites-attract rubbish. She took a large gulp of her wine.

'Achha, beta, Nandini is coming over to spend the night,' said Nina to Gayatri.

'Again? How come? I thought Amar was back.'

'I don't know, she just said she's not well, so she thought she would come.'

Gayatri smiled. 'I'm sure she wants to spend time with Tarun and Prom before they leave.'

'There,' said Nina as the doorbell rang, 'that must be her.'

After a few minutes, when there was still no sign of Nandini, Gayatri got up to look for her.

'Upar gaya, kamre mein,' said Malti Didi, when Gayatri asked her where Nandini was. 'Ro raha tha.'

Gayatri walked up to Nandini's room and knocked on her door. There was no answer. She entered the room, it was empty. She went

towards the bathroom door. She could just about hear Nandini's soft
sobs from inside.

'Chhoti,' she called softly.

The sobs stopped suddenly, giving way to the sound of running
water. 'I'm coming, Didi,' Nandini answered, her voice sounding
normal.

Gayatri considered whether to ask her why she was crying, but
decided against it. 'Achha, I'm waiting.'

'You go, Didi, I'll come down.'

'It's okay, I'll wait. Anyway, I'm just getting annoyed downstairs—
Tarun Bhaiya is trying to grill me about Vikram.'

Nandini emerged from the bathroom after a few minutes. Gayatri
could make out that her eyes were still wet, and … Is that powder
on her nose? When they were younger, it used to be hilarious to see
Nandini emerge from the loo after a crying session, with a completely
white nose courtesy Johnson's baby powder. Her make-up skills have
improved only slightly since then, thought Gayatri as she pulled her
sister into a hug. Nandini burst into sobs immediately.

Gayatri clicked her tongue worriedly and held her, stroking her
head.

'What happened, Chhoti?' she asked gently. 'Don't cry like this,
please. Her own eyes filled with tears as Nandini's sobs became louder.

They sat on the bed. Nandini sobbed for a few minutes, her face
against Gayatri's neck. Gayatri did not press her to talk, just handed
her some tissues and rubbed her back as she started to calm down.

'God, Didi,' said Nandini when her tears had subsided. 'I'm so sorry.
I don't know what came over me. I think I was just missing all of you,
and … I don't know … and then I saw you …' She blew her nose loudly.

Gayatri smiled. 'Don't worry, you're here now. Wash your face and
dry your eyes. Then come down and have a glass of wine. Or three.'
She kissed Nandini on her cheek. 'You'll come down on your own?' she
asked, standing up.

'Yes, I'll come in a bit.'

'Okay,' said Gayatri. 'And don't overdo the powder and end up looking like a circus clown.'

Nandini gave a little laugh through her tears, her heart almost choking with gratitude because Gayatri had not probed further.

Akshay concentrated on his breathing, placing one foot in front of the other on the jogging track. Late-night runs were his fix for everything that went wrong during his day. He felt addicted to the moment when, after a few minutes of jogging, he became numb to the pain that seeped into his muscles.

As he neared the end of his run, he started sprinting. His legs now felt like rubber, he could hardly feel them and yet, he knew he was in control, increasing his speed ever so slightly with each stride. At the end of the track, he slowed down, then stopped. Panting, he doubled over from the waist, and let his arms hang loose towards the ground. His breaths sounded loud and sharp against the quiet calm of the night.

His thoughts strayed towards his conversation with Gayatri that day. What had Ms Holier-than-Thou said in her latest lecture? 'Keeping quiet is cowardly', or something like that. She thought all he did was carry messages from 'goondas', hobnob with the likes of Sadhuji and work for criminals. She made him feel so small, petty, corrupt.

What bullshit, he thought. He was just doing his job. He knew many of his father's clients were not the cleanest of people, and of course, money changed hands frequently, judges were bribed and cops were handled … But those are professional hazards, he defended himself, they have nothing to do with me, personally.

He took a few more deep breaths as he stretched his tired muscles. He was not one to waste time lying to himself. He knew that he was drawn to Gayatri despite the way she thought—or maybe because of it. He remembered the rush of contempt for Sadhuji he had felt in his father's office—the thought of Gayatri being at the receiving end of Sadhuji's violent agenda was making him feel things he never imagined a hardened lawyer like him would.

He straightened and bent from side to side. But then, there was Vikram. *Either she is so dumb that she can't see through him, or she's a hypocrite. She needs to get a grip on reality.*

And so do I, he sighed ruefully, blinking through the sweat that stung his eyes.

11

THE NEXT MORNING, Amar called Nandini from office. 'Why haven't you come into office?' he asked angrily.

'I have a fever,' she lied, annoyed by his tone.

After a pause, Amar said, 'You're behaving very weirdly, Nandini. What the hell is going on?'

'Nothing, I told you I'm not well. Instead of asking how I am and if I need anything, you're ready to fight as usual.'

Amar took a deep breath. 'I'm not fighting, just saying your behaviour is really odd. You left so suddenly last night … When I told Mummy today that you had gone home, she was shocked. Please don't do stuff like this.'

Him and his mother. 'Amar, I'll talk to you later. I've just had some medicines and want to sleep.'

Amar could sense Nandini was lying. She just wanted attention, and he wasn't going to give it to her. Let her sulk, he thought. 'Fine.'

'Bye,' said Nandini, and she hung up. She hoped Amar wouldn't turn up at her house. She didn't want to face him until she had shaken off her feelings of doubt about their marriage—but far from fading, they seemed to be taking clearer shape.

'This issue has been very well-received. Great job, both of you,' said Kanthan, smiling at Gayatri and Farah.

'Thanks, Kanthan,' said Gayatri. 'Farah's piece has more than fifty comments online, plus five or six letters. And most of them are actually about the article right?' She looked at Farah.

Farah nodded. 'Yes. The first time sensible comments have outnumbered the abuse. We also had that bulk order from IHTL for all their institutes.'

'Great,' said Kanthan, 'and who knows, in a few years we may even break even.'

Farah and Gayatri laughed. Kanthan had always been particular about surviving on the funding provided by their sponsor, an academic publishing house which had never, in all the years of running his journal, attempted to exercise editorial influence. He had consistently refused offers of funding from all other sources.

'Anyway,' said Kanthan. 'Gayatri, this week we are focusing on the school trips that we're organizing?'

'Yes, that, and Farah's working on the submissions to the Indian History Congress.'

The landline phone on Kanthan's desk rang, and as he picked up the receiver, Gayatri and Farah got up and left the room.

'Did you hear about Preeti?' asked Farah as they walked down the stairs.

'Yeah, she's having such a horrible time with her pregnancy, no?'

'She'll have to remain in the hospital for another two months, can you imagine? She can't leave until she delivers the baby.'

Gayatri shook her head. 'This is scary. I don't think I'm going to be able to have kids, at this rate.'

'Don't worry, Vikram will change all that,' said Farah, smiling.

'Very funny.' Gayatri's brow furrowed as she pictured herself and Vikram with a child, and his mother.

They walked out to the veranda together and sat down.

'How is Zaheer?' asked Gayatri.

'Okay. Busy with his residency at the hospital. But he calls every day.'

'He will come back, right?' asked Gayatri. 'I mean, I don't want to make this about me, but I really don't want you to move to the US.' She smiled.

'You know, we've always talked of living here once he completes his degree, with our parents and siblings, but ...'

'But?'

Farah sighed. 'But things are changing. He's been telling me we should seriously consider moving. That India is turning into an unpleasant place for people like us.'

'And what do you think?'

'I told him this is where we belong, where our roots are. But honestly, sometimes, I don't know what to think.' She paused. 'Anyway, we're thinking of getting married when he comes to India in June. He may go back for a bit before we decide where we finally settle down. And if a baby happens during this time, then at least I'll be done with it.'

'Done with it?'

Farah shrugged. 'I really want kids. And hearing all these scary stories about PCOD and women giving birth to preterm babies, I just get scared. Look at Preeti, on bed rest for three months.' She paused. 'If you want kids, you should think about this stuff too. Marriage or no marriage. Sara's having a baby with a sperm donor.'

Gayatri winced. 'This is the ultimate proof of social forwardness. Now I'm feeling the pressure to have babies even without a husband.'

Farah laughed. 'Seriously, it's true. But things with Vikram are getting final, right?'

Gayatri shook her head. 'I don't know.'

Leela arrived with two coffees. 'Thank you, Leela,' they said in chorus.

'He's very different, Farah,' said Gayatri slowly a few minutes later.

'In what way?'

'Many ways, like I know you'll say this sounds silly, but I never thought I could marry someone who doesn't like to read.'

Farah shook her head. 'That's too much now, Gayatri.'

'I know, I know,' Gayatri said quickly, 'which is why I ... you know ... I didn't say no. I know I can't have a long list of stipulations. In addition to everything else, must have a great library.'

'Or look at it this way: if you meet someone who likes reading, then you marry him even if you dislike everything else about him.'

'Oh god no, I'd end up with someone like Akshay then.' She wrinkled her nose. 'I hate him, but I know he reads.'

'That would be fun,' said Farah, laughing. 'Did he get in touch with you again after that day?'

'No. But my parents have invited Amar and him over for dinner on Sunday. They are really worried about Nandini ... she's just planted herself at home.'

'Has she fought with Amar or something?'

'I think so, though she denies it. Listen, Faru, I was meaning to ask you to come over on Sunday too. Nandini was also saying she hasn't met you in a while.'

'Okay, that'd be nice, I'd like to see her.'

'Great,' said Gayatri. 'Maybe you can keep Akshay occupied too. If he gives me one more lecture about playing it safe, I will sock him in the face.'

On Sunday evening, Akshay turned his car into the Mehras' lane and parked outside their gate. After spending the past few days ignoring all thoughts of Gayatri with steely resolve, he had found himself accepting this dinner invitation far too eagerly.

Amar was glad that Akshay had agreed to accompany him. Had he come alone, the excessive attention that the Mehras paid him would have made it difficult to talk to Nandini. He meant to take her back tonight if she would come. He had called her many times over the last few days, trying to persuade her to see sense, that it was not right for her to stay at her parents' house for so long just after they were married, but the moment he brought up any societal niceties or his mother's advice, she just exploded.

Gayatri opened the door. She gave Amar a hug as he entered.

'How are you, Didi?' he asked.

She smiled. 'Fine. Everyone's in the drawing room.'

Akshay walked in behind Amar. He was wearing a long black kurta with jeans, which were neatly folded upwards at the hem, and black sandals. 'Hi, Gayatri,' he said, his resolve to avoid all thoughts of her suddenly seeming childish.

Gayatri smiled formally, and then held out her hand. He looked at it for a moment, then took it gently, holding on a few seconds longer than necessary before letting go.

'Have you noticed the way Amar is looking at Nandini?' Gayatri whispered to Farah a few minutes later as they set the small plates and napkins down on the centre table, next to the mutton shammi kebabs and the dhokla. 'I feel bad for him. I'm going to tell her to stop ignoring him. It doesn't look nice.'

'Yeah, do that.' Farah nodded. 'Though I was actually wondering why Akshay keeps looking at you,' she added with a smile.

'He doesn't, don't be silly.' Gayatri looked towards Akshay and caught his eye. She looked away immediately. *What thoughts is this crazy Farah putting in my head?*

They served the snacks to everyone, Gayatri ensuring that Farah handed Akshay his plate.

Prom made her way to Akshay, curious about him after her conversations with Gayatri. After an exchange of pleasantries, she asked him about work, and learnt that they had a few common acquaintances. He was polite and attentive while they discussed life in Delhi and the US.

'Gayatri told me you've been a great help on all their problems at the journal, with Sadhuji and all that,' she said a few minutes into the conversation.

He shook his head. 'No, I didn't do anything. She'—he looked at Gayatri—'is more than capable of dealing with an army of Sadhujis by herself.'

Prom laughed. 'That is true.'

When she walked away from Akshay a while later, she had a far more favourable view of him than Gayatri would have liked.

Nandini spent the first half of the evening avoiding Amar. She pulled Farah down to sit with her in one corner.

'Listen to me, Farah,' Nandini was saying, 'I'm younger than you and Didi, but I'm the only one with the experience. You'd better explain to Zaheer the terms on which you want to live with him *before* you guys get married, and please don't live with your in-laws.'

Farah smiled. 'Right now, I'm having a tough time convincing him to stay in India after the wedding.'

Nandini folded her hands in a gesture of resignation. 'Just go, I'm telling you. If it means you guys get to live on your own, just do it.'

Nina joined them just then, interrupting this discussion much to the relief of Farah, who was increasingly afraid that Amar or Akshay would overhear Nandini's complaints.

Gayatri was walking into the drawing room from the kitchen, when her phone buzzed. It was a message from Vikram. 'What's up?' She immediately regretted opening it, instead of just checking the preview. Now she would have to reply.

'Nothing, just a dinner at home, so a bit busy,' she replied.

Her phone buzzed again. 'Well thanks for being so concerned about me <smiley face>. I've just come home after five back-to-back meetings. <exhausted face>'

Gayatri winced. She hated his excessive use of those ugly yellow faces; it was hardly a big deal but it really bugged her. She replied, 'Ok. Get some rest.' As she typed, she wondered if she had become emotionally frigid. Perhaps she was simply incapable of feeling that 'in love' thrill any more.

'That's it?' he typed back immediately.

That's it? What does he want me to say? Surely he doesn't expect me to say something romantic. And I really don't—

Her phone buzzed again.

'Ha ha. Just kidding. You carry on, I'll speak to you tomorrow.'

She smiled. He wasn't all that bad.

'Ohhoooo!' Tarun Bhaiya's voice startled her. 'Bade smiles aa rahein hain. Long distance message?' His loud laughter rang out.

She reddened and smiled awkwardly. 'No, no, Bhaiya,' she said, 'just a friend. Some joke.' She glanced at Akshay out of the corner of her eye. He was looking at her.

'Tell us also … this joke,' said Tarun, with exaggerated innocence. 'We also like a laugh.'

'It's really not that funny,' said Gayatri, turning redder.

'Tarun!' interrupted Prom sharply. 'Come, let's call Binoy. I just remembered it's his birthday.'

Gayatri looked at Prom gratefully as Tarun followed her out of the room. She could not get herself to look at Akshay again, although she suspected his eyes were still on her.

After dinner, Gayatri managed to get Amar to pull up a chair next to Nandini and her. Nandini seemed clearly off-colour as he sat down.

'Didi,' he started almost immediately. 'This is not fair. I want my wife back now.' He smiled good-naturedly, but they could all sense tension.

Gayatri smiled. 'Oh, we will be only too happy. Please take her off our hands.'

'I told you, na,' said Nandini, 'I want to spend some time with Prom and Tarun Bhaiya. I'll come back soon.'

'They leave tomorrow, don't they?' asked Amar, his tone now serious. Nandini pursed her lips.

'Didi, please talk to her,' said Amar. 'She's been behaving so strangely. Ever since she insisted on coming back here.'

'Amar, there's no need to involve Didi in this. We are adults, we can sort this out ourselves.'

'Sort out what, you need to talk at least. You just walked out randomly at night, no fight, nothing. Not even telling my mother. At least tell me what the issue is,' whispered Amar angrily.

Gayatri stood up. Having them discuss their problems in front of everyone did not seem to be a great idea. 'Listen, you guys, why don't you go for a walk outside?'

'No, Didi, I don't want to,' Nandini said stubbornly.

'Nandini, just go. Please. There's no harm in talking.' She touched Nandini's shoulder lightly. 'Chhoti.'

Nandini got up reluctantly and followed Amar as Gayatri looked on worriedly.

'Some trouble there, no?' Akshay sat down next to Gayatri, startling her. He had a plate with chocolate mousse, gulab jamuns and ice cream.

'No, no, must be something stupid,' she replied without looking at him. 'You know how when you're young every problem seems ten times bigger.'

'Is there any reason you've been avoiding me all evening?'

'Avoiding?' Gayatri shook her head with exaggerated innocence. 'No, why would I do that?'

'I don't know. That's why I was asking,' he said calmly, taking a bite of the mousse.

'I'm not—'

'Gayatri,' Akshay interrupted, 'whatever you think of me—though I don't understand why I seem like such a criminal to you—I don't mean any harm. I hope you know that at least.'

Gayatri nodded. It wouldn't do any good to get into an argument with him, here.

'I was meaning to ask you something. About an article you wrote.'

Gayatri looked at him with slightly raised eyebrows.

'You gave me a few back issues, remember? When you asked me to speak with Sadhuji's men.' Akshay settled back into the sofa comfortably. 'I thought your piece on the caste system's impact on art and music was really good. I ordered one of the books you had referenced.'

'Thanks,' Gayatri said, a little suspicious of his sudden interest in her writing.

'How much input do you guys have on the articles written by others?'

'The professionals, not much. But the amateur articles, we end up doing a lot of fact-checking and editing. And rewriting, to be honest.'

'Yourselves?'

'Some parts, yes, but we also have a couple of interns to help us.'

'Oh,' said Akshay nodding, and taking the last bite of the mousse. 'This chocolate thing is really good.'

'It's from Elma's,' said Gayatri flatly, thinking of Nandini and Amar. She wasn't in the mood for small talk.

Amar and Nandini returned just then, looking tense, and walked to different corners of the room.

'Do you really not know what happened between them?' asked Akshay.

'No.' Gayatri shook her head worriedly. 'But I'm sure they'll sort it out. It happens to all married couples.'

'And how would you know that?'

Gayatri looked at him witheringly. 'Well, I do have eyes and a brain. You don't need to be married to know what it's like.'

'And what is it like?' asked Akshay, innocently.

Gayatri opened her mouth to say something but then shrugged. 'I guess neither of us really knows.'

'That's true.'

'Don't you get a lot of pressure to get married?' she asked.

'Used to. My parents gave up a few years ago.'

Gayatri nodded. Before she could think, she asked, 'And you didn't … I mean, there was no one—' She broke off.

'There was someone, a few years ago.' He paused. 'But it ended badly.'

Gayatri was curious, but she didn't probe further. 'And your parents are okay with you not marrying at all?'

'My mom is not, to be honest, but she's accepted that there isn't anything she can do about it.'

'Lucky you,' said Gayatri. 'I wish my mom would take a leaf out of her book.'

Akshay smiled. 'You seem to have put up a brave resistance.'

'It hasn't been easy, I assure you.'

'So ... er ... is Vikram still around?'

'Haan?' said Gayatri, a little surprised. She looked away. 'No, he's back in London.'

'Oh.' Akshay set his plate down. 'He is a banker, isn't he?'

Gayatri nodded.

'Is he planning to move back to India?'

'I think so. His firm wants to expand their client base. They want to tap into the Indian savings market or something.'

'You know what he does then?' Akshay asked, looking at her carefully.

'I guess. Invests for people. They invest with him, and he reinvests their money. Why do you ask?'

Akshay stood up. 'No reason. I'll go get some more dessert.'

'You'd better be careful with Akshay, Gayatri,' said Farah as she got into her car.

'What do you mean?' asked Gayatri, standing at the car window.

'You know what I mean.'

'I don't.'

Farah smiled. 'Okay. Don't tell me I didn't warn you. I know you.'

'Thanks for the warning, Aunty. But I don't need it.'

Farah shrugged as she pulled out of the driveway with a smile, and drove away.

Gayatri looked back to see Amar and Akshay being escorted to their car by her whole family. Nandini was nowhere to be seen. She waited for the procession to reach her and gave Amar a hug, saying softly, 'Don't worry. Whatever it is, it'll be okay.'

'Thanks, Didi,' he said.

She saw Akshay standing behind him.

He smiled at her, a little wryly. She smiled back. Just as his smile brightened, hers vanished abruptly.

The next morning, Akshay was walking down the stairs to his basement office when he saw Neelam coming up. He went back up the couple of stairs he had descended to let her pass. She reached the landing, stood close to him and asked softly, 'Where is Aunty?'

He bristled as he took a step back. 'I don't know,' he said coldly.

She reached out and touched him lightly on the chest.

He twitched sharply and grabbed her hand. She winced in pain. He clenched his jaw and let go of her hand, looking around to see if anyone was watching. 'You lay a finger on me once more, you'll regret it.'

'Oh, I don't think so,' she said with a smile, still wringing her hand in pain.

'Neelam?' called Rupi just then, from the other end of the room.

Akshay stepped aside quickly and hurried down the stairs.

Neelam walked up to Rupi, touched one cheek to hers and kissed the air. 'Hi Aunty, Grewalji sent me for the cash.'

'Sit, I'll just get it,' said Rupi.

Neelam sat on one of the sofas in the living room. Spotting someone dusting a cabinet, she said, 'Suno, zara ek coffee de dena.'

Rupi entered a few minutes later with an envelope and handed it to Neelam. 'What will you have?'

'Oh, I already asked for a coffee.'

'Good,' said Rupi, nodding. 'Count kar lo.'

'Oh no, Aunty. I know how particular you are, it must be correct.'

'I'm getting old now,' said Rupi with a smile. 'Even I can make mistakes.'

'But you still look the same as when I met you all those years ago. I don't know how you manage to keep your skin looking like that,' said Neelam as her coffee arrived. 'How are Amar and Nandini doing?' she asked, reaching for the cup.

'Fine,' said Rupi. 'Newly married, you know how it is.'

Neelam raised her eyebrows disdainfully. 'I have forgotten every moment of my newly married days. They were hell.'

Rupi nodded. 'Luck ki bhi baat hai. Not everyone ends up with the perfect spouse.'

'Oh, I don't know if *anyone* ends up with a perfect spouse actually,' said Neelam.

Rupi hesitated for a few seconds before saying slowly, 'One has to work on a marriage.'

Neelam remained silent as she sipped her coffee.

'And then,' continued Rupi, 'as you grow older, you realize marriage anyway has more value as an alliance than anything romantic. That realization changes many things.'

Neelam smiled, a hint of pity in her eyes. 'That's true.'

Rupi Grewal caught the look of pity. If she hadn't, she wouldn't have gone on to say, 'After all, the security and comfort that come with marriage are not comparable to anything else. I feel the women who are with men who refuse to marry them are the ones in real trouble.'

Neelam was slightly taken aback. Rupi had never been so direct.

'Look at Akshay,' Rupi added. 'I don't need to hide from you the number of girls that come and go.' She shrugged. 'I just wonder why they would be with someone who is so clear from the start that he won't marry them.'

'Still going on?' Neelam asked stiffly. 'Isn't he too old for all that?'

Now it was Rupi's turn to pity Neelam. But she didn't like to stoop to using her son as a weapon. 'Come, let's talk of something else,' she said. She couldn't, however, resist adding, 'We are both too old for all this.'

That night, Rupi walked up to Akshay's apartment after dinner. The door was open. She knocked and entered his bedroom.

'Hi, Ma,' he said, glancing up from his laptop. He was lying in bed. 'It's late. Everything's okay?'

'Hi, beta,' she said. 'Yes, yes, I just wanted to see you.'

'Come, sit,' he said.

'How are you, beta?' She sat down at the foot of his bed. 'I feel like I haven't spoken with you for so long.'

Akshay frowned. 'Did Papa tell you to talk to me?'

'No,' she lied. Her husband had spoken with her that morning about Akshay's changing attitude, knowing well that his wife was better at dealing with such matters. Mr Grewal might have his areas of weakness, but they were one team after all.

'I'm sure he did,' said Akshay. 'He's just upset because I asked him a few questions the other day. Don't worry.'

'Kya poocha?'

Akshay shook his head. 'Leave it.'

She persisted. 'Something to do with Sadhuji?'

Akshay nodded. 'Nothing is hidden from you, I know, Ma. This business is becoming dirtier. There is no … no line any more. Today it's bailing out the people who murdered a journalist, even destroying evidence. Tomorrow what? And for what?'

'He wants to rise fast in the party, in government. You know his ego.'

'His ego,' muttered Akshay shaking his head. 'I don't think we should help Sadhuji threaten and murder people. Fine, we've helped a few crooks avoid jail, but their deeds were done and it didn't … I don't know … it didn't have such a direct impact.'

Rupi looked at him questioningly.

He hesitated for a few seconds, then said, 'You know, Gayatri— Nandini's sister—she runs a really well-respected history journal. Sadhuji's men threatened her and her publication as well.' After a pause, he said quietly, 'That murdered journalist could have been her.'

'Does she know that Sadhuji's men were behind this murder?'

'She's very smart, I'm sure she's guessed.'

'Beta, even so, for your father's sake, don't—'

'Ma,' Akshay interrupted, his expression grave. 'I did what he told me to this time, but I don't know if I will again.'

Rupi looked at him worriedly. 'This will be serious, beta. He won't be able to take it.'

'Then he should get a grip and stop himself.'

'Akshay, before doing anything foolish, think of me. Don't do anything that could put a distance between us.'

He leaned forward and squeezed her hand. 'Don't worry, Ma. I won't let that happen. Why don't you try talking to him? Counsel him, Ma—this is going too far.' He paused. 'There has to be a line, even for him.'

She nodded. 'I'll talk to him.' She paused before speaking again, 'There is one more thing … Neelam. I saw her with you this morning. What did she want?'

Akshay lowered his gaze. 'I don't know. She's been trying some stunt for the past few weeks.'

'I wanted to slap her when I saw her touch you. She will sink to any low.'

'I'm sorry you had to see that.'

'Sometimes I curse the day I invited her into this house. She seemed so helpless then, all those bruises …' She sighed. 'You know, I still remember how happy I felt when Papa said he was helping her file a case against her husband. And then when he gave her a job, I really thought—'

'Don't think of it, Ma. What's done is done.'

'Don't worry. It doesn't hurt, beta. Not one bit. I'm almost glad that she is in your father's life. It decreases the burden on me.' She paused and looked towards the window. 'It's what she did with you that I can't forgive.'

Akshay smiled. 'It's so far back in the past, I don't even remember it now.'

'But I do,' said Rupi, standing up. 'I'll go now. I need to give your father his medicines.'

As the door closed behind his mother, Akshay's eyes hardened. Of course he remembered the day he had heard them, his much-older girlfriend and his father, together in the office. He remembered the moaning, the groaning. They could have at least locked the main door. The memory, the sounds, his brain had preserved them all too well.

12

Vikram sat across Akhil at The Bridge, an elite restaurant overlooking the Thames. It was a cold December day, the chilly London air biting whoever dared to venture out.

Akhil had ordered oysters. Vikram dutifully picked up the hard shell, squeezed some lemon onto the oyster, and popped the slimy mixture into his mouth. He tried to swallow it without tasting it. Oysters always reminded Vikram of his grandfather telling him that he used to eat two raw eggs every morning. 'Nice,' he lied.

'Meri billi, mujhi ko miaow?' Akhil laughed. 'Saale, jhoot mat bol. English bolni sikhayi hai tujhe.'

Vikram let out a laugh and shook his head. 'Pata nahin, sir, aap kaise karte ho.'

'Karna padta hai, beta. Aur phir aadat ho jaati hai, yaar,' Akhil replied, expertly allowing an oyster to slide into his mouth. He was something of a Jekyll and Hyde personality: when happy, he talked like a desi truck driver, and when displeased, he retreated into some impression of an English lord.

Vikram nodded. 'Haan, I eat so many things I never thought I would now, even eggs were a no-no when I was growing up.'

'Okay, now tell me about the meetings scheduled for Delhi,' said Akhil. He couldn't bear it if the conversation steered to a topic unrelated to him for more than five seconds.

'Sir, there is some delay at Grewal's end. The first meeting is now scheduled for the tenth of January. We'll have to commit to an approximate amount to Jain by then, I think, he will expect that.'

'Matlab we tell him that total contribution from here is X amount, and X minus about fifteen per cent reaches the party. That's fine. When will you give me the final figure?'

'I should have it this week. I think we should have at least forty crore committed.'

Vikram watched Akhil pop another oyster into his mouth and lick his lips. It reminded Vikram of people eating golgappas in South Extension Market. He thought of making a joke about that, but didn't think his boss would appreciate it. Akhil could be sensitive about his desi roots.

'Karte hain, behenchod!' said Akhil, shaking his head. 'Once we send this money in, things will move for us like crazy. Sky is the limit, yaar.'

Vikram nodded. You had to admire the guy, he thought. His ideas were simple but effective. Vikram was lucky to have been picked up by him, otherwise, he'd be stuck working with some medium-paced gora, trying to play by the rules. Truly, luck was the difference between geometric and exponential growth.

'What about that Sadhuji?' asked Akhil.

'He will expect a kickback, sir.'

'Kitne pe aaya abhi?'

'Seven per cent.'

Akhil shook his head. 'Kya laalchi sadhu hai, saala.'

'Don't worry, sir, I'll get it to three per cent.'

Akhil grunted as he sipped his champagne. 'And you broke off with that girl?'

Vikram waved his hand and mumbled something inaudible.

'So you didn't. Be careful. Zyada Majnu banne ki zaroorat nahin hai.'

Vikram bristled under his calm smile, and changed the topic.

'I've booked my ticket for next week,' said Vikram, smiling into the phone. He was lying on the sofa in his living room.

'Oh, okay,' replied Gayatri.

'I was wondering … Do you want to go somewhere for a weekend when I'm back?'

Gayatri hesitated. 'Let's see when you come, and anyway, we'll need to be quite sure about each other for my parents to allow me do that,' she said with a nervous laugh. 'I mean, we should talk, you know, see how we feel.' She winced as she spoke.

Vikram was quiet; he didn't understand her hesitation.

'Anyway, how's work?' she said quickly. 'Did you manage to set up your meetings in Delhi?'

'Yes,' he said flatly.

She could sense he was put off by her reluctance. 'I was meaning to ask you,' she said, trying to change the topic, 'are you going to invest the money you raise in India in foreign stocks? Isn't that a bit complicated in terms of RBI regulations?'

'Huh?'

'No, I just read in the papers today that they've increased the limit a person is allowed to remit abroad each year. You're planning to invest that money for people, right?'

'Er, yeah, something like that,' said Vikram.

'Then why do you need to meet with these politicians?'

'Oh that, that's just courtesy. All businessmen do it. You never know when the government will turn on you.' He paused. 'So it usually doesn't do any harm to just meet with them beforehand.'

'Achha,' said Gayatri. Akshay had made her paranoid about Vikram's work for no reason.

'Gayatri, listen, that's the doorbell,' lied Vikram. 'I'll call you in a bit.' He sat up. He was not pleased with her asking him so many questions about his work. If she was going to start asking him about RBI remittance schemes, then he would need a proper story. He had almost forgotten she was a lawyer by training.

He shook his head, wondering again about his liking for her. A girl like her wouldn't understand why he was doing this. Why he needed to do this. What growing up in that shitty neighbourhood in that shitty suburb of that shitty town had done to him. She just wouldn't understand.

The next day at the office, Gayatri was distracted. Farah was busy on work calls for most of the morning, so they couldn't take their usual coffee break together.

'Faru, shall we go out for lunch?' she suggested as Farah finished a conversation with a contributor.

Farah looked at the clock on her computer. 'We could.' She yawned.

'Let's try that new Parsi place in Def Col.'

'Good idea,' agreed Farah.

When they reached the restaurant, they got a table immediately.

'Wow, I love the menu,' said Farah. 'I'll have one of those Pestonjee drinks.'

'They don't taste as nice as the bottles look,' cautioned Gayatri.

'Never mind. I remember having these in Bombay as a kid.' They ordered their food and sat back.

'Faru,' said Gayatri.

'Y-e-s,' said Farah, slowly drawing out the word with a smile. 'Tell me.' She could make out that Gayatri needed to talk about something.

'I'm confused.'

'Akshay?'

'No!' Gayatri said, looking offended. 'Has everyone gone mad?'

'Then?'

'It's Vikram.' She paused. 'I'm not feeling it, you know. When I speak with him, it's like he's on a different planet.'

'Did you feel more when he left?'

Gayatri nodded. 'I think so.'

'Is it a case of out of sight, out of mind?'

Gayatri shrugged. 'Maybe, or maybe I'm just too old to feel fluttery and buttery.'

'Buttery? What the hell is feeling buttery? It just sounds gross.'

Gayatri laughed. 'You know what I mean.'

'Listen, Gayatri, you have to think this through and figure out the answer. Either you like this guy enough to spend the rest of your life with him, or you don't.'

'I know.' Gayatri sighed. 'What bothers me is that there isn't anything I can point to and say that *this* is why I don't want to be with him. He's doing well, he seems like a nice guy, he is nice-looking ... and he seems to like me.'

'Then?'

'Then I don't know.' She swallowed. 'That day when Akshay came home, he made me feel very weird.'

'See! I knew it.'

'No, no, not like that.'

The waiter appeared with their drinks. Farah closed her eyes as she took a sip of her raspberry soda. 'You're right, it's too sweet. But I love it!'

Gayatri smiled as she stirred her fresh lime soda with a straw.

'Haan, so tell. Why did you feel weird?' asked Farah.

'He asked me about Vikram's work, if I knew what he does. I got a little worried. It made me think that I don't know anything about him, really.'

'And what about Akshay staring at you through the evening, like a school kid, and all that cosy chatting? That didn't bother you?'

'Farah, no!' protested Gayatri. 'He's just being normal now, I think. He used to be so rude when we first met, remember?'

'And what do you think has brought about this change in him?'

'I have no clue. What I do know is that I don't like him.' She paused. 'No, it's more than that. I don't respect him.'

'And you respect Vikram?'

'What's not to respect?' asked Gayatri. 'Look where he's come from. He studied hard, got an MBA, and now he works at a bank. He has no powerful father to support him. Unlike Akshay, who just feeds off his dad and is content to serve crooks. I know enough lawyer-betas like him who think they own the world.'

Farah looked at her friend thoughtfully.

'You're lucky, Farah. You met Zaheer and there was no confusion.'

'No, but you remember how in the beginning his mother was not happy with the age difference? When I'm only a year older than he is.'

'You're right,' said Gayatri, nodding. 'I guess everyone has their own issues.' After a few seconds she said, 'Achha, I forgot to tell you, the *Indian Age* guys called again today. They want me to write a long feature on the Nigar Baba shrine, now that there is a Hindu–Muslim angle to the story after the shrine was demolished. They actually told me that they won't be responsible for trolling and threats. Can you imagine—newspapers have to warn writers like this now?'

'Did you agree?'

'I'll do it, I think.' Though she didn't like to admit it, the thought of telling Akshay about the piece had crossed her mind.

Their food arrived just then.

'Yum, yum yum,' said Gayatri as she took a bit of the dhansak.

'I know,' said Farah. 'Good call.'

'The eggs are also sooo good,' said Gayatri, her mouth full.

After a few minutes of eating in silence, Farah said, 'On the Vikram thing, don't complicate matters. Just try to figure out how you feel about him.'

Gayatri nodded. 'You're right.'

Farah smiled. 'My god, the mutton is so soft.'

'It is good, na? Give me someone who can cook like this and I'll be with him instead!'

Nandini had finally decided to go back to her in-laws' house that day, having run out of excuses once Prom and Tarun left for the US. Gayatri drove Nandini there.

After speaking of this and that for a few minutes, Nandini started talking of Amar, and their fights and arguments. Gayatri listened until Nandini's monologue came to an end, then said, 'But you love him, right? So you must make an effort for him. See, Chhoti—'

'Why am I the only one making an effort, Didi? What about him?' asked Nandini, adamantly, turning in her seat towards Gayatri. 'Maybe you think I'm being stupid and selfish, but the way I see it, we are equals. We both work at the same firm, in fact, I earn more than him. If anything, he got the job because of his father. I actually worked hard to get to where I am.'

'But, Chhoti, that's unfair. Amar's also very capable. He may not have gone to the best law school, but he went to a good college, then did an LLM. Why are you assuming he didn't get the job on his own merit?'

Nandini shook her head. 'Even if he did, he wouldn't have made partner on his own for sure. I've heard the way people talk about him at work. And I've had to speak up for him with our boss many times. Anyway, Didi, the point is, after slogging my ass off for twelve to sixteen hours a day, why can't I have a place to chill, to relax? Why do I have to sit in front of his parents like a doll and entertain their guests? Do you know how many people, especially these political types, come home? Almost every day, someone or the other is there. And I have to get dressed, and come and say namaste. And if I don't, he fights with me.'

Gayatri frowned.

'Didi, I can see you don't understand. It sounds petty, small, mean, I know. But this is how I feel.'

'Then talk to him.'

'He doesn't listen. The obvious answer is for us to move out, get our own place. But he loses it as soon as I mention it. So aggressive ...'

Gayatri sighed. 'Did you guys talk about all this before the wedding?'

Nandini shook her head. 'He only said we'd have a separate floor for ourselves. Which we do ... I just imagined it would be different, you know.'

'Chhoti, see, the best advice I can give you is that it's only been two months. Give it some more time, and keep an open mind.' She glanced at Nandini. 'I know Amar loves you a lot. He will find a way out.'

Nandini looked out of the window. She had known what her sister would say, and yet she was disappointed.

The rest of the journey was completed in silence. When they got to Devaki Sadan, Gayatri squeezed Nandini's hand. 'Don't worry, Chhoti. I'll call you once I get home, okay?'

'No, Didi,' said Nandini, pulling her hand urgently. 'Come inside with me, please. Just for five minutes. It'll be easier for me if you're there.'

Gayatri hesitated. She didn't feel like going in and meeting Mr and Mrs Grewal, but seeing the desperation on her younger sister's face, she couldn't refuse.

Akshay was sitting in the living room when they entered. Gayatri felt an odd lightness in her as he stood up and walked towards them.

'Welcome back, Nandini. We've missed you,' he said with a warm smile.

'Hi, Akshay Bhaiya,' she said. 'Amar is upstairs?'

'Yes. I'll tell Santram to call him.'

'No, no, I'll go up. I want to put away my things in any case.' Nandini turned to Gayatri, 'Didi, you want to come with me?'

Before Gayatri could answer, Akshay said, 'Why don't you bring Amar down? I'll get Gayatri a glass of water.'

Nandini nodded and went up the stairs.

'What can I get you?' Akshay asked Gayatri.

'Nothing, thanks, I'm good.'

'Something? A drink?'

She smiled politely. 'No, thanks.'

'If you're worried about offending your sister's in-laws, they're out.'

'No, no, it's not that. I just … I have to get back home soon.' She wouldn't have minded a drink, but she knew it wasn't right. Not here, and not with Akshay. 'I … No,' she said firmly.

He shrugged. 'Okay. Keep me company while I fix myself one?'

Gayatri hesitated. There was no sign of Nandini, but she didn't want to interrupt if she and Amar were talking. She followed Akshay into the drawing room. He noticed her eyes sweep the room distastefully.

'What's wrong?' he asked, consciously.

'No, nothing.' I have to be careful around him, she thought, he catches everything.

He brought a glass of water for her, and a drink for himself.

'So,' he said, sipping his drink. 'What's been happening?'

'Nothing since I saw you two days ago,' she said. There is definitely something odd about the way he's behaving, she thought. She glanced around the room again, then looked back at him. In his plain lawyer clothes of white shirt and black trousers, he stuck out in the opulent décor.

'Do you think they've sorted themselves out?' he asked, his eyes darting upwards.

Gayatri shook her head. 'I don't know. Just adjustment issues, I think. Both need to understand the other.'

He nodded. 'I keep telling Amar to get a separate place. He doesn't listen.'

Gayatri was surprised. Was Nandini making it that obvious? 'I hope Nandini is behaving, I mean, she—'

'Of course,' said Akshay, interrupting her. 'I didn't mean it like that at all. I just don't think this kind of arrangement is viable these days.' He took a sip of his drink. 'If someone were to tell me to go live in someone else's house, I wouldn't be able to. Not for any amount of love. It's bound to create stress.'

Gayatri glanced at him. There it was, that feeling of discomfort she had begun to feel when he was around. She tried to concentrate on his words.

'Have you seen it?' he was asking.

'Haan? What?'

'*The Office*. The American one.'

'I have,' she said. 'A few episodes. But I prefer the British version.'

'Well, I thought I did too, but just keep going with it, I promise you, it gets better.'

She nodded politely. 'Listen,' she said, suddenly. 'I've been meaning to tell you … You told me to tell you if I was, you know, dealing with anything controversial?'

He nodded.

'So the *Indian Age* has asked me to write a piece on this shrine near Delhi.' She paused. 'Basically, it's an old shrine of a pir called Nigar Baba. He was from Iran, and travelled to India in the twelfth century.'

Akshay was listening intently.

'The shrine was in a Hindu locality, in the house of a Hindu family. The family allowed a chaadar to be offered each day by a representative of a Muslim family that safeguards the shrine. Then, the Hindu family sold the house. The buyers broke the shrine overnight. There was a fight, and a little boy was set on fire.'

Akshay nodded. 'Yeah, I remember reading about it in the papers. Horrible.'

'They asked me because I wrote an article on Nigar Baba a few months back. I haven't agreed to do the piece yet. I thought I'd do some research, maybe visit the place and then decide.'

Akshay took a deep breath and set his glass on the table. 'Please don't do it,' he said gently.

Gayatri frowned. 'Look, I'm just letting you know because you asked me to tell you.' She placed her glass on the table as well. 'Anyway, I'd better get going.' She stood up quickly. 'Will you do me a favour and tell Nandini that I left? I don't want to disturb her if she's talking to Amar.'

Akshay followed her as she made her way out. At the door, she said, 'No, no, there's no need, please stay.'

He didn't reply, and followed her instead to her car.

'Bye,' she said flatly.

He touched her arm gently, saying, 'Listen, Gayatri.' She paused, took a deep breath and turned around, looking at him defiantly. He looked directly into her eyes for a few moments. 'I know I can't stop you from doing this. All I ask is that you be careful, and think about your safety. And that of your family and friends. This may not be the right time to write such a piece.'

She glanced down at his hand, which was still touching her arm, and took a step back.

'Come on,' he said, holding out his hand.

After a moment of hesitation, she took his hand grudgingly.

'You know,' he said, pausing for a few seconds, 'you're quite scary, Gayatri Mehra.'

She opened her mouth to say something rude, then closed it again. She smiled despite herself. The tension dissolved. Suddenly conscious of her hand in his, she pulled it away and got into the car, after a quick 'Goodnight'.

Nandini sat on one corner of the bed, sulking. 'You could have at least got off the sofa to give me a hug.'

'You could have come over to me yourself,' replied Amar. His eyes were trained on his screen.

'Is this all I mean to you? I've come back after so many days and you're not even looking up from your laptop.'

Amar slammed his laptop shut with a bang. Nandini flinched, startled by his sudden movement.

'What do you want me to do? You just randomly leave one day, acting like I've done something wrong, but refuse to tell me what it is. Do you have any fucking idea how that fucking feels?' asked Amar, his face flushed with anger. 'And you have the guts to tell me what I should be doing?'

Nandini's eyes filled with tears.

'There is no point in crying, Nandini. Just because my tears don't flow as easily doesn't mean that I'm not hurt.'

'You don't understand anything,' she said through her tears.

'Do *you* understand how it feels to be basically abandoned by your wife after a couple of months of marriage? What the hell, Nandini?

Can't you see that you need to tell me what's wrong? I can't bloody know what's going on in your brain. Did you think of what I would tell everyone—why Nandini decided to pack her bags and go home suddenly?'

Nandini shook her head. 'I just had to. And it was only a few days.'

'Well, fine,' said Amar. 'Then I just have to behave like this.'

He picked up his laptop and left the room, banging the door shut behind him.

13

Mr Grewal was sitting at a large six-seater wooden table in Sadhuji's ashram. This set of private meeting rooms contrasted starkly with the public areas of the Ashram complex: the rustic white notes of the shrines and meditation halls were replaced by expensive leather and chrome.

Grewal stared vacantly at the table before him, sitting with his shoulders slightly slumped, looking nothing like the confident senior advocate striding down the corridors of the Supreme Court. He nodded as Sadhuji entered the room and sat down opposite him.

'That behenchod Chauhan is screwing me over,' said Grewal. There was no need for formalities when they were alone.

Sadhuji stroked his long white beard calmly. 'What did he say?'

'That targets have not been met from my side,' replied Grewal angrily. 'This, after I delivered bloody fifteen crore to the party, Sadhuji.' He shook his head. 'I don't know if that idiot knows how to count.'

'How much more does he want?'

'He says Aastha Malhotra has delivered twenty-eight crore for the same ticket.' Grewal looked disgusted as he continued, 'Chauhan just threw up his hands and said, "What can we do, bhai? It's like a tender process. She has bid more." Ek toh I don't know what that madam elephant has done to get backing from the Sardas. They have just *poured* money on her. A behenji who didn't even go to college competing with someone whose juniors are now High Court judges can—'

'Anyone else left for you to ask?'

Grewal shook his head. 'No. And now I have to manage the expectations of the people I got the contributions from, make sure their work is done.' He paused. 'Ab to bas I'm depending on Vikram's money to get me across the line.'

Sadhuji stayed silent for a few seconds before saying, 'It will happen. When is he coming back from London?'

'I think he has a meeting with Cheema in two weeks.' Grewal clenched his jaw. 'Ek toh it's so difficult to talk on the phone these days. These wiretaps have made life miserable. One doesn't know which haraami is listening in.'

Sadhuji smiled serenely. 'Sab theek hoga. Don't worry.' He added, 'I'll also send more calls for contributions.'

'I need the ticket, Sadhuji,' said Grewal slowly, his face tense. 'That's what Chauhan had promised ... what you had promised me.'

'It will happen. No one can change your kismat.'

Kismat, scoffed Grewal inwardly as he looked at Sadhuji. This rascal refuses to get out of character even when we are alone. 'Let's hope so,' he said aloud.

'Let me work out what additional funds we can arrange,' said Sadhuji. 'Once Bhargav gives me the final figures, should I pass them on to Akshay?'

'No, no, tell Bhargav to talk to me directly. That's another problem. I can't understand what is wrong with Akshay. Behaving like a bloody girl.'

Sadhuji tilted his head questioningly.

'He says it's too dirty,' continued Grewal with a shake of his head. 'He thinks I'm putting the whole family at risk.'

'Has something scared him?'

'Kya scared, Sadhuji? After that journalist's murder, some screw in his head has come loose. I don't know why he's so fixated on that case. Goes on about drawing lines and being careful. He's gone mad.'

'Maybe we shouldn't have told him to help with the bail for my men,' said Sadhuji, thoughtfully.

'My son, my own son, Sadhuji. Why shouldn't he help? Thinks he's too good for this. Bloody fool.'

There was a long pause before Sadhuji asked, 'Will he … I mean, can we give him something?'

'Matlab?'

'You know, buy him a flat, a BMW, something he likes.'

Grewal let out a hollow laugh. He didn't say anything, just shook his head.

Sadhuji pursed his lips, unaccustomed to anyone talking to him without being overly respectful. He said tersely, 'Well, you will have to find some solution for Akshay.' He paused. 'Like we have for that Neelam woman. Have you done the needful?'

Grewal shook his head. 'Not yet. I'll do it soon.'

'The election is not that far away.'

'It's not easy, you know that.'

'Oh, I don't know about that. I never keep just one woman in my life. That, I've always told you, is a recipe for trouble.'

'She's not like that,' Grewal protested weakly.

'They are all like that. Have you tried to talk to her about the house in Mashobra?'

'I did bring it up a couple of months ago, but she got hyper—crying, screaming. So I let it be. But I will do it, Sadhuji. It's been sixteen years with her, such a long relationship takes some time to break.'

Sadhuji looked down at his hands, absently touching the coloured gemstones in the rings on his long, pale fingers. 'Time,' he said slowly, 'is the one thing I can't help you with.'

Neelam walked into Grewal's office without knocking. He had returned from the meeting with Sadhuji just a few minutes back.

'Haan?' He looked up.

She closed the door behind her. 'Where were you? I tried calling you so many times. You didn't pick up.'

'Me? Oh, just some meeting.'

Neelam's forehead creased into a frown. Walking around his desk, she stood behind his chair and started to massage his shoulders.

He leaned forward, saying, 'No need, no need right now.'

She removed her hands and waited. He turned his head to look at her. 'Come in front, why are you still standing at the back?'

'What is going on?' she asked, rooted to the spot.

'What do you mean? Talk to me from there,' he said irritably, pointing to the chairs across the desk. 'You're giving me a crick in my neck.'

She walked slowly to the other side of his desk. 'What is happening?' she demanded.

'Nothing. What do you mean "what is happening"?'

'Is there someone else?' Her beautiful, perfectly symmetrical face was crumpled with anger.

'Someone—' Grewal sighed in exasperation. 'Are you mad?'

'I'm not. Something's been wrong for more than a month now. I'm not a fool.'

He took a deep breath. This was not the right time to tell her. He held out his hand. 'Come.'

She didn't move.

'Come, baba,' he said, ignoring her glassy stare. He patted his leg. 'Come now, Neelu.' She took his hand and let him pull her onto his lap. He took a deep breath and smelled her hair. 'I'm stressed, you know that.'

He put his arms around her stiff, unyielding body. It would be tough for him to give up this addiction.

Twenty minutes later, Neelam emerged from Grewal's office, straightening her sari. She walked into her room, closed the door behind her and sank to the floor, crying noiselessly.

After some time, she got up and poured herself a glass of water. She wiped her eyes and fanned her face with a sheaf of papers, the cool air soothing the red in her cheeks. She took out the small compact she always carried in her bag. Checking her face in the mirror, she applied powder on her chin and nose until she felt she looked normal.

She was surer than ever: he was thinking of dispensing with her completely.

Anil Bhargav sat in the reception area of M.C. Chaddha's office in Greater Noida. Everything had a shine to it: the table, the walls, even the lips of the receptionist which were arranged in a distasteful expression as she looked at him. A life-sized photograph of Sadhuji in a golden frame dominated the room, his right hand frozen in a gesture of continuous blessing.

A short man with a large paunch hurried towards Bhargav from one of the rooms down the long hallway, and held out his hand. 'Please come, sir.'

Anil Bhargav stood up haughtily. 'I have been waiting fifteen minutes.'

'New girl, sir, sorry,' said the man apologetically, glaring menacingly at the receptionist.

Anil Bhargav followed the man down the hallway and into a small room. A dark, moustachioed man, sitting at the head of the table that took up most of the space, rose hurriedly.

'Please come, sirji, please sit,' he said, gesturing to a chair. 'Myself Chaddha,' he added, holding out his hand.

Anil Bhargav shook his hand and sat down.

'Sirji, will you have chai, coffee, juice?'

'Chai.'

'Dengue,' Chaddha addressed the other man. 'Vishnu ko bol, do chai. Achhi wali.'

'Yes, sir,' said Dengue, handing over a business card to Anil Bhargav before he left the room.

Bhargav took the card. It read: Darshan Gogia, Chief Legal Officer, Chaddha Buildcon Limited.

'Dengue?' he asked, puzzled, turning the card over.

Chaddha bared his paan-stained teeth in a smile. 'Oh, ji, we call him that here. Pyaar se, you know. He has had dengue every year since 2008.' He sounded almost admiring. 'Every single year. His platelet count drops, the doctors give up, his wife and children are crying, and then he recovers.' He shook his head. 'Chamatkaar.'

Anil Bhargav looked at the card again.

'This is January–February. Good time for him. Once rains come, he is infected for a few months. Then back to work. Anyway,' said Chaddha, clearing his throat, 'Sadhuji told me you had a proposal for me.' His paan-stained teeth appeared again in all their red–brown glory. 'I cannot refuse Sadhuji anything. I'll say yes without hearing only. Anything, ji.'

'Thank you,' started Anil Bhargav. 'Sadhuji sent me here to you specially to make this request. The thing is that we know that nowadays putting away your hard-earned cash is not easy. Kabhi FCRA, kabhi FEMA, kabhi notebandi.'

Chaddha chuckled. 'FEMA better than FERA, sir. Now no jail time at least.'

Anil Bhargav ignored him. 'Sadhuji is looking for some donations, you know—'

He was interrupted by a peon bringing in tea. Once the peon had left, Chaddha leaned in and said, 'Bhai, koi chakkar nahin. Whatever Sadhuji says I will give.'

Anil Bhargav looked at him intently, wondering whether he should try for one, or take a chance with two.

'In my business,' Chaddha continued, waving his hand, 'there is so much black, ji. You know real estate. I am always looking for some way to use it. And if it helps Sadhuji's cause, I am in.' He closed his eyes and murmured, 'Jai Swamidev.'

'Okay, then, will two be okay?'

'Arre, done, ji.' Chaddha nodded without flinching.

I should have said four, thought Bhargav.

'Bhargav sahib, I know you are thinking ki yeh aadmi toh bewakoof hai, he would have agreed to more. Asal mein ji, I am so indebted to Sadhuji for everything. Just six months back, I was nothing, totally finished.' He waved his left hand dramatically. 'I was wanting to kill myself. Then my bhabhiji said, "Bhaisahib, come with me to my Sadhuji, he will take care of you." I didn't want to go, but my wife also forced me, ji.'

He smiled. 'Bas, ji, that was it. Within three days, I had a partnership offer from Welal Builders, from Dubai.' He raised his eyes upwards with an adoring smile. 'Jo bhi I have now, Sadhuji has given me. Three big projects are going on together. It is all his, ji, nothing is mine.'

Anil Bhargav nodded. 'Jai Swamidev,' he said.

'Sach. I am a new devotee, and now I curse my luck that I didn't come to Sadhuji's durbar earlier.' He reached under his collar and pulled out a laminated photo of Sadhuji etched in a gold locket as proof of his devotion.

'We are coming out with many more items,' said Bhargav, the astute marketer in him unable to resist. 'Sadhuji does not like it, but we know his devotees want to feel close to him.'

'Yes?' said Chaddha eagerly.

'A new range of photos of Sadhuji in gold-plated frames, and also a set of watches. They will be expensive, of course, but the money all goes to Sadhuji's causes. He himself lives like a sanyasi.'

'Jai Swamidev!' chanted Chaddha, smiling.

Dengue entered the room. 'Come, Dengue,' said Chaddha, standing up. 'Bhargavji, Dengue will handle all the details.' He patted Dengue's back. 'Four months of the year, jab Dengue ko dengue ho jaata hai, no legal work is done in this office. Maybe I will take Dengue also to Sadhuji for his blessing.'

Rupi Grewal poured her husband's fourth drink of the evening.

He swirled the single malt over the ice cubes slowly. 'Politics is a really dirty sport,' he was saying. 'Everyone involved is a bloody bastard.' He took a sip. 'What kind of a business is this where I ... *I* ... have to prove my worth for a ticket to a bloody tenth fail?'

'This is politics, na. You have to pay your dues,' Rupi said. 'And you have Sadhuji on your side. He has helped us so much over the last thirty years. He has never failed you.' She paused. 'I don't understand why managing this ticket business is so tough for him. I thought the Ramanis backing you would be enough?'

Mr Grewal shook his head. 'He can't interfere in the finances of the party, that's above his pay grade. The highest bidder gets the ticket. The

Ramanis will just move their backing to whoever is getting the ticket.'
He sighed. 'Anyway, more than Sadhuji, it's that boy Vikram who has
turned out to be a godsend for me. He's turning out to be more useful
than my own sons. Forget Amar, he was always useless, good only for
that sarkari corporate law set-up,' said Mr Grewal derisively. 'But I had
higher hopes from Akshay. He's toh become a hurdle in my path now.'

'Don't talk like this about your sons. Amar is a good boy. There is
nothing wrong with being in a steady job, with a happy marriage, a
normal life.'

Mr Grewal was not listening. 'Did you try to talk some sense into
to that Akshay? I hope you've told him that any more of his flashing
eyes and judgemental nonsense, and I'll throw him out. Bloody idiot!'

'You should be careful,' Rupi said quietly, looking at the carpet.
'He's the only one who is actually looking out for you.'

Mr Grewal glanced at her before letting out a hollow laugh. 'I don't
need that kind of looking out. I don't need a mummyji at this age.'

Rupi Grewal glanced at her drunk, ugly, fat, old husband, and
wondered whether Akshay was right after all.

Neelam waited until the last intern left; now it was just her and Akshay
in the office. She let a few more minutes pass and then walked into his
room casually. He didn't look up.

'Still working?' she asked, her tone sweet.

His head was bent over his papers. The frown on his forehead
deepened.

'You've always been so hard-working,' she said, sitting down in one
of the chairs across his desk.

'Get out of my office,' he said quietly, not looking up at her.

'Ak—'

'Get out!' growled Akshay, pushing his chair back suddenly as he stood up, his face burning with fury. 'Don't force me to do something I'll regret.'

'That's exactly what I want you to do,' said Neelam unflinchingly, her freshly painted red lips parting in her beautiful smile. 'Everyone's left.'

Akshay took a deep breath and placed his hands on the desk. 'What the hell do you want? Money? What is it?'

She raised her kajal-lined eyes to him. 'I want you, Akshay. I want you back,' she said softly, leaning forward in her chair, as if to convince him of her sincerity.

Akshay looked at her in disbelief and shook his head. Slowly, as if each word took immense strength to utter, he said, 'Just get out of here. If it wasn't for my father—' He broke off and swallowed.

She stood up and walked towards him, her sari-clad frame silhouetted against the bright lights outside the door.

'Don't come near me,' he said angrily, standing up straight. 'I'm warning you.'

She took another step. He walked around the other side of the desk and headed for the door. She hurried forward and barred his way. 'No,' she said calmly, folding her arms before her chest.

Clenching his teeth, he pushed past her roughly and strode down the corridor.

'I'll keep doing this,' she called from behind him. 'I'm telling you, until you listen to me, I'll even … I'll tell your father.'

He paused.

She walked up behind him. 'I don't want to do this, but you—'

'No,' he interrupted, still facing away from her. 'What do you want? Tell me and end this rubbish.'

'Can we sit, at least?'

'No. Say what you have to. Quickly.' He turned to face her.

'You remember that night when we were returning from that client meeting … how many years ago now?' she said softly. 'You were just twenty-three, I think. I told you, let's stop and chat, and you parked the car—'

'Get to the fucking point,' he said through clenched teeth.

'Akshay, please,' she said, lowering her eyes as they glimmered with tears. She swallowed and looked up at him pleadingly. 'You know what a terrible time that was for me with the divorce. It was your father … no, your mother, who introduced me to this world, encouraged me to study law, then work here—'

'Why the hell are you going on about this shit? Just tell me what you want.'

'I'm sorry.' She paused. 'Look, I know you really loved me, and I hurt you by … by—'

'Can't you see? I don't give a shit any more. It's been more than fifteen years. Can you please tell me what you want? Otherwise I'm leaving,' he said, taking a step towards the door leading to the stairs.

'I want another chance,' she said. 'I know you haven't got over what … what we had.' She looked at the ground and said, 'I want to correct the mistake I made all those years ago.'

Akshay stared at her for a few moments, his mouth slightly open in bewilderment, then shook his head. 'I have to go. Save yourself some humiliation, and remember what a mess you've made of my family before repeating this nonsense.'

'I've made?' she asked, her voice rising. 'I've made? What about your father? Why do you blame only me?' She took a step closer to him, her eyes red with a shade of madness. 'You listen to me. I will not let your father ruin me, abandon me like this.'

Akshay shook his head. He turned away, but she caught his arm and pulled him around roughly. 'I'll ruin him first. I'm not a fool. You tell your father that.' Her mouth was curled into a sneer.

It was the first time Akshay had seen her look anything less than beautiful. He shook off her hand and walked up the stairs.

'If I'm going down, I'm taking your father with me, his career, his life. I have proof of all the dirty things that that dirty old man did to his son's girlfriend. And, by the way, that's what got him off in the first place.'

Akshay stopped, despite himself.

'You think he didn't know about us?' she yelled, unable to control herself. 'Of course he did. He knew, Akshay Grewal. Your father knew.'

Akshay ran up the rest of the stairs and opened the door to his apartment, banging it shut loudly behind him.

14

'MA,' SAID AKSHAY, entering his parents' room the next morning. 'Can I talk to you for a second?'

Rupi Grewal looked at him over the rim of her spectacles. She had been examining the weekly household expenses. 'Of course, beta. What's the matter?'

Akshay closed the door behind him, his face troubled. 'Ma, listen, I'm sorry for what I'm going to say, but I don't know whom else to talk to.'

Rupi's expression changed to one of concern.

Still standing, Akshay continued, 'This Neelam, she is … Please warn Papa about her.'

'What do you mean?'

'She's talking about leaving him, and … trying to get back with me—' he broke off.

Rupi's eyes hardened. 'Now? After all that Grewalji has done for her?' she said indignantly. 'Her house, her staff, he pays for everything. Her trips abroad. What has he not given her?'

Akshay lowered his eyes. What had his family come to? 'Ma, I'm sorry to drag you into this, it's not fair, I know—'

'It's not your fault, beta,' she said. 'Your father has got into this mess himself. Let me see if I can talk to him.'

Akshay left the room and dragged his feet up the stairs to his apartment on the first floor. The whole house was full of miserable people. Amar and Nandini couldn't stop fighting; his father was going to get screwed by his mistress; his mother was busy defending his father against the mistress; and he himself was increasingly drawn to someone who was set on marrying someone else.

The next day was a Sunday. Akshay woke up to muffled noises. Amar and Nandini were at it again. After forty minutes of trying to ignore the warring sounds, he decided to call Amar.

'Haan, Bhaiya?' said Amar, feigning cheer, oblivious to the fact that his brother was aware that he had been fighting with his wife almost continuously for the past two days.

'Do you want to play squash today?'

Amar hesitated for a moment, before saying, 'Okay.'

'We'll leave in half an hour?'

'Perfect.'

As soon as Akshay hung up, the voices resumed. When he was ready, he went up the stairs to their flat. Knocking on the door, he called, 'Nandini? Amar?'

Nandini let him in after a few seconds. She was smiling, looking normal. 'Hi, Bhaiya,' she said sweetly. 'Come, sit. Amar is just getting ready.'

These two should go to Bollywood, thought Akshay as he sat down. 'Why don't you come with us, Nandini? What will you do at home alone? You can play something at the club, or swim, or take a book and read?'

Nandini smiled. 'No, no, I'll just finish some work.'

'Leave your work today, you work the whole week,' he said kindly. 'Take a break. Or if you want, we'll drop you off at your parents' place and pick you up later. It's on our way.'

'That's not a bad idea, actually.'

Amar emerged from the bedroom, less successful at concealing his bad mood than Nandini. 'Let's go, Bhaiya,' he said, not looking at her.

'Nandini is coming with us,' said Akshay. 'We'll drop her at her parents' place.'

Amar sighed exasperatedly. 'She can drive herself. Why should we tie ourselves up—'

'Amar,' said Akshay firmly, 'let's go.'

Akshay had narrowly avoided getting hit by the flying ball a few times already. He continued to play, hoping the hard hitting would help Amar let off some steam.

Amar grunted loudly and smashed the ball forcefully into the wall. The ball ricocheted and came directly at Akshay again.

'Whoa, relax, Amarinder!' called Akshay, using the name he had teased his brother with when they were younger.

'Don't call me that, Bhaiya,' shouted Amar, throwing his racket across the squash court, where it landed with a loud thud.

'Amar … Kya hua, yaar?'

Amar swallowed and walked to pick up his racket with a shake of his head. 'Sorry. Just lost it for a second.'

'Chal, let's forget the game and go get a beer.'

'But we've hardly—'

'Chal, na,' said Akshay, putting a sweaty arm around his brother's shoulders and towing him along.

Half an hour later, Amar's good cheer seemed to have returned as he sipped his second beer. 'Sorry, Bhaiya,' said Amar, 'I was playing like a maniac, I know. I've been a bit stressed at work. This deal we are closing—'

Akshay nodded. 'Don't worry.' He paused. 'Nandini's also busy?'

Amar shrugged. 'Must be.'

'Are things okay with you guys?' Akshay ventured cautiously.

Amar smiled blandly. 'Yeah.'

Akshay nodded and took a large swig. 'That's good, Amar. Nandini's a great girl—'

Amar slammed his beer mug down on the table. Some of the other people in the club restaurant turned in their direction. Akshay smiled at them apologetically, then turned back to Amar with raised eyebrows.

Amar glared at his beer mug. 'Sorry,' he muttered. They sat in tense silence for the next few minutes. 'Fuck it!' Amar said eventually. 'I'm not happy, Bhaiya. I thought marriage would be … different. But this … this is just fucking hell.'

Akshay took a deep breath. 'It's too early, Amar. Abhi toh you guys just got married. It will take time to settle. Every relationship has bad patches, yaar. Plus work has been so stressful—'

'No, Bhaiya, Nandini will kill me if she learns that I've spoken to you, but there's really no point hiding anything.' He looked out of the window. 'This was a mistake. When we were dating, things were fine, but this marriage thing is hurting her—her ego or something. But what can I do? She has to live with us, and she has to say namaste to Ma and Papa every day. She gets pissed at such silly things, and kuch bhi hota hai toh her solution is to just walk out. "Bye, I'm off to my parents' house." What the fuck is that?'

'What's the problem, though?'

'We just can't stop fighting. Most of it starts over something stupid. Like one day she wanted to go out for dinner, but Khan Uncle had come home, so we had to eat downstairs. She got so mad, saying she had left office early, and that I always do this, blah blah blah.'

'Had you planned to go out beforehand?'

Amar nodded, 'Haan, but she should also understand, na. Khan Uncle is so important for Papa. Could we have just left when he specifically asked to meet her?'

'What else?'

Amar hesitated. 'You know, Bhaiya,' he said, 'the thing that really pisses me off is that she's started acting ... you know ... *smart* about her work and dissing me.'

'But both of you are partners at the same firm.'

'Yeah, but she is equity and I'm not there yet. She is also Ramjee's pet. He loves her more than his own bloody daughters. She keeps getting promoted.'

'So?'

'So she's started dissing me,' said Amar angrily. 'Like, once, she said that I don't have to work for my deals. Basically, she's saying clients come to me because of Papa. Then, in front of her junior, she said that I can't understand her transactions.' He looked at Akshay. 'I wanted to slap her right there. She had the guts to say that *I* didn't understand some stupid structure she has put in place. I told her that it was a bad structure, tax-wise. You should have seen her then, Bhaiya. Madam intellectual fucking giant can't take criticism. She thinks I'm not as smart as her. And that's bloody condescending.'

Akshay sipped his beer thoughtfully.

'Basically, Bhaiya, there are two alphas in this relationship. In most relationships, sometimes even gay ones, one partner dominates, na.

That's for a reason. It's because people can't love each other if they're too busy competing.'

'Amar, dekh,' said Akshay slowly. 'I can see what you're pissed off about.' He paused and then continued. 'I would probably react the same way in your situation.'

'I'm sure there's a but coming.'

'But,' continued Akshay, 'I also know Nandini is a good person. And you guys were really happy before you were married.'

'*I* was, Bhaiya,' said Amar, shaking his head, 'but maybe she wasn't. She told me the other day that she had lots of doubts about marrying me. She said she should have listened to her sister.'

'Gayatri?'

'I can't even blame Gayatri Didi, in a way,' said Amar. 'Looks like she's the only one who could see that we were not suited to each other.'

'Dekh, Amar, shaadi toh ho gayi. Maybe you need to see some things from Nandini's point of view.'

'Kya? What should I see?' asked Amar aggressively. 'She just went off to her house for ten days, Bhaiya. She didn't tell me anything, just gave some lame excuse about not being well. Who does this sort of shit? Why can't she get off her high fucking horse and see some things from *my* point of view?' He ran a hand through his hair in frustration. 'Both of us work, both come back tired. I don't bloody tell her to press my legs or cook me food. She has help, drivers, whatever she wants …'

'Amar, Nandini is an intelligent girl, of these times. You have to give her some space. If she doesn't want to come down and hang out with Ma and Papa, don't force her, yaar. Imagine if you had to go and live in her house. You come back from work tired as a dog, just want to get a drink or sit in bed and watch something, and then her dad says my business associate is here, get dressed, come down, make conversation.' He looked at Amar. 'She also has a point, na,' he said gently.

'I don't know, Bhaiya,' said Amar, sounding tired. 'That's the way this works. What can I do? I can't change society. We have to live in this world. And the fact of the matter is that this world is not gender neutral. No matter what she does at work, or how much she earns.'

'What you can do,' said Akshay carefully, 'is be a little supportive of her. I know she has hurt you, and even I would get pissed off if someone kept putting me down. She has to change that, agreed. But that doesn't mean that you don't have to change.' He paused, looking at Amar to gauge whether he was listening. 'Marriage is hard work, yaar. It's not like you find your life partner and suddenly it's all good. I know it's tough to adjust at this age, but you have to remember why you married her. And be calmer. I hope it hasn't … you know … come to anything physical?'

Amar looked away.

'Amar, are you crazy?' said Akshay, widening his eyes. 'Yaar, this is not okay.'

Amar looked at his brother. 'She hit me first, Bhaiya, slapped me. She's no saint.'

Akshay was quiet, wondering how to react. 'Amar,' he said after a few moments, 'take things calmly now and try to start afresh. Why don't you guys go out tonight, just the two of you? Have a good time, have a few drinks, you know.'

'Nothing will happen even then. She's become frigid. And I don't feel like … like doing anything with her.' Since his marriage, it had become awkward to talk or even joke about sex with his brother.

'No, no, not like that,' said Akshay. 'Just go out and get drunk. Talk, loosen up.'

Amar shook his head.

'It'll be good for both of you. Come now. Let's go pick up Nandini, then you guys go out. Cheer up, yaar,' Akshay said, getting up and patting Amar on his back. 'And bring on some romance. Everyone fights. It will end.'

As soon as Nandini reached her parents' house, she had gone straight to Gayatri's room and entered without knocking. Her sister was curled up in bed, watching something on her laptop.

'Oh, Chhoti, I didn't know you were coming … sit,' she said loudly—she hadn't taken off her earphones. 'Let me finish this episode, just two minutes left.'

Nandini sat on the edge of the bed and looked around the room. Didi is so lucky, she thought glumly, no one interferes in her life at all.

Gayatri pulled out her earphones. 'I'm so addicted to this, Chhoti,' she said. 'You should watch it. It's called *Zindagi aur Hum*.' She smiled, her face glowing.

'Didi, you're so useless. Totally lost in your world.'

'What to do?' said Gayatri with mock sadness. 'We who have no romance in real life must make do with make-believe.'

'You have Vikram, na. There will be lots of romance soon, don't worry.'

Gayatri was silent for a moment, before saying, 'Anyway, how are things with you? You didn't message to say you were coming.'

'Haan, Amar and Akshay Bhaiya went to play squash, so I got dropped off here.'

'They'll pick you up?' asked Gayatri, with more than a touch of interest in her sister's plans.

Nandini nodded. Gayatri could see she was looking a little low. 'Do you want chai?'

'Cold coffee,' Nandini said. 'I know it's freezing, but I've been dreaming of Malti Didi's cold coffee.'

Gayatri dialled a number on her cell phone and said, 'Malti Didi, ek cold coffee aur ek chai bhijwa dijiye, please. Kamre mein.'

'You've started dialling them on their mobiles?' asked Nandini.

Gayatri smiled sheepishly. 'Everyone has phones now, and I just can't be bothered to get out of bed in this cold.'

'Didi, you're so lazy,' said Nandini, wistfully.

'Achha, how are things with Amar?'

'Okay-okay,' said Nandini, shrugging.

'What okay-okay? Have the fights stopped?'

'No.'

'Then?'

'Then what? We'll go on like this only, until it ends.'

'Don't be stupid, Nandini. It's hardly been any time since your wedding.'

'I'm sick and tired of this, Didi. And anyway, you're the one who had said he's not good enough for me. I'm just coming around to your point of view now.'

Gayatri opened her mouth to protest, then closed it again. After a few moments, she said, 'Nandini, I was wrong. Amar is a good guy and he loves you. And that's what counts at the end of the day, na. What are you going to do with someone who is brilliant, but a jerk at home?'

Nandini looked down at her hands in her lap. 'He is not that good.'

'What do you mean? Did he say something to you?'

When Nandini did not respond, Gayatri pressed on. 'Nothing physical, na?'

Nandini pursed her lips.

Eyes widening, Gayatri asked, 'Really?' She gazed at her sister thoughtfully. 'And, by any chance, did you also hit him?'

Nandini looked at her sister with a frown. How does she know?

'You did. Before or after?'

'Before,' said Nandini, sulkily.

Gayatri took a deep breath. 'That does not, in any way, condone his hitting you,' she said, 'but, Chhoti, please, do not create these ugly scenes. This is a serious matter. We all hope that he will be so good as to not retaliate even if you hit him. But with what face can we criticize him if you go around hitting him?'

'I don't know, Didi,' said Nandini, lying back on the bed with a sigh. 'I know I shouldn't have. But it's so frustrating. He doesn't understand anything.'

Their conversation was interrupted by a knock at the door. Malti Didi entered, and placed a tray with the cold coffee and tea on the bed, petting Nandini's head on the way out.

Gayatri handed the tall glass to Nandini and picked up her own cup.

Nandini took a sip. 'I'm ashamed of myself for that hitting episode. And I drew blood, like, I scratched him on his face. He just, you know, defended himself, like swatted me away.'

Gayatri shook her head. 'Just see,' she said disapprovingly. 'Anyway, I'm glad you know you were in the wrong.'

'But, Didi, the thing is, when I react like this, and then he retaliates, the actual issue disappears and it becomes about behaviour—like you said this, you did that, you hit me. What about the real issue? Why were we arguing in the first place?'

'So what was the issue?'

'He said to me, "That's a dumb way to think about this deal." He's telling *me* that, Didi. Me. In front of my junior.' Nandini shook her head. 'I'm the one who's worked my ass off to get where I am, the one who has such loyal clients. What does he have? A shitty practice in an area that requires you to be a robot, no thinking whatsoever. And anyway, any deals he gets are just because of his dad—'

'You told him all that?' Gayatri broke in.

'Yes,' said Nandini defiantly. 'I did.'

Gayatri winced. 'Chhoti, you shouldn't have. You know how much something like that can hurt.'

'Didi, everyone says this in the office. It's so embarrassing. I hate it. And, on top of that, he never apologizes for anything, just walks off, even if I'm crying. He obviously doesn't give a shit. How can I ... no, *why* should I stay married to him?'

'Chhoti, listen, I know you're having a hard time right now, but try to remember the good times. When you started dating, remember when he surprised you on your birthday with that trip to Udaipur? He is sweet, he loves you so much—and no matter what you say, you know you love him. These chhota-mota things will get sorted. Just be patient.'

'No, Didi, it's too much for me. I cannot live in that house any longer. The more time I spend with him, the less I like him.'

Gayatri sighed. 'For now, just try to reconnect with him. If you guys don't remember why you love each other, you won't be able to make the compromises you both need to make for each other.'

Nandini bit her lip and said in a resigned tone, 'I think we've lost whatever we had.'

'In two months? Are you out of your mind? Of course you haven't.'

'I'm telling you, Didi, I don't think I love him any more. I'm wondering if I ever did.' She closed her eyes as she sipped her drink. 'This is good. Even the cold coffee in their house is weird.'

'Uff, forget the cold coffee. Okay, remember that fight we had? When I was trying to tell you to think hard before you decided to get married? You said you loved Amar, that he made you feel happy, and you didn't want to think beyond that.'

Nandini was quiet for a few moments as her eyes filled with tears. 'I remember. But he's changed. It's not the same any more. He's become so unbearably bossy all the time. And that triggers something in me—I can't take it, I become a monster myself.'

Gayatri put down her cup of tea and slid over to Nandini. Placing an arm around her shoulders, she said seriously, 'Chhoti, you know that marriage is a big deal, na?'

Nandini nodded, a single tear trickling down her cheek.

'It's not like dating, where you can break up after a fight or two. What I'm trying to say is that you guys are newly married with your whole lives ahead of you. Amar has to work at it, and so do you.'

Gayatri squeezed Nandini's shoulders. 'Be brave, sweetie. If Amar can't see what you're saying, maybe it's the way you're saying it. Try saying it with love.'

Nandini glanced at her sister through her tears. 'And how do you know all this? You aren't even married,' she said with a weak smile.

'Maybe it's because I'm not married that I can see all this.' She wiped Nandini's cheeks. 'Come, now wash your face and let's sit with Ma and Papa. And when Amar comes to pick you up, please tell him that you want to go out. Have some fun. I'm telling you … you guys need a relaxed night out, a break from fighting.'

Nandini sniffed.

'Good girl,' said Gayatri, standing up. 'Now come. Wash your face, and cheer up.'

Two hours later, Amar called Nandini from the car. After disconnecting, he turned to Akshay, clicking his tongue irritably. 'She is saying to come in, yaar. I don't feel like it,' he said, 'but I think she was sitting with her parents, so I didn't want to say no.'

Akshay stared at him for a long moment.

'Why are you looking at me like that?' asked Amar.

'Don't you get it? She also must feel like this sometimes, na.'

'Pata nahin,' he said, shaking his head tiredly. 'Bhaiya, come with me.'

'What will I do? You go. Bring her out.'

'No, no, please, just come. I'm … please come. She said her parents are there, and I don't want to say anything stupid. Right now, even the thought of seeing her face is bugging me.'

'Okay, come,' Akshay said, getting out.

Amar stood behind him as he rang the doorbell.

It was Gayatri who opened the door.

Tea was organized, and they all sat down in the living room. Amar was a little stiff, but Akshay tried to make up for it by talking to Ashok and Nina attentively.

After a while, Gayatri turned to Amar. 'So, where are you guys planning to go tonight?'

Nandini glared at her sister, then looked at Amar. 'I was … I was just telling Didi that maybe we could go out tonight.'

Amar glanced at her in surprise. He nodded. 'Okay, why not.'

Nandini looked down with a slight frown. He was behaving like he was granting her a favour. He'd better not be thinking she was trying to make up with him. 'Didi, you also come na, please?' she said.

'No, Nandini, you guys go. What will I do with you?' Gayatri laughed, a little too loudly, trying to mask her irritation. 'I don't want to be a kebab mein haddi.'

'Come na, Didi, please,' said Nandini.

Gayatri shook her head.

'Actually, Didi, why don't you come,' said Amar, stiffly.

'Let's all have dinner together,' Nandini said. 'Bhaiya will also come, yes?'

'Yes. Bas, Bhaiya, it's done,' Amar said as Akshay started to protest. 'Gayatri Didi, please, let's all go get a drink. Even your parents are going out for dinner. What will you do alone? Just come, please. We'll go home, change and pick you up in an hour.'

Akshay frowned at Amar, and Gayatri glared at Nandini.

'They are so unbelievably stupid,' said Gayatri, shaking her head. 'I think *I'll* need to get drunk to survive this horrendous evening.' She took a long swig of her drink.

'Second that,' said Akshay.

Amar and Nandini had started to argue within a few minutes of arriving at the rooftop bar in Connaught Place. Akshay had finally suggested that he and Gayatri move to a separate table. He glanced at Amar and Nandini, and signalled to a waiter to refill the glasses on both tables.

Gayatri, now considerably loosened by the rum inside her, said with a slightly silly smile, 'We are both useless, actually. The only advice we gave them was to get drunk.'

Akshay shrugged. 'I don't know what's wrong with them. Though it must be tough for Nandini, at nearly thirty, to adjust to this family set-up.'

'Please,' said Gayatri, stuffing a piece of chicken tikka in her mouth, 'Nandini is no saint. I know how she talks to Amar, she can be vicious.'

They were silent for a few moments before Akshay said, 'Shall I tell you something?'

Gayatri nodded, still chewing.

'Today, when Amar was talking to me about Nandini, I wasn't sure whether I was doing the right thing by telling him to stay and give it a chance.' He shook his head. 'So many marriages fall apart before kids come along and we say, good for them, at least they figured it out in time. Maybe these two aren't right for each other, who knows?'

Gayatri nodded slowly. 'I know what you're saying. They sound pretty miserable.'

They both looked in the direction of their siblings.

'Well, things seem to have improved,' said Akshay. 'See, Nandini is smiling slightly.'

'It's the alcohol. What are they drinking?'

'Whisky.'

'Both of them?'

Akshay nodded.

'If we see any signs of fighting, we'll tell the waiter to send them a different drink. Or LIITs. They'll be making out before long.'

Akshay smiled. Gayatri was definitely a little high.

'Why are you looking at me like that?' Gayatri asked. 'I'm telling you, alcohol really works like magic for the brain. Everyone needs a drink sometimes. I think people who don't drink don't really know themselves.'

'Really?' asked Akshay, enjoying this version of Gayatri.

'Yeah,' she said, with alcohol-induced carelessness. 'See, now don't think I don't know I'm slightly drunk. I do, but I'm okay to let go and have fun. Even with you.'

'Even with me?' he repeated, laughing.

'Yeah, even with you. See, you're so uptight'—she pulled a face as she spoke—'and condescending usually. But after a few drinks … you're not so bad.'

'Ah, okay. Next time I'll take care to only appear in your presence when we're slightly drunk.'

'I think all political conferences should start with everyone downing a few shots. There is no way, no way, there won't be some progress. We may not solve Kashmir, but there will be some concessions: trade, movement, tourism. I mean look at us—we basically don't like each other, but in this moment, I'm okay to have a conversation with you.'

Akshay was quiet for a moment, then he looked directly at her and said, 'I like you.'

Gayatri seemed to not have heard him over the loud music. 'Anyway,' she continued, 'I hope these two can work something out now.'

Akshay took a large sip from his glass. 'They just need to spend some time—' His eyes widened as he looked towards Amar and Nandini. 'Oh wow.'

Worried, Gayatri quickly turned in their direction. 'Oh,' she said, her face muscles relaxing in relief. 'Thank god.'

Amar and Nandini were sitting very close, their lips pressed against each other's.

'Actually, yuck,' said Gayatri, grimacing as she turned back. 'I can't look. It's like seeing my daughter with someone.' She popped another piece of chicken in her mouth. 'But it's definitely better than the fighting.'

'It is a bit gross, I agree. Amar and I have nine years between us. You and Nandini have four, right?'

Gayatri nodded. They sipped their drinks in silence for a couple of minutes, before Gayatri spoke. 'Amar generally talks to you about … stuff?'

'We don't get much time to have heart-to-hearts these days, but we did have a long chat today. And their room is right above mine, so whether I like it or not …' he trailed off, stretching his lips into a resigned expression.

'Oh, that must be awful.'

Akshay signalled to the waiter for another round.

'Are you sure?' she asked worriedly, looking at her phone.

'Of course,' said Akshay, taking her phone and putting it face down on the table. 'Bhaiya and Didi also need a break from these idiots' problems. And it's only ten.'

Gayatri nodded with a small smile. A troublesome thought was fighting its way to the top of her mind, but she'd managed to quash it without registering it so far.

'So, why haven't you got married yet?' asked Akshay.

Gayatri was slightly surprised by the question. 'I don't know,' she said. 'I had a longish relationship in my twenties. Three years. But it didn't lead to marriage for whatever reason.'

He nodded.

'You?' she asked.

'No reason, never really wanted to, you know … with anyone.'

'You told me you had one serious—'

'I did. It didn't end well.'

'What happened?'

'She cheated.' Akshay looked down at his glass.

They sipped their drinks in silence for a few minutes, then started talking about their time studying law.

'I've been meaning to ask you something, Gayatri,' Akshay said. 'How is it … I mean, at some level I still can't understand why you do what you do. I know yours is a respected journal, popular with a certain section of society. And the library, I loved it, really. But still—' He broke off.

'Because I love it. I wake up in the morning excited to go to work. I love the research, the stories, the writing, losing myself in a different world.' She smiled. 'It's purely selfish.'

'But,' he picked up a fork and began drawing an imaginary picture on the table, 'is that enough? You may love what you do, but everyone wants to shine, to do well, to be … you know … to be recognized. At least, everyone intelligent.' He looked at her. 'Will you achieve that here?'

'How do I explain?' She took a deep breath. 'I don't value public achievement like I used to. I don't set much store by what other people say or think about me. All I care about now, is that my day goes in a way that makes me happy. And studying history makes me happy. I come home with my brain full of things I didn't know in the morning.'

'So that's it? You'll be happy to die a researcher, having published a few papers. Nothing more?'

Gayatri sipped her drink and shrugged. 'I'll be happier dying having published a few papers and enjoyed each day of my life, than earning middling fame as a lawyer and cribbing all the way.'

'Why didn't you want to litigate?' he asked.

'Never mind.' She shook her head.

'Why?'

'You'll take it personally.'

'I won't. Really.'

'I ... I thought it was pointless. I just couldn't see the moral justification for someone paying you to argue their point of view. Where you are aligned morally with the argument, okay, but that's not how a lawyer's life works, right? It's not the Article 14 and 19 cases that you deal with every day, it's rape and murder and property disputes and bloody mergers and acquisitions. Defending rapists and murderers and cheaters. Drafting some pointless plan so that some imaginary thing can merge with another imaginary thing—it's all such a construct, nothing is real.' She shook her head. 'And there is so much muck, with judges and cops and ...' She paused to look at him. 'You know better than anyone.'

Akshay sipped his drink, seemingly lost in thought.

'I mean,' she said, 'I read somewhere that you're defending that guy who works at CPD? The one accused of raping his junior?'

Akshay's forehead creased with a frown.

'Frankly, I don't know how you can stand there defending someone like that guy.'

He leaned back in his chair and swirled the leftover liquid in his glass. 'I don't have a noble reason for doing what I do,' he said, his gaze fixed on his glass. 'But frankly, I'm a little surprised at your naive view of a lawyer's role, considering you've studied and practised law.'

She gave him a sharp look.

'My job, and I'm talking specifically of criminal defence law now,' he said, 'even at its worst, is to defend to the best of my ability. That's it. Who I defend, whether they are guilty, I am not supposed to care.' He paused. 'If you take your righteousness to its logical conclusion, lawyers would be judges, and where would you be then, when a not-so-powerful someone needs a defence and there's no lawyer willing? Yes, it's tough work and, honestly, it's dirty work, but irrespective of individual motivations, someone's got to do it.'

She was staring at the table, but Akshay could tell she was listening.

'And, as for the work itself, it can be really exciting,' he continued. 'A loophole in the law, picking through the investigation, trying to understand another human being's psyche. The importance, the recognition, that's separate. You become the difference between jail-time and going home. It's huge. It's the feeling a doctor gets, maybe. Except that the doctor is always on the right side. Here, sometimes we're right, sometimes not.' He paused. 'Plus, one has to earn a living.'

Gayatri spoke after a few seconds. 'I didn't mean to criticize what you do, and I know a large part of why I can do what I do is because I'm part of the privileged few.' She sipped her drink. 'Anyway, since we're talking about the choice between law and history, I'll tell you something. There was this historian, Jadunath Sarkar, whom you may not have heard of, who said that a historian is like a judge. Evidence is presented before you, and there are certain rules you need to follow to evaluate it—you weigh the evidence and present your verdict, not argue a point of view. Your work is what you believe is the truth. And, for whatever reason, I guess I'm more comfortable doing that kind of lawyering and judging.'

Akshay nodded, looking at her very intently, intensely even.

She said, 'So I guess you need to perform your function, and I, mine. Everyone has their own path, right?'

Akshay remained silent. She held his gaze for a few seconds, before he turned to look at Amar and Nandini. She turned towards them as well.

'Well, if they can spend an evening happily with each other, the effort's been worth it,' she said.

Half an hour later, Amar and Nandini stumbled out of the bar into the dimly lit, pillared passageways of C.P.'s Outer Circle, with Akshay and Gayatri trailing behind them. As they turned a corner of the wide corridor, Gayatri stopped, saying sheepishly, 'Akshay, listen, I'll just run back to the loo. Two minutes. You carry on with them.' Before he could respond, she had turned and walked away briskly.

Akshay called out to Amar and Nandini. They were holding on to each other, giggling and stumbling as they tried to find their way to the car. He told them that Gayatri had gone back to the bar, and that he was going there too. He had to explain this to them a second time before they, in their drunken states, understood what he was saying.

Hoping to catch up with Gayatri, he jogged back towards the bar, but she was already out of sight. He waited for her downstairs, slightly angry with her for setting off by herself, that too in the middle of these dark, lonely passageways, where every pillar seemed to provide cover for a dangerous shadow.

A couple of minutes later, he spotted her at the top of the stairs. Trying to descend swiftly, she stumbled on the last step. He held out his arm to steady her, but Gayatri, not knowing he had followed her, let out a frightened screech.

This was her nightmare scenario, the reason she didn't venture out alone after dark in Delhi too often.

'Gayatri!' he said, holding on to her arms. 'Relax, it's me.' Slowed down by alcohol and fear, Gayatri took longer than usual to register that it was Akshay. She was still struggling against him, trying to land a blow with her elbow, when a ragged-looking man with matted hair appeared out of the darkness.

'Kya ho raha hai? Madam, aapko yeh tang kar raha hai?'

'Nahin, Bhaisahib, main inke saath hoon,' said Akshay. He put one arm around her shoulders lightly as she collected herself.

'Police chowki agle block mein hai—'

Gayatri, now calmer but still slightly breathless, said, 'Sab theek hai, Bhaiya, thank you.'

Akshay took out a hundred-rupee note from his pocket and held it out to the man.

'Nahin,' replied the man, 'main toh bas madad ke liye aaya tha,' and shuffled back into the shadows.

Akshay, followed the man a few steps away to his sleeping spot and pressed the money into his hand, then quickly returned to Gayatri.

As they walked down the corridor, he gently covered her shoulders with his arm. Gayatri didn't move away, his arm felt warm and comforting in the cold winter night. She felt a strange lightness in her stomach, but put it down to the alcohol in her.

'Maybe I should have let him take you to the police chowki,' she said, a minute later, with a small smile.

'Ha ha,' he said drily. 'And maybe you should enrol in a karate class. That flapping around like a clumsy duck won't scare away an assaulter. Actually, I should have just—'

'What?'

'Nothing,' he said, removing his arm just as they stepped into the bright lights of the car park, where Amar and Nandini were waiting.

15

THE NEXT DAY was a Monday. Gayatri woke up feeling that something was not quite right. She remembered walking with Akshay's arm around her shoulder the previous evening, and squirmed slightly.

She reached for her phone immediately and typed out a message to Vikram. 'Can we speak when you have a few minutes?'

She received no reply from him until evening, when he texted to say: 'Sorry, been working round the clock. I'll call when I can', leaving her irritable, more so because she didn't know what she would say to him when they did speak.

Gayatri and Vikram kept missing each other until she finally caught him late on Wednesday night.

'Sorry, I've been so busy,' he said. 'It's just these meetings for the India trip. I have to tie in some investment commitments from here, you know, so it's tough. Akhil's wife is also complaining.' He paused, then added, 'Like you.'

Gayatri swallowed uncomfortably. 'Vikram, listen, I wanted to speak … uh … actually … because I need to talk to you about something.'

'What?'

'Vikram, I'm … I mean, this … I'm not sure about us,' she blurted out quickly.

'What do you mean?'

'See, I wanted to be clear that … I mean, I'm not sure yet, Vikram.' She paused. 'We should be clear on where things stand. I don't want to, you know, give you the wrong impression.'

He frowned. 'Have you met someone else?'

'No, no, of course not,' she said, too quickly. Although the memories of the evening with Akshay had faded over the past couple of days, blurred as they already were by the alcohol ingested that night, a strange sense of disquiet had persisted.

'Then?'

'Nothing, I just want to make sure that you understand that I'm not sure about … about us. I just want to be honest with you.'

Vikram was silent.

'Look, I'm sorry—' she began apologetically, only to be cut off by him.

'So you're not sure. So what? I'll come back and we'll figure it out.'

'No, but—'

'No buts, baby, just chill. Doubts will come and go. We'll talk when I get to Delhi, and if it makes you feel any better, then you should know I'm fine with you taking your time. We'll make a decision when I come next week. Okay? I can't wait to see you. Achha, listen, Akhil is calling me, let me take his call. I'll call you back.'

She was quiet. She didn't like being called 'baby'. This conversation had not gone as she had envisaged. But she couldn't deny that Vikram was right in a way. There was nothing happening between her and

Akshay, and she did like Vikram; so why was she doing this? She didn't quite know.

She nodded and said softly, 'Okay.'

Gayatri tossed the phone on her bed and stared out of the window. She had expected an unpleasant conversation, and really should have been happy that Vikram was so understanding. But she just felt hollow.

Gayatri's words swirled in Vikram's head long after he had gone to bed that night. He tried to remember her tone, and wondered what she was thinking. He didn't know whether he was more furious or hurt. Staring at the ceiling, he wondered how and when a girl like Gayatri, whom he hadn't even found attractive at first, had acquired the power to affect him like this. Wide awake in the darkness, he remembered the feeling he had when he pulled her towards him the day before he left for London.

He got out of bed and made himself a drink. Walking to the windows in his living room, he sat down on the carpet cross-legged, his eyes focused on the lights twinkling on the white and blue Tower Bridge in the distance. He thought of his early motivation for meeting her, the contact with Grewalji, his father's smile when she had come home. Vikram took another swig and closed his eyes.

The thing was, she was a higher form of being—unscathed, secure. She represented what he wanted to be. She had something he didn't.

He opened his eyes and picked up his phone, calculating how soon he could go back to India.

Later that evening, Gayatri entered her grandmother's room. She kissed her and sat down on a sofa.

'How was your day, Dadi?'

'Okay,' said Dadi. 'My sisters had come over for lunch. They ate my head with their non-stop chatter.'

Gayatri smiled weakly.

'What happened?' asked Dadi.

'Nothing.' Gayatri shook her head.

'Something is wrong,' declared Dadi.

She wondered how her grandmother could tell. It's probably because she actually concentrates on people, thought Gayatri. Not like everyone else, who has half their mind on their phone anytime they talk to you.

'Dadi,' she said slowly. 'I'm not sure about Vikram. It's stressing me out.'

'No one is forcing you … well, no one apart from your mother,' she said with a withering look. 'You don't need to marry him if you don't like him. But you must ask yourself if you're not just making excuses. If you're used to this life, and are too lazy to adjust somewhere else. That is not the right reason to say no. You are a girl, and I feel that you must have a family of your own, your children, your home. You want that, don't you?'

Gayatri shrugged.

'There isn't anyone else?'

'No, of course not.' Why is everyone asking me this?

'See, Gayatri, when I met your grandfather,' Dadi said slowly, looking fondly at one of the many photos of her husband placed in her room, 'I didn't know him at all. I had seen him only once, in a darkened cinema hall in Lahore. I still remember the movie that was playing, *Bandhan*. It had Ashok Kumar in it.' She looked at Gayatri. 'I was lucky. Most people my age weren't as lucky as me in whom they married. But, beta, times have changed. You are not expected to make marriages in this way today.'

'But what should I do, Dadi? I can't make up my mind. I almost wish I didn't have a choice.'

'But you do, and you must use this choice wisely, beta. Make your decision based on your future, not on fear and other people's stories.'

Gayatri lay down on the bed and placed her head in her grandmother's lap. Dadi stroked her hair gently. 'Don't worry, it will all turn out fine. You are such an intelligent, sensible girl. You will make the right choice.'

After a sleepless night, Gayatri came down early for breakfast the next day. Nina was already at the table. Gayatri sat down and spread out a newspaper before her, hoping her mother would not bring up Vikram.

'Listen, Gayatri,' said her mother. 'This Vikram—'

'Ma,' started Gayatri with an exasperated intake of breath, 'please don't—'

'No, no,' said Nina, pouring black tea from a kettle slowly. 'It's not that … It's just that I met Shama yesterday. She was telling me a little more about their family. You know, she said that they have only recently become well-off, and their lifestyle and habits are not really like ours. I just felt … I don't know whether you will be able to adjust to them. I mean, we haven't met them yet, but when you went there, did you also think …' She trailed off.

So Shama Aunty's antennae had finally caught on to Vikram's not-so-affluent past.

'No,' said Gayatri innocently, enjoying her mother's discomfort. 'They seemed normal, I mean, reasonably normal. Some things were different, like they had covers on the sofas, plastic crockery, you know, but nothing extraordinary.'

Nina nodded. 'It's good if you feel like that, but, you know, there may be adjustment issues later and I don't want to make you go through that.'

Gayatri felt a surge of anger against her mother. Suddenly she is all modernity and understanding. Just a hint that these people may not be what she considers to be her social equals and she starts swinging like a pendulum. She only thinks of herself, not me. 'Well, I like him a lot,' she said aloud, taking perverse pleasure in the worry on her mother's face. 'That should count, no?'

'Of course, beta, but in arranged marriages, you know, we do see whether the families match and all that. That's how it happens.'

'You should have thought of all that before you introduced me to him,' said Gayatri flatly.

'I know,' said Nina, in a troubled voice, oblivious to her daughter's anger. 'This Shama has put us in a fix.'

'Not "us". Just you. I'm not going to consider such stupid things when I'm making this decision,' Gayatri said firmly, getting up from the table.

'Where are you off to? It's only seven-thirty. And today is New Year's Eve. I thought you told me you were taking the day off?'

'No, we have to get next month's issue out, so Farah and I decided to work today. I'm going to pack my breakfast. I'll just end up fighting with you if I sit here.'

'But why will we fight, Ga—'

'Bye, Ma,' said Gayatri, walking past her mother.

Gayatri parked her car and walked towards the office, her mind preoccupied. It was a dim, smoggy winter morning, and the city was dark and overcast.

As she neared the office entrance, she noticed that the glass pane in the main door was broken and the door was ajar. Pushing it open, she entered and switched on a light. Her eyes widened as she looked around. There was broken glass everywhere. The windows had been shattered, the pictures slashed and thrown on the floor. Both Farah's and her computers lay smashed on the ground.

Instinctively, she took a step back. She was reaching for her phone in her bag, when she heard some shuffling towards the stairs leading to the basement. The noise grew louder as three well-built men, their faces half-covered, appeared at the top of the stairs. Two of them held iron rods in their hands, and the third held a hockey stick. They stopped suddenly as they caught sight of her.

She stumbled backwards, saying, 'Kya, ye kya kar…' but she trailed off as a cold dread filled her. Breathing heavily, she wondered if she was dreaming. She glanced towards the main door, gauging whether she could make a run for it. Before she could decide, one of the men wielding an iron rod walked up to her quickly, blocking off any chance of escape. She stared at him blankly, frozen in place.

'Tu kaun hai?' he growled in a Haryanvi accent.

She swallowed, her body now rigid, fear sitting like a physical weight in her stomach. The man's eyes—all she could see of his face—seemed calm and unafraid. She backed away slowly until she was standing against a wall. There was a window beside her, but she knew it would be bolted. One of the other men was making a phone call while his companion stood by.

'Udhar hi raho,' she said, her voice quavering.

Although she could only see his eyes, she felt as if the man smiled as he walked towards her, saying menacingly, 'Agar bola hota ki ladies-log honge, hum tayyar ho kar aate.' He looked at his mates. One of them sniggered.

Gayatri's hand was shaking as she held it up weakly and said, 'Idhar mat aana. Maine police ko bula liya hai, woh abhi aa jaayegi.'

The man's eyes narrowed, the calm confidence in them instantly replaced with anger. 'Madarchod,' he spat and raised his iron rod high.

Gayatri closed her eyes and screamed loudly as he brought it down heavily on the window behind her, shattering the glass. She felt stabs of pain in her arms as pieces of glass pierced through her clothes and skin. Crouching down, she buried her face in her knees. Her body was trembling. She wondered if this was how she would die, at the hands of this faceless man. He squatted down next to her and, after a few seconds, touched her arm. She looked at him and let out another scream. His eyes looked capable of any insanity.

Then suddenly, as if it had all just been a bad dream, the three men ran out of the door and vanished. Shivering uncontrollably, Gayatri waited until she heard the sound of a car starting in the distance. A few seconds later, she stood up shakily and stumbled out of the door to the garden. She sank down on the cold, wet grass and wept.

Forty-five minutes later, Gayatri was sitting in Kanthan's study as a doctor and a nurse tended to the wounds in her arm. Kanthan and Farah were sitting by in gloomy silence.

'How come the police haven't reached yet?' asked Gayatri. Her voice was unsteady and her face was pale.

'They should be here any minute,' said Farah.

Gayatri looked at Kanthan's stricken face and said softly, 'Let's be thankful they didn't go upstairs. With the kids here—' She broke off, not wanting to worry him further.

He shook his head sadly. 'I feel like such a coward, Gayatri. I couldn't think of any better way to protect the kids than to stay upstairs and call the police.' He paused, tears welling up in his eyes. 'I didn't realize you were downstairs until I heard you scream.'

'I know, Kanthan. I don't know why I had to come in early today, of all days,' said Gayatri as the nurse instructed her to hold her arm straight.

Kanthan nodded. 'It happened so fast. Just fifteen minutes. I can't believe how much destruction they managed in such a short time.'

'You did the right thing, Kanthan,' said Farah, 'by packing your family off to your brother's house immediately.'

Gayatri winced as the nurse pulled out a piece of glass from her left arm.

'Bas, that was the last one,' the woman said kindly, before giving Gayatri a tetanus shot.

Farah walked over to Gayatri and stroked her hair. Gayatri noticed she had tears in her eyes.

'Faru, what's wrong with you now?' asked Gayatri, willing her voice to be strong. As her friend shook her head miserably, Gayatri clicked her tongue, 'I think we need to get over this shock. Let's think of what we should do now. I was thinking of calling Akshay, he may be able to help.'

Farah nodded, 'Yes, that's a good idea. Why don't you call him now, it'll be good if he is here when the cops come.'

Gayatri rose gingerly to leave the room, and dialled Akshay's number.

'Hey,' he answered cheerfully.

'Hi, Akshay, listen,' she said in a low tone, 'I'm sorry to bother you like this, but the thing is ... uh ... our office was vandalized ... everything is smashed and—'

'Are you okay?' he interrupted.

'I'm fine. I mean, they broke a window near me, but—'

'What! Gayatri, are you hurt?'

'No, I'm fine.'

'And the others? Farah, Kanthan?'

'They're fine. Those men didn't go upstairs, thankfully.'

'Have you called the cops?'

'Yes.'

'I'm coming. I'm leaving right now.'

'Thanks. Thanks so much, Akshay,' she said gratefully.

'Don't worry, okay, Gayatri? I ... I'll be there soon.'

'Okay, bye,' she whispered, suddenly close to tears.

She composed herself and went back into Kanthan's room. 'He's on his way,' she said, sitting down, trying to speak calmly.

Kanthan shook his head. 'This is no country for people like us.'

Twenty-two minutes later, Akshay parked his car and entered Gayatri's office. He had broken most speed limits and jumped a few red lights on his way. He saw Gayatri standing on the front lawn with three khaki-clad policemen. He noticed white bandages on her left arm as he walked towards her with brisk, long steps.

Gayatri hadn't anticipated the rush of relief that washed over her as soon she saw Akshay. She stepped away from the policemen mid-sentence. He put an arm around her shoulders. 'You okay?' He glanced down at her face, which was buried in his chest for a brief moment, before she pulled away awkwardly, speaking with a sudden formality. 'Yes, thank you, Akshay. Thanks for coming so quickly.'

He nodded, looking at her arm with concern. 'How did this happen?'

'One of them broke a window next to me and some pieces of glass went in. I'll tell you later in detail. Let's deal with these cops first.' She walked back to the policemen before he had a chance to ask more questions.

'Arre, Sharma sahib,' said Akshay, following her and shaking hands with one of the policemen.

'Akshayji,' said the policeman. 'You know these people?'

'Haan haan, Gayatri is my ... my brother's ... She is family.'

Gayatri noted the change in the policeman's tone upon Akshay's arrival. 'Goondagardi ka mamla hai,' said Inspector Sharma. 'There have been some instances in the university also in the last few weeks.'

Akshay nodded.

'We will take some photos and then take Mr Kanthan's statement here itself.'

'Where is he?' asked Akshay, looking around.

'Upstairs,' answered Gayatri.

'You all right, Farah?' asked Akshay, spotting Farah approaching them. 'Why don't you both sit here in the veranda? I'll go around with the cops while they click the photos.'

Farah nodded gratefully and sat down, while Gayatri turned to follow Akshay and the cops.

'Aap bhi baith jaaiye, madam,' said Inspector Sharma, looking back at Gayatri.

'Why?' she demanded.

'Aap rest karo, we will do our job. Akshayji is also here.'

'Thank you,' said Gayatri coldly. 'But this is my office, and I'd like to be there while you look around.'

Akshay sighed. This inspector didn't know whom he was trying to patronize. He said quickly, 'Sir, Gayatri bhi lawyer hai. I don't know the place all that well, she and Farah run it.'

Inspector Sharma looked at Gayatri doubtfully.

'I'll show you the damage,' she said, leading them into the office.

'Aaiye, sir,' said Akshay, smiling at Inspector Sharma.

Despite Akshay's presence at the police station, the recording of Gayatri's and Farah's statements turned out to be a long process, and they were all exhausted by the time it was over.

'Akshay,' said Farah tiredly as they walked towards his car. 'It doesn't look like these cops are going to be much help in finding the people who did this, no?'

Akshay shrugged and said quietly, 'I don't know. It depends on who's behind this.'

They climbed into the car.

'Anyway,' said Gayatri, fastening her seat belt, 'things would have been so much more difficult without you, Akshay. You've given us your whole day, thank you so much, really. You must have had other work, and today is New Year's Eve of all days—'

'Don't be silly, Gayatri,' he said. 'I'll follow up with Sharma in a day or so. My guys talk to him regularly on other cases.'

They were silent for most of the drive back to the journal's office. Akshay parked the car outside the gate. As Gayatri and Farah got out, he asked, 'You guys will be okay?'

'Yes,' said Farah. 'Thanks so much for today, Akshay.' She walked inside, saying, 'I'll just see whether Leela is still here.'

Gayatri walked around the car to Akshay's open window, and rested her hand on the sill. 'Thank you,' she said.

'You don't need to thank me,' he said. He paused for a long moment before saying softly, 'When that guy broke the window near you … touched your arm'—he clenched his jaw—'it must have been terrifying.'

She looked at him and nodded, blinking back tears. 'It was. I froze. It was as if I was watching a movie of how I would die.'

He placed his hand on hers. 'You're very brave, Gayatri.' He squeezed her hand as he spoke.

She swallowed. 'That guy,' she said, 'I don't think I'll ever forget his voice, or those eyes …' She looked away. 'He was like an alien, you know, the kind of goonda I've only heard about or seen in films.'

Akshay started to unlock his door to get out, but she shook her head. 'No, no, I'm okay. Uh, listen, I haven't told anyone at home yet. They'd just panic. I thought I'd tell them myself when I get home.'

'Okay,' he said, nodding. 'Though I heard a cop at the station on the phone with a reporter, so be prepared for this to make the news.'

'Oh no,' groaned Gayatri. After a pause, she said, 'Listen, can I ask you something?'

He nodded.

She extricated her hand from under his. 'Why did you go so much out of your way for us today?'

'What do you mean?'

'I mean … do you know something about who did this?' she asked softly. 'It's Sadhuji, isn't it?'

He looked away with an angry shake of his head. 'Why are you so suspicious of everything, Gayatri?'

She bit her lip sheepishly.

'Why does everything have to be motivated? If the cop was telling you to sit, it's because he's a chauvinist. If I'm helping you, it's because I'm guilty. Why the hell do you insist on looking at the world like this?'

She swallowed. 'No, it's just—'

'It's just what?' he demanded.

'I—'

'And the worst is, where you should be suspicious, there you act as if nothing's wrong and you're happy to go along with it.'

'What do you mean?'

He looked at her reproachfully. 'Nothing. Forget I said anything.'

'No, tell me, what did you mean?'

'Nothing, Gayatri, it's none of my business what you do or who you choose—' he broke off. Taking a deep breath, he mustered a smile and said, 'It's getting late, I should get back to work.' He patted her hand gently. 'And let's not talk of unpleasant things. I think you've had enough for the day.'

She looked upset.

'Bye,' he said, pushing the gear stick to reverse with his left hand. 'I'll follow up with the cops.' He added with a small smile, 'And take care of your arm, okay?'

She stared after his car as he drove away, before walking inside slowly.

16

THE NEXT MORNING, there were loud knocks on Gayatri's bedroom door.

'Haan?' she called groggily, poking her head out from beneath the razais.

Ashok Mehra entered. 'Is this true?' he asked his daughter, pointing to his phone.

'What?' She sat up sleepily. Her eyes focused on a news report open on his phone. She sighed as she saw the headline. 'Yes, Papa.'

'What happened to your arm?' he said in alarm.

She looked at her bandaged arm. 'Nothing, some glass broke on it. While we were cleaning up.'

Ashok Mehra looked very angry and very worried. 'Did you go to a doctor?'

She nodded, 'Of course, Papa. I thought I'd tell you myself when I got back, but you were out for New Year's and I just crashed.'

'And you didn't think it important to call us? Someone forwarded me this news report on WhatsApp … that's how I get to hear?'

'I'm sorry, Dad,' she said. She could see why he was angry. She described the incident in more detail, leaving out the part where she encountered the attackers. She had texted Akshay the previous night to try to have that part left out of the news reports.

'You're sure you're okay?' Ashok asked, after she had finished.

'Yes, Papa. I swear.'

'But why didn't you call me, beta?'

'It was okay, Dad. Akshay was also there to deal with the cops, and I didn't want to worry you unnecessarily.'

'Akshay? How come he was there?'

Gayatri shrugged. 'I called him. He knows the cops and was anyway helping me with some stuff on the journal. Why are you so surprised?'

'So you don't know then?'

'Don't know what?'

'Nandini came back at about three in the morning. She was crying and screaming. She wants to leave Amar.'

'What?' said Gayatri, her eyes widening. 'But … how … I mean, they were fine that day …'

'I don't know. Both my daughters were waiting for the same day to give me the shocks of my life.'

Gayatri got out of bed and put her arms around her father. 'I'm sorry, Dad. I didn't want to worry you. And I was so tired, I just came up to my room and slept.'

He put his arm around her, and kissed her on her head. 'Beta, please take care. No matter how liberal your mother and I are, we are not okay with you doing something that is dangerous.'

'I know, Papa, I'll be careful,' she said. 'The cops are keeping an eye now. It was probably just some gang of thieves. And I'll speak with Nandini. Don't worry, must be one of those ups and downs.'

'I hope so,' said her father.

Gayatri's eyes, hidden from her father, reflected the worry she was trying to mask with her words.

A distraught Nina was waiting for Gayatri when she went downstairs for breakfast. Before her mother could say anything, Gayatri hugged her, apologizing for not calling the previous day. After being thoroughly questioned and giving her mother sound reassurances that her arm was all right, Gayatri asked about Nandini.

Nina said tiredly, 'She came home in a real state. I thought maybe Amar had hit her or something, but she said no. She just kept saying she doesn't want to go back.'

'And how was she this morning?'

'She seemed normal ... She said she had work in office though it's a holiday, ate her breakfast. So I also didn't say anything. Maybe she will go back to Amar's house in the evening.'

'Does Dadi know?' asked Gayatri, sitting down on a chair. 'She'll be very upset.'

'Huh,' said Nina derisively. 'What upset? She will blame me for this, you just wait and see. Anything that goes wrong with her son or granddaughters is all my fault.' She glared at Gayatri as she continued, 'Anyway, for your part, I hope you know that it's only because of your father that you are not being forced to quit your job right now. I tried telling him that our daughter should be married and settled at this age, not getting injured with windows breaking all around her. But he doesn't understand.'

'Don't worry, Ma, it looks worse than it is. Achha, I have to rush,' she said standing up. 'I'll see you later. Good luck handling Dadi.'

As she left, Gayatri said a silent prayer of thanks that her parents did not know how the window had broken.

Akshay knocked on his father's office door. 'Papa?' he said.

A familiar grunt sounded from within.

Akshay entered and closed the door behind him. 'Do you know anything about this vandalism at Gayatri's office?'

'Haan?' said Mr Grewal, looking up from the papers on his desk. 'What happened?'

'Some goondas entered and smashed everything.'

'She is okay?'

'Yes, she's okay. But those goondas … they were Sadhuji's people?'

'How would I know? And even if they were, it's not our business. You seem to be spending more time on this girl's matters than on your work.'

'But, Papa—'

'Akshay,' said Mr Grewal, removing his spectacles, 'you know how the real world works. It may be Sadhuji's men, who knows? Didn't you warn Gayatri anyway? She should have listened.' He paused. 'Meanwhile, I understand her sister has left the house after a fight with Amar.'

Akshay looked surprised for a moment, then shook his head. 'That's not the point. Papa, all I know is that this is not worth it. If that makes me dumb or naive or whatever, then fine. First that journalist was murdered, then all that trouble at the university, now this. And we are the ones bailing out Sadhuji's men. Don't do it, Papa.'

'Don't do it, Papa,' mimicked Mr Grewal. He let out a dry laugh. 'These days, I'm beginning to think that even Amar may be smarter than you.'

Akshay sighed. 'Papa you can think what you like, but this game is too dirty. People's lives are involved. People we know.'

Mr Grewal looked at Akshay's face closely. 'You know what I really think? I think what's happening is fine. You think these left-wingers give a damn about anything? They are also angling after some vote bank or the other. That fellow running their journal is also probably being paid off by someone or the other.'

'Irrespective of that, you just can't continue to support Sadhuji through this kind of shit. You need to put a stop to this.' Akshay tried to keep the frustration out of his voice.

Mr Grewal narrowed his eyes. 'You son of a bitch. Think you're smarter than me?'

Akshay, though taken aback by his father's words, held his gaze steadily.

'No one has the guts to speak to me like this,' shouted Grewal. 'No one.'

'Yes, I know. My mother definitely doesn't. And, as for the other people in your life, and you know whom I'm referring to,' Akshay said pointedly, 'they will also screw you over.'

Grewal's face turned red.

'Maybe this is not the time, Papa, but you need to be careful about Neelam, she will—'

'You … you have the guts to … Get out! Out!' roared Mr Grewal.

Akshay left the room, banging the door as loudly as he could behind him. Mr Grewal's face as he glowered at the door, and Akshay's face as he walked away, wore identical expressions of rage and hurt.

Back in his apartment, Akshay paced around the living room. He closed his eyes, flexed his hands and took a deep breath. Would I have gone along with this if not for Gayatri, he wondered. He rubbed his forehead. It was all a circle. She judged him, he judged his father, and his father now judged him back. He remembered Neelam's words, that his father had known about their relationship. But that didn't have anything to do with this. No, that was separate.

At half past twelve that day, Gayatri entered Southern Delights, a South Indian restaurant near Nandini's office. Nandini was already there.

'What happened in your office, Didi?' asked Nandini as soon as Gayatri sat down. 'And what happened to your arm?'

Gayatri repeated her version of the incident for the third time that day.

Nandini sighed. 'I'm sorry, it must have been awful.'

'It's okay, we'll deal with it.' She looked at Nandini. 'Now, tell me what's going on with you and Amar? I thought things were good after we went out that night?'

'Same story. We were at a New Year's party, and we started fighting there only. Lots of shouting and screaming. In public.' Nandini spoke very matter-of-factly.

'What about?'

'I told him that we need to move out of his house, that's the only way to save our marriage. He got hassled. Then someone at the party hinted to him that I had to put in a word with my boss to keep his bonus at the same level as mine last year. That is true, but I don't know how anyone found out.'

'He got upset?'

'Very angry. But he would have been equally angry if his bonus had been less than mine. He's an insecure prick. Anyway, when we reached home, I said something which just blew his fuse.'

'What?'

Nandini pursed her lips, then said, 'Now, don't be shocked. His dad. He's having an affair with this woman called Neelam who works in his office. I told Amar that he was the only idiot in the whole house who didn't know. Even I can see it, and I barely moved in a couple of months ago.'

'Oh god,' said Gayatri, closing her eyes and shaking her head.

'And then—'

Gayatri looked up at her. 'There's more?'

Nandini nodded. 'He pushed me so hard onto the bed when I said this, I really thought my back was broken.'

Gayatri's eyes widened.

'But I got up, and kicked him back.'

Gayatri put her head in her hands again and let out a groan.

'This is what marriage is, Didi. This is the shit that it is. I can't believe I did this to myself.'

'What a mess ...'

'Don't worry, Didi. I'm definitely not,' said Nandini, sipping the buttermilk from her glass. 'I'm done with this marriage bullshit.'

Akshay was walking out of the Delhi High Court complex when Gayatri called him to ask if he could follow-up with Inspector Sharma. She deliberately didn't mention Amar and Nandini.

Forty-five minutes later, Akshay called her back. 'He's not answering my calls, Gayatri.'

'Okay,' she said. 'Thanks.'

'I'll try again in a while.'

'Don't bother, I'm going to drop in at the police station on my way home,' she said.

'Why? Let him call back. There is no point in irritating them.'

'I want to put some pressure on them, or they'll just keep sitting on their asses.'

Akshay paused for a moment, and said, 'I'm just leaving my chambers at court. Why don't I meet you there?'

Gayatri hesitated. 'No, it's okay ... You've already done so much.'

'It's ten minutes away, I'll meet you there. You know he probably won't see you otherwise.'

Gayatri took a moment to grudgingly admit to herself that that was true. 'Akshay, thanks so much. I know with Amar and Nandini—'

'Forget about that. Let them sort out their issues. Let's keep this separate.'

'Fine,' she said. 'But thanks again, you've really gone out of your way—'

He cut her short. 'It's no trouble. I'll see you there?'

'Yes,' she said. 'I'm leaving now.'

Two hours later, Gayatri and Akshay walked out of the police station. 'These cops are so crooked,' she said bitterly. 'He seemed so unconcerned about everything.'

'That's the way they are, Gayatri. It's not special treatment for you.'

They walked towards the parking lot and paused at the point where had to part ways to go to their own cars.

'I still think there has to be some way of getting through,' she said. 'Maybe meeting the commissioner of police, or speaking to the press? Kanthan said he has asked someone he knows to try and get a meeting with the commissioner—'

Akshay interrupted her. 'Listen, I've been on my feet in court most of the day. Can we go sit somewhere and talk?'

She looked towards her car hesitantly.

'You don't have to. It's just if you wanted to discuss anything,' he said, starting to walk towards his car.

'No, no,' said Gayatri, not wanting to appear rude after everything he had done. 'I was just ... uh ... let's go. We can go to Café Turtle. You know it?'

'Yes, in the bookshop in Khan Market?'

Gayatri nodded. 'We can drive separately and meet at the coffee shop.'

Gayatri arrived at the first-floor bookshop a few minutes after Akshay. She glimpsed him disappear behind a bookshelf. Turning the corner, she saw him reading the back of a slim hardcover. He replaced the book when he saw her. Together, they climbed the stairs to the cheerful and warm coffee shop.

'What will you have?' asked Akshay as they sat down at a table. 'No rum here, I'm afraid.'

She smiled sheepishly, remembering the evening they had gone out. 'I'll have a filter coffee.'

He signalled to a waiter. 'Two filter coffees, please,' he said.

After a few seconds of silence, Gayatri asked, 'You read poetry? I saw you downstairs with that book.'

'Oh. No, actually, I don't read much poetry. I picked up that book because I like the writer. Vikram Seth. You've read him?'

Gayatri nodded. *A Suitable Boy* was her favourite book. Akshay had probably read his travelogue, she guessed.

'I've only read one of his books,' said Akshay. '*A Suitable Boy*. I fell in love with it.'

Gayatri raised her eyebrows.

'What's that look?'

'No, it's just that I love that book too.'

'You don't have to be disappointed that we like the same book,' he said, with a smile. 'Anyway, I'm sure that's a pretty common opinion.'

The waiter placed their coffees before them.

'If it's any consolation, I read it by chance,' he continued. 'I found a copy of it in my college library.' He took a sip of his coffee and continued. 'It was beautiful. Smooth, thin, white pages bound in a maroon hardcover. I had time back then.'

Gayatri smiled, remembering her own experience of being immersed in the world of that book. She brought her attention back to the present. 'So, this Sharma, do you think I pissed him off?'

'No, the truth is, you probably don't matter enough to piss him off. He is working on many cases, being pressured by many people, and truly doesn't give a shit about this case.'

Gayatri looked away trying to conceal her irritation. Akshay went on, 'It's the way things work, Gayatri. I once met a senior police officer who told me that to be a police officer was to lose your humanity. Dead bodies, criminals, terrorists, that's their everyday world. Nothing shocks them any more—things that move ordinary people have zero impact on them. The only thing that moves them is money, or pressure from above.'

'So what are we supposed to do? Accept these people coming and vandalizing our office, and just keep quiet?'

'Yes,' said Akshay simply. 'There is a lot of money and political pressure competing with your frustration. Unless you can put together a movement to create publicity or are willing to pay, nothing will move forward. I can guarantee that.'

She nodded, but he could see she didn't really understand.

He's so cynical, she thought as she drove home. But he has good taste in fiction. He was the first man she had met who had actually read and liked *A Suitable Boy*.

What did it mean when someone else loved a piece of art that you loved, she wondered as she stopped at a red light. Probably nothing. She looked over at the car next to hers, and saw a man talking energetically into his handsfree speaker. That guy could have loved *Malory Towers* or *The Magic Faraway Tree* as a child, but that didn't say anything about anyone other than Enid Blyton.

The light turned green. But maybe, she thought as she shifted her car into first gear, loving the same work of art means that you share some sensibility, or at least an experience. Something that you don't share with everyone.

Just then a motorist cut into her lane, causing her to brake suddenly. 'Fuck,' she cursed as she swerved out of his way, losing her train of thought.

Amar grit his teeth as he sat across from Nandini in her room in her parents' house. It had taken all his willpower to go over and apologize. But his mother had insisted, and she was right. His father would strangle him if Nandini and he were to separate within a few months of marriage, just when he was preparing to contest his first election.

Nandini sat on a chair, her arms crossed combatively.

'Look,' began Amar, 'you said some very nasty things about my dad, and … and *her*. How can you forget all that?'

Nandini did not answer.

He continued, 'I'm sorry. I said I'm sorry. I should never have pushed you, okay.' He waited for her to say something, but she remained silent. 'And I'm not even saying anything about you hitting me back. That was fine, justified. I deserved it.'

Nandini glanced at him witheringly. 'Achha?'

'Nandini, please. Let's go away somewhere for a few days. Away from my parents and the house. Let's just spend some time with each other.'

'Amar, look I'm sorry, but I'm done with this marriage.' She shook her head. 'We are not right for each other. These fights, this aggression, we can't live like this. We'll just destroy one another.'

'Nandini, don't say that,' he pleaded. 'This is just the beginning, it will get better.'

'No. These last two months have changed the way I think about you, Amar, about us. I'm sorry, but that's what it is.'

'Okay, okay,' he said. 'Let's give things one last shot. A trip to Goa, all by ourselves. And if you still feel it's not working, then fine, we'll see what needs to be done. One last shot, Nini, please?'

Nandini's expression softened a little bit. Amar saw his opening. He crouched by her feet on the floor, holding her hand. 'Come on, baby, just for one or two nights. I'll book tickets for tomorrow. I'll pick you up from here, no need to come home.'

She looked at him and sighed. She tried to feel hopeful, but just felt exhausted.

He picked up his jacket, saying, 'I'll book the tickets and let you know when you should be ready. I love you.' He left the room before she could change her mind.

Later that night, Rupi Grewal entered her elder son's room. Akshay, sitting at his desk, turned to face her.

'You spoke to Amar?' she asked.

He nodded. 'He's taking Nandini to Goa for a couple of days. Let them try to sort things out.'

'I really don't know how these girls of today operate,' said Rupi, shaking her head. 'Anyway, what's happened between you and Papa?'

'Why?'

'He seems very upset with you. He said something about Gayatri. What does she have to do with all this?'

'Ma, I ... nothing. Her office was vandalized yesterday and she was injured, all by Sadhuji's goondas.' He paused. 'I can read about this stuff in the papers, and not go for a protest march. But I will not actively work for and defend the people that do this.'

'Beta, you know better than anyone how things work and what your father's connection with Sadhuji is. He cannot change Sadhuji or the party's thinking just because this girl is related to us.'

He shrugged. 'Fine, but I've changed my … I don't see these things the way he does. And I don't want to just go along with what he's doing any more. It's too much, too real now. I can't be a part of this.'

Rupi said gently, 'This is an important time for your father, beta, with the fight for the ticket and then the elec—'

'He's being reckless, Ma. This will come back to bite him,' Akshay said forcefully. 'And I hope you've warned him about Neelam.'

They were both silent for a few seconds, then Akshay took a deep breath and said slowly, 'Ma, there is something else.' He paused. 'She said Papa knew. About me and her. Did he? Tell me the truth, Ma.'

'No, beta,' said Rupi, looking away.

'This is important, Ma. Please don't lie. I need to know.'

His mother sighed. 'What is the point of this now?' She looked at Akshay furtively, her eyes giving the truth away.

Akshay winced. 'Fuck.' He took a breath. 'Sorry, Ma.'

She covered his hand with hers and said pleadingly, 'Beta, he didn't know the extent to which you were involved. He thought it was just an infatuation. He was also so much younger then. Everything is not so black and white.'

Akshay swallowed hard. He got up and put on his running shoes.

'Beta, wh—'

'I'm going out, Ma. I need some fresh air.' He kissed her on her forehead and left the room.

17

'So she's gone?' asked Farah, wrapping her hands around the coffee mug to make the most of its warmth.

'Yes. Amar picked her up this morning. One thing less for my Dad to worry about. He's still fretting over what happened in the office.'

'My parents too,' said Farah. 'My mom told me to quit. She said next time if they come and find me here, they'll carry me off and kill me. I had such a hard time convincing them not to tell Zaheer.' She sighed. 'He'll get more adamant that we move to the US, and I don't want that.' Farah sipped her coffee. 'But, you know, Gayatri, it's strange … somehow, now I feel less scared. I'm thinking, let's publish what we have to. We can't live in fear.'

Gayatri smiled wryly. 'And here I was going to say that if I was in your mother's place, I would also have reacted like her.' Her phone buzzed. She frowned as she looked at it. 'Oh god. Vikram … I completely forgot about him.'

'He's still in London?'

'Yeah. I think he's coming back tomorrow.'

'That's good.'

Gayatri was quiet.

'What?' said Farah.

'Nothing.'

Farah took a sip of her coffee, and waited.

Gayatri knew Farah would not probe her. After a few seconds, she said, 'I told him I was not sure about us, because after that evening when I went out with Akshay and Nandini and Amar ... I ... I don't know.'

'Oh,' said Farah.

'No. No "Oh",' Gayatri insisted. 'There's nothing there, and there never can be, you know that. Nandini's life is complicated enough already.'

'But?'

'But nothing. I just don't feel comfortable with Vikram any more, that's all.'

'Your mother won't be happy if this Vikram thing ends.'

'Oh, you'll be surprised,' Gayatri said. 'She's so unbelievably shallow. Now she's been dropping hints about breaking it off with Vikram because she's heard from that cow Shama that his family is not so high-flying after all.'

'Don't be so hard on Aunty, Gayatri. She means well.'

'Maybe, but I'm not telling her about my doubts about Vikram anytime soon. Let her stew. And anyway, if I say no now, they'll just make me meet someone else. That's the last thing I need. So I'm not going to say anything.'

'But, Gayatri—'

'Ohho, Faru! Never mind all this. Let's go in now,' she said, getting up.

Neelam stood by Mr Grewal's desk, looking at him petulantly, her hands on her hips.

'What is this, Neelam?' he was saying. 'Every day some new tantrum.'

'It's not a tantrum. Why can't I handle things for this party like I always do?'

Mr Grewal had just told her that Rupi was in charge of arrangements for his sixty-fifth birthday party.

'Neelu, try to understand,' he cajoled. 'You know how politics works. What was fine earlier may not be okay now.'

Neelam jerked her head to one side scornfully. 'Who do you think doesn't know about us? The whole town knows. Your wife—'

'Yes, but these things don't need to be spelled out. Appearances should be kept up.' He looked away from her, towards his computer. 'I don't want to discuss this further.'

'I know where this is going. First, you suggest this *cottage*,' she said, using air quotes, 'in Mashobra. Now suddenly your wife is doing the things I always did.'

Mr Grewal looked up at her. 'Don't be silly now.'

'You can't get rid of me like this, I'm telling you. Seventeen years I've—'

'Neelu, really, this is not the time—'

She decided to take a chance. 'Why don't we see how damaging your relationship with me really is? I can just go public with it and see what happens.'

Mr Grewal spoke after a few moments. 'Don't lower yourself to this level, Neelu. I don't need to tell you how the men get out unscathed, as if nothing happened. And the woman gains nothing but infamy, that too, if she's lucky.'

She looked at him accusingly, her eyes brimming with sudden tears. 'I can't believe you're saying these things to me. Me … whom you charmed and bullied and ...' Her voice dropped to a whisper, 'And loved, I thought.'

'Neelu, listen. You know better than to threaten me. And you know I love you. I'm just presenting reality to you. I will always take care of you, protect you ... you know that.' He pushed his chair back and stood up. Walking around his desk, he stood against it and pulled her towards him. 'I'm here, Neelu, like always. Trust me.'

She put her, head on his shoulder and started to sob. He stroked her hair gently. 'Nothing will change between us. It may be good for you to take a break. At least go and see the cottage in Mashobra. You will like it. Deodars as far as the eye can see. It's not a jail, it's what I know you've always wanted.'

He drew her slightly away from him, and tilted her chin upwards with his finger. Looking into her eyes, he repeated, 'I need you now, to support me. Don't let me down.'

After wiping her eyes with a tissue, she took a step back and said, 'Okay.'

'Neelu—' Mr Grewal reached for her again, but Neelam left his office before he had a chance to say anything further.

Sitting at his desk with his room door ajar, Akshay caught a glimpse of Neelam as she walked quickly past his room. He tried to focus on his computer screen for a few moments, then suddenly pushed his chair back and walked up the stairs to the driveway, out of the gate, and away from the house. He looked weary, tired as he was fighting the surge of hurt that had overwhelmed him since his conversation with his mother.

Neelam's words reverberated in his head: 'Your father knew.' He kept walking as memories surfaced. In all these years, he had never allowed himself to visit those quarters of his brain where these memories were stored, but there they were, all the better preserved for having been quarantined.

He had been twenty-two, and she twenty-eight, an elegant new presence in his father's office. Strikingly beautiful with her oval face and large eyes, her slim figure was always dressed gracefully in a sari, with a small round black bindi perfectly placed between her eyebrows. In the midst of her divorce, she had been melancholic, and seemed a far cry from the girls in his college with their mindless chatter and frivolous concerns. She had lived in the real world and struggled against a violent man. How he had hated her husband then.

Akshay pushed open the revolving gate of the park where he jogged every day and sat on a bench, staring ahead vacantly. It was on the periphery of this very park that she had asked him one night, on their way back from a client's house, to stop the car. He remembered his heart pounding as he steered the car into a narrow space. That kiss, in the car parked a few metres from where he sat now, on a dark Delhi winter evening, had felt like his first kiss.

He remembered how protective he had felt towards her, proud that this beautiful, intelligent, older woman had chosen him. He remembered the stolen moments with her on walks and drives, and in nooks and crannies of the office, working late. And then, after two wonderful years, Neelam had gradually retreated from him. He hadn't understood it at first. He thought she was bored of him, and he was determined not to make a fuss, to behave like a man. It wasn't until he heard those sounds from his father's office a few weeks later that he realized.

He grimaced as those sounds resounded in his ears now, shocking him with their vividness even after all these years. Papa and Neelam. Neelam and Papa. He remembered charging out of the office in angry tears, and then running back after ten minutes, convinced that he was mistaken. He had returned to find Neelam in his father's office, flushed and guilty.

Akshay sat still for a few minutes with his back hunched and his teeth clenched. He forced himself to dredge up more memories with her: in the park, on a visit to a client's house in Moradabad, in her house, in his flat. The times she tried to speak to him afterwards. He thought of the relationships he had not been able to have for years after, for want of trust; of the nights he had spent trying not to imagine his father and Neelam together; and of the one thing that had saved him until now: that his father had not known that Akshay loved her.

He grit his teeth and braced himself for a few seconds, but the truth didn't destroy him. He blinked and focused on the world before him. Everything was as before. Nothing was affected by him or Neelam or his father. The trees, squirrels, the old mali manoeuvring his water pipe that was entangled in loops. A few birds flew towards the ground, and, just for a second before they landed, they paused, all together. He had never noticed that before.

He turned his head up at the January sky, blue for a change. He let the waves of anger wash over him, their intensity tempered by the suspicion that really, he had known all along.

That evening, Akshay was on the phone in his office when he saw Mann gesturing wildly from the door. 'I have to go now,' he said as he hung up.

Mann entered. 'Sir, Anil Bhargav called. He wants us to go to the Rajpur Road police station and get them to cool off on the university vandalism case. He has heard the cops have some leads, which may be related to his people.'

Akshay stared at Mann absently.

'Sir?' said Mann. 'Shall I speak to Sharma? Find out kitne mein karega? Last time, it was around two.'

Akshay stood up and walked out of his room. Mann followed him down the corridor into Mr Grewal's office.

'Papa,' said Akshay, entering. He had managed to avoid his father all day.

'Yes,' said Mr Grewal coldly.

'I won't do this.' There was a rough edge to his voice.

'What?' asked Mr Grewal, though he knew well what Akshay was talking about.

'I'm not going to negotiate with the cops for Sadhuji's men.'

'Fine.' Mr Grewal took off his spectacles. He looked at Mann, standing behind Akshay. 'Mann, you go. Leave your boss out of this. Report back to me directly.'

Mann glanced at father and son in confusion.

'Go,' said Mr Grewal in a loud voice.

Mann left the room quickly, closing the door behind him.

'Why are you still standing here?' asked Mr Grewal.

Akshay struggled with himself for a few seconds before saying, 'Papa, please listen to me. You need to see if there is a better way to do this—'

'Are you daft?' said Mr Grewal banging his hand down on his desk. 'There isn't, okay? No *better* way. And I want this. So fuck off if you can't support me.'

Akshay remained silent for a few seconds before saying. 'I can't. Not through this. And I can tell you the reason as well.'

'I don't want to hear your bullshit reasons.'

Akshay ignored his father. 'You were partly right. Things have changed since I met Gayatri.'

Mr Grewal was silent as he processed this information for a few moments. Then he smiled scornfully. 'You, my son, are the biggest idiot I have seen. A girl. You've let a bloody woman talk you into standing against me? Your own father! Behenchod, I've given you everything. Everything! A ready-made practice, a name, contacts, even a bloody future in politics if you want. All on a fucking platter. And you meet some stupid girl, who doesn't have the good sense to back down from danger, and you suddenly have the guts to defy me?'

'Papa, leave Gayatri out of this. She doesn't know of any of this. But she has helped me draw a line that I don't want to cross.' He paused, and continued in a softer tone, 'I don't think you will understand, but she is brave in a way that makes me ashamed of myself.'

His father smiled disdainfully. 'How good is the sex?' he asked. 'That great?'

'Don't. There's nothing like that between us.'

'And what about Vikram? I thought she was marrying him?'

'Papa, stop,' said Akshay, his voice rising.

'I didn't think you would stoop to stealing someone's fiancée. But looks like I don't know you after all.'

'But I know you,' Akshay said after a pause. 'Fuck this little charade. I *know*, Papa. It's been many years, but I know that you knew about her and me.' Akshay's voice rose with each word. 'You fucking knew. And you still fucking went ahead and did whatever the fuck you wanted to do.' He spat out every 'fuck' with a hateful force.

Mr Grewal looked disoriented for a moment, then averted his eyes. Akshay stared at his father for a few moments, breathing heavily, willing him to deny the accusation.

Hearing in his father's silence what he already knew, he left the room.

18

'I THINK IT'S COME out well,' said Farah, scrolling down the layout displayed on her computer screen. She looked up at Gayatri who was standing behind her chair, one hand resting on her hip. 'So strange, na, just a few days have passed since those men came and broke this whole place, and we are back to normal. Life just goes on.'

'True,' said Gayatri. 'I just hope the cops catch those assholes.' She glanced at her phone as it vibrated. 'It's Nandini, I'd better take this.' She walked out to the veranda with her phone.

'Didi?' said Nandini when Gayatri answered. 'Where are you?'

'In office, why? How are—'

'Are you alone?' Nandini was speaking very softly.

'Yes, Nandini, what's wrong?'

'Didi, this is just so pissing off, you won't believe it,' Nandini said exasperatedly. 'I'm fucking pregnant.'

'What?' said Gayatri. Her eyes widened as she processed the news. 'That's great, sweetie,' she said, her eyes brimming with tears. 'I ... I can't believe—'

'Didi, no, please,' Nandini interrupted, her voice hard. 'Don't get all emotional on me.'

'But, Chhoti, this is so great! I want to hug you! My little baby is having her—'

'Didi!' hissed Nandini. 'No. I can't be with Amar.'

'Wha—'

'Didi,' said Nandini impatiently, elongating the last syllable of the word. 'Are you there?'

Gayatri opened her mouth, then closed it. Her stomach sank a little. She said, 'Chhoti, please relax. Come home, and we'll speak. For god's sake, don't do anything stupid in Goa.'

Nandini was silent.

'Chhoti, do you hear me, do not do anything stupid. I mean don't go to a doctor or—'

'I'm not going to do anything in Goa, Didi, I'm not an idiot. And we're coming back today anyway.'

'Does Amar know about the baby?'

'No,' Nandini said flatly. 'And it's not a baby, it's a pregnancy.'

'Okay, when are you going to tell him?'

'I'm not. Telling him is the end of any choice for me in the matter, I—'

'Okay, okay, listen to me,' Gayatri interrupted her. 'Please keep the peace until you're back. You're landing this evening, right?'

'Yeah.'

'I'll come and see you today, and we'll figure this out.'

'Okay,' said Nandini after a pause, her voice breaking slightly. She let out a soft sob.

Gayatri closed her eyes. In that moment she felt as if she would do anything, anything, to make Nandini feel better. 'Chhoti, relax okay. We will sort this out, I promise.'

'Okay, Didi, I'll hang up now,' said Nandini.

Gayatri down after hanging up, her head in her hands.

Her phone buzzed again. It was Vikram. She composed herself. 'Hi,' she said into the phone.

'No calls, nothing from you,' said Vikram. 'You don't seem happy I'm back.'

Her mind still on Nandini, she said, 'Uh ... I had messaged you to thank you for the flowers. I thought you might be tired.'

'I'm never tired for you,' he said cheerfully.

Gayatri winced and quickly changed the subject. 'Did you manage to wrap up everything in London?'

'Yes, mostly. Now I have to get to work here. So when are we meeting?' he asked. 'Can I see you today?'

'Actually, I promised Nandini that I would go and meet her today,' said Gayatri apologetically.

Vikram was silent. He had expected her to keep herself free today. 'That's fine, maybe you can text me once you're done with her. I'll come by, even if it's late. We can do a coffee or something.'

'Er ... okay,' said Gayatri. 'I'll let you know.'

'Fine,' said Vikram, unsatisfied.

Gayatri hung up and blew out her cheeks in a loud sigh. 'Oh god,' she muttered, walking back to her desk.

Gayatri got to Nandini's house at six-thirty that evening. Nandini broke into sobs as soon as she saw her older sister. Gayatri hugged her and led her to the sofa.

After Nandini's sobs subsided, Gayatri fetched a box of tissues and a glass of water for her. 'Here.'

Nandini sipped the water and wiped her nose. 'I'm such an idiot,' she said, shaking her head miserably.

'I know,' said Gayatri. 'Aren't you on the pill or something?'

'I was, but then I stopped. We were fighting so much, and there was no point … We weren't doing anything anyway.' She paused. 'But a couple of nights last month, we had too much to drink and … and I don't know. Then I missed my period, and I don't know why, but it struck me literally on the plane on Saturday that I could be pregnant. I was completely mindfucked. I went for a walk once we reached the hotel, and bought a testing kit and—'

Gayatri sighed. 'Anyway, you need to relax now. This is not the end of the world, you know.'

'Didi, listen,' said Nandini, placing her hand on Gayatri's, looking desperate, 'I cannot be with him. I just can't.'

'But didn't you guys get a chance to sort things out in Goa?'

'Didi, I … It doesn't matter. I just know I've made a mistake. I've been thinking a lot about why I don't want to be with him, and I don't … I … The truth is, I just don't respect him. I can see it so clearly now. I can't believe I was so stupid.'

'Chhoti, look. Maybe you're overreacting because of this preg—'

'Didi,' Nandini interrupted, looking at her sister angrily. 'I didn't expect the "you're hormonal" bullshit from you at least. I know what I know. I just cannot be with him. I'm not stupid.'

'Okay, tell me why exactly.'

'First, he refuses to see sense and move out of this house. I keep telling him I can't live here, but no.'

'Chhoti, that's something you can discuss more—'

'Wait, na, I have lots more. I'm not finished. I hate the fact that I'm always having to stop myself from being promoted at work, getting a larger bonus, I'm always pushing myself down. And for what? What is he contributing to my life? I'm earning enough to live a good life on my terms, and yet he expects me to kowtow to his parents? Why the fuck can't I—a twenty-eight-year-old corporate lawyer—decide my own plan for the evening? And, Didi, you should see the way he behaves after all this, the fights we have, the ego he has ... For what? He thinks because he's a man, he can get away with bullying me. And I can't forget that slap, that push—that's just finished everything for me.'

Nandini was out of breath now.

Gayatri said calmly, 'Okay. Don't you think you contribute to these situations also, that you can also make an effort to make things better?' She glanced at the closed door of the bedroom. 'And could you please speak softly?'

'Don't worry, he's gone somewhere with Akshay Bhaiya. Bhaiya's also had some huge fight with their father, he said he needed to talk to Amar. Anyway, forget all that. I just see Amar differently now, as if I've woken up from a dream.'

Gayatri was momentarily distracted by her comment about Akshay having had a fight with his father. 'Look, Chhoti,' she said after a beat, 'the fact is, when you're an adult, and you make certain decisions, you have to take responsibility for them, remember why you made them, and try to remain faithful to them. You can't take people along with you, and then throw them out when you're tired of them.'

'So just because I made one wrong decision, now I should spend the rest of my life being miserable?'

Gayatri paused briefly, considering whether Nandini was actually right. 'But, Chhoti,' she said, 'what about the baby?'

'Don't say baby, Didi. It's just a few cells right now.' Nandini looked away. 'It doesn't have to become a baby.'

'What are you saying? That you'll abort it? Without telling Amar?'

Nandini shrugged. 'It's better than telling him now, fighting like mad for the rest of our lives together, then splitting up and becoming single parents.'

'Chhoti, listen, calm down. I don't know if you've thought this through.'

'Why? How do you know how much I've thought about this?'

Because this is exactly how much you thought when you decided to marry him, said Gayatri to herself. Instead, she said aloud, 'Listen, let's take this step by step. Why did you marry him?'

Nandini took a deep breath, and said, 'Because I used to have fun with him, and he was nice and sweet. And he asked me at a time when all my friends were getting married, and there was no reason to say no.'

'Okay, so is he less nice now, or less fun?'

'Now nice and fun are not important. I hate him. I don't respect him. Fighting, fighting, fighting every day, mistrusting every decision he makes, and now this baby ... I can't live like this. Maybe it was my mistake, fine. I didn't realize what I wanted.'

Gayatri sighed as she rubbed her forehead. 'This is not a joke. Marriage is serious stuff, families are involved.'

'I don't care.'

'And the baby ... Okay okay, your pregnancy ... whatever ... you're okay to ... to just let that go?'

'Yes,' said Nandini firmly. 'Didi, whatever happens with us, I can't have this baby now when I'm not sure about us. It will be madness. My whole life is at stake. His too.'

'Okay, here's what I think you should do. Talk to Amar, tell him how you feel. Not all this I'm-too-smart-for-you stuff, but that you need a bit of space, that you guys need to move out of here.'

Nandini frowned. 'I've already tried speaking with him ... many times. I'm past all that now. It's not about living in this house or somewhere else,' she said. 'I've stopped loving him. I don't even *like* him any more.'

Gayatri moved closer to Nandini on the couch and took her hand. 'Listen, this baby belongs to both of you. I get how it impacts you

more, but it's his too. You can't do anything stupid without letting him
know, it will kill all trust in your marriage.'

Just then, the door opened, and Amar and Akshay appeared in the
doorway. Gayatri stood up quickly.

'Oh, hi, Didi,' said Amar. He sounded tired.

'I just came to say hi to Nandini,' said Gayatri. 'And you,' she added,
looking at Amar. Her face was frozen in a plastic smile.

An awkward silence stretched between them for a few seconds.
Finally, Akshay cleared his throat and said, 'Are you around for a while,
Gayatri?'

'No, no,' she said. 'I was just leaving.'

'Okay, come, I'll walk you down,' he said.

Gayatri nodded. 'Chhoti, why don't you come home for a day or
so?' She smiled at Amar. 'You won't mind, na? We've been missing her.'

'Up to her,' said Amar, not looking at Nandini.

'Come for a night.' Gayatri squeezed Nandini's hand. 'Maybe
tomorrow?'

Her sister pulled her into a hug that was tighter than usual.

'I love you. I'll call you.' Gayatri patted Nandini on her cheek and
went down the stairs, Akshay following her.

On the first-floor landing, Akshay said suddenly, 'I just need to
drop this bag off.'

Gayatri looked back. 'I'll make a move, then.'

'Wait,' said Akshay. 'Don't go.'

Gayatri frowned, her mind still occupied with Nandini.

'I mean … I want to speak to you. About a few things.'

'Uh, okay, I'll wait here,' she said.

'No, no, come in, please.' He pushed open the door to his flat.

Gayatri hesitated, but then followed him in. He went straight into
a room, leaving her in the living room. Pulling out her phone, she
typed a message to Nandini, 'Don't speak to him right now, wait until
you are calmer. I'll call you, or you come home for a couple of days.

We'll figure things out.' She looked around as she replaced her phone in her purse. Akshay's flat was very different from his parents' house downstairs—all light blues and greys and straight lines.

Akshay emerged from his room. 'Come, let's go outside. We can talk there.' She followed him to the balcony just beyond the living room.

'Do you mind if I smoke?' he asked.

She shook her head. 'I didn't know you smoked.'

'I don't. I mean, only rarely.' He pulled down a packet of cigarettes from the ledge above the window.

Gayatri looked at him distractedly. He lit a cigarette, took a deep drag and blew out the smoke, careful to turn away from her. They stood in silence. Gayatri wondered what he had to say. He seemed nervous.

'Do you have some news from Sharma?' she asked.

Shaking his head, he said, 'It's very unlikely anyone will be caught, much less charged by the cops for this.'

'But—' she started, frowning.

'Listen,' he stopped her. 'That's not what I wanted to talk about. I ... uh ...' His eyes looked into hers directly for a few moments. He opened his mouth, and then closed it again, swallowing.

She looked away. Surely he isn't ...? She was afraid to complete the sentence in her own head. Nandini was on the verge of leaving Amar. And what about Vikram?

Akshay glanced at her as she stared steadfastly at the garden below. She was gripping the rail of the balcony tightly. 'Gayatri, the thing is—'

'Akshay,' she interrupted nervously. 'Vikram got back to India today.'

He looked at her silently for a few seconds. 'Are you still seeing him or ... whatever it was?'

Gayatri nodded. 'Yes, I think so. I mean, he's just come back ...' she trailed off as her phone began to ring. She pulled it out of her bag and looked at it. 'I have to take this. May I?' she asked, pointing to the door leading to his living room.

He shrugged. She stepped back into the living room, and whispered into the phone, 'Hello? Chhoti?'

'Come back and pick me up, Didi,' Nandini said in a weak voice. 'What happened?'

'I told him the truth. About the baby and that I want to leave him. He went mad. I've locked myself in the loo. I don't want to see him. I can't do this, Didi. He is crying outside. Please come.'

Gayatri closed her eyes. 'Fuck. Okay, stay there,' she said. 'I'm still downstairs. I'll be there in a minute.' She thought for a few moments, before going out onto the balcony.

Akshay looked at her troubled face, and asked, 'What happened?'

She shook her head. 'Nandini and Amar ... they are ... maybe you should come up too. She says Amar's crying.'

Akshay winced and shook his head to one side in irritation. 'These two,' he said. 'Can't they behave like adults? I'm sorry, I know she's your sis—'

'No, I know what you mean, it's fine.'

He went up the stairs. They could hear Amar yelling. Akshay knocked on the door loudly. 'Amar!' he shouted. 'Amar!'

Amar opened the door a few seconds later, his face wet with tears. He was surprised to see Gayatri standing behind Akshay. She walked past him into the bedroom and tried to open the bathroom door, but it was locked. She dialled Nandini on her phone. 'Come out. I'm outside your bathroom.'

Just as the bathroom door opened, Amar rushed towards it. Nandini slammed it shut immediately. 'Didi, tell him to leave, or I won't come out,' she called from inside.

Amar looked at Gayatri pleadingly. 'Didi, how can she? We're having a baby and she wants to break up?'

She put her hand gently on his shoulder, and shook her head.

'He's gone,' she said as Amar backed away into the other room.

Nandini opened the door and peeped out, then stepped into the room gingerly.

'Take her down to my place,' said Akshay.

'Bhaiya, why—' called Amar from the other room.

'Amar yaar, relax na,' said Akshay. 'Both of you need to calm down, then you can talk to her. She's not going anywhere.'

Gayatri led Nandini down the stairs to Akshay's flat. Nandini sank down on a sofa and broke into loud sobs. Gayatri remained silent, her arms around Nandini. As Nandini quietened down, Gayatri said gently, 'This is not the way, Nandini.'

'I know, Didi,' said Nandini in a miserable voice. 'But you know me, I can't pretend. I exhausted my capacity for that in Goa. Did you see how mental he is?'

'It's understandable, Chhoti. You told him he's going to be a father and then you say you want to leave him in the same breath.'

Nandini started sobbing again. 'Then what should I do? Everyone just blames me. I'm the bad one.' Gayatri sighed as she got up to get her water.

Akshay was at the door when she re-entered the living room. She gestured for him to stay outside. After Nandini had had some water, Gayatri made her lie down on the couch, and gently stroked her head. 'Just close your eyes and relax now. I'm here.'

A few minutes later, she got up and slipped out of the door. 'She's asleep,' she said to Akshay. 'This is madness. How is Amar?'

'Devastated,' said Akshay flatly. 'Is she really pregnant?'

Gayatri nodded, her face a mixture of worry and despair. 'I'll go up and talk to Amar.'

When she opened the door to Amar's flat, she saw him sitting on a couch, staring blankly into space. 'Why is she doing this to me?' he asked helplessly.

Gayatri's eyes filled with tears. 'I'm sorry, Amar, on her behalf,' she said. 'You know pregnancy makes a woman's hormones jump around a bit ... Maybe ...'

He dropped his head in his hands. Gayatri sat on a chair near him and put her hand on his shoulder. 'You have to be strong, Amar.'

Amar looked at her with tears in his eyes. 'Is she going to ... finish ... abort this ... our ...?' He shook his head. 'Please tell her not to.'

'Just give it some time, Amar, don't worry,' she said, tears now streaming from her eyes.

'I just can't believe this,' he said, still shaking his head.

Gayatri reached out and held his hand.

Akshay walked in a few moments later.

'I want to be alone for some time,' Amar said, wiping his tears. Seeing their worried expressions, he added with a weak smile, 'Don't worry, I'm not about to kill myself. I just want to be by myself.'

Gayatri stood up reluctantly. 'Okay, but only if you leave your door open,' she said.

19

'SHE'S STILL ASLEEP,' said Akshay, walking out to the balcony.

Gayatri was sitting on the ground, her back against the wall and her arms wrapped around her legs. She glanced at her phone. 'It's going to be nine. I thought I'd stay till she wakes up, but—'

'You have to stay, please. I can't handle these two alone,' said Akshay. 'Just call home and make some excuse.'

'I've done that. They know I'll be late.' She watched as Akshay pulled out a cigarette and reached for the lighter under the planter. 'I thought you rarely smoked?'

He lit the cigarette and inhaled deeply. 'One of those days,' he said with a weak smile. 'I'm going to get myself get a drink, I need one. Would you like something?'

Gayatri hesitated.

'Would you?' he asked again. 'Old Monk, or would you like a whisky?'

'Old Monk is fine, thanks.'

Akshay walked back inside. Gayatri looked up at the gulmohar tree that slanted towards the balcony, sage and wise. She remembered Nandini telling her about the tree, how she loved that it leaned into her kitchen upstairs. Akshay came back with their drinks and sat on the ground beside her. The next few minutes passed in silence as they slowly sipped from their glasses.

'How's work?' he asked after a while.

Gayatri looked at him and shook her head. She wasn't in the mood for small talk.

'We may as well talk of something while we wait,' he said.

She sighed. 'Our next issue is due to be published this week, so we're quite busy.'

'Are you planning to write that article on the Nigar Baba shrine?'

'I'm doing the research,' she said, taking a sip of the rum.

'It's a complicated issue.'

'It's not *that* complicated,' said Gayatri sharply. 'A shrine was destroyed for no good reason. A boy was burned.'

'You know,' he said after a few moments, 'I was once arguing a case for a small Hindu organization. They were supporting some men who were charged with trespassing and stealing two idols from the National Museum in Delhi. The men claimed that the idols were originally installed in their village by some warrior ancestors of their clan ... I think they were called Kelamdars or something. The idols were then seized by the British in a skirmish, and placed in this museum. Poor guys, they managed to escape from the museum, but got caught a day later.'

'So you're saying these people had the right to barge into a public museum and steal whatever artefacts they liked?'

'I didn't say that. What I'm saying is that when I spoke to them, I realized that the way they saw it, this was a truly righteous act. As courageous as that of any freedom fighter battling the British.' He paused. 'When I went to the jail to meet them, I was expecting thugs. What I saw was two intelligent, quiet men, giving me dates and cogent details. They genuinely believed that the idols' rightful place was in their village temple. I remember feeling stupid then, for prejudging them.'

Gayatri shook her head. 'But there is a constitution, and there are laws. Whatever justice they want, nothing can justify breaking the law.'

Akshay was quiet for a few seconds before he spoke. 'You're not going to like what I'm going to say, but sometimes I wonder at people like you. You're intelligent, educated and yet unable to recognize the biases that colour your world views. Where is the open-mindedness that any liberal worth their name should have? At least base your decisions on issues, not ideology.'

Gayatri started, 'But—'

He interrupted gently, 'Everything is not black and white, the real world is grey. Okay, tell me, have you or haven't you been upset by election results in India and the world over recently, with all these right-wing governments coming to power?'

Gayatri nodded slowly, wondering where he was going with his point.

'So, even though democracy is itself a liberal system, when the person elected doesn't quite fit your version of who should be in power, you are upset. You protest every move, even though these are people elected by democratic majorities, all within the system.'

She frowned. 'So we should sit back and let injustice rule, let the mobs go mad—as long as that is what the majority wants? Who will speak for the minority?'

'No, what I'm saying is that these elections show that there are millions of people with a vote who think differently from you, and even me. What good does it do to sit in our cocoons, passing judgement, acting like only one section of society knows what's good for everyone else? What makes you intellectually superior to them? Sure, speak up for minorities, fight for the rights of those who don't have a voice, but also recognize the impact your prejudices have on your views.'

She remained silent.

'I'm not saying that there should be riots and khoon kharaba, and if I could I would kill the fucker who vandalized your office and had the guts to touch you with my own bare hands. But there is a need to empathize, understand. Otherwise, even in all your self-righteous fury, you're just a stuck record without any hope of progress.'

Gayatri shook her head, her thoughts oscillating between feeling insulted by his words and puzzled at his intense anger at the thug. Just then, her phone buzzed. Akshay caught a glimpse of the caller's name. Vikram. 'Do want me to …?' he asked, gesturing towards the living room with his finger.

'No, no,' said Gayatri casually as she answered the phone. 'Hi.'

'Hey,' said Vikram. 'What about that coffee? Are you back—'

'No,' she said quickly. 'I'm still at Nandini's. This will take a while, I'm sorry.'

There was silence at the other end.

'Hello?' said Gayatri, uncomfortably.

'I'm still here,' said Vikram drily.

'I'm sorry, I'll explain when I see you. It was an emergency. Tomorrow?'

'Fine.'

'Bye—' Gayatri said even as the line went dead.

A few moments later, low voices sounded from the living room. Akshay peeped inside and came back. 'Amar is here, they're talking,' he whispered.

'Oh god,' said Gayatri, with a sigh. 'I hope they don't create another scene.'

They waited quietly for a while.

'You know,' said Gayatri softly, finishing her drink, 'we're definitely better off single.'

'Oh, I don't know,' said Akshay, looking at her.

She glanced at him sideways. 'Even after all this drama?'

'Maybe. It's a question of finding the right person. These two …
maybe they're just not right for each other.'

'Nandini is really immature,' said Gayatri shaking her head.

'Actually, I don't blame her so much.'

'Really?'

'Of course, I want them to stay together,' he continued softly. 'But
if they are fighting like this so early in the marriage, is it worth being
together and having a baby? The child will be miserable. The parents
will have affairs. It can get really shitty.' He took a large sip of his drink.
'You know, I was hurt pretty badly by someone a long time ago.'

Gayatri shook her head. 'I think all that whisky is making you tell
me things you'll regret tomorrow.'

'No,' he said slowly, staring blankly at his glass. 'Maybe it'll give me
the courage to say the things I regret not saying.'

Gayatri looked at her feet nervously, remembering their conversation
earlier that evening.

He smiled weakly at her. 'Don't look so scared.'

She smiled back, despite her nervousness. 'You're quite high.'

'Not enough.' He leaned his head against the wall and looked up at
the sky. A few stars were visible, along with a half moon.

'Don't worry so much about these two,' Gayatri said, trying to
sound optimistic. 'I think with the baby coming—'

'It's not just them, you know,' he said. 'I had this massive … I don't
know what to call it … fight, I guess … with my father.' He drained the
last of his whisky and set the glass down next to him.

'What happened?'

'Lots of stuff, old things, new things. It all just came out in one go.'

Gayatri didn't know what to say. 'You should try to forget the past,
especially where your parents are concerned. They can never really
mean badly—' she said, not entirely believing her own words.

'Oh, you'll be surprised,' he interrupted, looking at her steadily. 'My dad,' he paused before continuing, 'started having an affair with someone I ... I was in love with. And he knew.'

Gayatri stared at him, unsure how to react.

'Please don't say anything. I probably shouldn't have said anything to you.'

She looked at the ground, embarrassed.

'Sorry,' he said. 'It's just ... I had that fight with Dad, and now these two...' He shook his head. 'And I think I've been drinking too quickly.'

Gayatri glanced at him. His hand rested on his leg as he stared into the semi-darkness. Her eyes softened as she placed her hand on his. Their fingers intertwined, naturally, as if they had done so a hundred times before. Akshay looked at their joined hands, for a couple of seconds then turned towards her. Gayatri leaned in slightly. He raised his hand to touch her cheek gently with his fingers.

The sound of the door opening drew them apart. Gayatri blinked awkwardly as Amar stepped into the balcony.

'Oh, Gayatri Didi, you're still here?' he said, peering at them. He looked tired. 'Nandini's gone up, for now. She's just so exhausted ... maybe it's also the pregnancy.'

Gayatri scrambled up. 'Oh, fine, let her rest. I'll speak to her tomorrow.'

'Thanks,' said Amar. 'Sorry for dragging you into this.'

Gayatri squeezed his arm and made her way downstairs to her car. Akshay went with her, and despite her protests, insisted on following her home given how late it was.

Their cars moved swiftly on the empty roads. As she drove, she was conscious of Akshay's car behind her, his headlights visible each time she looked into her rear-view mirror. Her head was too full of worry for Nandini again to dwell on what had happened—or not happened—between Akshay and her. She parked outside the gate and waved a quick goodbye, willing him to turn around and leave, but he got out of the car and waited while she called for the watchman. She could sense his eyes on her, and felt her face and neck grow warm.

The watchman unlocked the gate and she went inside quickly, saying, 'Thank you, Akshay, good night.' Closing the gate without waiting for a reply, she almost ran into the house, exhaling in tired relief once she was inside.

But the feeling that something between them had changed that night lingered.

Akshay drove back slowly. He remembered how happy his whole family had been at Amar's wedding. How had things come to this, he wondered, thinking of Amar and Nandini and his father and Neelam. He turned on the radio and flicked through a few stations, before settling on a station playing old Hindi songs.

The notes of Hemant Kumar's '*Jaane voh kaise log the*' filled the car.

Jaane voh kaise log the jinke / Pyaar ko pyaar mila
Humnein toh jab kaliyan maangi / Kaanton ka haar mila

As the song played, he remembered having Gayatri's hand in his, that near-moment on the balcony. He had forgotten what it felt like to hold a woman's hand for the first time: light head, somersaulting insides. The song was still playing when he emerged from his reverie.

Gham se ab ghabraana kaisa / Gham sau baar mila

He reached home but stayed in the car till the song finished, his eyes closed, his heart heavy.

The next afternoon, Gayatri and Farah were sitting in their usual spots in the veranda, eating lunch.

'So, she's still at her in-laws' house?' Farah asked, concerned. Gayatri had just finished telling her about Nandini.

Gayatri nodded. 'I spoke to her this morning. She sounded calm. She said she's thinking things through.'

'Will you try and see her today?'

'You know, last night I thought I would be rushing to her place this morning, but after speaking to her, I'm thinking I should let her be for a bit.'

'Are you sure? What about your parents, do they know?'

'They have no clue. They had to rush to Bombay this morning. My Dad's masi passed away.' She ate a spoonful of her dahi. 'Chhoti actually sounded better. Maybe she's sorting things out with Amar. I don't think I should interfere.' She paused. 'I hope Akshay's also left them alone.'

'Was he there yesterday?'

Gayatri nodded. 'Thank god he was, actually. I don't think I could have managed the situation on my own.' She suddenly remembered their conversation on his balcony, and that stupid moment when she took his hand—

'Gayatri, why are you turning red?' asked Farah.

Gayatri swallowed and shook her head. 'Nothing!' She paused. 'I … It's just … This Akshay is also crazy. Faru, I think he … you know … he's trying to tell me … I don't know …'

'It's quite obvious to me, Gayatri,' said Farah with a small smile.

'Don't smile like that, Faru.' Gayatri rolled her eyes. 'I think he's mad, but I think he … Likes? Has feelings? I don't know—what's the word at this age?' She stopped, and then continued, 'And I can't understand why. I thought I was the sort of girl he looked down upon, disliked even.'

'Nonsense!' said Farah. 'Anyway, will you tell Vikram now?'

'What?'

'About Akshay.'

'There's nothing to tell. It's not like anything can happen between us.'

Farah looked at Gayatri. 'Are you sure?'

'He's still the same guy who works for people like that bloody Sadhu, who literally destroyed our office.' His words about wanting to kill that goonda crossed her mind.

'He's also the same guy who's gone out of his way to help us in our mess with Sadhuji, all for your sake,' Farah pointed out. 'Anyway, you shouldn't let Vikram think you're going to marry him—just because you don't want to be rude.'

Gayatri played with the rajma chawal on her plate with her fork and nodded. 'I'm going to talk to him. I'm just dreading the conversation.'

'And what about Akshay?'

'What about him?' asked Gayatri, looking up at Farah sharply. 'Even if there was anything between us, which there is not,' she added emphatically, 'our siblings are on the verge of a divorce, and he's thinking we ... He's mad. He needs help. This is not some Bollywood movie, where we will end up together. It's not possible.'

'You should think about this a bit more, instead of ignoring your feelings,' said Farah calmly. 'You don't have to decide now, but don't push him away just because of other people.' She paused and added disapprovingly, 'And please don't keep Vikram hanging just because you think it will keep Akshay away.'

Not too far away, in a private flat on Prithviraj Road that few people knew about, Mr Grewal waited for an audience with Sadhuji. He had been waiting for some time when Sadhuji walked into the plushly furnished room, looking fresh in a long white kurta. Anil Bhargav entered after him, carrying a black bag.

Sadhuji looked at his visitor expectantly. Grewal rose with an imperceptible sigh and bent towards Sadhuji's feet. This charlatan will not tire of his power games despite my age, he thought.

'They've asked for a commitment of seventy-five crore,' Grewal began immediately.

'Who "they"?'

'Chauhan,' said Grewal, knowing well that Sadhuji would have been informed of this already.

Sadhuji stroked his beard. 'Hmm. And you will have this done through Vikram?'

Grewal nodded. 'He will arrange fifty. I spoke with him on the phone. He's met with Cheema too.'

'Good.' Turning to Bhargav, Sadhuji said, 'Give him the list of people then, that should cover the balance.'

Bhargav pushed a dirty pink file towards Grewal with the names and bank details of Sadhuji's wealthy devotees. Now that's worth the backaches I get touching his feet, Grewal thought as he leafed through it. He closed the file and said, 'Thank you, Sadhuji. This should work.'

'And your lady? Have you done the needful?' asked Sadhuji.

Grewal glanced at Bhargav. Sadhuji had never spoken of Neelam in front of anyone else.

'It will be taken care of,' he said.

'She should leave as soon as possible. These are the loose ends that one tends to trip on. Aaj kal internet par kuch bhi chhap jaata hai.'

Grewal nodded, bristling with anger.

20

The next morning at a quarter past nine, Akshay made his way up to Amar's flat and rang the doorbell. Nandini came to the door after a few moments. She looked pale and drawn.

'Is Amar at home?' he asked, walking in.

She shook her head. 'He's left for work.'

'How are you?'

'Fine.'

'Do you need anything? Medicines or … I don't know … Do you need to see a doctor?'

Nandini smiled wanly. 'Thanks, Bhaiya. I'm okay. I'm planning to go see a doctor today.'

He put his hand on her head awkwardly, said, 'Take care,' and left.

He dialled Amar on his phone as he walked down. Amar told him he had an urgent meeting in the office and that he would be back in a few hours to check on Nandini. He warned Akshay not to tell their parents about the pregnancy, Nandini had made him promise to do so only when she was ready.

After his conversation with Amar, Akshay messaged Gayatri. 'Have you spoken to Nandini?' He stopped by his flat to pick up some files, and then went directly down to the office.

As he switched on his computer, his phone buzzed with a reply from Gayatri. 'Not today. Why?'

He clicked his tongue in irritation and called her. 'You haven't even checked on her?' he asked, when she answered.

'I thought I would leave them be for a day or two, let them sort things out together. She sounded calm when I spoke to her yesterday, she said she's discussing things with Amar. I didn't want to interfere.'

'Gayatri, please call her or come over. I just saw her and she's not looking well.'

'Where's Amar?'

'He's not here. He had some meeting.'

Gayatri sighed. 'I'll leave now.'

Three hours later, Gayatri and Nandini were on their way back to Devaki Sadan after visiting a doctor's clinic. Nandini had insisted on going to someone other than their usual gynaecologist. 'I hate her,' she had said.

Gayatri glanced at Nandini as she steered the car to the left. 'Aren't you even a little happy?'

Nandini was staring blankly out of the window. She shook her head.

'The doctor did say that you may feel low and irritable, it's a by-product of being pregnant.'

Nandini remained silent.

After a few minutes, Gayatri asked, 'Do you want to eat something?'

Nandini shook her head.

'Say something Nandini, don't be quiet like this.'

'There's nothing to say, Didi. I told you how I feel the other day. Things haven't changed.' She turned on the radio in the car.

'Achha, listen,' Gayatri said, turning the knob to lower the volume, 'why don't you come home for a few days? It'll give you some space to sort yourself out.'

Nandini nodded. 'I will.'

'Do you want to come today?'

'No,' said Nandini firmly. 'Maybe after Amar's dad's birthday on Sunday. It's a big party, so I've got to be here.' She paused. 'I believe your Vikram is also invited.'

Gayatri's thoughts drifted to her dinner with Vikram the previous night. He had just refused to take her seriously, no matter how much she tried to explain that she didn't think things were working for them. One thing he had said had stayed with her though: Vikram told her that Mr Grewal was very upset with Akshay as his son had made it clear that he didn't want to help on Sadhuji's matters any more.

She turned into Devaki Sadan and parked the car. Getting out of the car, she walked around to the other side and held the door open for Nandini.

'I'm not disabled, you know, Didi. I can get out of a car on my own,' Nandini snapped.

Gayatri willed herself not to react. When she got into her car to leave, she texted Akshay saying she had taken Nandini to the doctor.

He replied immediately. 'Okay, good. How is she feeling?'

'From the way she's been biting my head off all day, I'd say fine, but otherwise depressed and low.'

'Okay. Don't react. Amar should be home soon. I'm in chambers.'

'I didn't ask where you were,' she replied quickly. Akshay read the message before she had time to delete it. Dammit, she thought as she stared at the screen, Nandini's irritability is rubbing off on me.

No response.

'I'm leaving,' she typed.

'Fine.'

'Will you check on them once you're back and call me?'

'Fine.'

She drove away, frowning at his curt responses.

Late that night, Gayatri saw a message from Akshay.

She opened it, and regretted doing so immediately. She had been avoiding reading her messages, so that Vikram wouldn't know she had checked them. He had been messaging her all evening.

'Hi. I checked on them. Seem okay.'

'Thanks,' she typed, and paused before pressing on send. She added, 'You're back home?'

In his room across town, Akshay smiled and frowned at the same time as he read her message. 'Yes. Why?' he typed.

'Just wanted to ask whether you saw them in person. Did you see Nandini?'

'No, she was asleep. Saw Amar.'

When she didn't reply, he sent another message. 'Don't worry, Gayatri. Let them take their time. We can't sort it out for them.'

Gayatri read his message, and nodded. 'That's true. Thanks. See you soon.'

'How soon?'

A sudden smile broke out on her face when she saw his message. 'Goodnight,' she replied.

'Goodnight, Gayatri,' he typed, also smiling.

The next day passed uneventfully, or so it seemed.

Nandini wasn't home when Gayatri called her in the morning. She told Gayatri she had decided to go to office.

Amar was in Gurgaon in client meetings all day.

Gayatri spent her day checking proofs for the journal from the printers, and hoping that Nandini was reconciling herself to having the baby and being with Amar. She had decided she would not pressure Nandini to tell their parents about the pregnancy until they were back from Bombay.

Akshay distracted himself from his falling-out with his father by burying himself in work.

Vikram spent the day with Akhil, guiding him with ease through meetings in central Delhi with the government's top brass. He checked his phone periodically for messages from Gayatri, but there was nothing beyond one about being busy with work.

The following morning, there was a knock on Akshay's office door. 'Yes,' he called out distractedly.

A junior lawyer in the office peeped in and said, 'Sorry to disturb you, sir, just wanted to say we are having a farewell lunch today for Neelam ma'am.'

'Neelam?'

'Uh … yes, sir. Actually—'

'Ah, yeah, yeah, of course,' Akshay said, masking his surprise. 'I won't be able to come. I have a meeting.'

Once the junior closed the door, Akshay stood up and started to pace around his office. So his father had fired her. Was this because of Akshay's warning? No, it had to be something else. He was too egoistic to heed any advice from him. He was probably getting rid of her in anticipation of his political debut.

Once again, his father wanted something badly, and didn't care who he ruined to get it.

Amar helped Nandini sit up in bed. 'We are going to the doctor now,' he said firmly.

'No, no,' she protested weakly.

'Baby, look at you. You've been so unwell all night.'

'I'm just feeling sick,' she said, willing herself to sound strong.

'I can't understand why you didn't call me yesterday if you were so sick. You really shouldn't have gone to office,' he said, touching her cheek.

'I didn't want to disturb you. And anyway, I know myself, na, I'm okay.'

'But—'

'Amar, listen, please,' interrupted Nandini, pushing his hand away. 'I'm just feeling sick. When I went to the doc with Didi, she said this would happen. Please don't panic.'

'But you've been going to the loo so often—'

Nandini looked at him angrily. 'Please stop this! Go to work if you can't help, but don't sit on my head like this.'

'Okay, okay, sorry,' said Amar. 'Achha, listen, I thought we could tell Mom and Dad today.'

'No,' said Nandini, sharply.

'Why?'

'Let tomorrow's event get over, Amar. A couple of days won't matter.'

'But why? They'll be thrilled.'

'I know, but I'm not feeling well today. Let's just get past tomorrow, and then we'll tell them.' She paused. 'I haven't even told my own parents.'

Amar sighed. 'Okay, whatever you want.' He leaned in to give her a kiss on her cheek.

Nandini stopped him with a hand on his shoulder. 'On your way out can you tell Shanti to bring me a piece of toast please?'

'I'm not going to office.'

'Don't be silly,' said Nandini. 'Please go, I'll call you if I need you.'

'No.'

'Please, Amar, just go.'

'But I—'

'Just go, please. Go get ready.'

He stood up and sighed. 'I can't understand you at all sometimes,' he said, walking to the bathroom.

The moment Amar locked the door, Nandini got out of bed and checked whether the bedsheet beneath her was stained. Since the abortion the previous day, there had been so much blood and pain—but all that, she could bear. What she couldn't do any more was keep up the charade of this marriage when she was so desperately unhappy.

Just a couple more days, she told herself, taking a deep breath.

Later that afternoon, Akshay returned from court to find the office almost empty. He remembered everyone had gone out for Neelam's farewell. Before long, he heard sounds of people trooping back. He tried to concentrate on his work, but couldn't. After another fifteen minutes, he walked with halting steps to Neelam's door, and knocked.

'Yes,' she answered from inside.

He entered.

Neelam looked up from the files in her hand. She frowned in confusion, wondering if he had mistaken her room for someone else's. 'I haven't left yet,' she said, regaining her composure and placing the files on the desk.

'I know.'

'What do you want?'

Someone knocked on the open door behind Akshay. 'Yes, Kritharth?' said Neelam, looking past Akshay.

'Ma'am, sorry, but Mr Khosla is on the line.'

'I'll call him back.'

Kritharth nodded, closing the door.

Akshay said, 'Can we speak if you're free?'

She was silent for a few moments. Then, she shrugged. 'Okay.'

'Why are you leaving?'

'Your father asked me to.'

'Where will you go?'

'He's bought a place for me near Shimla.' She paused, and continued softly, 'He says the view of the deodars is lovely.'

Akshay opened his mouth, but said nothing.

'Anyway, what do you need?' she asked with a small, tight smile. 'This is hardly the place to scream and shout at me for the last time.'

'No, it's not that. I wanted to … Actually I want to … say goodbye.'

Neelam looked at him disdainfully. 'What do you want me to do with that?'

'Nothing, I just—'

'Is this really all you wanted to say? Or did you want to gloat over my suffering? I don't mind giving you that pleasure, you know. I owe you that.'

'No, Neelam, I've not come here for that.'

'You must have enjoyed the last few times I tried to talk to you, and you had the power to push me away.'

Akshay shook his head. 'No, I don't know if I'll see you again, and … and a part of me wants closure.'

'I did what I had to, Akshay,' she said tiredly. 'I'm not proud of how I made you feel, but I'm not ashamed either. I had my own struggles which you would not have understood at that age, at that stage of your life.'

Akshay nodded. 'I'm not going to lie,' he said slowly. 'You know what it did to me when you … left.' He swallowed as he tried not to think of his father. 'But I also know that I was not thinking of you then, Neelam, it was all about me.' He paused. 'I never thought I'd say it, but maybe I can imagine what you went through, and the choices you had to make.'

She looked away. 'You're wrong, Akshay,' she said. 'There was no choice. He was powerful, he had what I needed. The money, the job, the security, the assurance of freedom from my husband. It was the only practical thing to do. What you and I had … considering the animal I was married to … being with you was …' She took a deep breath. 'Maybe the happiest I've been.'

He stayed silent.

'But I knew what I needed to survive,' she continued. 'And no, it wasn't a brave decision. But I don't care. I didn't have the courage or energy to fight one more battle with the world, to be with someone barely out of college. I decided that the best thing to do was to give your father what he wanted.'

Akshay dropped his gaze.

'I'm sorry, Akshay.'

He looked at her again. 'If it was anyone else—'

'I know,' she said. 'But you should also know that I don't regret my decision. It was the right thing to do—perhaps the only thing to do. And your father has kept me happy for so many years.' She paused. 'Until now. It was after he told me I had to leave for Mashobra, that I tried to speak to you those few times. But I really don't know what I was trying … one last desperate attempt perhaps.'

Akshay was taken aback by the hatred that had crept into her voice suddenly. It was so unlike the Neelam he knew. It hit him how these years had changed her, ravaged her even.

She looked at him and her gaze softened. 'Anyway, you didn't feel like this a few weeks ago,' she said.

'No,' he said, nodding. 'I didn't.'

'What's changed?'

'I don't know, I feel …' he paused, 'distanced from what happened between us, reconciled even, in a way that I didn't before. You've started to seem human to me.'

'That's good. I'm happy for you.' She looked around the cramped space and then raised her eyes to his. 'It's not easy, you know, to be the bad one, so clearly the one at fault.' She lifted her slim index finger to dab the corner of her eye. 'And just see where I've ended up.'

He opened his mouth to say something, but she interrupted him. 'Don't. I'm fine, and maybe like you, I've accepted that nothing is ever purely good or purely bad. My husband, you, your father, you all brought some good and some bad into my life, just like I did to yours.'

He nodded.

'And your father … Don't be too hard—'

'Leave him out of this,' he said quickly.

'What do you mean?'

He gazed at her intently. 'Neelam, once, there was something between us that had nothing to do with him. It was for the sake of that time in our lives that I came to speak to you, keeping him and everything else aside.'

She stared at the table for a few seconds and then nodded as she looked up at him.

'If there's anything—' he began.

'There isn't,' she said softly, shaking her head. 'Thank you, Akshay.'

'But—'

'No, Akshay,' she said firmly, 'there's nothing.'

21

VIKRAM LEFT MR Grewal's cabin after a long meeting and settled down in the conference room. Unzipping his bag, he rummaged in it, and then cursed as he realized he didn't have the charger for his laptop. He poked his head out of the room and looked down the corridor. Akshay's door was ajar.

Walking up to the door, he knocked and said, 'Hey, Akshay, sorry to bug you, but do you have a charger for a MacBook Air by any chance?'

Akshay looked up. He had noticed Vikram around the office the last few days. He nodded. 'Yes, upstairs in my flat. Do you need it now?'

'Actually, yes, my computer is completely out of charge,' said Vikram apologetically. 'If someone else has one—'

'Probably not. I'll get mine,' said Akshay, standing up.

'Thanks so much.' Vikram followed him out.

Akshay didn't quite know how to tell him to stay in the office without being rude. They walked up to the flat, and Akshay went to his room to get the charger. When he returned, Vikram was standing by the living room window.

'This house is massive,' he said, looking outside. He pulled out a packet of cigarettes. 'Do you mind if I have a smoke? Downstairs, one has to stand on the road ... Unless you're in a rush?'

Akshay shrugged. 'Sure.' He opened the door to the balcony and stepped out.

Vikram leaned against the wall and held out the packet to Akshay, who took a cigarette. Lighting his own, Vikram said, 'You know, there was a time I couldn't afford cigarettes. No offence, but back when I was in college, I hated guys like you. I came from Ghaziabad, in my shitty clothes, carrying a shitty bag.' He exhaled through his nose and mouth. 'And you guys came in your dad's cars and with your cool friends from all the cool schools, speaking in an English so fast that it seemed like a completely different language from the English I knew.'

Akshay exhaled smoke and leaned against the parapet. 'I can imagine that. Though I didn't have a car. I took the bus. And I worked every day in my dad's office after college.' He shrugged. 'Anyway, everyone has a perception of themselves that suits them. Including me.'

Vikram nodded. 'You know, I remember, one time when I was in college I saw some people drag a guy out of a huge white car and start to beat him up. I think it was a Merc.' He paused to exhale. 'I didn't know why he was being beaten. But I was so frustrated with these rich kids and their possessions that I joined the mob. Got in a few solid kicks. It felt so good.'

Akshay looked at Vikram quietly and stubbed out his cigarette.

'Anyway, that was then,' said Vikram. 'Now, I hire idiots like those rich kids. And the girls I've dated wouldn't look twice at those losers.'

Akshay thought of Gayatri. 'What's your plan generally, here in India?' he asked. 'Do you intend to go back to London?'

Vikram shook his head. 'If all goes well, I won't have to go back.'

'Workwise or ...?'

Vikram smiled. 'Work and pleasure. Let's see how things go.'

'Ah.' Akshay nodded.

Vikram glanced down at the garden where several men were perched atop ladders and bamboo sticks, setting up a shamiana for the evening's party. 'I have to say, I really admire your dad. He's built such a successful practice, so much wealth, all by himself.'

Akshay remained silent.

'And now,' continued Vikram, 'the sky is the limit. In politics, he can make as much as he wants.' He paused. 'As long as he rids himself of all liabilities.' He gave Akshay a meaningful look. Bhargav had discussed Sadhuji's worries about Neelam with Vikram. 'Scandals, affairs, that kind of thing. You know how messy politics can be.'

Akshay stiffened, wondering how it was that someone introduced to them so recently was brazenly talking of his dad's relationship with Neelam.

'Anyway,' said Vikram, enjoying Akshay's discomfort, 'why don't you come along for some of these meetings with Sadhuji? We could use your help—'

'Shall we head downstairs?' asked Akshay in clipped tones. 'I have a call in five minutes.'

The fading evening light lent an emerald-like sheen to the large, dressed-up lawns of Devaki Sadan. Round tables with black-and-white tablecloths dotted the green grass, a vase of white flowers placed at the centre of each one. Chairs covered in white satin, with thick black sashes tied around the back, surrounded the tables. The starkness of the black-and-white décor and waiters' uniforms was softened by bright yellow fairy lights that were strung on the bushes along the edge of the lawn, and on the great big gulmohar tree. Angeethis were placed every few feet to allow guests to stay warm as they chatted. The Grewals had pulled out all stops for this event.

Akshay stood in a corner of the garden with an acquaintance from court. He was dressed in a black kurta and slim white pyjamas. Guests were starting to troop in; waiters weaved in and out of the crowd, balancing trays of chicken tikka, skewered prawns, spring rolls and aloo cutlets.

Akshay saw his mother gesturing to him.

'Beta,' she said as he walked over, 'did you check the number of bottles at the bar?'

'Yes, Ma. I've got the numbers written down.'

'Okay, I've sent Mohan for five more single malts. Papa said to serve it only to the people who ask for it, not to display it at the bar.'

Akshay nodded.

'Now go and stand with your father,' she said, gesturing with her chin towards a group of people surrounding Mr Grewal.

'He's with his people. I have nothing to do there,' said Akshay.

'Then go and stand at the entrance.'

'He wouldn't want me there, Ma.'

'You shouldn't talk like this.'

Akshay gave her an apologetic look. 'I'm here if you need me to do anything.'

She sighed. 'Achha, where are Amar and Nandini? I feel as if I haven't seen them for days.'

'They're here somewhere. I thought I saw them ... '—he scanned the crowd—'there they are, talking to Poonam Aunty.'

'Okay, good.'

'Hi, Rupi!' A lady tapped Mrs Grewal's shoulder and Akshay took the opportunity to slip away.

At half past eight, Gayatri and her parents entered Devaki Sadan. Gayatri was dressed in a black salwar–kameez with small silver sequins all over, a beige shawl draped over one shoulder. Mrs Grewal greeted them and led them towards her husband. Gyan Singh Grewal graciously offered Ashok a drink, before he was pulled away by another guest. Ashok, Nina and Gayatri settled down at a table in a corner of the lawn. Surrounded mostly by lawyers and politicians, they felt slightly out of place.

'Can you see Nandini anywhere?' asked Nina.

Gayatri looked around, then shook her head. 'No. There are so many people here, she must be busy.' Nandini had been a little distant with her for the past couple of days.

A few minutes later, Nandini arrived at their table herself and hugged her parents, holding them tighter than usual. She kissed Gayatri, but avoided catching her eye. Ashok shifted one seat down so that Nandini could sit between him and Nina.

Amar, who had been right behind Nandini, touched their feet and sat next to Gayatri. She smiled at him, trying to gauge how he was feeling. He seemed calm and normal, though a little less chirpy than usual. He started to talk to her about work, as if the drama of the previous few days had been forgotten. Maybe this is how things are, she thought, continuing the conversation mechanically, relationships come back from the brink, and everyone behaves like nothing happened.

After a few minutes, a man dressed in a dark-blue safari suit came up and whispered a few words to Amar. He nodded, and looked at Nandini. 'Come, Nandini,' he said. 'Papa is calling us to meet Sadhuji.'

Gayatri looked around at the crowd. It had occurred to her, on the way, that Sadhuji would be here today. There was no way she was going anywhere near him.

'You also come, no, Mom, Dad,' said Amar, looking at Mr and Mrs Mehra. Ashok and Nina nodded politely and stood up. Amar turned to Gayatri and offered her his hand to stand up. 'Didi?'

'No, Amar, you all go, I'm fine.'

'Gayatri,' said Ashok. 'Come with us.'

Unable to come up with an excuse, she stood up reluctantly and walked with her family towards Sadhuji. As they drew closer, she caught a glimpse of his face, a smug smile plastered across it. She recalled the mess that his goons had created at her office, and imagined him coolly directing many such operations, murders even, all with that smile on. She tried to slow down, but Mr Grewal and her father were behind her, shepherding her towards Sadhuji. Her stomach sank further with each step.

Suddenly, she felt a hand touch her arm. It was Akshay. 'Gayatri, can you come with me, please? There's someone looking for you.' She looked at him in surprise as he pulled her away.

'Come,' he said, guiding her to a tall table on the other side of the lawn. 'I saw you being taken towards Sadhuji.'

'It's just the whole situation … that …'

'I know,' he said.

She nodded, trying to breathe through her relief at not having to encounter Sadhuji, and also processing the fact that Akshay had sensed her discomfort from some distant corner of the garden.

Akshay glanced at her. She was looking exceedingly pretty in her simple black salwar–kameez. Her long earrings were tangled in her hair as usual.

Gayatri could sense his gaze on her. She looked away, to where her parents were now standing with Mr Grewal and Sadhuji.

A waiter came by with drinks on a tray. Akshay told him to pour them two rum-and-Cokes.

'No,' Gayatri protested.

'Why?'

She shook her head, but then accepted the drink poured by the waiter. After a few seconds' silence, she said, looking around, 'This is a big party.'

'The big ones are yet to come,' he said, looking towards the entrance. 'Ah, they've started. See …? Devender Kumar.'

'The CM?'

He nodded. 'They will all come for fifteen minutes each, maybe stay for the grand cake-cutting.'

She nodded. 'Listen, Akshay, I'll be okay now. You should go be with your father.'

'I'd rather be here,' he said calmly.

She stared down at the table, not sure what to say. She felt his eyes on her again.

'Gayatri?' he said softly.

She raised her eyes to his, but he didn't say anything. Serious and earnest, he looked very handsome in the evening light.

He sighed and said, 'There's no point in pretending. I know that you know already.'

Gayatri's cheeks felt warm despite the chill in the air.

'And,' he continued slowly, 'I want to tell you that irrespective of what's happening between you and Vikram'—he held her gaze steadily—'that I am … I have … fallen in love with you.' Even though she had known what he was going to say, her cheeks burned when she heard his words, her stomach felt light. She looked away.

He continued with an embarrassed smile, 'I can't remember being this nervous in a while.' He swallowed. 'Look, I know the mess our families are in, with Nandini and Amar, and I know that this is very awkward for you. Don't say anything now—'

She turned to him abruptly. 'Then why are you saying all this now?'

He said simply, 'I can't help it.'

'Nothing can happen between us, Akshay.' She lowered her gaze once again.

'Because of Vikram?' he asked, taking a step closer to her.

Gayatri could smell his cologne. 'Because I don't—' She broke off as she looked up at his face.

They were silent for a few seconds.

'Do you really not?' he asked softly.

Her eyes flickered for a second as they focused on something behind him and she took a step back. Akshay turned around and saw Vikram approaching them.

'Hi,' said Vikram to Gayatri, leaning in for an awkward hug. He shook Akshay's hand. 'Why do you guys look so morose?' he asked cheerfully, draping his arm casually around Gayatri's shoulder.

Akshay gathered himself and smiled at him.

'We were just … uh … talking about work,' said Gayatri, moving to pick up her glass and shrugging off Vikram's arm

Vikram shook his head and looked at Akshay. 'I wish she'd talk to me about work. It seems like I don't know anything about her. But she has told me how you helped her through that bit of muck she got herself into. She gets into a lot of trouble considering she's like an academic, no?'

Gayatri shuffled awkwardly, but Vikram continued, oblivious, 'Akshay, where's Grewalji?'

Akshay pointed to the crowd near Sadhuji. 'I think he's there.'

'Is that Ravi Kapadia?' asked Vikram, squinting.

'I think so,' said Akshay. 'Anyway, I'll leave you two to it, I'd better go see … uh … see to the … food.' He walked off.

'Come, let's go that side,' Vikram said.

Her eyes still on Akshay's retreating figure, she said, 'No.'

He glanced at his phone. 'Why can't you come with me and meet a few people? As it is, I've been texting you and—'

'Look, Vikram, I don't want to. And anyway, I don't have to go anywhere with you and do anything. I've already tried to be clear with you, but you refuse to listen. This has been over for a while.' Gayatri regretted the way the words left her mouth, but didn't say anything to Vikram to assuage their impact. Her mind was too cluttered with her own feelings for her to be sensitive to Vikram's.

He looked at her angrily. 'I really don't know what the hell is wrong with you. Anyway, I have enough work to do here, and no time to waste running after you. Fuck this good-girl shit!' He walked away.

Gayatri closed her eyes and tried to compose herself.

A few minutes later, Gayatri spotted her parents eating their dinner. As she walked towards them, she caught a glimpse of Akshay speaking to someone. He seemed normal, not ruffled in the least.

'Why is Vikram here?' her mother whispered as Gayatri sat down next to her.

'I don't know ... He's started some work with Gyan Uncle.'

'What work?'

Gayatri shrugged irritably. 'How do I know?'

'So you two ... you're not ...'

'Ufff, Ma, no, there's nothing any more, it's off.'

Nina nodded in satisfaction. 'You've told him?'

'Yes,' Gayatri replied flatly.

'Achha, earlier, when we were going to meet Sadhuji, where did you disappear with Akshay?'

'Why are you asking me like that?' said Gayatri quickly, and a shade defensively. 'He wanted to introduce some colleague of his who ... uh ... wants to do history.' She looked away, her eyes scanning the crowd for Akshay. There he was, standing with Mrs Grewal. His eye caught hers across the distance, and she turned away, hurriedly and guiltily.

What had he said? She tried to remember his exact words. *I've fallen in love with you.*

'Why is your face going red?' asked Nina.

'Huh?' said Gayatri. 'Nothing.'

Nina looked at her carefully. 'You're feeling okay, na?'

'Of course, Ma. I was just standing near an angeethi.'

'Anyway, Gayatri, listen, Chhoti is not looking okay to me. Has she spoken to you? Is something bothering her?'

'I don't know,' said Gayatri. She wished Nandini would just tell their mother about the pregnancy so she didn't have to lie. She glanced at her parents' plates impatiently, willing them to eat faster so they could leave.

A tap on a mic, followed by a low 'hello, hello' interrupted the din of conversation just then. About half of the guests turned towards the sound, while the remaining continued their conversations.

'Ladies and gentlemen,' said a voice. 'Please.' The crowd quieted down further.

Gayatri and her mother craned their necks to get a look at the owner of the voice. 'It's Rakesh Purohit,' said Nina. 'He comes on those TV debates for BSD.'

The voice continued, 'Please join us in wishing a very happy sixty-fifth birthday to Grewalji.' A round of applause broke out in the crowd. 'There are many distinguished leaders among us. Devenderji, Harbansji, Priyaji, and of course, Sadhuji,' he finished, folding his hands and bowing slightly towards Sadhuji. Nodding benevolently, Sadhuji held up a hand in a symbol of blessing. Purohit finished, 'Please join the BSD family and the rest of Grewalji's family to cut the cake, and wish him a successful year.'

Rupi Grewal and Amar took their places next to Mr Grewal, who sliced into the giant cake while the crowd applauded. Gayatri spotted Akshay standing at the edge of the crowd around his father, making no attempt to move closer. Various people fed, and were fed, cake. Soon, the VIP politicians started to leave with their muscular PSOs trailing behind them, their safari suits doing nothing to conceal the obvious bulge of their guns underneath.

Gayatri fidgeted impatiently until her parents finished their food and were ready to leave. She followed them to the corner of the lawn where the Grewal family was sitting at a table, eating dinner. She noticed that Akshay wasn't with them.

Rupi Grewal stood up graciously. 'Ashok, Nina, come, sit with us'.

'No, no, Rupiji, we've already eaten,' said Nina, smiling politely. 'Just came to say goodbye, and thank you.'

Ashok nodded in agreement. 'Yes, we should make a move,' he said formally.

'No, I insist, please sit with us,' said Rupi firmly. 'At least have a cup of tea or coffee.' She waved them over to the two empty chairs at the table. Gayatri stood awkwardly behind Nandini as two waiters pulled out the chairs for her parents. One of the waiters came up to her and gestured to the next table, just a few feet away where a few people were sitting, engrossed in food and conversation. She followed him, wishing the evening would come to an end.

As she neared the table, she realized Akshay was sitting there with a few other people she did not recognize. She did not look at him as she sat in the only vacant chair next to him, and pulled out her phone to appear busy. Akshay acknowledged her with a smile, and continued to eat. How can he act so normal, as if nothing out of the ordinary has happened, she wondered.

Her thoughts were interrupted by a male voice. 'You are the girl who came to the Ashram, isn't it? From that history journal.'

Gayatri looked up. It was the man seated across from her.

Akshay wiped his mouth and spoke. 'Uh, Gayatri, this is Bhargavji, secretary of the SSP.'

'Akshay had spoken to me that time when you needed help. You are Nandini's sister, eh?'

She nodded coldly. Her skin crawled at the thought that she was sitting at the same table as the people responsible for the vandalism at her office, for that frightening encounter.

'I hope things are clearer now, with Kanthanji,' Anil Bhargav said as he scooped up some dal with a piece of roti.

Gayatri remained silent. She glanced towards the next table where Sadhuji was sitting. Kartar Singh Doljat, not Sadhuji. Just a guy from some village in Punjab, she reminded herself.

'I hope you understand the situation better now, and are more open to others' voices,' Bhargav continued. 'This liberal, Marxist, one-sided view of history has to be corrected. We are looking for historians actually, to help us educate others.'

Akshay noticed Gayatri flinch and quickly said, 'Bhargavji, Gayatri is set where she is, and she is—'

'Actually,' interrupted Gayatri angrily, 'let me tell—'

Akshay placed his hand lightly on hers under the table. 'No,' he whispered softly.

She clenched her jaw.

'But why not?' said Bhargav, calmly. 'Let her say.'

Oh fuck, thought Akshay, taking a deep breath. He squeezed Gayatri's hand, but she shrugged it off.

'Why not what?' she said challengingly.

'Why not work with us? We are also very interested in history. We have set up an online resource with many rare books, all available for free. It's all about spreading the truth, isn't it?'

'Gayatri,' Akshay said softly to her, 'he's just baiting you. Please don't fall into his trap.'

Well, I'm fucking baited, she thought. She smiled innocently. 'You think I'm up for sale like you?' Her tone was polite but sarcastic.

Bhargav looked amused. 'I see.'

'No, you don't,' said Gayatri. 'You don't see that I know it was you and your low-level goondas who came into our office and broke everything like cowards. You don't have the intellectual capacity for a discussion, so you have to resort to using goondas with iron rods and hockey sticks. And then you have the guts to ask *me* to work with you?'

Bhargav shrugged calmly. 'Broke? Broke what?'

Akshay gestured with his hand to Bhargav to stop. He wouldn't put it past Gayatri to reach across and hit him. 'Please, not here, not now,' he whispered to her.

Her eyes flashed. 'I don't give a fuck any more about anyone. I'm done.'

'We didn't do anything, Gayatriji,' insisted Bhargav. 'No matter what you believe, there are certain things that are beyond the remit of individuals in organizations.'

'Bhargav sahib, bas ab,' said Akshay. 'Please.'

Bhargav picked up his glass of water, and took a sip. 'Akshay, you should be telling this madam not to accuse people of crimes just like that. People like these, they go around touting lies for their foreign masters, catering to one small elite section of society, trying to mislead every—'

Gayatri shook her head and stared at him incredulously. *'We mislead?* We are an academic journal. Rigorously edited, publishing academically credited people.'

'What academic credentials? Same Marxist historians everywhere, saying, "Oh, history is economics, Hindus and Muslims have always been brothers." Criticizing our own Hindu past, not willing to look at anything positive about India unless it was done by a Muslim conqueror. Then it is great. What is the need to lie in the face of facts, I would like to know?'

'That's not the point, I'm not here to defend any type of historian,' said Gayatri. 'But we are free to publish the views we want, we don't take funding from the government and are not answerable to anyone. Who are you to tell us what to publish and what not to?'

Just then, an acquaintance of Akshay's came up to their table. Akshay stood up to greet him, and was reluctantly pulled away to meet someone else.

Bhargav did not give up. 'By that logic, we are also free to tell our views. Why only your views should be published?'

'Please go ahead and publish what you want yourself. But all you can do is goondagardi and threaten people with weapons … a rational discussion is beyond you.'

'What goondagardi you are going on about?' Bhargav asked in a low voice. 'Do you people really listen to anyone with a different view? Isn't that also goondagardi of a different kind? Have you ever considered why people like you are ashamed of your own culture? Why anything with "Hindu" in it is treated as something deserving of revulsion?' He paused. 'And, if anyone else expresses a view that is not in line with yours, you explode into your righteous fireworks.'

'Look,' said Gayatri, 'if you disagree with us, write to us, we will publish your articles based on merit, we will engage with you that way.'

'Okay,' said Bhargav, challengingly. 'If someone sends you an article in Hindi, will you even look at it?'

Gayatri shook her head, slightly discomfited. 'We are an English-language journal.'

'Maybe, but you are also a historian. You are supposed to engage with ideas. Just because they are written in a different language, a language that you should know well, given it is your mother tongue, doesn't make the ideas any lesser.'

'It's not just about language,' she said, faltering momentarily since there was some truth to what he was saying. 'If the ideas are bullshit and based on some indoctrination to serve some political purpose, why should we engage?'

Just then, Akshay returned to the table.

'Madam,' said Bhargav, now leaning in. '*You* think it is bullshit. There is a difference.' He paused. 'If I tell you now that I admire Veer Savarkar, your reaction will be: "Get lost, I know your kind." You will say Godse was his follower and wonder how I can support Gandhi's killer? You will raise a hue and cry … He is right wing, Hindutva … All that.'

Gayatri shook her head and opened her mouth to respond. Bhargav spoke before she did. 'I tell you Savarkar was an enlightened man, a brave man. That is my opinion, and it has a basis. Do you know, when he was studying in the UK, he used to attend each and every Parliament session when India was discussed, and then he would report back home in a newspaper. He used to say that we can't sit in chains forever, begging for Home Rule, that the moderates were wasting time.' He wiped his mouth with a napkin and continued. 'He was so impressed by the suffragettes in the UK ... He wrote that we need to learn from the women over there, they are tying themselves up, fighting, showing the men in power what they can do. He asked for independence, complete freedom, maybe decades before your own beloved heroes.'

Akshay looked at Gayatri warily, expecting her to explode any second.

'Have you read about his life?' continued Bhargav. 'Probably not, but you, and others like you, will focus on quotes taken out of context and condemn a man because *you* are indoctrinated. There is no attempt on your part to look at individual issues, to acknowledge the possibility that, as an individual, you may have a different view from others in your cosy coterie. Then how do you expect the people you insult and deride to respond? This is what your arrogance causes: people talking *at* each other, and not engaging.'

Gayatri shook her head. 'No serious historian disputes facts. Do you think we don't know he had progressive views on certain issues, cow worship, the caste system? But the way to engage in debate is to actually debate by writing and speaking ... Not by beating down your opponents with threats and violence.' She took a breath and continued calmly, 'Look, if you believe there is a distortion, correct it in the right manner. Because academics, honest ones, don't know how to deal with goondas.'

'We are doing that, madam. Trying to spread the word, write, but what to do—people like you don't even want to listen, let alone publish us.'

Gayatri frowned. 'So you create an army of trolls and idiots who have no credibility, who tout ideas that they don't understand, incite people to turn against and even kill each other? All this just to correct some historical record that you think isn't right? You really expect us to believe that it has nothing to do with the political parties that you are associated with, which get voted into power because of the ideas people like you propagate?'

Bhargav clicked his tongue. 'You don't understand, madam, and that is the problem with your type of people. You live in a nice central Delhi house, but you claim to understand the history of India. Nothing you understand. How many lower-caste people do you know other than maybe the help you employ in your house? How many villages, or even small towns in India have you visited? There is a very big difference between book knowledge and lived experience. It's people like you who need to question yourselves, your ingrained biases, and look at things afresh.'

'Gayatri,' Nina's voice interrupted the conversation. 'Let's go.'

Gayatri turned to see her parents standing up and nodded. She looked back at Bhargav, who sat watching her calmly. Taking a deep breath, she stood up and followed her parents as Amar walked them out.

After a few seconds, Akshay excused himself and went quickly to the driveway, where the Mehras were waiting for their car with Amar. Akshay quietly walked up to Gayatri and stood behind her. In a low voice, he began, 'Listen, about tonight, don't—'

She turned around and looked up at him, her gaze not angry and hard like he expected, but with an expression he couldn't read. 'It's fine,' she said, softly, sounding tired. He didn't know whether she was thinking of him, or her conversation with Bhargav.

They stood in silence for a few moments. When the car pulled up, he held the door open for her. He gave her a small smile while she tucked her feet in and closed the door.

As the car drove away, Gayatri craned her neck and looked back. Amar was walking inside, but Akshay stood rooted, his hands behind his back.

22

Dear Amar,

The pregnancy is over, I aborted it. I'm sorry.

I know you won't understand why I had to do this, but I hope in time you will realize that this was the right decision for all of us.

I'm going back to my parents' house. We can deal with the formalities whenever you are ready.

I know it's cowardly of me to run away, but I think it's the best thing to do for now.

Please take care of yourself,
Nandini

Nandini placed the handwritten note on the bed when Amar was in the bathroom, and left the apartment quietly with the bag she had packed before the party last night. She had considered telling Amar face to face, but she knew he would fly into a rage, maybe even hit her. It wasn't worth it, she had concluded, and it made no difference to the outcome; she had already decided to leave.

On her way down, she rang Akshay's doorbell and told him what she had done, her gaze lowered but her voice steady. 'Bhaiya, I'm telling you so you can take care of Amar,' she ended.

Stunned, Akshay, remained standing at the door even after she began to descend the stairs. A few seconds later, he reached for his phone.

Gayatri was on her way to office. Seeing Akshay's name flashing on her phone, and recalling the previous evening, she let it ring for a bit before answering.

'Hi,' she said awkwardly.

'Gayatri.' Akshay's voice was hard.

She was taken aback by his tone. 'Yes?'

'Did you know?'

'What?'

'Your sister has gone and aborted the baby. And she's left a fucking note for Amar, telling him about it.'

'What?' whispered Gayatri in shock, slowing the car down. 'How … Who told you?'

'She did. Just now, on her way down, with a packed bag.'

'Oh fuck. Oh fuck, oh fuck, oh fuck.' Gayatri pulled over on the side of the road. Akshay was quiet. 'Now what?' said Gayatri. 'I … She is such a … oh god.'

'I'm going up to Amar.'

'Yes, of course,' said Gayatri, her voice barely escaping her throat. 'I'll … I'll call Nan—'

He hung up.

Nandini answered on the third ring. 'Didi, just stay out of this,' she said. 'I knew he would call you.'

'But, Chhoti—'

'Just. Stay. Out.'

'I ...' Gayatri sighed. 'Where are you? What about Mom and Dad?'

'I'm going home now. I've told Dad not to leave for office today. I'll tell them myself.'

'Are you okay? I mean—'

'I'm fine,' she said brusquely. 'I have no regrets. Please don't come back right now. I want to handle this on my own, in my way.' She hung up.

Gayatri closed her eyes and rested her forehead on the steering wheel, wondering what to do. She remained still, her eyes closed for a few seconds, until her phone rang again. It was Kanthan.

They had finally got an appointment with the commissioner of police.

An hour later, Gayatri and Kanthan reached the Delhi Police Headquarters, housed in a tall building, which was shared with the Public Works Department. Gayatri squared her shoulders as they entered, determined to focus on the task at hand. They went through the security formalities and walked towards the filthy lift lobby. Not even the police could ensure cleanliness in a city like Delhi.

There was no signage when they got off the lift. After mistakenly entering the Public Works offices, they turned around and made their way to the correct office. Two and a half hours passed before they were told to go inside. Commissioner of Police Ranjit Alhawat gestured to the chairs opposite him and asked them to have a seat.

'Bataiye, Kanthan sahib,' he said graciously, getting to the point like a man who had things to do. 'What can I do for you?' He ignored Gayatri completely.

Kanthan introduced Gayatri, and handed him the letter they had prepared, setting out the key facts of their case and explaining the situation.

Alhawat nodded, picked up the phone and dialled a number. 'Mr Kanthan, from *Indian History*, koi journal hai, is sitting in my office. He is saying no action has been taken on an FIR he registered two weeks back. SHO kaun hai?'

As he spoke, Gayatri and Kanthan glanced at each other, slightly hopeful at the authoritative tone of this voice. Maybe those lazy, corrupt cops were in fact accountable to someone. The commissioner continued, flicking to the first page of the letter. 'FIR was filed in PS Underhill Road, No. 14567/187...' The conversation went on for a few minutes, punctuated by the occasional murmur from the commissioner.

He put the phone down, and rested his forearms on his desk and intertwined his fingers. Though Kanthan looked at him expectantly, it struck Gayatri that the commissioner's pose was a clue, from Bollywood movies and real life, that he was not inclined to help.

'Mr Kanthan,' he said, 'we are aware of the case, and are progressing the investigation. The IO is looking into it. It takes time to analyse the evidence in any matter. We are doing everything we can ...'

A few more minutes of opaque official-ese later, they were politely shown out.

Gayatri and Kanthan left the room and walked down the stairs. 'No one is going to move a finger,' she said.

Kanthan shook his head. 'And just think, this is how he behaves with us, we who were able to pull strings to meet him. What hope do ordinary people without this access have?'

Back home a few hours later, Gayatri entered the study, bracing herself to see the impact of Nandini's return on her family. Her parents were sitting in their usual chairs; both seemed to have aged a few years since she had left for work that morning. Her father had a tray with a bottle of whisky and ice laid out before him, her mother looked miserable.

Gayatri put her bag down and slumped into a chair. They sat in silence for a few seconds, before her father said, 'What's done is done. We just have to deal with things as best we can.'

Gayatri nodded.

Nina's eyes welled with tears. Ashok took her hand. 'There is no choice, Nina, this is not something that we can resolve by talking to Amar. There is only one way now … divorce.'

Nina pulled a tissue from the box and wiped her nose. 'But is there no way—?'

'Ma,' said Gayatri, gently. 'Dad is right, there's no chance of a reconciliation now that Nandini has … done this.'

'And she will find someone else in time,' said Ashok. 'She hasn't committed a crime, she hasn't killed any—' He stopped abruptly, then cleared his throat. 'It will take a few weeks, maybe months, but it'll be okay.'

'And your mother?' said Nina, looking at Ashok. 'How are we going to tell her?'

'I will tell Mama tomorrow morning myself,' said Ashok. He looked at Gayatri, 'No mentioning this to Dadi today, okay? Just be normal when you see her. I've told her Nandini has high fever.'

Gayatri nodded. 'Where is Nandini?'

'Upstairs.'

'I'll go up to her.'

'Don't be too harsh on her, okay? I think she's had enough.'

Gayatri knocked on Nandini's door. 'Chhoti?' she called.

'Come in, Didi,' Nandini answered a few seconds later.

Gayatri walked in. The room was dark, except for a dim bedside lamp. Nandini was curled up in blankets. Gayatri sat on the bed beside her. She looked unwell.

'How are you feeling?' Gayatri asked, stroking her forehead lightly. Nandini nodded. 'Fine, Didi, better.'

'The procedure ... was it ...?'

'Horrible. Lots of blood.'

'Chhoti—'

'Didi, please don't. Please. I know what I did was horrible, terrible ... I'm a monster, not a normal woman. I've ...' She paused as tears filled her eyes quickly. 'Who's finished my own—' She swallowed. 'I'm not asking for sympathy, I did it for my selfish reasons. I'm sorry for the impact it has had on everyone, but I don't want to hear anyone's views on it.'

Gayatri nodded, stroking her forehead. 'Just rest now.'

'I've been lying down the whole day.'

'Do you feel like doing anything, watching something?'

Nandini shook her head.

Gayatri stood up with a sigh.

'Are you angry with me, Didi?' asked Nandini.

Gayatri looked at her and said, 'Honestly, Chhoti, I was, but I'm not any more. I just feel like I've failed you.'

'This is not about you.'

'No, not like that, I just ... I don't know.'

'I couldn't tell you, Didi. You would never have helped me do this, and I was sure this was the only thing to do. I didn't want to wait.' Nandini blinked back tears.

Gayatri was silent for a few seconds, then said, 'I can't say that I agree with your decision. But what's done is done. We have to move on.'

Nandini nodded.

Gayatri bent over and kissed her forehead. 'This will pass, Chhoti. For all of us. It's a bit clichéd, but true, that time really does heal everything. Goodnight.'

Gayatri's eyes were full of tears as she closed the door of her sister's room behind her.

23

It took a few weeks for the Grewal and Mehra households to start limping towards some semblance of normalcy.

On his mother's insistence, Amar left for the US to stay with his sister. She thought a change of scene would be good for him. Mr Grewal and Akshay resumed their duties in office and court. While Mrs Grewal declined all social engagements, relatives called and visited her, shaking their heads in commiseration, their ears cocked for any previously unknown, juicy detail of the split. Though Rupi appreciated these visits from family and friends, she was unable to vent her feelings against Nandini satisfactorily; no one outside the immediate family knew of the aborted pregnancy.

Mr and Mrs Mehra had tried to ring up Amar's parents several times, but their calls were neither answered nor returned.

Gayatri spent as much time at home as possible. She worked hard to persuade her mother not to discuss the divorce with Nandini.

'How easily we've gone from calling it "the marriage" to calling it "the divorce",' Nina had commented sadly.

Dadi had not reacted to Nandini's return as feared. She was quieter than usual for a couple of days, avoiding all calls and visitors, and then she simply got back to normal. She did not try to speak to Nandini about the abortion, nor did she ask Gayatri about it. Dadi's sisters and cousins visited her, murmuring and nodding over-sympathetically, to atone for their curious whispers on the phone about extramarital affairs and speculation about the boy's sexual orientation.

Nandini braved the ordeal of going to office after she learned that Amar had left the country for a while. Though she found it taxing to be equanimous in the face of her colleagues' fake sympathy, which gave way to vicious gossip about her when she wasn't present, staying at home with her upset mother and occasionally running into Dadi's visitors was unbearable.

Ultimately though, she found that there wasn't a great deal of difference between the attitude of her highly educated colleagues and Dadi's unsophisticated cousins.

It was Mann who told Vikram about Nandini and Amar.

Entering the room where Vikram was waiting for an appointment with Mr Grewal, Mann explained the situation sombrely. As he listened, Vikram's thoughts strayed to Gayatri and Akshay. He had been seething since the day of the party, when he had seen them together, standing so close to each other, blushing and smiling. Even from a distance it was clear that they'd been flirting. He was furious with himself for letting a girl like Gayatri get to him, make a fool of him. Now let's see them getting together, he thought, clenching his jaw to suppress a smile.

'Vikram?' said Mann as he noticed Vikram's eyes glazing over.

'Haan? Uh, yeah …' Vikram shook his head sympathetically. 'That's really sad, I can't believe it. Everything seemed okay that day at the party. How is the family doing?'

'Amar has left for the US.'

Vikram nodded. 'But why did she leave?'

Mann shrugged. 'Kya pata, girls aaj kal are on another planet.'

'And how is Mrs Grewal?'

'Ma'am is upset of course, but she is dealing with it. These things affect the whole family, na.'

'There will be a divorce I imagine?'

Mann nodded. 'I thought I'd tell you so you'd understand that sir may be a little distracted at the moment.'

'Thanks, uh … yes. I'll keep that in mind.'

'Last week's meeting with Akhil has given me the confidence,' said Mr Grewal to Vikram, 'that the two of you can deliver the funds.'

Vikram smiled in the oily, subservient manner he had acquired over the past few weeks. 'Sir, that's quite unfair. When I gave you those figures, you didn't believe me?' This is like flirting, he thought as the words left his mouth.

'No, no, it's just more confidence. I need to get this in the bag now. This ticket won't come for free.'

Vikram nodded. 'I need to follow up on some of the requests from the contributors too, sir. We may need to start speaking to some of the sectoral regulators on some approvals.' He looked at his laptop. 'I think the first calls will be to I&B, and iron and steel.'

Mr Grewal grunted. 'It'll be done.'

'Sir, uh … will Akshay be involved in this? Shall I ask him—' He knew very well that Grewal didn't want Akshay involved at all.

'No,' said Mr Grewal firmly. 'He won't be. In fact, I was thinking maybe you could take on a more direct role in these dealings.'

Vikram looked at him, his eyes widening very slightly.

'I can send you to the relevant persons directly as my man.' Grewal paused, gauging Vikram's reaction. 'You can take a cut, you know. All work is paid work. And there is enough to go around, even after Sadhuji's fees.'

'Cut?'

'Half per cent.'

'Of the entire tranche?' asked Vikram. Grewal nodded. Vikram was silent as he calculated how much that would amount to. 'And Akhil?'

'You handle that. I am offering you a consultancy role.' Grewal leaned back in his chair. 'It will be all cash, so whether you share the whole or part of it with Akhil, I leave to you.'

'One per cent,' Vikram said confidently.

Mr Grewal smiled. This was exactly what he would have done had he been in Vikram's place. 'Done. One or two cycles like this, and you'll get a feel for how to take things forward yourself. Maybe without Akhil …'

Vikram nodded.

'I'll tell Mohan to arrange a desk for you here in my office. Whenever you need to come in.'

'Thank you, sir.' Vikram stood up.

'And … uh,' Grewal hesitated. 'One more thing I wanted to talk to you about. You may have heard from the Mehras that my son and Nandini—'

Vikram interrupted him, 'I heard, sir. I'm sorry.'

'Whatever your plans with the elder sister, I don't think we should let personal relationships get in the way of business.'

'Absolutely, sir,' said Vikram, smiling. 'No question.' Mann really is an idiot if he thinks this old fox is even mildly disturbed by his son's impending divorce, Vikram thought as he left the office and walked down the corridor, mulling over Grewal's unexpected offer. He stopped outside Akshay's room. Maybe just a peek, at one half of the pair of unfortunate lovers?

He knocked.

'Yes?' called Akshay.

'Hi,' Vikram said cheerfully as he entered. Seeing Akshay's startled look, he said, 'What happened?'

'No, uh … nothing. I wasn't expecting you,' said Akshay, standing up.

'I was just leaving. I came to meet your father. There's so much going on with his ticket contributions, I'm sure you're aware.'

Akshay shook his head. 'I'm … uh—'

'I wanted to say how sorry I am to hear about your brother and Nandini.'

Akshay nodded. 'Thanks.'

'It creates so much unpleasantness for the whole family,' he sighed and added, 'for both families actually.'

Akshay nodded distractedly.

'Gayatri is also so upset, poor thing,' said Vikram, watching Akshay intently. 'Of course, things will not be the same now. I just thought, you know, since both of you are such good friends I'd …' He trailed off.

Akshay said abruptly, 'Vikram, er, I'm sorry but I have a deadline, so I'd better get back to work.'

'Sure, sure, sorry,' said Vikram, backing out. 'Best of luck for the deadline.'

Akshay sat back in his chair, trying to slow down his racing mind.

Vikram spent the next few days working closely with Grewal's office, meeting people, and learning to say the right things, in the right manner, to those people. Anil Bhargav accompanied him to every meeting. The fact that people he had only read about in newspapers and seen on TV before this were now just a phone call away gave Vikram a heightened sense of power. It was almost a revelation to him that they were, in fact, human, and had needs just like him. And now that he was able to fulfil some of those needs, they were deferential to him.

As he exited South Block with Bhargav after a meeting with a joint secretary in the I&B Ministry, Bhargav said to him, 'This is the final stretch before Grewalji gets his ticket. Some money has come from you, and some from us, but now we have to make sure the matter is finished neatly.'

'I know,' nodded Vikram. 'We will deliver, almost half the amount has come in already. With foreign investment, one has to be more careful. There are forms, RBI restrictions, all that. We have to channel it through existing Indian companies—'

'That is all okay,' interrupted Bhargav as they approached their car. 'There is a lot of money riding on your shoulders right now. Grewalji thinks you have enough skin in the game to finish the job. He has a more ...' he paused, 'business-like way of making people do their job, more ... civilized. Even in a delicate situation like this.'

Vikram was silent.

Looking straight ahead, Bhargav said, 'You know the carrot-and-stick theory?'

Vikram nodded.

'Sometimes, carrots work, but sometimes sticks are necessary. Grewalji prefers to use the first approach, but we are not afraid to use sticks if we have to.'

'I understand,' said Vikram quietly.

'Good.'

'Akshay hasn't called at all?' Farah asked Gayatri. They were sitting in the office veranda with their mugs of coffee.

'No,' she replied with a sigh. 'And I don't think he ever will, after all this.'

'I know it'll be tough for the families to accept, but if both of you know you want to be together—'

'I never said anything about me, Farah,' said Gayatri sharply, 'I just told you what he said that day.'

After a few moments of silence, she turned to Farah, 'You're really annoying, Faru. You start something, and then just drop the topic.'

Farah looked at her with a half-smile. 'You want me to insist that you're in denial about Akshay?'

Gayatri clicked her tongue in exasperation. 'Of course not. I'm just saying that given what's happened between Nandini and Amar, even if I did like him, and that's a *big* if, we would never be able to work this out with our families.'

Farah shrugged. 'You know best. You seem to be making decisions for him also, but please, remember that these chances at love don't turn up very often.'

'If he wanted, he would have called by now, right? His not calling is a clear sign that he's not interested now. And I can hardly blame him.' Her casual tone belied the furious churning of her insides.

'I hope he knows you're not with Vikram any more?' Farah asked.

Ignoring her question, Gayatri said, 'Speaking of Vikram, he messaged me yesterday.'

'Vikram? I thought you guys broke up?'

'We did, that day at the party. But after hearing about Nandini, he's generally being sweet and friendly.' Gayatri shrugged. 'Asking about her and my parents, you know. He's even asked me to meet him for a coffee tomorrow.'

'What did you say?'

'I couldn't say no. He's been so nice, even after I was so awful to him.'

Farah sighed.

They were silent for a few minutes. Then Gayatri said, 'Faru, we have to do something.'

'About Akshay?'

'No, silly,' said Gayatri irritably. 'About our case and that bloody Sadhu. These cops definitely won't lift even a finger for us.'

'What can we do?'

'See, we're sure it was this Sadhu. We have to either dig up some dirt on him, or convince some reporter to write about this.'

'I don't think we'll manage either, realistically speaking. And we already tried once through that friend of yours at *National Express* ...' Farah trailed off.

'I'm going to try again. I'm not done with that fake Sadhu yet,' Gayatri said, determined.

The following day, Gayatri sat across from Vikram in a café in Khan Market. As she dabbed her mouth with a tissue, she thought how wrong she had been about him. He was being so nice and friendly, genuinely concerned for Nandini.

'Shall we take a walk in Lodhi garden?' he asked as he paid the bill.

'Now?' She was surprised.

'It's a nice afternoon. And I haven't been there in many years.'

Gayatri hesitated, and then agreed. 'Okay, maybe just a short walk.'

They descended the steps from the coffee shop and made their way to the other side of the road.

As Gayatri and Vikram entered the park, the noise of the traffic outside gave way to the chirping of birds. The sunshine and greenery radiated a feeling of laziness that is peculiar to mid-day winter in Delhi. Many people were lying in the sun, shirking work for an extra half hour after lunch in the garden.

'It's always so nice to walk here in the winter sun,' Gayatri began. 'This may be one of the last afternoons—'

Vikram interrupted her. 'You know,' he said casually, 'you're a fucking bitch.'

Gayatri halted abruptly. 'Excuse me?'

Vikram stopped a couple of steps ahead. He turned around and drew closer to her. 'You. Are. A. Fucking. Bitch.'

Gayatri stared at him, confused.

'No one's ever told you that?' he continued, in a faux-sympathetic voice.

'What ... What are you—' She looked around her, now scared. There were a few people on the grass, in the distance.

She started to walk away, but he grabbed her arm. 'Wait!'

'Let go of me,' she said firmly, regaining more of her composure with each passing second, 'or I'll shout.'

He clenched his jaw and released her arm.

'You're a psycho, Vikram. I don't know what I was thinking, agreeing to meet you.'

'Is that so? Maybe if you ever got off the mountain of morality you live on, you'll see the hurt you cause others. Coming to my house, pretending to be kind to my dad ... We don't need your fucking pity. I actually thought you could be ... And you, without any fucking reason, just ...'

'Just what?' said Gayatri, incredulously. 'I tried to tell you again and again. Yes, there was a point where I thought we might have a future together, but ...' She took a step back from him and swallowed. 'Even when we met after you came back from London, I told you clearly how I felt, but you just refused to listen.'

'Maybe if you had told me the truth, that you and that fucker Akshay were up to some shit behind my back, I would have dropped you like the piece of shit you are. Like he has, I bet, after what your sister's done.'

'Look,' she said, 'despite your ugly behaviour today, I'm sorry if I hurt you—'

'Hurt me?' He laughed mockingly. 'An average-looking woman like you, stuck on the shelf, nose buried in some fucking history book … you have high hopes.' He took a step closer to her.

Gayatri retreated immediately, raising her finger as she said, 'I'm warning you, I'll shout if you come any closer.'

She tried to turn and walk away, but he was too quick for her. He grabbed her arm again, twisting it hard this time. Vikram's face was tense with rage, and the muscles in his neck bulged out ominously. She opened her mouth to scream, but no sound emerged.

He spoke through clenched teeth, in a voice drenched with hate. 'Who do you think you are? Why the fuck did you keep responding to my messages and calls, and lead me on like this?' His fingers dug deeper into her flesh. 'You're just a fucking nobody who thinks she's saving the world by writing in some dumb journal that no one reads. The world is run by people like me, you get that?'

Frightened and angry, Gayatri willed herself to remain calm. Mustering all her strength, she kneed him hard. He flinched and she pulled herself out of his grip, backing away.

Vikram followed her, repeating, 'The world is run by people like me.'

Gayatri looked back at him as she walked away, a mixture of fear and disgust in her eyes. She quickened her steps until she was trailing a group of women heading towards the exit.

Vikram went off in the opposite direction. This hadn't given him as much satisfaction as he had thought it would.

24

NEELAM SAT AT a mahogany desk in the cottage nestled among the deodars. Grewalji was right. She really did love this place. The air outside was cold and clean. The wooden interiors were comfortable and cosy, warmed by bright sunlight that streamed in through large windows. She had enjoyed the month she had already spent here, away from Delhi. It had given her the time and space to think.

She took a sip of the green tea that one of her staff, also arranged by Grewalji, had brought her a few minutes back. After setting the cup on the desk, she read for the third time the draft of the email open on the laptop in front of her. With her finger on the mousepad, she guided the pointer to the 'Send' button. The email was addressed to a friend of hers, a member of an Opposition party well-known for its squad of internet trolls. Now that the elections were approaching, they were hungry for scandals they could make use of.

She tapped lightly on the mousepad.

The same day, an anonymous Twitter account published a video that showed Gyan Singh Grewal with a woman. '#BSD #Sexual Harassment' said the tweet accompanying the video. The woman's face had been blurred professionally; it was not clear even to those who knew of the affair if that was Neelam. A barrage of tweets followed, speculating whether there were others whom Grewal had similarly targeted.

The video was removed by Twitter, but not before an industrious few had downloaded it and circulated it on WhatsApp groups. It was reported on by the legal press; many television channels and the newspapers the next day were full of salacious details and speculation based on the tweets accompanying the video.

As soon as the video went viral, Grewal frantically tried to push his position, through friends, that it was morphed and motivated to quash his political ambitions. A day later, he put out the line that even if the video wasn't morphed, there was no evidence of any wrongdoing; at worst, it was a private matter. His office obtained an injunction against the publication of the video, but the order came too late to make a difference. Regardless of the legal outcome of the matter, any chances of his getting a ticket were destroyed.

Sadhuji and the party made no move to help him.

The day after the scandal broke, Rupi left Delhi for her parents' home in Chandigarh, unwilling to entertain the same sympathizers she had just a few weeks ago, this time mourning her humiliation. She didn't say when—or if—she would be back.

Mr Grewal, already shattered, lost hope completely when people who mattered refused to answer his calls. He confined himself to his bedroom, curtains drawn. Other than Santram, his longtime aide, he didn't let anyone in, not even Akshay.

On the sixth day after the scandal broke, Akshay was bathing when he heard someone knocking frantically on his bedroom door and calling for him. Rushing out, he followed a panicked Santram down the stairs to his father's room where another servant and the guard were pounding on Mr Grewal's bedroom door, to no response.

Akshay looked at them and swallowed, trying not to imagine the worst. 'Get something to break it down.'

The guard brought a large iron rod, and together with Santram and Akshay, managed to pry the door open. Akshay rushed in to find his father lying on the bed, seemingly lifeless. He shook him, calling, 'Papa' a few times, but got no response. He checked his breathing and heartbeat, and nodded to Santram, saying, 'He's breathing. Jaldi, mera phone lao.'

Akshay looked around the room and saw a few strips of medicines on the bedside table. Squinting at the names, he could make out at least one brand of sleeping pills. He removed the socks on his father's feet and made him lie down straight on the bed. As he wiped his father's face with a wet towel, he noticed just how old he had grown.

He stood up and drew the curtains to let in some light, and waited anxiously for the doctor.

Several kilometres away, Vikram too was waiting anxiously in Anil Bhargav's office.

Since the video had been published, he had not been able to eat or sleep. His calls to Grewal and Bhargav had received no response, paralysing him with fear and an inability to predict the impact of the scandal. Akhil had been livid, demanding to know who was going to get their clients what they had paid for. Vikram had avoided further calls from Akhil. He had visited both Grewal's and Bhargav's offices; at both places, he was told they were out of town. His attempts to connect with the few BSD functionaries he had met were also unsuccessful. Finally, after days of incessant calling and messaging, Bhargav had replied, asking him to come and see him.

Now, unkempt and unshaven, Vikram waited for an hour and forty minutes in the reception area for Bhargav. A security officer patted him down and requested that he leave his mobile phone outside, before allowing him to enter.

Bhargav waved at Vikram to sit.

'Sir,' started Vikram helplessly, taking a seat opposite Bhargav.

'Yes, what is it?' asked Bhargav in an impatient tone.

'Sir, the amounts … I wanted to check what we plan to do next. I mean, I have to either return those amounts to my clients or we can—'

Bhargav raised his finger. 'Not "we"—"I". Sadhuji is not involved in Grewal's affairs. We don't know what your arrangements were with him.'

'Sir,' said Vikram, pleadingly. 'Aise mat kahiye. The money, it all went through Grewalji and you to the party.'

'Then ask the party. I don't know anything about any money. Do you have any documents, bank transfers, notes connecting us to you? As far as the party is concerned, electoral bonds can be from anyone, these are legitimate donations. They are not conditional on anyone getting a ticket.'

Vikram swallowed. 'Sir, please, I have done whatever you asked of me. I cannot … I mean, those amounts … they were huge. It is not something I can repay. All those people we met together, they all—'

'Ask them, then,' Bhargav said smoothly. 'They will welcome you with open arms in South Block. It's not our problem, Mr Gera. We don't know anything about this matter. Go work it out with Grewal.'

'But, sir,' started Vikram, his eyes filling with tears.

Bhargav looked at him for a few seconds, and then said, 'If you want my advice, go underground for some time. Some cases may be filed, but these people sitting abroad cannot do much here in India. And anyway, what can they say? That they want their bribe money back? You said that you had disguised ownership of the companies very well, so there is not much anyone can really do.'

'But, sir, my career, my reputation—'

'Forget about them,' Bhargav said witheringly. He picked up the phone and asked his secretary to send his next appointment in.

Vikram made no move to get up. 'Sir, please—'

Bhargav looked beyond him and waved someone in.

Vikram turned around and saw two guards approaching. He got up slowly and walked out of the room, unable to believe the mess he was in.

Dr Nadir left the room after Gyan Singh regained consciousness. Akshay followed him out to the door.

'Beta,' the doctor said, turning to him, 'you will have to keep an eye on him. This time, it was just a few pills. But coupled with his drinking and your mother not being here … See, I am his friend, so I can be honest with you.'

'Yes,' said Akshay nodding, 'thank you, Uncle, I understand, I'll take care.' He sighed and returned to his father's room. Santram was getting ready to sponge his father, so he signalled that he would come again later.

Back in his flat, he stood in the balcony and lit a cigarette. He was up to at least ten a day now. He dialled his mother's number, and told her about his father's overdose and Dr Nadir's visit. She listened to him silently, then changed the topic, unwilling to discuss her husband.

As Akshay hung up, he felt lonelier than he had in a very long time.

Later that morning, Akshay made his way down to his father's room. Mr Grewal was lying in bed, under the razai, seemingly asleep. Akshay walked up to him and put a hand on his shoulder, 'Papa?' he said.

His father didn't move, but Akshay could sense he was awake. He sat down next to him. Some minutes passed before Mr Grewal opened his eyes and stared at the ceiling.

Akshay was not used to seeing his father look so helpless. 'Papa, chalo now. Let's deal with this.'

Mr Grewal turned on his side, away from Akshay.

'Papa, listen to me. You can wallow like this for one day, or one year. But ultimately, we have to face what's out there, and deal with it. This is not the first time a scandal has broken and it won't be the last. In a few days, everyone will have forgotten about it and things will go back to normal.'

Mr Grewal was silent.

'Papa,' said Akshay gently, 'I am here, na. I promise, I will sort this out for you.'

When Mr Grewal didn't respond, Akshay turned him around to face him. His body felt limp, his eyes were blank. As Akshay gently stroked his forehead, Mr Grewal closed his eyes, and took a few deep breaths. The desire to end his life that had preyed on him since he had seen the video loosened its grip ever so slightly.

Gayatri read about the video in the newspaper. She had a feeling that the lady in the video was the woman Akshay had been involved with, but she couldn't be sure.

Now, as she sat with Farah, she wondered about Akshay and how he was holding up.

'Did you see the papers today?' asked Farah, interrupting Gayatri's thoughts. 'The Bar Council is thinking of suspending Nandini's father-in-law's license.'

Gayatri nodded.

'Any news of Akshay?'

Gayatri shook her head.

'And how are you feeling about that?'

Gayatri was silent.

'Gayatri?'

'Miserable,' she said quietly. 'He must hate me along with Nandini.' She looked at Farah helplessly. 'I didn't realize that I had actually ... Until this—' she broke off.

Farah squeezed her hand sympathetically, not needing Gayatri to complete her sentence. They were both quiet for a while, before Gayatri said, 'I know it's terrible, this scandal, but I really hope Vikram has got screwed in all this. I think his whole rotten business was dependent on Gyan Uncle getting the ticket.' She jerked her chin to one side derisively. 'It will serve him right, the asshole.'

Akshay intended to speak to his father about an action plan for getting back on his feet as soon as he recovered some physical strength. He saw an opportunity a few days later, when his father agreed to come up to his flat for a drink.

Gyan Singh looked on as his son arranged the cushions on a sofa so he would be comfortable. He hadn't forgotten how things had stood between them before this episode. Being taken care of in this manner made him feel small. He had a sudden impulse to tell Akshay to leave him alone and return downstairs; that would, at least, spare him this immediate humiliation. He decided against it, and settled into the sofa.

He had always thought Akshay was like him, nimble-minded and ambitious, a loyal lieutenant who would one day succeed him as one of Delhi's top criminal lawyers. Now, as he fought back a sting of tears, he realized his son was better than him in so many ways.

Mr Grewal's thoughts were interrupted as Akshay handed him a drink. They took a few sips in silence. It was Mr Grewal who finally spoke. 'I don't know what to do, beta,' he said slowly. 'My life has disappeared. I didn't think that I would lose heart like this, but these'— he waved his glass weakly—'the past weeks have made me question my whole life.'

'It may seem like that now, Papa,' said Akshay, 'but you know this will pass. We'll get over this. Other people have gone through worse and survived.' He paused. 'In fact, everyone has known about Neelam for many years, and they all know that these stories about offering to arrange a judgeship, harassment, they're all rubbish. This will run its course. We'll be fine.'

Mr Grewal shook his head. 'I don't think so.' He repeated softly, 'I don't think so. Not for an old man like me.' He sighed. 'You know, your mother … She was a very happy woman when we got married. I loved her, but there were other women. I bullied her, just like my father had bullied my mother.' He shook his head and continued, his voice breaking, 'And now, she has left me. The worst is I don't know if she'll ever come back.'

'Of course she'll come back, Papa, just give this time to die down,' said Akshay. 'I think it just got too much for her … First with Amar and Nandini, and then with all this.'

Mr Grewal drained the last of the whisky in his glass.

Akshay made him another drink. 'Papa, there's no point going over every mistake you've made in your life. You can't change the past.'

Mr Grewal eyes filled with tears. He poked clumsily at them with weak fingers, trying to wipe away the tears. 'This … It has broken me. I didn't think that everything I did adds up to nothing, but that's the truth. Neelam … I can hardly blame her, she was so upset at being sent away, but I truly didn't care because I thought her feelings were expendable, not as important as what I wanted, what I deserved—'

Akshay interrupted gently, 'If it makes any difference, I don't hold anything against you, Papa. Really.' He knew it was the shock of the scandal and the alcohol that were fuelling these thoughts. 'Papa, today is 16 February,' he said. 'By 16 March, you will be standing in court, arguing as usual. Ma will have come back. Amar as well. Just think of that.'

His father grunted, lost in thought.

Akshay continued, 'I have engaged Alok Sehgal to figure out a media strategy. He is coming tomorrow—'

'I will not meet anyone.'

'You don't have to. I'll deal with it.' He paused. 'Also, Papa, I was thinking … do you want to leave Delhi for a few days?'

Mr Grewal shook his head. 'What good will it do for me to leave a house or a city? I'll be alone wherever I am.'

'What about Vikram?'

His father shrugged. 'Vikram will have to salvage what he can in this mess. A lot of money has already gone to the party, they will figure a way to deal with him.' He took a sip of his drink. 'Beta, I want you to do something. Vikram has been calling, he even came to the office the other day. We still have some cash that he had given. Whatever is sitting with us, please return it to him. I don't know how he'll channel it back to the UK … I'll leave that to him.'

Akshay nodded. 'I'll do that. Shall I tell Santram to lay our dinner?'

'Wait,' said Mr Grewal. 'There's something I want to ask you, but I don't know if I should. You may mind it.'

'What?'

'Gayatri … and you … Is there any …? I know you liked her.'

Akshay shook his head. 'I haven't spoken to her since Nandini left.'

'Her parents tried to call us, you know, but your mother didn't want to speak to them.'

Akshay nodded.

'Beta, if there is any way—'

'No, Papa, right now, we are falling in ditch after ditch. I am just focused on getting some stability back for us as a family. The last I heard, she was with Vikram. So there's no point anyway.'

Mr Grewal closed his eyes and rested his head back on the sofa. 'You know,' he said after a few seconds, 'that bastard of a Sadhu could have helped me. When I think of all the scrapes I've pulled his gang of goondas out from …' He shook his head, smiling faintly.

'What?'

'I was so angry with him when he stopped taking my calls, I actually thought of using those documents I had kept. You remember? From the days I didn't fully trust him.'

Akshay nodded. 'I think that was when he was brokering that large land parcel from the Punjab government. When he pocketed almost seventy per cent, was it?'

Mr Grewal nodded. 'Some ridiculous amount like that. And remember when that woman was trying to blackmail him with those photos? We have those also somewhere.'

Akshay nodded slowly. 'If these were to leak somehow, would he know it was you?'

Mr Grewal thought for a few moments and said, 'He'll know about the photos … It was our office that paid off that woman. That land deal, he wouldn't know. But, beta, all this is faltu ki baat. What good will it do to release this now?'

25

A FEW DAYS LATER, Gayatri rushed into the office, very excited. 'Faru!' she said, putting down her things on her desk.

Farah looked up from the text she was proofing. 'What happened?'

'You know Chiki, na?'

'Who?'

Gayatri clicked her tongue impatiently. 'Chiki Pirzada. My classmate who works at the *National Express*. She's the one I've been hounding to have someone write a story on Sadhuji.'

'She's agreed to do a piece?' asked Farah.

'No, she's not writing anything. But she was hinting that Sadhuji will be hit with something hard soon, something really big.'

'Hinting means what?'

'Ohho, she can't tell me specifics, na, but she knows I hate that guy. She would have helped us earlier if we had had some concrete evidence. Anyway, she told me to wait and watch for a week. She said it was some old land-acquisition scandal.'

'I wouldn't be so hopeful,' said Farah, shaking her head. 'This Sadhu knows so many people. He'll just pay someone and get away with it.'

'Farah, stop being so cynical. After so many weeks, I've finally had some good news. Don't spoil it, na.'

'Let's see. He deserves the worst, that's for sure,' Farah said. Glancing at Gayatri, she smiled. 'It's nice to see you getting back to your normal self.'

Gayatri switched on her computer. 'I know. I don't want to jinx it, but things do seem to be getting back to normal.'

'How's Nandini?'

'Better. She's just completely immersed herself in work now. I think it's doing her good. She's not her chirpy self yet, but I think she'll get there soon.'

'And the divorce?'

'It's a long procedure. They have to go to court in two weeks, and then they may be referred to mediation, then they have to show they stayed apart for six months, and I don't know what all.'

'Oh, that sounds quite torturous. Is Amar back from the US?'

'No, but he's signed the divorce petition.' She paused, then said, 'Akshay is coming over this evening with it, for Nandini to sign. And to discuss the next steps.'

'Akshay?'

Gayatri nodded. 'My dad told me in the morning.'

'How come ... I mean their family hasn't been in contact with yours at all, right?'

'I was also surprised. But Mom and Dad are happy he's coming. They've been feeling so bad about the way things were left with the Grewals. I just hope he's civil,' she said, sitting down and scrolling through her emails.

'I'm sure he'll be more than civil,' said Farah, with a teasing smile.

'No, Farah,' sighed Gayatri. 'I think things will be very, very different when we meet now. My sister has broken his younger brother's heart, aborted their baby and basically ruined his life. There is no way he thinks about me the way he did earlier.'

That afternoon at three, Vikram arrived at Mr Grewal's office. He went straight to Akshay's room, knocked, and entered.

'Hi,' said Akshay, standing up. Vikram looked ill. His eyes had dark circles around them, and an air of defeat hung around him. 'Thanks for coming in, Vikram. I'll get straight to the point. We still have some of the cash you had delivered. It's yours to take back.'

Vikram stared at Akshay blankly.

'Look,' said Akshay, 'I'm sorry about all this. The cash, it's not the whole tranche ... about forty-five per cent is what we've calculated.'

Vikram remained silent.

'Have you spoken to anyone about the rest?' asked Akshay.

Vikram shook his head. 'I just ... I ...' He took a deep breath. 'I spoke to Sadhuji's man, that Bhargav. He just refused to acknowledge anything ... I don't know—' He broke off and looked at Akshay. 'You were sensible to stay out of this muck.'

'I may have also been in it, if it wasn't for ... Anyway, most of it is just bad luck.' Akshay paused. 'So what will you do about the remaining cash?'

'I have a few ideas. This amount helps a lot, it will buy me some time at least.'

Akshay nodded.

'Uh, Akshay, listen, about Gayatri—'

Akshay shook his head. 'I'm not in touch with her ... In fact—'

'Neither am I,' interrupted Vikram. 'I'm sure you will see her at some point when this mess clears up.' He sighed. 'I said some really shitty things to her the last time I saw her. I was just really pissed off with the way she rejected me for you. When you do see her, apologize to her from me.'

Akshay stood still for a few seconds, processing Vikram's words. 'Come,' he said, finally. 'Take the cash from upstairs.'

Akshay arrived at the Mehra residence at exactly seven that evening. Mr and Mrs Mehra received him graciously, both looking sombre. Without wasting time on pleasantries, they expressed regret over Nandini's actions as soon as they sat in the living room.

'We are truly sorry, beta,' finished Ashok Mehra.

'Uncle, please' said Akshay. 'Don't embarrass me.'

'No, no, beta,' said Ashok, 'Nina and I have wanted to come over and apologize to your parents for so long now. I can't tell you how bad we feel about everything that has happened.'

Akshay shook his head. 'There's nothing for anyone to apologize for. Not even Nandini.' He paused. 'Uncle, I don't know whether Gayatri told you, but we both knew of the pregnancy before Nandini went and … And even though Nandini's wish to leave Amar then and there seemed cruel to us at the time, I think her decision to go through with the abortion was the right one for everyone. It was really courageous in a way.'

Nina said, 'No, beta. We weren't able to sleep for so many nights, thinking of what poor Amar must have gone through.'

'Aunty,' said Akshay gently. 'I'm not saying it wasn't terrible, but it may work out for the best in the long run. Even for Amar.'

'Thank you, beta,' said Ashok. 'You don't know how much this means to us.'

'Whenever your parents are ready—' started Nina.

Akshay interrupted her, 'Aunty, right now, they're not in a position to deal with anything. But Papa knows I'm here with you, and he asked me to send you his regards.'

Both Ashok and Nina nodded gratefully.

'Is Nandini here?' asked Akshay. 'We can get started on the paperwork at least.'

'I'll just call her,' said Nina, standing up and leaving the room. Akshay nodded, wondering whether Gayatri was home.

Nina walked up to Nandini's room, opened the door and motioned for her girls to come down. As Nandini emerged from the room, Nina suddenly pulled her into a tight hug and kissed her on her forehead.

Akshay stood up as Mrs Mehra and her daughters entered the living room. Nandini looked at him, half-apologetic, half-scared. He walked over to her and gave her a hug. She pulled away gratefully, tears streaming down her face.

Akshay looked at Gayatri, but she just stared at the floor.

Once they had taken their seats, Akshay began to explain the divorce process to them. As he was talking, Gayatri wondered, not for the first time, how they had all landed up here. Less than four months ago, she had been arguing with Akshay at the wedding over serving alcohol, and now he was explaining to them the steps for getting a divorce. She stole a quick glance at him. He seemed calm, not hassled in the least. She swallowed as she remembered the party at his house, when had he told her ... But so much had happened between then and now.

'Gayatri?' Her father nudged her.

'Haan? Sorry, I just ... er ...'

'Printer,' said her father. 'He needs a printer.'

Gayatri looked at Akshay and then at her father. 'Sure,' she said nervously, standing up. Akshay picked up his laptop and followed her to the study.

Gayatri stopped beside the printer, her back to the bookshelf, eyes on the floor, wondering if it was best to leave. Akshay put his laptop on one of the shelves and stood facing her. A few seconds later, he took a small step towards her. She waited for him to say something, but he was quiet. He placed a finger under her chin and lifted it gently. Gayatri raised her eyes to look at him. She didn't know what she had expected to see, but she hadn't expected the mix of tension and apprehension she saw in his face.

'You okay?' he asked softly.

She nodded, slightly breathless. 'You?' she whispered.

'I've not been okay,' he said with a half-smile, taking one of her hands in his.

She raised her free hand to gently place it on his cheek. 'I'm sorry about everything.'

He took her hand from his face, and kissed her palm. Breathing a little heavier now, she pulled her hand away.

He pushed a strand of hair behind her ear. 'I'm still in love with you, Gayatri,' he whispered, leaning in closer to her.

'And I …' she started.

Just then, footsteps sounded in the corridor. They both jumped apart. Gayatri bent over the printer, and Akshay fumbled with his laptop.

Mr Mehra entered. 'It's not working?'

Gayatri said, 'Just a second. Some paper was stuck.' She handed the printer cable to Akshay. 'Connect and try again,' she said, slipping out of the room, trying to hide a smile.

The next morning, Farah swivelled around in her chair as Gayatri walked in. 'What happened?' she asked suspiciously.

'What?' said Gayatri smiling broadly.

Farah's eyes widened and she jumped up to give Gayatri a hug. 'I knew it!' she cried.

'*Did* you, now?' Gayatri was laughing.

'Chalo, this saga is over finally.'

'What over? Now we have to tell everyone. Akshay is insisting we do it in the next couple of days. He says we're too old to sneak around.'

'I agree,' said Farah, settling back in her chair. 'Anyway, now or in a month, it's all the same. Get it over with.'

Gayatri nodded. 'We were talking until three in the morning. I felt like a teenager.'

Farah giggled. 'Soooo sweet. Doesn't your jaw hurt? I'm sure that crocodile-size smile was plastered on your face the whole time.'

'Very funny,' said Gayatri, still smiling.

Akshay was waiting in his car outside Gayatri's office at six. She closed the gate behind her and got in. Though they had spoken for so long at night, she had not seen him since they said a formal goodbye to each other in front of her parents the previous day.

'Hey,' he said as she fastened her seatbelt.

She smiled at him. 'Hi.'

'What happened?'

'Nothing,' she replied, still smiling. 'Why?'

'You look strange with this slightly demented smile on your face. I'm used to seeing you all angry and worked up. I'm not sure I can take this happy-smiley version of you.'

Gayatri frowned. 'That better?'

He nodded.

'Now drive.' On Gayatri's insistence, they drove to a part of Delhi where they were unlikely to encounter anyone they knew, and entered a Café Coffee Day.

As they sat down, Akshay looked at Gayatri and shook his head. 'I can't do this, okay? I'm just telling you.'

'What? It's good, we can explore new parts of the city. Would you have ever come here otherwise?'

Akshay shook his head again. 'Listen, I refuse to sneak around like this. I feel like I'm cheating on someone. And it's taken us fifty-five minutes to drive to this part of town. Let's just come clean to everyone. We'll deal with whatever happens.'

Gayatri took a look at the menu and ordered a coffee. Akshay waved the waiter away irritably. 'Okay, okay,' she said. 'Don't spoil the mood. We'll tell them.'

'Tonight. I'm going to talk to my dad tonight.'

'Tonight?' said Gayatri, her eyes widening in alarm.

'Yes,' said Akshay firmly. 'You can take a day or two, that's fine.'

She sighed. 'And how do you think everyone will react?' Without waiting for him to answer, she said, 'My mom will go ballistic. Nandini also, I think. Dad will be fine, but just because someone will have to calm them down. Actually, no one will believe me, considering how mean and condescending you were to me in the beginning.'

'Mean? Me? No way!'

'Oh please! You were like "I'm such a busy lawyer, and my dad is forcing me to help these stupid girls who study history as a hobby." So irritating you were.'

Akshay smiled and lay his hands on the table, palms up. She put her hands in his.

'I was stupid,' he said, 'I didn't know how much one headstrong girl with an obsession for history would change me.' His face grew serious. 'Really.' He looked at her hands in his. 'You know, even dealing with Neelam … You know her, right?'

Gayatri nodded. 'She's the one you were telling me about that night?'

'And the one who leaked that video of my dad.'

'I had a feeling it was her.'

'Anyway, I don't know what it was about you or us, but it gave me the strength to deal with these ghosts of my past, something I hadn't been able to do for more than a decade.' He squeezed her hands. 'Thank you.'

'Ma'am, your coffee,' the waiter placed her coffee on the table. Akshay released her hands irritably. 'See?' he said. 'This is like being in school or college. I can't do this.'

As she stirred her coffee, Gayatri said, 'Okay, we'll tell everyone.' She shook her head. 'I can't believe all that has happened in these past few months.'

He nodded.

'You know,' she continued, 'I've been thinking about the whole run-in with Sadhuji, trying to process what happened and why. You can't imagine how much I hate that man, when I think of Megha's murder, and our office all broken and smashed.' She paused. 'But sometimes, I also think about that man who cornered me in the office and broke that window on me. His eyes, they'll never leave me.' She shuddered slightly. 'I keep wondering what his life was like, where he grew up, why he does what he does. Somewhere, it makes me feel this huge sense of disconnection with the world.'

'As in?' Akshay reached across and took her hand in his lightly.

'I don't know how to explain it. You remember that article on the Nigar Baba shrine I was planning to write?'

He nodded.

'Well, when I visited the site of the shrine, I spoke to many people. Some of the villagers were completely terrified. They actually believed that the Baba and his shrine had protected them from evil … and I was so surprised to see that these people included Hindus as well, not just Muslims.' She sipped her coffee and continued, 'Then I spoke to some older people in the village, who told me stories about a sort of natural stone shivling adjacent to the shrine, which was destroyed in the early 1900s by some mob. One old man cried as he told me how his own father had died shielding the shivling. They were still angry about it, and so they didn't empathize with those who were upset at the destruction of the shrine.' She paused. 'It put me in mind of our conversation that night on your balcony, about biases.'

'So now you've switched sides?'

She frowned at him. 'Of course not, whoever destroyed the shrine should be punished.'

'Then?'

'When I went to the village, I was very sure of the story as I would write it. It was there already ... a poor minority oppressed because someone had demolished their centuries-old shrine. But as I spoke to the people, I realized that the story is more complicated than that, and a five-hundred-word article with a deadline of a week would not do it justice.' She took another sip of her coffee. 'Basically, I see that I have prejudices too, and that sometimes I don't recognize them.'

Akshay smiled. 'Very self-aware of you.'

'Even when I met Anil Bhargav that day at your house, remember? That long conversation at dinner?'

'Of course, I remember,' said Akshay. 'I really thought you would lose it completely.'

'To be honest, I was really taken aback that someone like him would have rational facts at hand, and be able to make arguments that were not completely unjustified. And a little ashamed that I used to look down upon him and people like him, thinking that they were just rabble-rousers with no capacity for an intellectual argument.' She paused. 'The worst is, I was shocked at his command over English.'

Akshay nodded. 'He's actually very intelligent. I don't know how and why he got stuck with Sadhuji.'

'Didn't you all?' asked Gayatri.

'I guess.' Akshay shrugged. 'You know,' he added slowly, 'it's so strange. In some ways, my world has gone from being murky grey to having some boundaries between the blacker and whiter sides of life. And yours has gone from a black-and-white space to having some space for greys.'

She nodded. Finishing the last of her coffee, she smiled at him. 'Shall we go home then? We have some explaining to do.'

Epilogue

Vikram stayed underground for a few months, emerging from hiding when he learned that his father had passed away. He was surprised that not many people remembered what had happened with him, and that no official complaint or charge was brought against him. He is in talks with a school friend to start a garment export business.

The *National Express* carried a series of articles on Sadhuji's land-acquisition scam, based on the papers from Akshay. Sadhuji was arrested and later granted bail. He was forced to close down his ashram in Chhatarpur while the ED investigates him. He has returned to Doljat, where people still have unquestioning faith in him.

Anil Bhargav, for his part, came away relatively unscathed. He became a regular face on prime-time TV debates, and even signed a book deal. His book, *My Struggles with Historical Untruths*, will be published soon.

The *Indian History Review* team started producing a podcast on Indian history, which became quite popular. Anil Bhargav featured as a guest on two episodes in the first season.

The BSD, following the instructions of an astute PR consultant, distanced itself from Sadhuji by suddenly ascribing its ideology to a freedom fighter rescued from historical obscurity. They hope to exceed expectations in the next elections.

Akshay was right about his father. Mr Grewal was back on his feet within a few weeks. Rupi returned to Delhi to a considerate and appreciative husband. Though she would never admit it, she finds herself missing Neelam sometimes, wishing for a few solitary evenings without Grewalji.

Nandini is dating again, much to the relief of Ashok and Nina.

Amar has applied for a master's degree in the US with the intention of settling there permanently.

Farah and Zaheer got married in Delhi. The wedding was preceded by long arguments about moving to the US, which Zaheer was very much in favour of, particularly after he learnt of the incident at the *Review*'s office. But his arguments, based as they were on fear, were no match for Farah's quiet confidence in her roots, the country she considered her homeland, and her determination to continue her work at the *Indian History Review*.

Gayatri and Akshay moved into a flat in Hauz Khas. Dadi announced the fact calmly to her sisters at a lunch. Their shock increased as their eighty-five-year-old older sister proceeded to lecture them on keeping up with the times. Akshay and Gayatri are enjoying the domestic rhythm of their lives together. Cribbing about the cleaning maid, dealing with their grumpy landlord, visiting Qureshi for their favourite kebabs and having Sunday biryani at Andhra Bhawan.

And as for Delhi, the city continues to blossom with bouquets of bright bougainvillea, champa and laburnum in summer; flood with water and traffic in the monsoon; and unhappily hide beneath the cover of grey smog in winter. Seemingly unchanged but ever-changing, it absorbs the corruption, the violence, the scandals, as well as the triumphs, love and celebrations, and finds a place for them somewhere in its long history.

Acknowledgements

First and most, Ankur, my first reader—for unending encouragement and inspiration, fierce enthusiasm, many rounds of tireless editing, giving me exactly the right advice at the right time, putting up with me, and for so much more. This book would not exist but for you.

Diya Kar—for the love you gave the book and its characters, and for your incisive and insightful judgement on all matters, which has made the book infinitely better. Thank you so, so much.

The entire HarperCollins team: Shatarupa Ghoshal—thank you for your superb line-editing; Devangana Dash—for the cover design; Jyotsna Raman, Akriti Tyagi and Rahul Dixit.

Rajni George, for encouraging me when I needed it the most, and for editing the book with love and expertise. I'll always be grateful.

Tamiksha Singh for reading through this book at different stages, and tolerating my stupid questions.

ACKNOWLEDGEMENTS

Neelini Sarkar and Sheila Kumar for your excellent editorial suggestions.

Vivek Shanbhag, Krishna Udayasankar, Rajeev Mehrotra, Andaleeb Wajid, Nayanika Mahtani, Puneeta Roy, Geeta Gujral, Gyan Nagpal and Runjhun Noopur for your kindness and generosity along the way.

Rajat, Sandip and Niti for your large-heartedness.

My four sisters: Suparna, Radha, Minna and Sunaina. I hope our love is reflected somewhere in the relationship between Gayatri and Nandini. Especially, Supi didi for her comments on the cover, and Sunaina didi for comments on the writing and her constant support.

My bua, Lakhi Banik, for her love and all things Bengali in our lives.

My son, Kabir, for cushioning the lows with his love, hugs, smiles and cards under the door.

My Badimama, who filled my head with her stories. I miss you.

And finally, my parents, for everything and more.